PRAISE FOR

THOSE WHO ʃAVE US

"Blum...paints a deeply moving tale of the extreme measures that Germans and Jews alike faced to survive and the risks some took to save the lives of others...Blum's beautifully lyrical, heart-wrenching story strikes a deep chord within those who read it, opening the reader's eyes to the grim realities faced during this horrible time by Jews and the Germans in the Resistance who tried to help them. This novel will leave no reader untouched."

—*Tulsa World*

"Moving."   —*Woman's Day*

"Eloquent."   —*Lifetime Magazine*

"I was much impressed by Jenna Blum's book. It is a powerful evocation of terrible events, moving and persuasive. But it is also a remarkable first novel, with memorable characters and an exemplary control over structure, bringing past and present together to great effect. I admired it...I should say that I only feel enthusiastic enough about a complimentary copy of a novel to write thus about once a year, if that—a further measure of the quality of this one!"   —Penelope Lively, author of *Moon Tiger*

"In the haunted first world of Jenna Blum's debut novel, time has healed no wounds, and no character is spared heartbreak. Yet from this bleakness emerges a story so fully human and affecting that we cannot resist its redemptive urges. Rendered with startling precision, in prose vivid as stained glass, *Those Who Save Us* is a gripping work that enchants, troubles and surprises. I wish I could stand beside it in bookstores and tell all readers: this powerful story will invade your dreams."
       —Christopher Castellani, author of *A Kiss from Maddalena*

"In her compelling first novel, Jenna Blum forces a moral re-evaluation on her characters and on the reader. Cagily plotted between past and present, guilt and innocence, *Those Who Save Us* is a moving, unsentimental page turner."
       —Alison Leslie Gold, author of *Fiet's Vase*

THOSE WHO SAVE US

THOSE WHO SAVE US

JENNA BLUM

A HARVEST BOOK • HARCOURT, INC.

Orlando   Austin   New York   San Diego   Toronto   London

Requests for permission to make copies of any part of the work
should be submitted online at www.harcourt.com/contact or
mailed to the following address: Permissions Department,
Houghton Mifflin Harcourt Publishing Company,
6277 Sea Harbor Drive, Orlando, Florida 32887-6777.

www.HarcourtBooks.com

Excerpts from this have been previously published in slightly different
form in the *Briar Cliff Review, Meridian,* and *Prairie Schooner.*

Library of Congress Cataloging-in-Publication Data
Blum, Jenna.
Those who save us/Jenna Blum.
p.   cm.
1. World War, 1939–1945—Underground movements—Fiction.
2. World War, 1939–1945—Germany—Fiction.   3. Germany—History—
1933–1945—Fiction.   4. Holocaust, Jewish (1939–1945)—Fiction.
5. German American women—Fiction.   6. Young Women—Fiction.
I. Title.
PS3602.L863T47   2004
813'.54—dc22   2003014777 √
ISBN 978-0-15-101019-6
ISBN 978-0-15-603166-0 (pbk.)

Text set in Garamond MT
Designed by Cathy Riggs

Printed in the United States of America

First Harvest edition 2005
P R T V W U S Q

This book is for my mother, Frances Joerg Blum,
who took me to Germany and gave me the key:
Ich liebe Dich, meine Mutti.

And it is in beloved memory of my dad, Robert P. Blum,
who would have said *Mazel tov.*

I had voluntarily joined the ranks of the active SS and I had become too fond of the black uniform to relinquish it in this way.

—RUDOLF HOESS, COMMANDANT OF AUSCHWITZ

THOSE WHO SAVE US

PROLOGUE

Trudy and Anna, 1993

THE FUNERAL IS WELL ATTENDED, THE NEW HEIDEL-burg Lutheran Church packed to capacity with farmers and their families who have come to bid farewell to one of their own. Since every seat is full, they also line the walls and crowd the vestibule. The men are comically unfamiliar in dark suits; they don't get this dressed up for regular services. The women, how-ever, wear what they do every Sunday no matter what the weather, skirt-and-sweater sets with hose and pumps. Their parkas, which are puffy and incongruous and signify the imminent return to life's practicalities, are their sole concession to the cold.

And it is cold. December in Minnesota is a bad time to have to bury a loved one, Trudy Swenson thinks. In fact, it is quite im-possible. The topsoil is frozen three feet down, and her father will have to be housed in a refrigeration unit in the county morgue until the earth thaws enough to receive him. Trudy tries to steer her mind away from how Jack will look after several months in storage. She makes an attempt to instead concentrate on the eu-logy. But she must be suffering the disjointed cognition of the be-reaved, for her thoughts have assumed a willful life of their own.

They circle above her in the nave, presenting her with an aerial view of the church and its inhabitants: Trudy herself sitting very upright in the front row next to her mother, Anna; the minister droning on about a man who, from his description, could be any fellow here; the deceased looking dead in his casket; the rest of the town seated behind Trudy, staring at the back of her head. Trudy feels horribly conspicuous, and although she means her father no disrespect, she prays only for the service to be over.

Then it is, and the congregation rumbles to its feet and stands in expectation. Trudy realizes that they are waiting for her and Anna to depart the church ahead of everyone else, as is proper. She pauses to mumble a final good-bye to Jack; then she takes Anna's elbow to help her from the pew. Anna allows Trudy to guide her past the ranks of impassive faces, but once they are outside she folds her arms to her sides and forges on alone. The two women take tiny cautious steps over the ice to Trudy's car.

Trudy starts the ignition and sits shivering, waiting for the engine to warm up. The interior of the Civic won't be comfortable until they have reached their destination, the farmhouse six miles north of here. The arctic air is like shards of glass in the lungs; it shakes Trudy to the bones until they threaten to snap.

Well, I thought that was a nice service, she says to Anna.

Anna is looking through the passenger's window at the horizon. The Lutheran Church is built on the highest ridge in New Heidelburg, all the better to be close to God. From this vantage point in the summer, the countryside below is a dreaming checkerboard over which it seems that one could, with a running start, spread one's arms and fly. Now it is a sullen and unbroken white.

Trudy tries again.

Short and simple, she says. Dad would have approved, don't you think?

Slowly, Anna turns her pale gaze on the windshield and then upon her daughter, staring at Trudy as though she doesn't know who Trudy is.

We must get to the house, she replies. I must set out the food. The people will be coming soon enough.

This is true; all around them, the New Heidelburgers are already climbing into their trucks and minivans. After a brief and respectful intermission to let the family members refresh their public faces, the townsfolk will descend upon the farmhouse, bearing casseroles and condolences. Trudy shifts into gear and accelerates out of the lot, noting Anna's hands and feet jerk up, just a little, at the unaccustomed speed. Although Anna has lived nearly fifty years in this remote rural area, where people think nothing of traveling half an hour to buy groceries, she has never learned to drive. She turns back to her window to watch the fields as they blur past.

To Trudy, who abandoned New Heidelburg for the Twin Cities as soon as she finished high school thirty-five years earlier, this landscape is a study in monotony, as bleak and inhospitable as the steppes of Siberia. Snow and mud, gray sky, line after line of barbed-wire fencing swooping along the two-lane road. Silos and trailers. Even the cows are nowhere to be seen. It is early yet, three o'clock, but night comes quickly in this part of the country; it will be full dark in an hour. The knowledge of this, and how she will spend that time, makes Trudy feel desperate to be in her own kitchen, her study, in her classroom lecturing disenchanted students, anywhere but here. She suddenly decides she will return to Minneapolis sooner than planned, perhaps tomorrow morning. For one of the odd things about death, Trudy has discovered, is that in its wake one must go about business as usual; it seems heartless and wrong, but now that the rituals of mourning have been attended to, the sole task left to Trudy is to try and comprehend the enormity of this sudden change. And this she might as well do in the comfort of her home rather than sitting in silence with Anna.

First, however, there is the reception to be endured, so Trudy pulls into the farmhouse drive. As they pass through the windbreak of pines, fingers of sun pierce the clouds, transforming the spindrift in the fields into glittering sheets and highlighting the outbuildings in what seems to Trudy a shamelessly dramatic, ecclesiastical way. She parks and helps Anna from the car but paces around the dooryard long after Anna has gone inside. It is here, reportedly, that Jack had his fatal heart attack; the coroner has assured Trudy that Jack was dead before he hit the ground. Yet Trudy wonders: Did Jack pause, bewildered by the pain ripping through his left arm, his chest? Did he have time to realize what was happening to him? Trudy hopes not; it would ease her mind to know for certain, but Anna, the only witness, is as usual not talking.

Trudy spends another minute peering at the tamped-down snow, trying to discern beneath it the path Jack followed so consistently from barn to porch that his boots wore ruts in the grass. But she can see nothing, and the sun fades behind a gauzy cataract of cloud, and finally Trudy sighs and climbs the steps into her mother's house.

For the house has always been Anna's, really. Jack and Trudy might as well have been boarders whose untidy but necessary presence Anna has patiently tolerated. After all, it is Anna who has scrubbed the floors, laundered the curtains, polished the windows with newspaper and vinegar, vacuumed the tops of doorways with a special attachment. It is Anna who has combated the farmwife's enemies of soil and excrement, chaff and blood. This is ultimately a losing battle, since it is an axiom of agricultural life that whatever is outside must come in, sooner or later. But Anna has managed, through great and stubborn effort, to enforce some measure of Teutonic cleanliness here.

After hanging her coat, Trudy joins her mother in the kitchen. The two women work in silent and hurried concentration, ferrying the food Anna has cooked during the past forty-eight hours into the dining room. This is a dim and cavernous space of which Anna is inordinately proud, with dark wainscoting and fleur-de-lis wallpaper and a high ceiling that seems to float in the gloom. The mirror over the buffet is a milky glimmer; the heavy drapes filter out what little natural light there is. Trudy can't recall the last time she was in this room. Sliding doors close it off from the rest of the house, protecting the prized oak furniture from the whips and scorns of everyday life. It has been reserved solely for company, which means that for the past several years it has not been used at all.

But it is the perfect setting for the occasion at hand, which demands the utmost in formality, and with this in mind Anna has been busy in here. The rug is striped from a vehement brushing. The sideboard and table are slippery with lemon oil. Soon their gleaming surfaces are hidden beneath trivets and Pyrex casseroles containing not the *Sauerbraten* and *Kartoffeln* of Anna's native country but the recipes she has learned to make: noodle hot dish, ambrosia topped with a fluffy mound of Cool Whip, Jello ring with fruit. An exercise in excess, since the neighbors will arrive any minute bearing more of the same. Yet protocol requires that Anna provide for them nonetheless.

Trudy sets a wicker basket of rolls on the table and turns to her mother.

Did you make coffee? she asks, the first thing she has said to Anna since entering the house.

Anna waves a distracted hand.

I will do it, she says. You go make sure I have not overlooked anything.

Jawohl, Trudy thinks.

She prowls from living room to kitchen and back again in a familiar circuit, even as she did as a girl, trailing Anna and asking questions to which Anna gave no answers. Naturally, everything is in perfect order. Upstairs, while checking for fresh hand towels in the bathroom, Trudy notices that Jack's shaving gear is missing; in its place are Anna's perfume bottles, each aligned a precise centimeter from the edge of the glass shelf. Trudy looks into her parents' bedroom next: the bed is neatly made, but the floor is covered with labeled garbage bags. Jack's clothes, ready for donation to the church. Trudy frowns and rubs her arms.

She returns to the living room, takes her coat from the closet, and escapes to the porch, where she stands huddled and shaking.

She strains her eyes toward the road. A heavy blue dusk has fallen over the land, compressing the sky into the ground. By now there should be headlights moving in somber procession up the drive, beneath the black branches of the pines that border it. But there are none, and the only sound is the wind whistling over the fields.

Trudy waits until it is too dark to see. Then she walks back inside, switching on lamps as she goes. She finds Anna still in the dining room, sitting at the head of the table. Trudy can barely distinguish Anna from the shadows around her; she is merely another black solid shape, like the furniture.

Trudy fumbles for the wall switch and the frosted cups of the chandelier shed a sallow light. One of its bulbs has burned out.

I don't think anyone's coming, she tells Anna.

Anna appears not to have heard her. She is toying with a placemat, combing its tassels into straight lines. She looks tired, Trudy thinks. She is, perhaps, more pale than usual. But the loss of her husband will not leave any visible mark on her. Anna's beauty is sunk in the bone. Although this is not Anna's fault, Trudy finds it almost a personal affront that her mother should continue to be so composed and resplendent even now, even at seventy-three, in widow's black.

Trudy starts to say something else—she has no idea whether it will be *I'm sorry* or *What did you expect?*—but Anna precludes this by nodding and getting to her feet. Without so much as a glance at Trudy or the untouched food, she proceeds through the double doors. Trudy hears nothing for a minute as Anna crosses the living room carpet; then there is the clocking of Anna's heels on the stairs and in the hallway overhead. After this, a creak of springs as Anna settles onto the bed she has shared with Jack for over four decades. Then, again, silence.

Trudy remains where she is for a while, listening. When there is no further noise, she wanders into the kitchen and pours herself some of the coffee Anna has brewed in an industrial-sized urn. Trudy stands by the sink, not drinking but letting the cup warm her fingers, which are still stiff from being outside. She gazes through the window in the direction of what she knows is New Heidelburg, though she can't see even the faint bruise of its lights on the horizon from here.

Trudy takes a sip of coffee. Why should she be surprised? she asks herself. Truth be told, she isn't. The townsfolk have already paid their respects to Jack in the church. And now that he is gone, they no longer have any reason to be nice to his widow or her daughter. As they have wanted to do for years, ever since Jack first brought Anna to this country, the New Heidelburgers have washed their hands of her.

Anna and Max,
Weimar, 1939–1940

1

THE EVENING IS TYPICAL ENOUGH UNTIL THE DOG BEGINS to choke. And even then, at first, Anna doesn't bother to turn from the *Rouladen* she is stuffing for the dinner that she and her father, Gerhard, will share, for the dachshund's energetic gagging doesn't strike her as anything unusual. The dog, Spaetzle, is forever eating something he shouldn't, savaging chicken carcasses and consuming heels of bread without chewing, and such greed is inevitably followed by retching. Privately, Anna thinks him a horrid little creature and has ever since he was first presented to her five years ago on her fourteenth birthday, a gift from her father just after her mother's death, as if in compensation. It is perhaps unfair to resent Spaetzle for this, but he is also chronically ill-tempered, snapping with his yellowed fangs at everyone except Gerhard; he is really her father's pet. And grossly fat, as Gerhard is always slipping him tidbits, despite his bellowed admonitions to Anna of *Do not! Feed! The dog! From! The table!*

Now Anna ignores Spaetzle, wishing her hands were not otherwise engaged in the mixing bowl so she could bring them to her ears, but when the choking continues she looks at him with some alarm. He is gasping for breath between rounds of *rmmmp rmmmp rmmmp* noises, foam flecking his long muzzle. Anna abandons the *Rouladen* and bends over him, forcing his jaws open to get at whatever is blocking his windpipe, but her fingers, already meat-slick, find no purchase in the dog's slippery throat. He seems to be succeeding in his struggle to swallow the object, yet Anna is not willing to leave the outcome to chance. What if what he has eaten is poisonous? What if the dog should die? With a fearful glance in the direction of her father's study, Anna throws on her coat, seizes the dachshund, and races from the house without even removing her grimy apron.

There being no time to bring Spaetzle to her regular doctor in the heart of Weimar, Anna decides to try a closer clinic she has never visited but often passed during her daily errands, on the shabby outskirts of town. She runs the entire quarter kilometer, fighting to retain her hold on the dog, who writhes indignantly in her arms, a slippery tube of muscle. Beneath guttering gaslamps, over rotting October leaves and sidewalks heaved by decades' worth of freeze and thaw: finally Anna rounds a corner into a row of narrow neglected houses still pockmarked with scars from the last war, and there is the bronze nameplate: HERR DOKTOR MAXIMILIAN STERN. Anna bumps the door open with a hip and rushes through the reception area to the examining room.

She finds the Herr *Doktor* pressing a stethoscope to the chest of a woman whose flesh ripples like lard from her muslin brassiere. The patient catches sight of Anna before the practitioner: she points and emits a small breathy scream. The *Doktor* jumps and straightens, startled, and the woman grabs her bosom and moans.

Have a seat in the waiting room, whoever you are, Herr *Doktor* Stern snaps. I'll be with you shortly.

Please, Anna gasps. My father's dog— he's eaten something poisonous— I think he's dying—

The *Doktor* turns, raising an eyebrow.

You may dress, Frau Rosenberg, he tells his patient. Your bronchitis is very mild, nothing to be alarmed about. I'll write you the usual prescription. Now, if you'll excuse me, I must attend to this poor animal.

Well! says the woman, pulling on her shirtwaist. Well! I never expected— to be forsaken for a *dog*.

She grabs her coat and pushes past Anna with a dramatic wheeze.

As the door slams the *Doktor* comes quickly to Anna and relieves her of her burden, and she imagines that he shares with her the faintest smile of complicity over his spectacles. She lowers her head, anticipating the second, startled glance of appreciation that men invariably give her. But instead she hears him walking away, and when she looks up again his back is to her, bent over the dachshund on the table.

Well, what have we here, he murmurs.

Anna watches anxiously as he reaches into the dog's mouth, then turns to prepare a syringe. She takes some comfort from the deft movement of his hands, the play of muscles beneath his thin shirt. He is a tall, slender fellow, bordering on gaunt. He also seems oddly familiar, though Anna certainly has not been here before.

As grateful as I am to you for rescuing me from Frau Rosenberg, I must point out that this is a most unorthodox visit, Fräulein, says the *Doktor* as he works. Are you perhaps under the impression that I'm a veterinarian? Or did you think a Jewish practitioner would be grateful to treat even a dog?

Jewish? Anna blinks at the *Doktor*'s blond hair, which, though straight, stands up in whorls and spikes. She remembers belatedly the Star of David painted on the clinic door. Of course, she has known this is the Jewish Quarter, but in her panic she has not given it a thought.

No, no, Anna protests. Of course not. I brought him here because you were closest—

She realizes how this sounds and winces.

I'm sorry, she says. I didn't mean to offend.

The *Doktor* smiles at her over one shoulder.

No, it's I who should apologize, he says. It was meant as a joke, but it was a crude one. In these times I'm indeed grateful for any patients, whether they're fellow Jews or dachshunds. You are Aryan, yes, Fräulein? You do know you have broken the law by coming here at all.

Anna nods, although this too she has not considered. The *Doktor* returns his attention to the dog.

Almost done, almost done, he mutters. Ah, here's the culprit.

He holds something up for Anna's inspection: part of one of her sanitary napkins, slick with spit and spotted with blood.

Anna claps her palms to her face, mortified.

Oh, God in heaven, she says. That wretched dog!

Herr *Doktor* Stern laughs and dispenses the napkin in a rubbish bin.

It could have been worse, he says.

I can't imagine how—

He could have eaten something truly poisonous. Chocolate, for instance.

Chocolate is poisonous?

For dogs it is, Fräulein.

I didn't know that.

Well, now you do.

Anna fans her flaming cheeks.

I'm not sure that I wouldn't have preferred that, she says, given the circumstances.

The *Doktor* laughs, a short bark, and moves to lather his hands at the sink.

You mustn't be embarrassed, Fräulein, he says. *Nihil humanum mihi alienum est*—nothing human is alien to me. Nor canine, for that matter. But you should be more careful what you feed that little fellow—for meals, that is. He is far too fat.

That's my father's doing, Anna tells him. He is constantly slipping the dog scraps from the table.

Now Herr *Doktor* Stern does give her another, longer look.

Your father—that's Herr Brandt, yes?

That's right.

Ah, says the *Doktor,* and lifts Spaetzle from the examining table. He settles the dog in Anna's arms. The dachshund's eyes are glazed; limp, he seems to weigh as much as a paving stone.

A mild sedative, the *Doktor* explains, and muscle relaxant. So I could extract the... In any case, he'll be up to his old tricks in no time, provided you keep him away from sweets and other, shall we say, indigestibles?

He lowers his spectacles and smiles at Anna, who stands returning it longer than she should. Then she remembers herself and shifts the dog to fumble awkwardly in her coat pocket for her money purse.

How much do I owe you? she asks.

The *Doktor* waves a hand.

No charge, he says. It is the least I can do, considering my last ill-fated interaction with your family.

He turns away, and Anna thinks, Of course. Now she knows where she has seen him before. He attended Anna's mother in the final days of her illness, the only physician in Weimar who would come to the house. Anna recalls Herr *Doktor* Stern hurrying past her in the upstairs hallway, vials clinking in his bag; that, upon spying the woebegone Anna in a corner, he stopped and chucked her under the chin and said, *It'll be all right, little one.* She recalls, too, that Gerhard's first reaction to his wife's death was to rant, *It's all his fault she didn't recover. What else can one expect from a Jew? I should never have let him touch her.*

You used to have a beard, Anna says now, a red beard.

The *Doktor* scrapes a hand over his jaw, producing a small rasping sound.

Ah, yes, so I did, he says. I shaved it off last year in an attempt to look younger. Vain in both senses of the word.

Anna smiles again. How old is he? No more than his midthirties, she is sure. He wears no wedding ring.

He opens the door for her with a polite little flourish. Anna remains near the apothecary cabinet, fishing about for something else to ask him, wondering whether she can possibly pretend interest in the jars of medicines and tongue depressors or the skeleton propped in one corner of the room, wearing a fedora. But the *Doktor* has an air of impatience now, so Anna gives a small sigh and takes a firmer grasp on the dog.

Thank you very much, Herr *Doktor,* she murmurs as she brushes past him, noticing, beneath the odor of disinfectant, the smell of spiced soap on his skin.

My pleasure, Fräulein.

The *Doktor* flashes Anna a distracted half-smile and calls into the waiting room: Maizel!

A small boy with long curls bobbing over his ears scurries toward Anna, his arm in a sling. He is followed by an older Jewish man in a threadbare black coat. Their forelocks remind Anna of wood shavings. She presses herself against the wall to let the pair pass.

As she emerges into the chilly night, Anna casts a wistful look back at the clinic. Then, with unease, she remembers her father. It is late, and Gerhard will be furious that his dinner has been delayed; he insists his meals be served with military precision. On sudden impulse, Anna turns and hastens toward the bakery a few streets away. A *Sachertorte,* Gerhard's favorite dessert, will provide an excuse as to why Anna has been out at this hour—she is certainly not going to tell him about the debacle with the dog—and may act as a sop to his temper.

Like everything else in this forlorn neighborhood, the bakery is nothing to look at. It does not even have a name. Anna wonders why its owner, Frau Staudt, doesn't choose to relocate outside the Jewish Quarter, since she is as Aryan as Anna herself. No matter; however run-down the shop, its pastries are the best Weimar has to offer. Anna arrives just as the baker is flipping the sign from Open to Closed. Anna taps on the window and makes a desperate face, and Frau Staudt, whose substantial girth is trussed as tightly as a turkey into her apron, throws up her hands.

She unlocks the door, grumbling in her waspish little voice, And what is it you want now? A *Linzertorte*? The moon?

A *Sachertorte*? says Anna, trying her most winning smile.

A *Sachertorte*! *Sachertorte,* the princess wants…I don't suppose you have the proper ration coupons, either.

Well…

I thought not.

But the widowed and childless baker has long adopted a maternal attitude toward the motherless Anna, and there is indeed a precious *Sachertorte* in the back, and Anna manages, by looking suitably pitiable, to beg half of it on credit.

This accomplished, she returns home as quickly as she is able, given that she is holding the pastry box under one arm and the dachshund, who is starting to squirm, in the other. And again Anna is in luck: when she sneaks in through the maid's entrance, she hears a rising Wagnerian chorus from her father's study. Gerhard is in a decent mood, then. Perhaps he has not noticed what time it is. Anna deposits the dog in his basket and frowns at the sideboard. The *Rouladen,* left out of the icebox this long, has probably spoiled. Anna will have to concoct an *Eintopf* from last night's dinner instead.

As she hastily assembles the ingredients for the casserole, she pinches bits from the cake and eats them. The cold night air has given her an appetite. It has done wonders for Spaetzle too, apparently, for he makes the quick recovery the *Doktor* has promised. He waddles from his bed to lurk underfoot; he stares with beady interest at Anna's hand, following the progress of *Sachertorte* from box to mouth. As Anna does not appear to be about to offer him any, he lets out a volley of yaps.

Quiet, Anna says.

She cuts herself a sliver of cake and eats it slowly, savoring the bitter Swiss chocolate and sieving her memory for more details of Herr *Doktor* Stern's house call five years earlier. She recalls that the red beard made him look like the Dutch painter van Gogh, whose self-portraits were once exhibited in Weimar's *Schlossmuseum*. Even now without it, the resemblance is striking, Anna reflects: the narrow face, the sad blue brilliance of the eyes, the weary lines etched about the mouth, not without humor. The artist in his final tortured days.

Anna sighs. In the time before the Reich, she would have been able to revisit the *Doktor* with some conjured malady. She might even, with careful planning, have encountered him socially. But now? Anna has no excuse whatever to visit a Jewish physician; in fact it is, as the *Doktor* himself has reminded her, forbidden. Not that Anna has ever paid much attention to such things.

She takes a disheartened bite of cake, and Spaetzle barks again.

Shut up, Anna tells him absently.

Then she looks down at the dog. Encouraged by Anna's thoughtful expression, he begins to wriggle and whine. Anna smiles at him and slices another piece off the cake, somewhat larger this time. She hesitates for a moment, the chocolate softening in her palm. Then she says, Here, boy, and drops it to the floor.

2

CHECK, THE *DOKTOR* SAYS.

Anna frowns at the chessboard, at the constellation of battered pieces on their cream and oak squares. This set, Max has told her, belonged to his father, and his father before him. One of the original black pawns has vanished, replaced by a stub of charcoal, and Anna's queen is missing her crown. She is also boxed into a corner.

Anna is not a complete novice at the game; she learned its rudiments as a girl, on the knees of her maternal grandfather. But Max's tutelage during the past four months has enabled her to better understand the logical ways in which the pieces move together, the clever geometric mesh. He has reintroduced her, too, to the keen joy of unadulterated learning, which Anna hasn't experienced since studying languages at *Gymnasium*. Now, as Anna falls asleep at night, she sees the board tattooed on her eyelids, rearranges the pieces into endless configurations. And she is improving.

But Max is so much better than she! Each match is still an exercise in humiliation. As, Anna is coming to feel, are her clandestine evenings here. Max is more complicated than the games they share. It is true that whenever Anna appears uninvited on his back doorstep, Max seems pleased to see her, invariably exclaiming, Anna, isn't it funny? I had a feeling you might stop by. And Anna has caught him assessing her with the healthy masculine admiration to which she is accustomed. But Max confines his compliments to sartorial observations, commenting on a new dress Anna is wearing or a silk scarf that brings out the blue of her eyes. His behavior is that of a fond uncle. It is maddening.

He watches her now over the rims of his spectacles, amused.

Are you willing to concede? he asks.

Not yet, Anna tells him.

She studies the board. Her hand hovers over one of her knights. Then she gets up and goes to the stove, which exudes tired whiffs of gas.

May I make more tea? she asks, reaching for the canister on the top shelf. The movement causes her skirt to rise a good three inches above the knee. It is an outdated garment, the Pencil silhouette long since out of fashion, but it is also the shortest she owns.

You're still in check, Anna, says Max. You wouldn't by any chance be trying to distract me with that fetching skirt, would you?

Anna glances back at him.

Is it working?

Max laughs.

That reminds me of a joke my father's rabbi used to tell, he says. Why does a Jew always answer a question with a question?

I don't know, says Anna, busying herself with the tea. Why?

Why not?

Anna makes a face at Max and looks around his kitchen while she waits for the water to boil. Like the rest of his rooms behind the clinic, it is small but neat, each cup hanging from its proper hook, the spices alphabetized in the cupboard, the floor swept. There are even plants on a step-laddered rack against one wall, yearning toward a strange lamp that emits a cold purple-white light. But there are some housekeeping tasks that Max has either neglected or hasn't spied at all: the diamond-shaped panes in the mullioned windows could use a good cleaning with news-paper and vinegar, and a finger run over the sill would come up furred with dust. Things only a woman would notice; this is def-initely a bachelor establishment, Anna thinks, and she smiles fondly at her chipped teacup.

As the teakettle stubbornly refuses to sing, adhering to the maxim about the watched pot, Anna turns her back on the stove and wanders to the plants.

What is this one called? she asks, bending over a dark green leaf.

She hears the scrape of Max's chair as he comes from the table to stand behind her.

That's *Monstera deliciosa,* he tells her, the Swiss cheese plant.

Ah. And to think I thought cheese came from dairy farms. And this one?

Max puts a casual hand on Anna's shoulder as they lean for-ward together. Anna catches her breath and looks sidelong at it, the long dexterous fingers with their square clipped nails.

An asparagus fern, says Max. *A. densiflorus sprengerii.*

Anna stares at a single frond questing toward the light, blind and sensitive and quivering under the onslaught of their mingled breath. When Max takes his hand away she fancies she can still feel its warmth, as though it has left a radiating imprint.

He points to another specimen with striped leaves.

Now this one, he says, glancing at Anna over the wire rims of his spectacles, is *Zebrina pendula,* otherwise known as a Wander-ing Jew. A donation from a former patient who is now, I believe, in Canada. Aptly named, don't you think?

Anna retreats a few steps.

I suppose, she says.

She resumes her position at the chessboard. Is Max smiling as he does the same? Anna moves her rook quickly, without forethought.

Max pushes his spectacles up onto his forehead as though he has another set of eyes there.

That's done it, he says, sighing. You've completely foiled my plan, young lady.

Anna watches him covertly as he canvasses the board, holding his head, hands plunged into his undisciplined light hair. He puts a forefinger on his rook.

Tell me something, he says. Your father. Is he a member of the *Partei*?

He has leanings in that direction, yes, says Anna carefully.

Max rubs his chin.

As I thought, he says. He impressed me as being the sort who would. He's an—opinionated fellow, yes?

You could say that.

Mmmm. And tell me something else, dear Anna. I've been wondering. Has it been very difficult for you, living alone with him these past five years? You seem so very...isolated.

The room is quiet enough that Anna can hear the bubble of the water in the pot. Despite the astonishing ease of these evening conversations, which Anna reviews each night as she lies in her childhood bed, this is the first time Max has asked her something this personal. She would like to answer. But her response remains bottled in her throat.

Max strokes the rook.

The death of a parent, he says to it, is a profoundly life-altering experience, isn't it? When I was a child, I often had this feeling of *God's in his Heaven: All's right with the world*—that's Robert Browning. An English poet. But ever since my father died in the last war, I've awakened each morning knowing that I'll never again feel that absolute security. Nothing is ever quite right, is it, after a parent dies? No matter how well things go, something always feels slightly off...

As Max talks, Anna is paralyzed by simultaneous realizations, the first being that nobody, since her mother's death, has ever spoken of it. At first, neighbors came bearing platitudes and platters of food, and there were well-meaning invitations from distant relatives to spend holidays in their homes, summers at their country houses. But nobody has ever had the courage, the simple human kindness, to ask her how she feels in the wake of the loss. To approach the matter directly.

And the accuracy of Max's comment about her isolation: how can he know this? Anna looks across the table at his narrow face. Although quiet by nature and an object of some envy because of the attention her looks drew from boys, Anna did have girlfriends for a time, school chums with whom she linked arms at recess, acquaintances whose classroom gossip she shared. But the rise of the Reich, coinciding with her mother's death, soon put an end to this. The activities of the *Bund deutscher Mädel,* which Anna joined with all the other girls, seemed insipid and made her vaguely uncomfortable; during patriotic bonfires in the Ettersberg forest or swimming parties with the boys of the *Hitlerjugend,* Anna would watch the happy singing faces and think of what awaited her at home: the cooking and cleaning, her mother's dark and empty bed. She began participating less and less, citing housework and her father's needs as the reason, and eventually her friends stopped coming up the drive to the house, their invitations too dwindling into a puzzled silence.

And so Anna is left with only her father, whose demands, once offered as an excuse, are certainly real enough. She thinks of Gerhard performing his morning toilette, wandering about the house in his dressing gown, clearing his throat into handkerchiefs that he scatters for her to collect and launder. She must trim his silvering beard daily, his hair fortnightly. His sheets, like his shirts, must be starched and ironed. She must prepare his favorite meals with no concern for her own tastes, the consumption of which Anna endures in a fearful stillness punctuated only by the snapping of Gerhard's newspaper, *Der Stürmer,* and explosive diatribes about the evils of Jews. How Anna wishes he had died instead!

Max pushes his rook across the board.

Check, he says, and looks up.

Oh, Anna. I'm sorry.

Anna shakes her head.

I didn't mean to upset you, Max says.

You haven't, Anna reassures him, finally finding her voice. I'm just startled by how well you put it. It's like being in a sort of club, isn't it? A bereavement club. You don't choose to join it; it's thrust upon you. And the members whose lives have been changed have more knowledge than those who aren't in it, but the price of belonging is so terribly high.

Max tilts his chair back and considers Anna for a long moment, scrubbing his hand over his face and neck.

Yes, he says. Yes, it is much like that.

Then his chair legs hit the floor and he stands.

Speaking of your father, he says, smiling, would you like to see how his dog is doing?

Anna gazes sadly at him, disappointed by this return to more superficial conversation. But as Max beckons to her, she obediently gets up and follows him.

After turning down the heat under the teakettle, Max takes Anna's elbow and leads her to a door at the rear of the house, which Anna expects to open into a garden. Instead, she finds herself in a dark shed smelling mustily of straw and animal. She hears a thick, sleepy bark, and when Max lights a kerosene lantern, Anna sees that he has constructed a makeshift kennel here. Including Spaetzle, there are five dogs in separate cages, and Anna catches the green glitter of a cat's eyes from the corner, where it presides over a heap of kittens. There is even a canary in a cage, its head tucked under its wing.

Anna walks over to Spaetzle.

Hello, boy, she says.

The dachshund snarls at her. Anna snatches her hand from the wire mesh.

I see his disposition hasn't improved any, she observes.

Perhaps it might, says Max from behind her, if you'd stop stuffing him with chocolate.

Anna flushes. I told you, that's my father's doing—

Ah, yes, of course, says Max. So you've said.

Anna turns to see him smiling knowingly at her. Face burning, she stoops to peer at a terrier.

So you are something of a veterinarian after all, she comments.

Max doesn't answer immediately, and when Anna is certain her color has receded she swings around again to look at him inquiringly. He is standing with his hands in his pockets, regarding the animals with an odd expression, both tender and grim.

I'm more a zookeeper, he says. And not by choice. Not that I don't love animals; I do, obviously. But these have been abandoned to my care. Left behind.

Left...?

By my friends, by patients who've emigrated, to Israel, the Americas, whoever will have them. People I've known my entire life—gone, *pfft!* Just like that.

Max snaps his fingers, and the canary lifts its head to blink at him with indignant surprise.

Anna digs a toe into the straw.

Circumstances are truly that bad for—for your people?

Worse than you can imagine. And they are going to get worse still. The things I have heard, have seen...

When he doesn't finish the thought, Anna asks, And you? Why don't you go as well?

She looks down and holds her breath, praying that he won't answer in the affirmative. But Max gives only a short, bitter laugh.

What? And leave all this? he says.

Anna glances up. He is watching her, his gaze speculative.

Loneliness is corrosive, he says.

Anna's eyes film with tears.

Yes, she says. I know.

She thinks that she might be able, in this moment, to go to him and put her arms around him, rest her head on his chest; she wants nothing more than to be able to stay here with Max forever, in this simple dark place smelling of animal warmth and dung. But of course this is impossible, and the thought only serves to remind her of how late it is.

God in heaven, it's hours past curfew, I have to go, Anna says, darting past Max into the house.

In the kitchen, while Anna fastens her hat, Max holds her coat out like a matador, flapping it at her; then he helps her into it. His hands linger on Anna's shoulders, however, while she fastens her buttons, and when she is done he spins her around to face him.

Where does your father think you are? he asks. When you come here?

Oh, it doesn't matter to him, as long as his dinner is served on time, Anna murmurs. He thinks I'm at a meeting of the BdM, I suppose. Sewing armbands and singing praise to the *Vaterland* and learning how to catch a good German husband.

And isn't that what you want, Anna? Max asks. Aren't you a good German girl?

Before Anna can reply, he kisses her, much more violently than she would have expected from this gentle man. He drives her back against the wall and pins her there with a hand pressed to her breastbone through the layers of cloth, making a slight whimpering noise like one of his adopted dogs might in sleep. Anna clings to him, raising a tentative hand to his hair.

Then, as abruptly as he initiated the embrace, Max breaks away and bends to retrieve Anna's hat from the floor. He smiles sheepishly up at her and quirks his brows over the rims of his spectacles. His face has gone bright red.

We can't do this, he says. A lovely creature like you should be toying heartlessly with fellows her own age, not wasting her time with an old bachelor like me.

But you're only thirty-seven, Anna says.

Max hands her the hat, one of its flowers crumpled on its silk stem. Then he lowers his glasses and gives Anna a serious look.

That's enough, young lady, he tells her. You know that's not the real reason why this is impossible. For your own good, you really must not come back.

Over Anna's protests, he pushes her gently through the door and shuts it behind her.

Anna stands on the top step, her hand between her breasts where Max's was not a minute ago. She is too nonplussed by the speed of the encounter and what he has said afterward to rejoice over it. She stares into the garden while she waits for her pulse to resume its normal rhythm, watching fat flakes of snow filter so languidly through the air that they appear suspended.

Naturally, Max is quite right. These evenings should come to an end before either of them get further involved, though the real obstacle—as Max has implied—is not that he is twice her age. The problem, not addressed head-on until tonight, is that Jews are a race apart. And even if Max is not observant, the new laws forbid more than Aryans visiting Jewish physicians: sexual congress between Jews and pure-blooded *Deustche* is now a crime. *Rassenschande,* the Nazis call it. Race defilement. It is like the poem Max read to Anna last week—how do the lines run? Something about a dark plain on which armies clash by night. She and Max are pawns on opposing squares, on a board whose edges stretch into infinite darkness, manipulated by giant unseen hands.

But if Anna can't recollect the poem in its entirety, she remembers how Max read it, with exaggerated self-mockery, pausing to glance ironically at her between stanzas; his little half-smile; the glint of mischief flashing like light off his spectacles. Anna laughs and runs her tongue out to catch the snow as she descends the steps toward the gate. Of course she will come back.

3

ONE MORNING IN MARCH 1940, ANNA WAKES WHEN HER father pounds on her bedroom door. She lies blinking and disoriented: What time is it? Has she overslept? Gerhard is never up and about before her. She turns her head to the nightstand clock, and when she sees that it is but an hour after dawn, she leaps from the bed, snatches the robe from the door, and runs into the hall. Gerhard is now nowhere to be seen, but Anna hears him crashing about downstairs.

Vati? Anna calls, following the noise to the kitchen. What is it? Is something wrong?

Gerhard is snatching plates from the china cabinet, holding each up for inspection before dropping it to the table.

This, he says, waving a saucer at Anna, this is what's wrong. Why is so much of the china chipped?

Anna clutches her dressing gown closed at the throat.

I'm sorry, Vati, I don't know. I have been very careful, but it is so old and fragile —

Gerhard tosses the dish next to its companions.

Nothing to be done, nothing to be done, he mutters.

He yanks open the icebox and thrusts his head inside, strands of silver hair hanging over his forehead.

Leftovers, he says. Carrots and potatoes. Half a bottle of milk. Half a loaf of bread— Is this all there is?

Why, yes, Vati, I haven't yet gone to the market today, it's far too early, so—

Gerhard slams the door closed.

There is nothing in this house fit for a chambermaid to eat, let alone decent company, he says. You must go immediately. Get meat. Veal or venison if they have any. Vegetables. Dessert! You must spare no expense.

Yes, of course, Vati, but what—

Gerhard charges from the room, leaving Anna staring after him. She has been an unwilling student of her father's erratic behavior her whole life, alert as a fawn, calibrating her every response to his whims. But nothing in Gerhard's mercurial moods has prepared Anna for his invasion of her territory, the kitchen; if asked prior to this, Anna would have said that Gerhard might not know even where the icebox is.

Anna!

Coming, Vati.

Anna hurries into the house and finds Gerhard standing in the downstairs WC.

Why are there no fresh handtowels? he demands, shaking a fistful of linens at her.

I'm sorry, Vati. I laundered those just last Sunday—

This is appalling, Gerhard says. They must be done again. Starched. And ironed.

He throws the towels at Anna's feet.

Yes, Vati, she says, stooping to collect them. I'll do it as soon as I get back from the—

And where is my best suit?

In your closet, Vati.

Pressed? Brushed?

Yes—

My good shoes? Are they shined?

Yes, Vati, they're upstairs as well.

Humph, says Gerhard.

He comes out into the hallway and glowers about, hands on hips, at the entrances to the library, the drawing room, the dining room, at the chandelier overhead.

After you go to the market, you must ensure that everything in this house is spotless. Spotless, do you understand? No pushing dirt under the rugs, Miss.

Why, Vati, I would never—

Gerhard rakes a hand through his thinning hair. In his atypical *dishabille*—he is still in pajamas—he reminds Anna of a big bear disgruntled at being awakened too soon.

Where is my breakfast? he demands.

I'll get it right away, Vati.

Very good, says Gerhard.

He pinches Anna's cheek and strides off in the direction of his study. A moment later Anna hears him burst into song, a snatch of the Pilgrim's Chorus from Wagner's *Tannhäuser,* bellowed at the top of his lungs.

Anna sneaks back upstairs and dresses hastily, then returns to the kitchen and adds to the bread a boiled egg and some cheese that has escaped her father's notice. Putting this on a tray with a pot of tea, she brings it to Gerhard's office.

Ah, thank you, Anchen, he says, rubbing his hands. That looks lovely. Even as you do this morning, my dear.

Anna sets the food on her father's desk and retreats to the doorway. She has learned to be wariest of him when he is smiling.

Will there be anything else? she asks, eyes on her shoes.

Gerhard slices the top off the egg and eats it with a mouthful of bread.

We will be having guests for dinner, he says, spraying crumbs onto the blotter in his enthusiasm, very important fellows on whom I must make the best possible impression. Everything, down to the last detail, must be perfect. Do you understand?

Anna nods.

Gerhard flutters his fingers: dismissed. Anna walks from the room as quickly as she can without actually running, leaving Gerhard to hum and mumble as he chews.

Tulips, he calls after her. Tulips are in season, aren't they? If you get to the market fast enough, you might be able to get a few bunches...

Anna patters rapidly down the staircase, pausing only to grab her net shopping bag and coat from the rack near the door. Safely out on the drive, she looks back over her shoulder at the *Elternhaus,* her childhood home: such a respectable-looking place, with its heavy stone foundation and half-timbered upper stories. One would never suspect its owner to be so volatile. Anna glances at the window of Gerhard's study and hurries down the road before he can throw it open to shout further instruction.

Once the house is out of sight around the bend, Anna repins her hat, which she has crammed onto her head at a crazy angle in her haste, and slows her pace. This is her favorite part of the day, these hours devoted to her errands, the only time she has to herself. During the journey into Weimar and back, Gerhard and his requirements are conspicuously absent, and Anna dawdles along indulging in her own daydreams. Until recently, these have been of the vaguest sort, centering primarily on the day Anna might escape her father's house to live with whatever husband he has chosen for her. Gerhard has exposed her over the past few years to a variety of candidates, but in Anna's mind the face of her spouse remains indistinct. Not that she has cared much who he might be or what he will look like, as long as he is quiet and kind. Nor has Anna ever thought of other aspirations, attending University for instance; what for? None of her peers would ever consider such a thing. *Kinder, Kirche, Küche*: children, church, kitchen; this is what all German girls hope for; this is what Anna has been raised to be. Her future is not for her to decide.

But lately her reveries have assumed a different, more concrete form. Given the war—the girls being requisitioned for agricultural *Landwerke,* Anna's potential suitors commandeered by the *Wehrmacht* and *Luftwaffe*—who knows what might happen? And there is Max. Perhaps, if things continue to worsen as he says, Max will leave after all—and take Anna with him. They could go to a warm place far away from this senseless strife, somewhere he could set up a small practice and they could live simply. Portugal, Greece, Morocco? Anna pictures them walking along a beach in the morning, talking while the fishermen set out their nets. They will linger in a café over lunch. They will eat strange fruit and fried fish.

This pleasant picture evaporates as Anna nears the center of Weimar, where she realizes that Gerhard's fitful humor seems to have communicated itself to the world at large. The weather itself is nervous, sullen fat-bellied clouds racing across a slaty sky, and in the market in the Rathaus Square, where Anna exchanges ration coupons for venison and vegetables, merchants and customers alike are cross and short-spoken. Nobody, it seems, will meet Anna's eye. Not that there are many people about; the streets are as quiet as if the city has been evacuated while Anna slept. Has there been bad news of the war? Anna clamps a hand to her hat, which the wind threatens to tug from her head, and recalls Max's observation that his charges become restless before any change in atmosphere. Perhaps her fellow Weimarians are responding in kind to a drop in the wartime barometer.

Anna ducks beneath the snapping Nazi flag over the doorway of the Reichsbank, taking shelter in the vestibule while she thumbs through her ration booklet. If she and Gerhard forgo sweets for the rest of the week, Anna calculates, she will have just enough to cajole some sufficiently impressive pastry from Frau Staudt for tonight. Anna steps once more into the raw afternoon and hurries back through the Square toward the Jewish Quarter. By now she too is uneasy in her own skin, wanting only to finish her shopping and return to her warm kitchen.

The Quarter also seems deserted—that is, until Anna spots Herr Nussbaum, the town librarian, standing on the sidewalk in front of his house. And this sight is so strange that Anna stops in her tracks, thunderstruck. For the elderly librarian, whose fussy vanity doesn't permit him to appear in public without the hat that hides his bumpy skull, is stark naked. He wears nothing but a large cardboard sign hung from his neck with a string, proclaiming: I AM A DIRTY JEW.

Anna would like to look away, but she can't help gaping at Herr Nussbaum's poor flabby old man's buttocks, the white tufts on his back. Before this, the closest she has come to seeing a man unclothed is a childhood glimpse of Gerhard in the bath, his limp and floating penis reminding her of a wurst casing half-stuffed—an observation that, when repeated to her mother, earned Anna a lashing and an hour in the closet. This current spectacle so offends Anna's sense of the rightful order of things that she cannot believe it is real. She looks wildly about to confirm whether anyone else is seeing it too. There is Frau Beiderman across the street, but the seamstress scuttles in the other direction with a businesslike air. Aside from her, there is only Anna and the naked Herr Nussbaum, standing with his hands cupped over his genitals against a luminous backdrop of shivering cherry trees, like a refugee from a dream.

Cautiously, after looking again this way and that, Anna approaches the librarian.

What's happening? she asks, voice low. Who has done this to you?

Herr Nussbaum stares resolutely at the house opposite, remaining quite still except to tremble in the sleet that spits like sand from the sky.

Anna drops her net bag of purchases to the pavement and starts to remove her coat.

Here, she says. Put this on.

The librarian ignores her. His long medieval face belongs over a ruff in a portrait, his gaze the sort that would follow the viewer to any corner of the room. Now the severe dark eyes that so frightened Anna as a child are terrified themselves, rheumy and watering from fear and wind.

Go away, he says, without moving his mouth.

What?

Get away from me with that coat, you stupid girl. They're watching.

Who?

Anna glances over her shoulder. On the ground door of the dwelling across the road, a curtain flutters, then falls back into place.

But you mustn't mind your neighbors, she whispers. If they had any decency, they'd take you in. You must be freezing—

Not them, you idiot, the librarian mutters through his wispy beard. The SS.

SS? Where? I don't see—

Everywhere. SS and Gestapo. Something has set them off; they're on a real rampage. Started going through the Quarter this morning looking for something, God knows what. And they haven't stopped since.

Anna's stomach turns to water.

Every house? What about the *Doktor*? Herr *Doktor* Stern? Did they—

The librarian gives a small fatalistic shrug: probably, it says.

You're just making things worse for me, he hisses. Go away!

Anna seizes her bag and runs down the street toward the clinic. It looks as it always does, with its soot-stained stones and bronze nameplate, and for a moment Anna is reassured. Then she touches the door in the center of the six-pointed Star, and it swings wide to reveal the reception area dark and empty behind it.

Max? Anna calls.

Well, perhaps he has no appointments this afternoon. Most

of his patients have emigrated anyway, and the remainder will not be seeking medical attention with the SS about. But—

Max?

Anna peers into the examining room. It is in wild disarray, the apothecary jars smashed, cotton wadding soaking up medicine on the tiles. The filing cabinet has been forced open to regurgitate its patient histories on the floor: GOLDSTEIN, JOSEPH ISRAEL, says the one Anna steps on, in Max's distinctive, all-capitals hand; 3 MARCH 1940, SEVERE HEMATOMAS FROM BEATING, COMPLAINT OF PAIN IN THE LEFT ARM—

Max! Max—

In the kitchen, a teacup lies on its side on the table, milky curds clinging to the rim. The plants have been swept from their perch, and there are large bootprints in the soil surrounding the shattered clay pots. Anna races upstairs to Max's bedroom, a place to which she has never been but often envisioned visiting under very different circumstances. It is small and impersonal and similarly despoiled, the mattress and pillows slit in an explosion of feathers, sheets on the floor. Anna picks one up in icy hands and buries her face in it; it smells of Max, of his hair and sleep. Then she flings it aside and descends the steps on legs that feel both rubbery and too heavy, as they sometimes do just before her time of the month, as though the blood in them is more responsive than usual to the pull of gravity. There is an unpleasant odor in the hall, reminiscent of sheared copper. It grows stronger as Anna follows it to the door of the shed.

The fanlight window over the clinic entrance brightens for a second with weak sunlight as she opens the door, enough to show her the animals before dimming again, and at first Anna thinks they are sleeping. Then her vision adjusts and she realizes they are dead. The dogs must have been shot or stabbed, for blood drips from the cages, the air thick with its metallic stench. The cat's fate is clearer: its skull has been crushed along with those of its kittens, whose corpses lie in a drift by the wall. Only the terrier, in the cage beneath Spaetzle's, is still alive. Its paws twitch; one brown eye rolls piteously in Anna's direction as it whines.

Anna takes a few steps toward it. Something crunches under her heel. She looks down, grimacing: Max's spectacles.

A high, outraged little note escapes Anna's windpipe. She scoops up the glasses and slides them into her pocket. Then she bends and vomits in the hay. When nothing is left in her stomach, she crosses the shed. She pauses in front of Spaetzle's remains, wishing she could feel something about the death of her father's dog. But as she can't, she lifts the terrier from its cage.

The animal is clearly dying, and Anna knows she should put it out of its misery with a swift twist of the neck or blow to the head. Instead she sinks to the ground cradling it, stroking the matted fur. So Max, for whatever reason, has been arrested. God in heaven, what if it is Anna's fault? Anna presses a bloody fist to her mouth, her eyes stinging with tears. What if, despite her caution, somebody has seen and reported the Aryan girl visiting the Jewish physician's house? But no; the SS would not be ransacking the entire Quarter if this were the case. Regardless, Anna must help him. What can be done for Jews who have been taken into protective custody? If only Anna had paid more attention to the rumors whispered around her during her daily errands. It is like trying to recall voices overheard from another room while one is dozing. Random beatings of Jews, roundups, detainments, deportations. The homes of Aryans who question the treatment of their Jewish neighbors suddenly empty and remaining so night and day, mail accumulating in their boxes, milk souring on the doorsteps.

But Anna remembers hearing that the SS can be bribed, particularly if the supplicant is pretty and desperate enough. She has used her looks for lesser things. And the safe in Gerhard's study surely contains something of value. Anna need only think of a way to get her father out of the house.

She sets the terrier's body down, its eyes having long since

filmed over. Then, after cleaning her sticky hands as best she can
with straw, Anna leaves through Max's back garden so as not to
be seen. The SS may still be abroad, and the last thing Anna
needs is to be detained for questioning as to why she is in this
district. The premature dusk is smoky and raw, its uniform gray-
ness an ally to Anna in her dark *Zellwolle* coat. She races through
the alleys of the forsaken Jewish Quarter, skirting tricycles and
ducking lines of washing, all the while clutching the spectacles in
her pocket.

4

THAT EVENING, GERHARD IS FORCED TO AMEND HIS DIN-
ner plans. He telephones his important new acquaintances and
arranges to meet them at a restaurant. After all, Anna hears him
explaining into the receiver, he doesn't want them to catch his
daughter's influenza. Anna has told him that it is rampant in
Weimar just now, the streets a symphony of sneezes, the shops
like TB wards. Gerhard's companions must be pleased with his
concern for their health, for Anna hears him humming as he
dresses and descends the stairs. The cloying fragrance of his *Kölnischwasser,* of which he has used a great deal, lingers long after
his car disappears from the drive.

Some time later, Anna creeps down to the kitchen. Breaking
into her father's safe has been useless, as the strongbox contains
only Gerhard's traveling papers and a gold pocketwatch that no
longer tells time. Anna sits dully in a chair, forcing herself to
nibble a wedge of cheddar while she considers alternate plans.
None comes to mind. Perhaps the watch would be worth something on the black market, but Anna has no idea who might be

involved with this risky venture nor how to find out. In despair she abandons the cheese on the table.

She is attempting an apple next when she hears a rap on the window near the maid's entrance. She freezes with her teeth half-sunk into the fruit. The knock comes again, faint but insistent.

Anna rushes to the door and flings it open to find Max standing there.

Oh, my God, she cries, dropping the apple, which wobbles unheeded across the floorboards. Oh, thank God you're all right—

Max tries to smile.

May I come in? he asks.

Don't be a fool, Anna tells him. She tugs him into the kitchen by the shirtsleeve.

Max props himself against the icebox as Anna secures the lock and begins whisking the curtains shut.

So you know, he says. About the *Aktion* this morning.

Anna turns to examine him. He is covered in mud, his hair plastered to one side of his head as if he has just awakened, and there is a shallow scratch on one cheek. Other than this, he appears unharmed.

I was in the Quarter and I ran across Herr Nussbaum, she says. And when I went to your house, I found the animals—

They killed them, Max says.

Yes.

Max frowns at the floor, his Adam's apple bobbing in his throat.

I was afraid of that, he says. I wanted to do it myself, the humane way, but there wasn't time.

Anna begins rummaging through the pockets of her skirt.

I have your glasses here somewhere, she says. I know you're hopeless without them—

Then, without warning, she begins to weep.

Max comes to Anna and takes her in his arms. This is the

first time he has held her properly, and Anna relishes it, damp and filthy as he is. She sways against him, closing her eyes, but Max stares at the wall over her shoulder, distracted.

How long will your father be gone? he asks, detaching her.

How did you know he's not here?

I've been in the bushes much of the afternoon. I saw him leave a half hour ago, off to dine with his friends, am I right? Top brass, all of them.

Max rubs his eyes. Dear God, of all the places I could have come, he groans. I'm so sorry, Anna...

He runs a hand down the side of his face, which rasps with stubble. I just need a bite to eat, he says. Then I'll be on my way.

Of course I'll fix you something, Anna says, collecting herself. But first we must get you out of those wet rags.

Anna—

Ignoring his protests, Anna leads Max from the kitchen and into the house, beneath the twisting, exaggerated shadows cast by the chandelier in the entrance hall, up the main staircase.

Here, she says, once she has shown him to the WC. Clean yourself up. I'll be back in a moment.

Then she ransacks Gerhard's bedroom closet for clothes he will not miss, keenly attuned all the while to the small splashes Max makes as he bathes and shaves, the noises she would hear each morning if they lived here together. It is ridiculous, given the circumstances, but there it is: the fierce joy that Max is in her house. Anna shakes her head at herself and returns to the WC with a pair of old tweed trousers and a shirt.

Thank you, Max says, accepting them. I'll be quick.

Anna ignores this, exiting to let him change but leaving the door open a few centimeters. From behind it, she says, So you left before the SS began the *Aktion*. How did you know they were coming?

Silence from the WC. Stealing closer, Anna watches Max remove his shirt. His skin is very white, blotched here and there with a fair man's spreading freckles; because he is so thin, his body looks much older than that of a man in his mid-thirties. His chest, however, is furred with a surprisingly healthy crop of reddish hair. He slides his trousers and briefs from his hips.

Please, Max, Anna says, touching her burning face. Tell me what happened.

Max dresses in Gerhard's clothes, which, Gerhard being a portly fellow, bag comically on his narrow frame. Then he opens the door all the way. Anna slides past him into the narrow room and perches on the lip of the tub.

I'm sorry about your father's dog, Max says. Jews aren't allowed to own pets. The animals were killed because they're considered contaminated by Jewish blood—

Anna makes a dismissive gesture.

Herr Nussbaum said the SS were turning the entire Quarter inside out, she says. You can't expect me to believe they were only looking for who might still have a dog or two.

Max contemplates Anna for some time, stroking his razor-reddened chin. Then he says, My being here is placing you in terrible danger. The less you know, the better.

Anna leaps to her feet.

You listen, she says, giving Max a small shove. Do I mean so little to you that you can't trust me? Were all those nights we spent talking and playing chess nothing more than that, only games?

Max sighs.

Of course not, he says. All right. Since I've already involved you by coming here—

Yes, tell me.

I did know about the *Aktion* before it happened. More than that, I'm afraid I was its cause.

I don't understand. How—

Max looks sternly at her. Quiet, young lady. Let me explain in my own way.

He sits beside Anna on the tub.

You know of the concentration camp?

Chastened, Anna nods.

There's been some talk, she says. It's up on the Ettersberg, yes?

Yes. In the forest on the mountain. Established for political prisoners and criminals and Jews and anyone else who offends the Nazis. They're put into this Buchenwald for re-education, which means they are used for slave labor. They are starved and beaten and then, when they're half-dead, they are considered dispensable.

What happens then? Anna whispers.

Why, they're dispensed with. But since it's a crime to waste ammunition nowadays, it's done by lethal injection. The SS kill them in batches, with needles to the heart. Evipan sodium, I believe. Or air. Afterwards, the bodies are cremated.

Anna tries to digest this and fails. It is too insane to be comprehended. She looks resentfully at the cold, skillful fingers on hers, then up at Max's dear, tired face, strangely exposed without his glasses, poised and watchful as that of a fox. The deep lines hashmarked about his eyes, the violet shadows beneath them. How can he inflict this on her? How can he come here, to her home, and dump this repugnant story in her lap?

That can't be true, she tells him.

Max attempts an ironic smile, but a muscle flutters near his jaw.

Oh, it's true, he says. I know it seems impossible. But it's happening as we speak.

How do you know? How do you know it's not just a rumor?

It's not a rumor, Max says wearily. I've been there. I've seen it.

He withdraws his hands from hers and fumbles in the pocket of Gerhard's trousers, producing a small cylindrical parcel.

What's that?

Film of the camp. There's a photography studio the SS use for identification shots of the inmates. Some of the prisoners have managed to take pictures of what goes on up there, don't ask me how. I have to make sure that this film gets to a safe place.

Where?

Somewhere in Switzerland. Exactly where, I don't know. It's safer that way.

So the SS found out you were working for this—Resistance network.

Yes.

And they were looking for the film.

Yes.

Max drops the little canister into Anna's palm. The waxed paper it is wrapped in is greasy to the touch. It will repel water.

Such a small thing, says Max. You'd never suspect it was worth so much blood.

Anna returns it to him, trying to parse this new Max with the man she knows, the good doctor to whom she has confessed secrets she never knew she had. All along, while she has been thinking only of beguiling him, he has been engaged in an infinitely more complicated and important game. She looks at the braided rug beneath her feet, suddenly shy.

Who else is involved? she asks.

Max slips the film back into his borrowed trousers.

I don't know the extent of the network. A handful in Weimar. Most beyond. Frau Staudt, for one—

Frau Staudt?

Anna pictures the baker trampling through the forest on the Ettersberg and begins to laugh helplessly.

I would have gone to her tonight, but I saw the SS outside the bakery, says Max. I couldn't think where else to go.

Anna gets up and kisses him on the forehead, inhaling, for a moment, the smell of his hair.

I'm glad you came to me, she says. So glad. Now come, time for bed.

Anna, are you mad? I can't stay here!

You'd rather go back to the bushes?

Max frowns, but he allows Anna to help him stand. He is shaking with fatigue.

In the morning, he says, as soon as things settle down, I'll find a safer place.

He follows Anna to her bedroom, where she bustles about, folding back the eiderdown and plumping the pillows. She turns to see him looking at the shelves of Dresden figurines and trophies from the League of German Girls, the embroidered samplers, the canopied bed in which Anna has slept since girlhood.

No, he says. It's too risky.

You couldn't be safer in heaven. My father never comes in here. I'll bring you some food.

Max glances at the doorway as if considering flight, and then at the high lace-curtained window, through which even he, skinny as he is, couldn't fit.

All right, he says. For one night, since there's no feasible alternative. But Anna, please don't trouble yourself with food. I'm so tired I can barely see.

As Anna starts to object, Max climbs into her bed without removing Gerhard's trousers.

Shhh, he says. He settles into the pillow.

Anna closes the door and moves about the room, shedding her clothes. She exchanges her slip for her shortest nightgown and eases in beside Max, who is lying with his back to her.

I forgot to give you socks, Anna whispers. Your feet are cold.

She rubs them with her toes. Max shifts his legs away.

Anna presses against him and rests her lips on the nape of his neck.

Max rolls over. No, Anna, he says.

Why not?

Anna senses that he is smiling.

I've already told you, you're far too young for me, Max says, and they both start to laugh, shaking with it and trying to muffle the noise against each other's shoulders.

It is then that Anna hears her father's unsteady progress up the stairs, the risers complaining under his weight. There is a soft thud as part of Gerhard, a shoulder or knee, hits the wall in the hallway. His labored breathing stops outside her room.

The door swings open. A slice of light falls across the bed.

Anna, Gerhard says.

Anna forces herself up on one elbow, though every instinct screams that she curl into a fetal position.

Yes, Vati, she says, mimicking a voice soft with sleep.

Gerhard braces himself against the doorframe. The medicinal odor of schnapps wafts to the bed.

Is there any bicarbonate of soda? he asks.

Yes, Vati.

I'd like some right away. And perhaps a digestive biscuit or two.

Of course, Vati.

They serve such rich food at the officers' club, Gerhard complains. Never a simple hearty meal. Tonight it was goose. You know how goose affects me. I had to leave early.

I'm sorry, Anna says.

Gerhard belches, releasing vapors of drink.

I'm feeling rather liverish, he confesses.

He turns with great care, then pokes his head back into the room.

What are you doing asleep at nine o'clock? he asks.

I'm not feeling myself either, Vati. A touch of influenza, don't you remember?

Ah, yes. Poor Anchen.

Gerhard sways, then waves a hand.

Bicarbonate, and quickly, he says.

Right away, Vati.

Gerhard shuts the door and lurches off down the hall.

When she hears *Die Walküre* from his study, Anna climbs from the bed and gropes for her wrapper. Her father will have to wait a bit longer for his medicine. She desperately needs to visit the bathroom. Before she leaves, however, she pats the quilt to determine where Max is and finds his arm. His muscles are so rigid that even through the goosedown they feel like bunched wire.

Impossible, Max breathes. This is impossible—

Anna bends to put her lips against his ear.

No, it's not, she whispers. I know where to hide you. I have the perfect place.

5

A WEEK LATER, HAVING FINISHED HER ERRANDS, ANNA IS standing in her coat in the upstairs hallway, before a small door. Behind it is what Anna has always thought of as the Christmas closet, since her mother used to store gifts for the holiday in this crawlspace. As a child, Anna was often unable to resist stealing the key from her mother's sewing kit and taking it to this door, which she would eye with a curiosity matched only by fear of the consequences should she be caught opening it. She waits in front of it now gripped by much the same emotions, the key clutched in her slippery hand.

She is counting slowly to five hundred, Gerhard's car having left the drive a few minutes earlier. Anna cannot be too cautious, although there is little chance that he will return and even less that he would find her if he does, once she has entered the closet. Anna is fairly certain that Gerhard doesn't even know of its existence. The *Elternhaus* is full of architectural oddities that its current owner has forgotten. Initially conceived of as a hunting lodge, it was never intended to be more than a seasonal outpost from which its builder, Gerhard's great-grandfather, could ride to hounds. But with each successive male Brandt the wheel of the family's fortune has spun further downward, and subsequent generations, camped full-time in the *Elternhaus,* have added their personal touches to its original sprawling floorplan.

And Anna, during her tenure as housekeeper, has cleaned every inch of it, often on stepladders or on her hands and knees. In the days following her mother's death, she sometimes had help in doing so: a series of maids hired by Gerhard — all named, oddly, either Grete or Hilde. But every Grete-Hilde departed within a month of arrival, perhaps owing as much to Gerhard's fickle attitude toward payment as to his tempers: when he was in pocket, he would dole out wages with the air of conferring a great favor; when not, promises. And by the time his financial situation became more stable — his legal practice bolstered by new friends he had made among the ranks of the Reich — Anna had fulfilled the positions of maid, cook, and laundress so nicely that Gerhard apparently never considered it necessary to seek more staff.

Therefore the unexpected breezes in the *Elternhaus* corridors, the ominous gurgles of its plumbing, are as familiar to Anna as the workings of her own body. She would be able to describe each idiosyncrasy of the house if marched through it blindfolded: the windowseats where there are no windows, the halls that lead nowhere, the hearts carved in the banisters by a fey great-uncle. And Anna knows about something else that she believes Gerhard, given his general neglect of his property, does not. She shifts from foot to foot; she has reached four hundred now, and she bounces the key in her palm. It is true that once Gerhard has left for his office in the city, he usually does not return until evening — and then accompanied by supposed clients, drunken fellows wearing the Nazi armband who shout and sing until all hours of the night. But better to be safe than sorry.

Finally, when two more minutes have passed and the only sound is that of water pattering from the eaves, Anna unlocks the door to the Christmas closet and steps inside. To her left is a wall with a high window that allows a dusty shaft of light to fall on another little door to her right. This conceals a maids' staircase connecting the upper stories of the *Elternhaus* to the kitchen, once enabling servants to scurry behind the wall to answer their masters' demands while remaining out of sight. Now, of course, Anna is using it for a different purpose. She knocks on the interior door, three soft raps, and pushes it open.

A few meters down, on the landing, Max shields his eyes with a hand. Even such indirect light is painful to him after hours in the dark. His upturned face is a pallid circle, and Anna pityingly thinks, as she gropes her way along the steps, of creatures living in caves so deep beneath the sea that they have never seen the sun and are white and blind in consequence.

Max rearranges his nest of blankets to make room for Anna.

You have brought spring with you, he says. I can smell the wind in your hair.

The landing is barely big enough for two. Anna wedges herself in beside Max, feeling the bony jut of his hip against her own, and removes her coat with some difficulty. Max buries his face in the cloth.

The past few days have been warmer, she tells him. The gutters are rushing like waterfalls.

I know, says Max. I listen to them at night.

Are you hungry?

Max laughs. Perpetually. But please, don't run off to the kitchen just yet. I'm more starved for company than food.

He puts an arm around her, and Anna imagines that, were he unclothed, she would be able to see his bones through his skin. He eats next to nothing of what she brings him. His stomach, he has apologetically explained, roils with nerves.

They sit in comfortable silence, Max rubbing a thumb over Anna's collarbone. It amazes Anna: she spends much of her time in this dim, elongated box, fusty with years of disuse and the unlovely exhalations of Max's chamber pot, and so, on a physical level, Anna's life has shrunk to its confined proportions. Yet here, in the dark, she feels herself expanding. For years Anna has trudged through her days like an automaton with only her day-dreams to occupy her, paying no mind to what happens around her unless it hinders her routine in some way. Now, as she walks beneath dripping trees and visits shops, she observes her sur-roundings with as much keen interest as if she were a visitor to a foreign land. She embroiders and rehearses overheard conversa-tions for Max, hoping to be rewarded by his barking laugh; she lays anecdotes at his feet like treasure. Her personal landscape has never been brighter nor her mental horizons wider.

I went back to the bakery today, Anna tells Max now. Frau Staudt has a terrible hacking cough. You should see the black looks the customers give her as she handles their bread.

Any news? Max asks, smiling at Anna's scowling imitation.

We didn't have much time alone. Only a few minutes. But new papers are being drawn up for you so you can be moved to Switzerland. Frau Staudt says to be patient; these things take time, she said. And money. They are trying to raise the money.

Max takes his arm from Anna's shoulders and stretches, wincing.

And the film?

She hasn't mentioned it since I passed it to her on Thursday. But I'm sure she would have told me if something had gone wrong.

Max sighs.

Dear Anna, he says. My sole regret about what I've done is having to involve you.

Anna performs a complicated wriggling maneuver that ends with her sitting behind Max, his back to her chest.

How many times do I have to tell you I don't mind? she says in his ear.

Max doesn't answer. As best she can in the gloom, Anna studies his profile. She yearns to toy with his hair, which has grown long enough to relax into curls above his collar. Observ-ing the way it wings back from his fine, bony face, Anna imagines Max wearing tails, attending an opera in Vienna, perhaps, or Berlin. She feels a sudden wretched longing for the things they will never know together.

You need a haircut, she says lightly, yanking a wayward blond tuft.

I'm sure I do, Max replies. Next time you go to town, why don't you bring a barber back with you?

No need for that. Tomorrow, when I sneak you out for your shave, I'll do it myself.

Thank you, but no. I'd rather grow it to my knees.

Anna rears up indignantly.

I cut my father's hair every fortnight! she reminds him.

I know. I've seen the results. I'll wait until I reach Switzerland.

Anna slaps Max on the shoulder. He turns, cringing exaggeratedly, holding a protective arm up over his face.

Ouch, he says. That hurt, you little brute.

Not half so much as you deserve.

Is that so, Max says.

Suddenly he grips Anna's biceps and pulls her forward, kissing her with the same desperate intensity she remembers from the January evening in his house. He hasn't permitted anything of the sort since then, so Anna is taken completely by surprise as he pushes her into a reclining position against the steps. He rips open her dress, buttons popping off and scattering into the stairwell, and tugs a cup of her brassiere to one side, and Anna gasps at the slipperiness and the nip of his teeth, which, in his enthusiasm, he uses a bit too hard.

Straining against her, Max fumbles to undo his trousers, and Anna feels a draft on her thighs as he lifts her skirt to her waist. She inhales sharply when he enters her. There is some pain, but not much. Anna wonders if she will bleed, as she has heard sometimes happens. She is not frightened at the prospect of surrendering her virginity, although she has always thought this would occur on her wedding night and hopefully to a Siegfried-like bridegroom, rather than a doctor whose ribs, clashing against her own, have no more meat than those of a washboard. Later, in the bath, she will discover a dark raspberry on one breast and that her pubic bone feels bruised. But now, as Max drives into her, knocking her head against a riser and uttering small whimpers, Anna repeats to herself that this is Max, her Max, and is grateful.

It is over within minutes. A drop of sweat falls on Anna's forehead, and another, and one in her eye, stinging. Max whispers, Anna...and goes slack on top of her. He is still for what seems a very long time. Then he rolls back onto the landing and Anna can breathe again.

Eventually Max draws Anna to him. They lie side by side, blinking into the column of light. Then Max props himself up on one elbow to look at her. Stretching his hand, he touches Anna's nipples with thumb and ring finger.

Like cherries, he says. Cherries in the snow.

Anna smiles.

Is there still snow on the ground outside? Max asks.

Some, Anna tells him. But it's melting.

Max nods and sinks back down, resting his head on her chest. Anna strokes his damp hair, marveling at how soft it is over the fragile cradle of bone. She holds him this way, in meditative quiet, until the crunch of gravel on the drive signifies Gerhard's return home.

6

IT IS MAY, AND HOT. IN THE ROOM BEHIND THE STAIRS, Anna and Max lie naked, panting like mongrels. The atmosphere is too close to allow them to hold one another in comfort, so Anna settles for lacing her fingers through Max's and hooking a friendly ankle over his. She gazes up into the stairwell. With the passage of months, the sun's position has changed, and a concentrated beam of light pierces the gloom as if in a cathedral. Its angle lets Anna know that she has only a few more minutes to spend here, listening to Max talk. He craves conversation, which, Anna occasionally thinks with some guilt, she prefers to more physical intimacies.

Max traces the length of her arm with a forefinger. You know what I love? he asks.

Tell me.

These freckles. So dark on such light skin. Like sprinkles of chocolate.

Anna rolls her eyes.

Why, thank you, she says. My other lovers like them too.

Ah, your other lovers, says Max. His grip tightens on her waist. We'll just have to do something to take your mind off them, won't we? Come here.

Anna obliges. A passionate tussle ensues but is interrupted when Max starts to sneeze. He hunches into a quivering ball, sneezing and sneezing. Eventually he stops and blinks miserably at Anna, who sees, even in this dim light, that his face has gone persimmon red.

Dear sweet loving God, Max says, sniffling. There is nothing more wretched than a summer cold.

How on earth could you have caught a cold?

I suppose it could be the dust.

Perhaps, Anna agrees. Or perhaps you're allergic to the idea of my other lovers.

She feels for her slip and wriggles into it, an awkward process in this small a space.

Speaking of which, she adds, it's time for me to go put the finishing touches on dinner. My father has another festive evening planned.

Max helps her fasten a garter. More suitors? he asks.

An endless supply of them. *Hauptsturmführers, Obersturmführers,* who knows what rank Vati's managed to dig up this time. He has such high aspirations for me.

Max sneezes again as Anna stands and smoothes her skirt, and she looks at him with concern. I wish I could get a doctor for you, she says.

He waves this away. I am a doctor, and it's nothing, believe me. But Anna, all joking aside, you must tell Mathilde to hurry with the papers. I can't stay here much longer.

I know. Just until the end of the war.

Max shakes his head. Please, Anna. Promise me you'll see Mathilde tomorrow.

I promise, says Anna, and begins to climb the steps.

I mean it, Anna.

So do I, she whispers down to him. Don't worry.

She smiles at Max and shuts the inner door on his imploring face.

As she steps into the hallway, Anna is assaulted by a wave of vertigo. She leans against the wall and presses her forehead with her fingertips. They are freezing despite the heat, and when she takes them away, they are slick with sweat. She too must be re-acting to the air in the room behind the stairs, which is hardly fresh. But how peculiar that she should feel ill only upon leaving it! Perhaps Max is right; the pressure of hiding him here is taking a physical toll on both of them. What a pair they are, sneezing and reeling. Anna walks shakily to her bedroom.

Here a rapid transformation occurs. Anna exchanges her housedress for one of blue silk, splashes her face with water from the basin on the bureau, and pins her long dark hair, wavy with perspiration, into a chignon. Then she assesses herself in the full-length mirror and sighs. As it is widely held that praise spoils children, Anna has rarely been told outright that she is beautiful, but she knows she is from the effect her looks have had on others: covert admiration, shyness, envy. She knows too that vanity is wrong, but she has always taken a secret pride in her slim waist and high round breasts, the pale eyes and curious light streaks in her hair that for as long as she can remember have won exclamations and candy from strangers. Since entering young womanhood, however, Anna has found this more bother than benefit, given Gerhard's constant parading of her before prospective marital candidates. And now Anna would pay a high price to be plain, for her looks pose an ever-greater danger to both herself and Max. If only she were ugly, Gerhard would not persist in bringing this new species of suitors to the house, hop-ing to further his own ambitions by pawning Anna off to a high-ranking Nazi husband.

However, Anna knows enough of what is expected of her to play her part, and what matters most at the moment is that no sign of how she has spent the afternoon shows on her face. Anna frowns at her reflection, counting to one hundred, until the feverish color has receded from her cheeks. Then she descends to the kitchen, where she garnishes the chilled soup with sprigs of parsley. She surveys the place settings in the dining room and tweaks a rose in the centerpiece vase. She sits in one of the chairs, folds her hands in her lap, and waits. By the time Gerhard and his friends arrive, Anna's demeanor is one of docile, vapid composure.

There are two guests this evening. Anna has never seen the big blond officer before; he is handsome enough, but he has the skewed nose and pugnacious stance of a boxer. She thinks, smiling sweetly at him, that he would have been a street brawler in the unsettled period between the wars, the sort who would have ended up in prison without the *Partei*. His lips are full, like halved peaches, obscene in that block of a face.

SS *Unterscharführer* Gustav Wagner, Gerhard announces; Gustav, my daughter Anna.

As Wagner bows over her hand, Anna asks, Are you perhaps related to the musician?

She sees the wet flash of Wagner's eyes as he glances up at her.

No, Fräulein, but I appreciate beauty in any form, musical or otherwise, he says, and Anna feels the flick of his tongue on her skin. She longs to rap him on his oiled hair.

And you have already met *Hauptsturmführer* von Schoener, Gerhard continues, turning to the other officer. On two occasions, I believe?

Three— von Schoener corrects him. His voice is a weak rasp, the result, Anna knows, of exposure to gas in the trenches of the first war. He coughs into a handkerchief and gazes at Anna with watering brown eyes. Anna has always been uneasy around dark-eyed men. She would rather that he, too, lick her proffered hand than stare at her this way. But von Schoener continues to stand stiffly to one side of the quartet, projecting longing at her from a distance.

If you'll be seated, dinner is ready, says Anna. Unless you'd care for a drink first?

Gerhard laughs.

No, my dear, we're quite lubricated enough already, he says. Gentlemen, this way.

With an expansive gesture that falls just short of a bow, he ushers the officers into the dining room. Anna escapes to the kitchen. As she does, she hears Wagner say, Well, Gerhard, I'd heard you were hiding a little treasure here, but I never expected anything like this. She has the face of an angel! and Gerhard's modest reply: Yes, she is rather fetching, if I do say so myself... But hiding her, Gustav? Such a dramatic accusation! I'm merely keeping her safe until the right fellow comes along. She'll make some lucky man a good wife...

Anna, fighting another swell of nausea, lets the door swing shut behind her. When she re-emerges, carrying the tureen of soup, the three men have seated themselves in the dining room, Gerhard at the head of the table, the other two to either side. Wagner lounges in his chair, but von Schoener sits upright, a mismatched bookend. He presses his handkerchief to his lips, watching Anna's every movement as she serves him.

Is this watercress? Wagner asks, dipping his spoon into his bowl.

Cucumber, Anna tells him. An antidote to the warm weather.

It's nice, Fräulein. A local recipe? They have nothing like this where I'm from.

And where would that be? Anna asks, taking her seat opposite Gerhard.

A small town in East Prussia. You probably haven't heard of it.

Anna revamps her image of the pre-war Wagner: he would have been a farmhand, then, tormenting the animals and perhaps the younger, weaker boys.

Wagner laughs nastily.

I've never understood why everybody considers East Prussia so backwards, he says. I see you now think I'm a hayseed, Fräulein.

Of course not, Anna murmurs.

Let's hope the *Führer* never asks you to be a spy, says Wagner. He slides the spoon over his lower lip, tonguing the silver concavity. You'd make a very bad one. I can see your every thought on your face.

Anna prays this isn't true. She forces herself to take some soup. Though she is normally fond of cucumber, the liquid coats her mouth, slimy as algae.

And have you left your family behind to fulfill your duties here? she asks, looking pointedly at Wagner's left hand, where a slim silver ring glints on his wedding finger.

Wagner's grin fades.

Yes, my whole family. This ring is— It belonged to my grandmother.

Really, says Anna.

Wagner applies himself to his soup.

We must all make sacrifices for the Reich, Gerhard says. His voice, sonorous from years of courtroom appearances, is modulated, but Anna knows that he is furious with her, as he has been ever since she told him that Spaetzle ran away. He conceals his anger well, even as his silver mustache hides a harelip; like many of his imperfections, it is invisible to the casual observer. But can't even these officers, acquaintances of a few months, see Gerhard's conceit, his sycophancy, the foppishness of his cravat and handmade shoes?

Apparently not, for Wagner tells Gerhard, I like your waistcoat.

Gerhard looks modestly down at the garment, which, embroidered with a hunting scene, would be more appropriate hung on a wall.

And this room—! Wagner waves his spoon, scattering green droplets. That chandelier is magnificent. Did you kill the deer yourself?

Of course, Gerhard says of the configuration of antlers above the table. He reaches for the decanter. I am an avid hunter, he adds carelessly, though Anna knows he has never so much as held a rifle.

The acrid smell of the officers' boot polish is suddenly overwhelming. Swallowing bile, Anna collects the empty bowls, sets her own full one atop the rest, and excuses herself to attend to the main course. She arranges the slices of venison on a silver platter with distaste: the flesh glistens, the pink of a healing burn, causing her stomach to perform an even more lively set of calisthenics. Averting her eyes, holding her breath, Anna brings the meat out to the men.

Do you know, she says to *Hauptsturmführer* von Schoener, I don't think I've ever asked you what brings you to Weimar. What is it you do here, specifically?

The *Hauptsturmführer* blinks. Tears trickle down his face, which otherwise remains immobile.

Desk work— mostly— he gasps. He coughs into his handkerchief, inspects the contents, then folds it into a small square. I'm really— no more than— a bureaucrat— I wouldn't dream— of boring you— with a detailed— description—

He again brings the handkerchief to his mouth, gazing at Anna over the linen.

False modesty is a bad habit, Joachim, Gerhard booms. He spears a slice of venison and sends Anna a significant look from eyes as small and greedy as a bear's. Translated, his glance means: This one is good husband material; his lineage is impeccable and his valor demonstrated, but because of his injuries, he will never leave you to be summoned to the front!

Anna doesn't return her father's smile. Having fulfilled her duties as a hostess, she is now free to eat without participating in the conversation. She focuses on cutting her meat and dropping it into the napkin on her lap, listening for useful tidbits that Frau Staudt might pass on to others in the Resistance. But the men don't oblige her. Rather than discussing the camp —with which, as SS, they are obviously affiliated—they analyze the *Führer*'s brilliance during the recent offensive into France. Anna would glean more information from the *Völkischer Beobachter,* the local paper.

Suddenly *Hauptsturmführer* von Schoener breaks off mid-gasp.

What is it, Herr *Hauptsturmführer,* Anna asks. Would you like more wine?

I thought— I heard— something— he says.

The group freezes, Wagner's fork halfway to his fleshy lips. From near the ceiling, from the direction of the hidden maid's staircase, there is a muffled thump—the sort of sound produced, for instance, by a person sneezing so violently that he has knocked his head against the wall.

Immediately Anna bends over her plate, coughing. The men turn in her direction, Gerhard annoyed, Wagner startled, von Schoener concerned. And Anna meanwhile finds that her act has become real: there is no morsel of food lodged in her throat, of course, but she can't catch her breath. In his consternation von Schoener starts to cough too, and the table begins to sound like the percussive section of a human orchestra.

Then Wagner is behind Anna, seizing her arms and raising them above her head.

Breathe, he commands. Deeply. That's it.

He reaches over her shoulder for a glass.

Drink this.

Anna obeys. A last convulsion forces some of the wine into her nose, but she is finally able to draw a shallow breath. As Wagner releases her and resumes his seat, she nods her thanks and daubs her tearstained face on her sleeve.

That's how we East Prussian hayseeds stop choking fits, Wagner says.

The men chuckle. Anna laughs weakly along with them. Her energetic charade has expelled Max's fluids, and she feels them sliding like egg whites between her thighs.

Anyone for seconds? Gerhard asks. He crooks a finger at Anna.

Anna doesn't move. The officers will have to wait or serve themselves. She fears she has stained her dress.

I couldn't— eat— another bite— says von Schoener. My— compliments, Fräulein—

Again, from behind the wall, there is a bump.

What *is* that? Wagner asks.

Mice, perhaps, suggests Gerhard. I suppose this house has its share of them, like all old houses. This one was built in 1767, you know, as a summer home for the Kaiser.

Anna closes her eyes. Even she hasn't heard this tale before.

Wagner chews mechanically, his fat lips bunching.

That's impressive, he says. But you really do need an exterminator, even so. To get rid of the vermin.

7

By July 1940, CONVERSATION AMONG THE CITIZENS OF Weimar is limited to one topic: the phenomenal success of the *Blitzkrieg* on London. No more whispered complaints of how hard it is to find a decent leg of lamb, a pair of real stockings, a good cognac; no mourning once-voluptuous figures or lamenting husbands absent at the front. Instead, the *Volk* go about with their chests thrust forward, heads high, greeting one another with smiles: Did you hear? Four thousand killed in a single air raid! Those Messerschmitts are a miracle, a marvel. That fat sausage Churchill must be cowering in his bunker. Our boys will be home by Christmas yet!

Yes, it's wonderful, murmurs Anna, shouldering her way through the cheerful throng in Frau Staudt's bakery. Yes, yes, I couldn't agree more; it's splendid news.

Once outside, she takes a deep breath, relieved to be free of the pungent stink caused by the rationing of bathwater and her own hypocrisy. Anna has always been impatient with the gloating over Reich triumphs, and never more so than today, when she has quite different news to impart to Max. She sets off for home at a trot, ignoring the Rathaus bells tolling yet another *Luftwaffe* victory behind her. How will she tell him? Not an hour ago, Anna will say, Frau Staudt informed me that the new identity cards and passes are ready—two sets, not one. You and I, my dear Max, will cease to exist, but Stefan and Emilie Mitterhauser will be traveling to Switzerland, where they can make their paper marriage real in a quiet ceremony.

No warm beach or fried seafood, then: instead and more appealing at the moment, the breezes of Interlaken. A simple suite of rooms, perhaps overlooking the deep quiet lake, the mountains ringing it with their snowcapped peaks. Cool and sweet and quite a contrast with the afternoon through which Anna walks, more slowly now. To move through this air is like fighting one's way through a dream: all Weimar gasps for breath in heat heavy as cotton wadding, the motionless atmosphere that precedes a thunderstorm.

Gerhard's car is not in the drive when Anna reaches the *Elternhaus,* so she goes straight to the Christmas closet.

Hello, Herr Mitterhauser, she calls, shutting the outer door behind her. How do you feel about a holiday in the mountains?

Her attempt at gaiety is muffled in the cramped space, as though the stagnant air has swallowed it. Without warning, the dizziness and attendant nausea attacks her. Anna puts a hand on the wall and waits.

When it has passed, she flicks sweat from her forehead and opens the inner door. You'd better start packing, she says. We leave tonight—

Then the feeble light from the high window penetrates the stairwell, and the strength runs from her legs like water.

For there are no sheets, with which Anna has replaced Max's blankets when the days grew hot. There are no scraps of verse pinned to the walls. No empty plates. No chamber pot. There is nothing, in fact, to indicate that anyone has ever been in the hiding space at all, except for the olfactory ghost of Max's perspiration and their lovemaking, a salty smell curiously reminiscent of onions.

WHEN ANNA HEARS THE SCRATCH OF GERHARD'S KEY IN the front door, it is nearly eight o'clock. She sits in his study, in his chair behind his desk, a position forbidden to her. She toys with Gerhard's letter opener as she waits for him, turning it over and over in her hands. The instrument is embossed with a family crest—not the Brandts', though Gerhard claims it is. Anna runs her forefinger over the curving blade, which is sharp enough to draw blood. The weather has broken; thunder rolls overhead, and as Anna has not bothered with the lamps the fading light that trickles into the room is wet and green.

Eventually Gerhard throws open the door to his study.

There you are, he says. Haven't you heard me calling you? Isn't it about time for dinner?

He fumbles for his pocket watch and makes a great show of checking the hour. Anna watches him. His pores ooze whiskey; his thinning hair has escaped its pomade and hangs in strands over his forehead. Under the influences of his new friends, Gerhard, once a teetotaler, has taken to emptying a bottle nightly. To the casual observer, he would appear a harmless buffoon.

Yet of course Anna knows Gerhard is anything but, and despite her current resolution to remain calm, her hand clenches on the letter opener. The blade slips, slicing the tender meat beneath her fingernail.

She sets the knife down and inspects the welling bead of blood.

I didn't make dinner, she says. And you know why.

Then she flinches, steeling herself for the tirade she knows will follow. But Gerhard—predictable only in his unpredictability—surprises her by saying nothing as he sinks into one the armchairs usually reserved for his clients.

How did you know? Anna asks.

Gerhard smothers a belch.

How?

The whiskers in the shaving basin, Gerhard says, were blond.

You took him to the Gestapo. To be exterminated, as Wagner suggested. Like any other vermin—isn't that right?

Gerhard's mouth drops open as if he is shocked and aggrieved by this accusation.

I did it for you, Anchen, he says.

At his use of her childhood name, Anna feels another surge of nausea. Her blouse and the roots of her hair are instantly soaked with perspiration. She stands and paces with one hand cupped over her nose, hoping that the comforting smell of her own skin will assuage the sickness. Behind her, Gerhard reclaims his throne.

How much did they pay you, your friends? Anna asks, rounding on him. Or did it merely increase your cache in their eyes? Did it cement your social position, bringing him into Gestapo headquarters? Did they award you a Knight's Cross with Oak Leaves and Swords?

She starts to weep, and her tears, coming at such an inappropriate time, make her even angrier.

You've killed him, she says, killed him as surely as if you put a gun to his head and pulled the trigger yourself—

Gerhard crashes a fist down on the desk blotter.

Enough! he bellows. Stop sniveling, you repulsive slut. You stupid, stupid girl! You're not only a whore, you're a stupid whore. Of all the men you could have spread your legs for, you chose a Jew?

Anna tries to defend herself but produces only a squeak. Ah, here is the tempest, no less powerful for being belated.

And to hide him here, here of all places, Gerhard shouts. While all along I was thinking only of you! Your safety. Your future. I should let you rot. Better yet, I should turn you in as well. In fact, I think I will. We'll go to the Gestapo right now—

He lunges from behind his desk and clamps a hand on Anna's shoulder.

Come along, he says; we'll go this instant. Is that what you want? Is that what you want, Anna?

The muscles in Anna's neck seize as her father's fingers dig into them.

No, Vati, she gasps. Please —

Gerhard puts his face an inch from hers. It is what you deserve, whore, he says. His spittle, smelling of liquor and herring, peppers Anna's cheeks. He pushes her away.

Did you ever once stop to think? he demands. Did you ever once consider the consequences for me? When you were discovered — and it was only a matter of time, believe me — you would have been taken into protective custody along with that filthy Jew, and what would happen to your old father then? Living alone with nobody to care for him, afflicted by chronic ulcers?

Anna braves a look at her father, a tall man running to fat, his head lowered bullishly as he glares. Max would have been no match for him. She feels in her stomach, as if it were Max's, the lift of anticipation when the door to the stairwell opened and then, when it revealed Gerhard instead of her, the catapult of dread. She grasps an end table and screws her eyes shut, trying not to vomit.

All right, says Gerhard. All right, that's enough.

Having assured himself of his victory, he can now afford to be magnanimous; his voice drops into the confiding register he uses when, having cowed a jury with the forceful oratorical tactics he has borrowed from the *Führer,* he wishes to befriend them.

You're damaged goods now, he tells Anna, tainted by that Jew, but nobody need know, thank God. We'll put the best face on things. Yes, we must think only of the future. *Hauptsturmführer* von Schoener — he is your future. He may be a weakling, but he is a kind man. Think of all he has already done for you! Who but Joachim spared you being assigned Land Service in some Godforsaken place? He knows the value of family, of keeping a family together. He would marry you tomorrow.

Anna opens her eyes and stares at Gerhard. Can he be serious? Will he never see her as anything but child or chattel? For the past few weeks, Anna has never been more aware of her own body: her swollen breasts chafing against her brassieres; the weariness that dogs her every step; the tiny aches and pains in her joints, as though she is a house settling; the constant nausea accompanied by the copper taste of *Pfennigs*. She is not yet that thick in the waist, and she wears dresses without belts. But can Gerhard truly have not noticed that she is four months pregnant?

But of course, he is the very definition of a selfish man. Anna moves to the chessboard by the window and turns on a lamp. The ivory and onyx squares glow. Perhaps Gerhard never really saw Max either, not as a human being, a fellow man with whom he might bend his head over these handsome pieces and engage in the strategies of small-scale, harmless warfare.

She touches the crown of the white king. Thunder mutters, distant now.

Think only of the future, she repeats. I suppose you're right.

Gerhard nods.

I'm so sorry, Vati, for the trouble I've caused you. I will make *Hauptsturmführer* von Schoener a fine wife.

That's my Anchen, says Gerhard.

I'm tired now, Anna tells him. I'd like to lie down. Forgive me, but would you mind getting your own dinner? There is a pigeon pie in the icebox.

Yes, yes, Gerhard says. He smiles, exuding an oily mixture of schnapps and forgiveness.

Anna puts her cheek up to be pinched and leaves the study without looking back.

In her bedroom, she switches on the lamp. Its shade is a globe of frosted glass, bumpy with little nodules. Her mother's choice, as are the flowered coverlet, the extravagant armoire. Nothing in the room is really Anna's. It is the impersonal chamber of somebody perpetually asleep.

Anna takes her old school satchel from the armoire and packs three changes of clothes. There is no need to bring more; by this time next month, these dresses will not fit her. She adds her hairbrush and a pair of comfortable shoes. She burrows into the bottom drawer of the bureau and retrieves her christening gown, rustling between yellowed layers of tissue paper. Then she steals down the back staircase and runs from the *Elternhaus* through the servants' door.

The road to Weimar is deserted, as gasoline is impossible to get without connections and it is long past curfew. The only vehicle that might pass now would belong to SS or Gestapo, and Anna has no desire to encounter either one. She quickens her pace, jumping at movements in the weeds, her palms slick. The night is moonless and black but for the occasional sullen flare of lightning on the horizon, over the hump of the Ettersberg where the camp is. On the outskirts of the city, the sounds of people's ordinary evenings drift from the houses: the thin cry of an infant, a sudden shout of laughter, a man calling to his wife for a glass of water. Anna hates them all.

As she walks along, her dress clinging to her like bandaging, the poem comes to her. Could it have been only twenty-four hours ago that she was in the stairwell, listening to Max recite it? He lay then with his arms crossed behind his head, eyes closed to invoke memory, unaware of Anna's smile as she watched him.   .

> *Ah, love, let us be true to one another!*
> *... And we are here as on a darkling plain*
> *Swept with confused alarms of struggle and flight,*
> *Where ignorant armies clash by night.*

When Anna reaches her destination, she bypasses the front entrance and rustles through shrubbery to the back. There she taps on the sectioned wooden door. There is no response, no movement within, no flicker of light in a window. Anna whispers the verse into the humid air and waits. After three repetitions, she knocks again, harder this time, and is rewarded by a scuffling sound. Anna closes her eyes: she is still there, then, thank God; she hasn't been picked up and taken away, the only woman who can now help her. The door opens an inch to reveal the cautious, scowling face of Frau Mathilde Staudt.

Trudy, November 1996

8

IT IS ONE OF THE GREAT IRONIES OF HER MOTHER'S LIFE, thinks Trudy Swenson, that of all the places to which Anna could have emigrated, she has ended up in a town not unlike the one she left behind. Of course, Weimar was and is much bigger than New Heidelburg, and it was once a government seat, and it provided a home to Goethe, Schiller, artists and museums. There is certainly no such sophistication about this little farm hamlet. But the countryside of southern Minnesota, through which Trudy is driving, resembles the land around Weimar: the same gentle hills and fields that former Buchenwald prisoners say could be seen from the camp. And Trudy imagines that the mentality of the two places is also similar. People ostensibly turning a blind eye to their neighbors' activities while really harvesting and analyzing every last detail of their lives. The ingredients for their dinners. The color of their underwear, purchased in the local Ben Franklin. Who is sick, who is well, who is adulterous. In the case of wartime Weimar, who had been taken away in the middle of the night.

Here and now, also in the evening but an ocean away and

fifty years later, Trudy is pushing the speed limit as much as she dares: seventy-five on the highway, thirty in the populated zones. These small towns are all speed traps, and the interstate is not much better. When she reaches the New Heidelburg limits she slows still further, though she is frantic with the need to press the accelerator to the floor. Crawling along Main Street, Trudy is aware of curtains twitching, of faces gathering at the windows of Chic's Pizza and Cathy's Chat'N'Chew. She pretends not to see them. She knows that not only her presence here but the reason for it will have traveled through the whole town by morning. In fact, Trudy can hear the conversations as clearly as if she were eavesdropping on the party line: *Did you see Trudy Swenson was here today? Nooooo. But I did hear her mother tried to burn the house down. Oh, you know, I heard that same thing! I guess Miss Big-City Swenson'll finally have to put that old witch in the home.*

Trudy doesn't realize she has been holding her breath until she reaches the other side of New Heidelburg, at which point she lets it out in a *foooooooof.* The speedometer's red needle creeps upward as she passes the last stand of trees, the defunct golf course, the Catholic cemetery—the town's papists segregated from the Lutherans even in death—and a smattering of farms. Then there is nothing, until a few miles farther the New Heidelburg Health Clinic looms suddenly in Trudy's high beams. The big red brick building, along with the nursing home crouched beside it like a mongrel dog, is completely isolated from the rest of the town, as if not only illness but old age—its dementia and vacancy and bed-wetting—demands quarantine.

Trudy turns into the clinic lot and parks, checking the dashboard clock. It is seven-thirty, two and a half hours since she received the call from Anna's caseworker. Trudy has made good time. She shuts off the engine and headlights and sits in the dark for a minute. Then she sighs, pulls her muffler up over her face, and sprints into the building.

The hallway is quiet and dim, the check-in desk awash in fluorescence. As distracted by worry as Trudy is, the scene reminds her of a Hopper painting: the zone of bright light and the woman sitting alone in it, the distilled essence of isolation.

The nurse looks up at Trudy's approach, inserting a finger in the paperback she is reading.

Can I help you? she asks.

I'm Trudy Swenson, says Trudy, slightly out of breath. My mother is here? Anna Schlemmer?

The nurse nods and reaches for a folder in the hanging files in front of her.

Room 113, she confirms. But visiting hours are over. You'll have to come back in the morning. I'm sorry, hon.

No, please, says Trudy. I have to see her. I drove all the way from the Twin Cities. I came as quickly as I could—

I'm sure you did, says the nurse. But I can't go against the rules. Your mom's in the trauma unit—

Trauma! Trudy repeats. I was told the smoke inhalation was only minor!

Well, that's true, says the nurse. There's nothing for you to be real concerned about. But at your mom's age, you know, we can't take any chances. That's why we're keeping her for observation.

She gives Trudy a sympathetic smile. Why don't you get some rest yourself and come back tomorrow? That'd be best.

Trudy stares at the nurse in frustration. For a moment she wonders whether the woman is deliberately barring her access to Anna—yet another slippery New Heidelburg trick. But no, although the nurse is about Trudy's age, Trudy has never seen her before. She is not from the town; she must live somewhere nearby, Rochester, maybe, or LaCrosse.

Couldn't I just sit with her for a minute? Trudy persists.

Listen, Mrs.— Swenson, is it?

Doctor, corrects Trudy automatically.

The nurse raises penciled brows.

You're a doctor?

Of history, Trudy says, smiling.

The nurse regards her with some pity, and Trudy has the

momentary and uncomfortable sensation of viewing herself as another might: a foolishly arrogant little blond woman in a pilled black overcoat, with a determined set to her jaw.

Please, she says.

The nurse sighs.

I really shouldn't, she says. But…All right. Just for a minute. This way.

Trudy follows the nurse down the hall. The woman is short and stout, like the teapot. Everything about her, from her plump compact body to her easy-care perm, conveys a cozy capability. To distract herself from what might await her in the trauma ward, Trudy imagines the nurse's life: she has at least two grown children and several grandchildren; on weekends they come over with casseroles of hot dish and brats, which they eat in the rec room while the nurse's retired husband drinks Pig's Eye and watches the Vikings. There would be a basketball hoop on the garage. The nurse is everything Trudy has been raised to be and nothing whatsoever like the person Trudy has become.

They stop in front of room 113.

Remember, not too long with her now, warns the nurse. And try not to wake her. She needs her sleep.

Thank you. I appreciate this.

The nurse lays a hand on Trudy's arm. Trudy looks down at it, the short pink nails, the freckled flesh bulging on either side of the wedding and engagement rings.

There's one other thing you might want to know, the nurse says.

What's that?

She's not talking. She hasn't said a word since she came in, not to the doctor, not to anybody. We had to get her information from her social worker.

Trudy nods.

That's nothing new, she says. But thank you for telling me.

Again, that glance of compassion. Then the nurse walks away, the rubber soles of her sneakers creaking on the linoleum.

Trudy waits until the nurse has turned the corner. Then she takes a deep breath and opens her mother's door.

Oh, Mama, she says softly.

Anna is asleep in a hospital bed, the light bar over it casting a white glare on her face. If they are so adamant about Anna getting her rest, why is this on? Trudy wonders. She steals across the room. At least Anna is hooked up to nothing more dire than an IV. There are no tubes snaking into her nostrils, no beeping machines. Trudy lifts a plastic chair to the bedside. She sloughs her coat and sits as near to Anna as she dares.

Trudy has not seen Anna since Anna's seventy-sixth birthday in August, and she is shocked by how much Anna has changed in three months. *Failing,* the older New Heidelburgers would call it. Trudy catalogues with indignant sorrow the weight loss, the age spots, the spreading bruise on her mother's hand from the IV. They are frightening and unfair, the ravages time wreaks. Yet even now, Trudy is struck by the extraordinary geometry of her mother's face: the sculpted cheekbones and square jaw. The pleasing symmetry of widow's peak and pointed chin. In Anna's gray hair, the light streaks—once blond, now white—providing the touch of oddity without which real beauty is incomplete. Ever since Trudy can remember, whenever Anna made one of her rare forays into public, people would gravitate to whatever room she was in, just to look at her. But they never got too close. Anna's loveliness, combined with how little she talked, set her apart from ordinary folk. Made them clumsy. Suspicious. Shy. Resentful: *Oh, she's stuck-up, all right. Thinks she's so much better than us.*

But Trudy knows there are other reasons for Anna's silence. Now Trudy inches farther forward and squints, as if by concentrating she could penetrate the surface to what really interests her: her mother's skull, hard as the casing of a walnut. And within this, like the meat of a walnut with its complicated folds, her mother's brain. What information is encrypted in that soft gray matter? Trudy wonders. She watches Anna's eyes roll back and forth like marbles beneath their papery lids. What is Anna seeing now as she sleeps? What scenes so shameful that she will never speak of them, has never spoken of them, not even to her own daughter? What memories so tormenting that they have finally—perhaps—become unbearable?

As if she senses this invasive line of questioning, Anna jerks and wakes. She focuses her pale eyes on Trudy, who is reminded of the ghostly stare sometimes seen from a dead relative in an old photograph, a gaze from which one can't turn away.

Trudy hastily sits back. Anna looks at her, or perhaps through her to somebody who isn't there.

Mama? How are you feeling?

Anna doesn't so much as blink. The familiar silence spins itself out, so complete that Trudy can hear the faint and insectile buzz of the fluorescent bar over the bed.

Won't you talk to me, Mama?

Anna says nothing. Trudy waits. Then she touches Anna's hand, carefully, mindful of the tubing threaded into the vein.

Please, Mama. Was it an accident? The house, I mean. The fire. Or…I'm sorry, but I have to know. Did you— Did you set it on purpose?

Anna turns her face away. Then she rolls her head to the center of the pillow, her eyes once again closed.

After another minute or two, Trudy stands and collects her coat from the chair.

I'm sorry to have disturbed you, Mama, she says. I'm leaving now. But don't worry. I'll be back soon. And I'll take care of everything.

She leaves the room, quietly shutting the door behind her, and walks through the trauma ward to the reception desk.

The nurse glances up and sets her romance novel aside. *Passion's Promise,* it is called.

How's our girl?

Better than I expected, says Trudy.

Still sleeping?

Yes.

The nurse nods with satisfaction. She's going to be just fine. Out of here in no time.

How long will you keep her, do you think? Trudy asks.

Oh, a couple of days at most. No more than that.

Trudy runs a hand through her hair. I see. I guess I'll have to make some immediate arrangements, then...Well, thank you for everything.

The nurse watches Trudy curiously as she buttons her coat.

Are you taking her to live with you then? she asks.

This suggestion so shocks Trudy that she involuntarily snorts laughter through her nose. She rubs a knuckle across it, hoping the nurse has mistaken the sound for a sneeze.

Oh, no, she replies. I don't think she's in good enough shape for that, do you?

Well, the nurse says dubiously, she seems pretty strong. Some of these older farm ladies go on forever, you know. If it was up to me, I might—

Trudy shakes her head.

It's out of the question, she says. I work full-time, I can't look after her, and even if I had enough money to hire somebody—No. It's impossible.

The nurse shrugs and opens her book again.

That's too bad, she says. I suppose she'll go to the Center then.

Trudy grimaces beneath the scarf she is winding around her face. The penitential building next door is hardly the sort of place in which one would want to spend one's golden years. But there is no use being softhearted about it. This is just the way things are. Trudy herself will end up in a similar institution one day. And now, for Anna, it is the only logical alternative.

Yes, the Good Samaritan Center, she tells the nurse, her voice muffled by wool. In fact, whom should I speak to about getting her a room? Because when my mother's ready to leave, I think it'll be best to have her transferred directly there.

9

AFTER THIS VISIT, TRUDY IS TOO WEARY TO FACE THE three-hour drive back to Minneapolis, with its attendant dangers of black ice and starving deer who wander onto the roadway. Besides, Trudy has more business in New Heidelburg; better to get it over with all at once instead of making another trip. Since the town offers nothing in the way of accommodation—it isn't exactly a tourist attraction—she spends the night in one of the cheap motels on the outskirts of Rochester, in an overheated room that smells of smoke and dirty hair. She sleeps restlessly and rises early, and after a complimentary breakfast consisting of a roll and coffee so weak Trudy can see the bottom of the cup through the liquid, she returns to New Heidelburg, where she stops first at the nursing home to arrange for Anna's room there. A single, of course; if Anna, that most private of women, were forced to endure a roommate on top of everything else, Trudy thinks, she would break her toothbrush glass and quietly eat the pieces.

This unhappy but necessary task accomplished, Trudy proceeds to the next: dropping by the town's real estate office to list

the farmhouse for sale and its contents for auction. This trans-
action too is concluded with surprising ease, although the realtor
wears on her sweater a Santa Claus pin with demonic, flashing
red eyes, which both fascinates Trudy and stirs in her a vague
anxiety.

She finds herself back out on the street much earlier than expected, and since she has no reason to linger, she again takes her
leave of the town, this time with a bewildering sense of anti-
climax. Trudy frowns, puzzled. She should be relieved, even
pleased; she will reach the university campus well before her office hours and afternoon seminar. Which is good, since after receiving the call about Anna yesterday she absconded from both
without so much as a note for the History Department secretary.
But as Trudy passes the Chat'N'Chew, the Starlite Supper Club,
the Holgars' dairy farm, the nagging feeling that she has forgotten something intensifies. The Lutheran cemetery where Jack
lies buried on the ridge comes into view; is it that she has neglected to pay her respects to him? Trudy slows but then notices
a plastic Santa head the size of a pumpkin impaled on the pointed
iron gates. Trudy shudders, turns up the heat on the dash, and
drives on.

When she sees the double rows of pines that lead to the
farmhouse, she realizes what has been troubling her. It is not,
she tells herself, that she is being sentimental; it would be a gesture of kindness to personally retrieve Anna's belongings and
bring them to the Good Samaritan Center, instead of having the
social worker do it. And although insurance and county apprais-
ers will be sent to the property to estimate its value, it is only
practical that Trudy assess the fire damage firsthand. She pulls
into the drive beneath the trees, wrestling with the steering wheel
as the tires of her Civic whine for purchase in the snow. Eventually she reaches the dooryard, parks, and gets out. Then she
stands examining her childhood home.

Since Jack's death three years ago, Trudy has made a point of
coming here four or five times a year—on Christmas, Easter,

Anna's birthday, Mother's Day—enough to satisfy her own requirements for daughterly obligation. But on these occasions,
her need to escape Anna's silence and return to normal life, as
urgent as the pressure exerted by an unrelieved bladder, has prevented Trudy from really looking at the house. Now, as with
Anna, Trudy is startled by how much and how quickly the farmhouse has decayed. It is still standing, but just barely. The paint
is blistered, the foundation sinking, the roof an accident waiting
to happen. The developers to whom it will probably be sold will
either bulldoze the house to make room for more arable land or
let it fall down by itself; to judge from outside appearances, they
won't have a long wait. It is a shame, really, as the property has
been in Jack's family for three generations. But it can't be helped.
Trudy certainly is not going to live here, and she can't afford to
maintain it.

Sorry, she mutters as she navigates the rotting steps to the
porch.

Inside, there are further signs of Anna's demise in the housekeeping tasks she could no longer handle. The carpet of which
she was so proud is stained and curling in the corners, the wallpaper bubbled with water stains. Trudy ventures into the kitchen
and winces at the black tongues of soot around the stove. Glass
crunches underfoot, and an icy current of air rattles the industrial-
strength blue plastic over the window. Some member of the
New Heidelburg Fire Department has smashed it with an ax.
An overly dramatic gesture, Trudy thinks. Why not just try the
door? The farmhouse, like most in the area, has always been left
unlocked.

Upstairs, she finds her parents' bedroom unscathed, though
dusty and cold. Trudy has not been in here since after Jack's funeral, and she looks sadly at the lopsided bed and battered
dresser. Even the view from the window is homely and unpre-
possessing: the south field, the barn, a square of blank sky. So
why is it that sometimes, while standing in line at the supermarket or in the midst of giving a lecture, Trudy catches herself

thinking of just this scene? It rises before her uninvited and hangs there, superimposed between her mind's eye and what she actually sees.

But she is wasting time. From the closet Trudy unearths a scuffed hard-edged suitcase, a relic from the fifties, and begins filling it with Anna's clothes. Cardigans, pumps, dresses, skirts. Anna has never once in her life worn slacks, no matter how brutal the temperature. Trudy turns next to the bureau, taking from it costume jewelry and pantyhose, gloves with the pricetags still attached, a pair of slippers wrapped in crackling cellophane. When Trudy reaches the bottom drawer where the undesirables are kept, she selects the least worn of Anna's cotton nightgowns. Then she pauses, arrested by some distant bell of memory. Has Anna kept it? Is it still there?

Trudy chews her lip. She should close the drawer again. Best to let sleeping dogs lie. She leans forward and yanks the drawer out as far as it will go, ignoring the protesting shriek of old wood.

She digs through the sleepwear and darned underpants and pushes aside, in one corner, a decades-old sanitary belt, and there, at the very rear of the drawer, she finds what she is looking for: a single wool sock. She lifts it out and unrolls it with trembling hands and shakes the hard object within into her lap. Then she sits on the cold floor and stares at this sole souvenir of her mother's wartime life.

It is a gold rectangle about the size and shape of a ladies' cigarette case, and indeed, at first glance, it might be mistaken as such. The back is smooth metal, the front etched with a horizontal band of zigzagging silver lines in an art deco pattern. In the middle of this is a circle of diamonds—two or three of them missing now, leaving tiny pocked holes—and in the center of this is a silver swastika.

To somebody of Trudy's historical knowledge, this might seem an incongruous gift, since during the Reich German women were discouraged, even forbidden, to smoke. But to Trudy it is not strange, since the case is not intended for cigarettes at all. She pries open the catch at its side to reveal, framed in balding maroon velvet, an oval black-and-white photograph. Of a young Anna, seated. With the toddler Trudy on her lap, wearing a dirndl, her hair in looped braids. And behind Anna, one hand possessively on her shoulder, an SS officer in full uniform. His head is raised in an attitude of pride, his peaked cap tilted forward so that his features cannot be seen.

How many times as a girl, as an adolescent, has Trudy done exactly this, while Anna was hanging laundry in the dooryard or busy at the stove or helping Jack with the livestock? Peering at the photograph, trying to tease the details from its background. There aren't many. The folding canvas chair in which Anna and Trudy sit. The curving bulk of the staff car at the officer's back, a dot that might be the Mercedes emblem on its hood. Behind his head, tiny waving lines the size of lashes: the fronds of the willows in the Park an der Ilm, where Trudy knows this picture was taken. Or does she? Does this photograph truly confirm her earliest memories? Or has she merely looked at it so often that she only thinks she remembers? Images substituting for reality.

Trudy wipes her eyes on her sleeve. They are watering and her nose is clogged, facts she decides to blame on the cold.

She gets up, her knees popping like gunshots, and takes the photograph over to the window. She tilts the case this way and that, an action she performed countless times in her youth, as if by doing so she could shake off the officer's hat and finally, finally see her father's face.

But since of course she cannot, other memories obligingly come in its stead.

Where is he, Mama? Why isn't he here with us? I miss him—

Be quiet, Trudie! Do you want Jack to hear you? Now I will tell you something very important. You must never say such things in this house. You must never speak of that man at all. You must never even think of him. Never. Do you understand?

But I don't want Jack. I want him—

Her mother's strong fingers, digging into the soft flesh on either side of Trudy's childish chin.

I said you will not speak of him. He no longer exists. He belongs to the past, to that other place and time, and all of that is dead. Do you hear? The past is dead, and better it remain so.

And this conversation, held in the barn where Jack spent most of his time:

Daddy, I have a question.

Sure, Strudel. What is it?

Promise you won't get mad?

Why would I get mad?

Because it's kind of a bad question.

I could never be mad at you, Strudel. Ask away.

Daddy, did you know my real father?

I don't know what you mean, honey.

Yes you do. My real father. From Germany. Did you ever meet him?

Well, Strudel, you're right, that's not a nice question. It hurts my feelings. I'm your dad.

I know, but—

And that's all there is to say about that.

Okay, but—

And you shouldn't talk about these things, Strudel. Not to anybody. But especially not around your mother. You know how it upsets her.

And so on and so forth. A conspiracy of silence, a wall that Trudy could neither penetrate nor scale. She has often wondered whether Anna and Jack conferred as to what they would say when faced with such queries or if they made their responses independently and instinctively. Not that it really matters. The denials are confirmation enough. And the photograph, the solid evidence. Of course Jack, despite his stumbling, kindhearted evasions, is not Trudy's father. No, her real father, though perhaps now as dead as her adopted one, is still with her. He is Trudy's blond hair, her love of organization, her penchant for chess and classical music and all the other tastes to which Jack and Anna never subscribed. Sometimes Trudy thinks she can smell him on her, the personal scents of the man coming from her own pores: fresh barbering, boot polish, the sauerkraut and venison he had for lunch.

What Trudy doesn't know is the nature of Anna's relationship with him.

Was she the officer's mistress? His wife?

If either, did she enter into the contract willingly? Did she care about him, even love him? Trudy can't quite bring herself to believe this. The very thought turns her stomach cold and closes her throat. But why else would Anna have kept this picture — and her silent counsel — all these years?

Trudy holds the image up to the light and squints at her young mother. Anna's expression gives nothing away. It is calm, perhaps a bit grave. Does this signify a secret satisfaction at having secured such a powerful partner? Could Anna really be so morally bankrupt as to have solicited the liaison with the officer, enjoyed it, relished it? Could there be, behind that beautiful face, a void?

Or perhaps Anna's expression conceals resigned acceptance. Or horror. Or is an external portrait of the internal deadening, the numbness, that accompanies repeated abuse. Trudy has read dozens of case studies of women who undertook desperate measures in times of war, in order to survive. Maybe the officer forced Anna. Maybe she had no choice. But if this is so, and Anna is a victim of circumstance, why has she chosen never to explain this to her daughter?

The past is dead. The past is dead, and better it remain so.

Trudy gazes at the photograph a minute longer, then shakes her head and decisively snaps the case closed. Enough is enough. There is nothing to be gained by once again asking painful questions to which there are no ready answers. Whatever Anna has done, Trudy has made her own life, and it is high time that she return to it. She has afternoon classes to teach.

Moving from the window, she sets the little gold case on the dresser and finishes packing Anna's things. A favorite brooch, an afghan, hairbrushes. Trudy snaps the latches shut and takes a last look around; she will not be seeing this place again. She hefts the suitcase and leaves.

She is halfway down the stairs when she suddenly turns, runs back up, and seizes the gold case. She slips it into her coat pocket. Then she hurries from the bedroom, this time for good, her breath coming and going in ghosts.

10

ALTHOUGH SLEET SLICKS THE ROADS ON THE WAY BACK TO the Twin Cities, Trudy manages to arrive on the university campus a few minutes before her scheduled office hours. This is a relief; Trudy hates being late, the way rushing from place to place frays her composure, leaves her sweating and disheveled with her socks falling down inside her boots. She is also grateful to see that no students are lying in wait for her. When Trudy is her best self, she likes talking to them—in fact, she delights in any sign of their intellectual effort, no matter how small. But the past twenty-four hours have been trying, and Trudy knows that were her pupils to seek her out now, she would be impatient with their ever-ringing cell phones, their fidgeting embarrassment at being in such close proximity to her; their improbable, grammatically incorrect, unpleasantly intimate excuses as to why they haven't turned their assignments in on time.

Today, Trudy thinks, with any luck, the weather or the demands of their mysteriously busy lives will prevent them from coming to see her. She needs the hour to shift gears from her personal persona to her professorial one. She helps herself to a cup of coffee from the History Department hot plate and hangs her damp coat, then assumes her usual post at her desk and pulls a pile of midterms onto the blotter. With an air of diligence, Trudy uncaps her red pen.

The Mother's Cross, the top paper is entitled, *An Examination of German Women as Breed-Horses of the Third Reich.* Trudy sighs and flips open the oaktag folder to the first page:

> *It has been argued and indeed perported by historians of the time period under discussion, that is to say the Third Reich, that during this time period the German woman was viewed by the Nazi Government as a Baby-Machine, that is to say she was valued for her fertilization abilities above all. A partickular Award was awarded to German women that produced three, six or nine Purebloded children, bronze silver and gold respecktively, and from this an implication can be drawn that the real station the German woman occupied during this time period was the stable. She was merely a Breed-Mare or Horse.*

Trudy refrains from scribbling, *Do you have the slightest idea what you're talking about?* in the margin and instead writes SPELL-CHECK so vehemently that her pen rips the paper. Then she closes the folder and pushes it aside. Perhaps she is not in quite the right mood for grading after all. She tilts her chair back and stares at the far wall, where the room's only decoration hangs: an archival photograph, enlarged to poster size, of American soldiers marching German civilians to Buchenwald a few days after the camp's liberation, where they will be made to bury the dead. The afternoon is gray and gloomy—not unlike the one beyond Trudy's window right now—and the Amis are in army-issue slickers, their prisoners in patched wool coats. Toward the rear of the column, clinging to an invisible hand, is a small towheaded girl who could be the identical twin of Trudy at that age. She might in fact be Trudy herself.

Trudy is gazing at the poster without really seeing it when

she hears the dreaded knock on the door. She tousles her hair, which from the feel of it is drying in stiff unattractive spikes, like whipped egg whites.

Come in, she calls, and arranges her features into what she hopes is a welcoming expression.

But it is not a student who enters; it is Dr. Ruth Liebowitz, Director of Holocaust Studies, from down the hall.

Have I caught you at a bad time, Dr. Swenson? she asks.

No, not at all. Why?

Ruth laughs. Your face, that constipated look you get when you're trying to seem helpful. You must be expecting a student.

Trudy pulls a mock scowl.

I was, yes, but mercifully nobody's shown up. Come on in, I still have—Trudy checks her watch—another twenty minutes. How are you?

Ruth drops into the chair on the other side of Trudy's desk and tucks her feet beneath her, catlike. Trudy watches her fondly. People meeting Ruth for the first time often mistake her for one of her own undergrads. Her small freckled face, her nimbus of frizzy hair, her uniform of sweater and rumpled khakis seem more appropriate to a freshman than somebody in Ruth's important position. And Ruth deliberately fosters this impression, using what she calls *my disguise* to her advantage whenever possible: on the first day of class, she sits among her students to hear what they say about her. In actuality, she is only nine years younger than Trudy.

I'm fine, Ruth says now. More to the point, how are *you*?

A little tired, but— What. Why are you giving me that look?

Ruth narrows her dark eyes.

Come on, kid. You skipped out on your classes yesterday. You weren't home last night. What's going on?

How do you know I wasn't home?

I called, says Ruth. Several times, actually.

Several times? What did you think, that I was dead on the floor?

Ruth glances away.

So I was a little worried, she mumbles defiantly.

Trudy hides a smile. Knowing that Trudy lives alone, Ruth is sometimes a bit overprotective, but it is also comforting to know that if Trudy were indeed dead on the floor, she wouldn't have to lie there for days before being found.

What if I had been entertaining a gentleman caller? Trudy asks.

Ruth looks delighted. Were you?

No, Trudy admits. She sinks back in her chair and rubs her eyes. I had to go to New Heidelburg. There was a situation with my mother.

Ruth's gaze sharpens further.

This is the difficult mother? The one I so rarely hear about?

Of course it's her. How many mothers do you think I have?

Ruth flaps an impatient hand. What happened?

She had a little accident.

What kind of accident?

Honestly, Ruth, what are you, the Gestapo?

Ruth maintains an unwavering stare. The historically impossible friendship between the two women, the unlikely alliance between a professor of German history and the head of Holocaust Studies, requires black humor, a way of acknowledging and thus defusing possible tensions. But neither has ever applied it to the other personally.

Sorry, says Trudy. I'm not quite myself today...My mother's all right, it was nothing serious, but it's obvious she can't live by herself anymore. So I had to arrange to put her in a nursing home.

Ruth screws up her face in sympathy.

That's rough, she agrees. I know how it is. When we put my aunt in a home, she didn't speak to us for six months.

My mother hasn't spoken to me in fifty years, Trudy says, and laughs.

Again Ruth gives her a penetrating look, but she lets the subject drop.

Well, kid, she says, unfolding herself from the chair, if you
want to talk about it, I'm here...Oh! I almost forgot the other
reason I came in here.

What's that?

Ruth braces her palms on Trudy's desk and sways forward.

We got it, she says dramatically.

Got what? Trudy asks.

Ruth gives the blotter an emphatic slap.

For the love of God, woman, wake up! The funding for the
Remembrance Project.

Oh, says Trudy. Oh, good for you. How much did you get?

Ruth rolls her eyes. Not as much as I'd hoped for, naturally.
But enough to contact area survivors, to hire interviewers and
videographers. I can cut corners by having one of my doctoral
students encode the tapes for the archives. And if all goes well,
next year I can ask for more money—the sky's the limit.

That's fantastic, says Trudy. Congratulations—

This is such a feather in our cap. This'll put our program on
the map in terms of recording Holocaust testimony, put us right
up there with fucking Yale. And not even fucking Yale has survivor interviews on camera.

I know, says Trudy. You must be so proud.

I am, I have to admit, Ruth says, grinning. Her teeth are tiny
and pearly and crooked; like baby teeth, Trudy thinks, *milk teeth,*
Anna would call them. This Project is my baby...But sometimes
I think, what am I, nuts? There's so much work to be done—

Well worth it, Trudy assures her. Let me know if there's anything I can do.

Ruth settles a pert khaki-clad hindquarter on the corner of
Trudy's desk, wrinkling the term papers.

Actually..., she says.

Oh, God, groans Trudy. I was just being polite, Ruth!

I thought you might want to try out, Ruth says.

Try out?

For an interviewer's position.

Me?

Yes, you.

Trudy shakes her head.

I don't understand, she says. Why would you want me? The Holocaust isn't my field of expertise.

Ruth waves this objection aside.

We have to get this off the ground quickly, she says, and we need historians who really know their stuff to be interviewers, and that means you. I think you'd be a natural. And you'd really be doing me a favor.

Trapped, Trudy swivels to the window and looks out. The quadrangle is deserted, the sleet being whipped sideways by a relentless wind, the Gothic red sandstone buildings gloomier than usual in the premature dusk. Her reflection hovers among them, transparent and watchful, a streetlamp in its throat.

It wouldn't matter that I'm not Jewish? she asks.

Well, of course you should be, since we are the Chosen People, Ruth says tartly. But no, it wouldn't matter.

Huh, says Trudy.

Then she swings back around, reaching over to tug the papers from beneath Ruth's behind and stuff them into her briefcase.

I can't, she says. I'm sorry, Ruth. I'm truly flattered you asked. But I have such a full courseload this semester, as you know, and now there's this situation with my mother on top of everything else...

She feels herself flushing. Anna's transfer to the Good Samaritan Center having already been arranged, there is nothing much left for Trudy to do except make a weekend visit to ensure that she's settled in. And this won't take much time. But Ruth doesn't need to know this.

And, as Trudy has expected, she buys the excuse.

Forgive me, she says, hopping off Trudy's desk. I forgot. But maybe, when things settle down with her...Will you at least think about it?

Of course, Trudy lies.

Ruth goes to the door.

Good, she says. Because I'm going to keep after you.

She cocks a thumb and forefinger at Trudy in imitation of shooting a gun. You know where to find me if you change your mind, she adds, and leaves.

Congratulations again, Trudy calls to Ruth's departing footsteps in the hall. They are rapid. Ruth does everything quickly.

Trudy smiles, then glances at her watch. She swears and leaps from her chair, tugs her still-damp boots on, and grabs her briefcase. Yanking the door open, she nearly collides with the student who is standing on the other side of it, head hanging.

Professor Swenson? the girl mumbles to the carpet between her feet. Can I talk to you a minute? I'm so so so so sorry I missed class yesterday, I had this really really really bad urinary tract infection...

11

DESPITE TRUDY'S TENURED POSITION, HER AFTERNOON seminar, Women's Roles in Nazi Germany, is in the basement, the bowels of the university's History Department. At the beginning of her course, Trudy routinely refers to the classroom as the Bunker—*Hi, folks, and welcome to our lovely Bunker!*—trying to alleviate first-day awkwardness and take the temperature of her new class. If it is a nice humorous batch, the quip earns a few smiles, even muted chuckles. More often, though, the students just sit stone-faced, extravagantly unimpressed by this feeble attempt to win them over. Trudy supposes she can't blame them. There really is not much to laugh about in the prospect of spending an entire semester in a cramped windowless room, beneath light grids that resemble old-fashioned ice-cube trays, in little orange chairs better suited to midgets than the average undergrad.

Truth be told, however, Trudy likes her classroom: the safety of being underground, the warmth of all those bodies packed together. This is her domain, where for fifty minutes three times a week she is in complete control. Where history is documented and footnoted, confined to text. Comprehensible, if only in retrospect.

As she does at the start of each class, she snaps a fresh stick of chalk in two and stands rubbing her thumb over the rough edge, surveying her captive audience. It is a chocolate box of personalities; at this stage in the semester, Trudy knows each student, if not by name, then by trait. The quiet girl who arrives early and does crossword puzzles with obsessive zeal. The brilliant sophomore with the cobweb tattooed on her face. The two boys—Frick and Frack—who always sit poised for escape near the door, as identical in movement as twins though they are not related; if one is sick or absent, the other is also.

How are you all today? Trudy asks.

She waits with her eyebrows significantly raised until she gets a few incomprehensible responses. This is typical. The class runs at four o'clock, a bad time, the doldrums. Her pupils are sluggish, their circadian rhythms demanding naps, their stomachs requiring dinner. They blink at their feet, owlish and surly; they slouch in their chairs, doodling in their notebooks—flowers, hearts, intricate geometric configurations—drawings that, as far as Trudy can make out, have nothing to do with the material at hand. At the moment, her eyes grainy from lack of sleep and her difficult drive, Trudy wants nothing more than to join them. Especially as today's subject, a survey of German women as to what they did during the war, hits a bit close to home.

Yet somebody has to be the teacher here, so Trudy glances down at her notes and lectures as animatedly as she is able. She talks, pauses, asks whether there are any questions, applies her squeaking chalk to the board, but all the while she feels a growing humidity beneath her turtleneck. Flop sweat. Every professor is prone to it, gives an ill-received lesson on occasion, and Trudy, no exception, knows there is no shame in it. But each time it happens inspires the same panic as the first.

She pushes her damp bangs from her forehead and looks at

her watch, which she has unstrapped and set on the lectern. Only ten minutes left, thank God.

Trudy bounces the chalk in her palm. So in the final analysis, she says, what did you take from today's reading? What point, if any, is the author trying to make about the way these particular German women acted during the war?

Silence.

Trudy frowns out at her students. Once they get going they are usually a talkative group, flirtatious even, which makes their apathy today all the more galling. Perhaps it is not her fault; perhaps they have fallen prey to Thanksgiving Syndrome, too much sleep and food at home, dread of upcoming exams. Trudy decides to prod them a little.

Come on, people, she says. Participation is part of your grade, you know...What did you think of Frau Heidenreich saying that the Jews brought the Holocaust upon themselves? Were you surprised that she still thinks this, even today?

Silence.

Is her attitude typical?

Silence.

Did anybody *do* the assigned reading?

Silence. Then, from the rear, a phlegmy yawn that sounds like a marble rattling in a vacuum cleaner hose.

Ms. Meyerson, Trudy says. If you must insult me in this fashion, please cover your mouth. I am tired of seeing your tonsils.

Some titters from the class. So they *are* awake, Trudy thinks.

Sorry, the offending student mutters. It's just that—

Just that what?

Of *course* the anti-Semite was typical, the student says, scowling ferociously at her notebook. All those women were anti-Semitic. They were, like, part of the whole war machine. They were the perps.

Excuse me?

The perpetrators.

Ah, says Trudy. So, German women were perpetrators. And you know something? I agree with you, to a degree. Many of them were. But was it entirely their fault? Were they not products of their culture—which as we've seen was rabidly anti-Semitic—as much as you or I are? Might they not have been forced into doing what they did by the war? Don't desperate times call for desperate measures?

Silence. A bead of sweat trickles down Trudy's ribcage.

All right, she says, walking out from behind her lectern to stand in front of the class. Let's try it this way. Let's make it personal. Let's say...you're an Aryan German woman, circa 1940, 1941. About the age most of you are—twenty, twenty-one. Your normal life has been rudely interrupted by the war. Your husband is off fighting for the *Vaterland,* or already dead. Perhaps you have a small child to care for. And suddenly the Jews in your community start disappearing. Maybe you see it happening, maybe—as many of these women claimed—you don't. But you hear the rumors. You gossip, as women do. You know. And you know too that the price of resistance, or helping Jews—hiding them, feeding them, whatever—is death. What do you do?

Now they are listening.

The right thing, somebody calls.

Which is?

Well, *duh.* Helping the Jews, obviously. Any way you can.

Oh, come on, scoffs another student. That's, like, so naive. It sounds good, but like you'd really help if you knew you'd die for it. But not just, like, die. Be tortured first. And they'd kill your kid too.

I'd still do it, insists the first.

No, you just think you would, argues the second. It's easy to say you'd do something when you're just, like, sitting here in your chair.

You see? Trudy interjects. It's not so simple, is it? Most of us are drawn to this time period thinking it was a war of absolute good versus absolute evil—qualities rarely found in their purest form—and that's true. But don't forget that history isn't just a study in black and white. Human behavior is comprised of ulterior motives, of gray shades.

Every face is uptilted toward Trudy, attentive, even rapt. In the front row, a pale boy is nodding.

In her excitement at having snared their attention, Trudy continues: Now, let's take our hypothetical situation a step further. You're still the same young woman, but the tide of the war is starting to turn. There's no fuel. You're cold. Rations are increasingly scarce. Your child is starving before your eyes. You're bombed every night by the British. The enemy is advancing, and all anyone talks about is how the Russians will rape and kill you when they arrive. But then, suddenly, you have a chance to be protected. By a, a high-ranking officer. An SS officer, even. What do you do? Do you use what you've got, as a woman, in the time-honored fashion, and become his...his mistress, say?

Somebody snorts. *No,* she says.

Not even if it means a better life for you and your child?

No, the student repeats. That's just *wrong.*

Yeah, says another student.

But—

All you have to do is hang on until the war is over. Most of them survived, didn't they?

Well, you know that in hindsight, says Trudy. It's easy enough to say now, but—

Being the guy's mistress, that's, like, *proactive* evil. It's as bad as turning in the Jews.

But you're not *thinking,* says Trudy, thumping the lectern in frustration. Or rather, you're not putting yourself in that woman's shoes. Aren't there some situations in which the ends justify the means...?

She falters and puts a hand to her throat, which is suddenly tight. The key to being an effective teacher, Trudy has always thought, is to believe in what one is saying. Now she can't look the student who has challenged her in the face.

Trudy shuffles her notes, coughs into her fist.

Excuse me, she says hoarsely. Long day.

Professor Swenson? somebody asks.

What now? Trudy thinks.

It's five-fifteen.

Oh, says Trudy. Thank you. Sorry about that, folks...All right, get out of here.

The room erupts with activity as the students begin shoving their binders into their backpacks and pulling on their parkas. Trudy claps her hands.

Don't forget to read the Goldhagen for next time, she calls.

As they file out, abruptly boisterous, Trudy turns to erase the board, scolding herself under her breath. What on earth was she thinking, bringing personal material into the classroom? She has broken one of her own cardinal rules: unlike many of her colleagues, who lace lectures with anecdotes of their families, travels, weekends, Trudy believes that a certain distance is necessary to maintain proper authority. She brushes in irritation at the chalk dust sifting onto her shoulders—teacher's dandruff—but succeeds only in leaving a wide white swath on the dark wool. Trudy swears anew. She almost always wears black, and she shouldn't.

Professor Swenson?

Trudy looks to the ceiling, praying for patience, then turns. Yes, she says.

There is a girl waiting on the other side of the lectern, cracking fluorescent gum. She is a freshman, Trudy knows, but she can never remember this student's name and therefore mentally refers to her as the Pretty Girl. And she is, with her wide blue eyes and pink cheeks and long blond hair, a combination that should be a cliché but instead adds up to simple perfection. Trudy has sometimes resented the Pretty Girl, not for her looks per se but because they have led Trudy to form precisely the subjective opinions a good teacher should never harbor: the student is so pretty she must be dumb; she is spoiled, used to getting what she wants because of her appearance; she would make an excellent poster child for the *Bund deutscher Mädel,* the League of German Girls. She is the last person Trudy wants to talk to just now.

What can I do for you? Trudy asks.

The girl braves a quick glance at Trudy. She wears glitter makeup, Trudy sees, a constellation of sparkles scattered across her rosy face.

I just wanted to tell you? the girl says to her sneakers. That I'm finding this class, like, really fascinating?

Why, thank you, says Trudy. That's the best thing a professor can hear.

She gives the Pretty Girl a cursory smile and makes a show of gathering her notes, tapping their edges against the podium to align them before putting them away. Her longing for the safety of her own home, to be in a hot bath washing off the residue of this afternoon's embarrassment, is so acute that her skin itches.

But the Pretty Girl persists, keeping pace with Trudy as she walks from the classroom.

My grandmother was in the war? she says. She was hidden by a Catholic family, passing as a Christian? She was a— a whatchamacallit, a submarine?

A U-boat, Trudy supplies.

Yeah, a U-boat, the girl says, popping a small neon-green bubble.

Trudy looks sideways at her.

You're Jewish? she asks.

Half, says the Pretty Girl. My grandparents were Hungarian Jews? I'm half-Jewish.

I see, says Trudy. Well, please give your grandmother my best regards.

I would, says the girl, but she's dead.

Oh. I'm sorry.

But I wanted to ask you? I'm still not getting something. Like, it makes sense when you explain it, you know, *historically,* but I don't get how those women could have done all those things. Like what you said about the SS officer. Or just not help-ing, pretending nothing was happening. How do they, you know, live with themselves afterwards?

That's a good question, Trudy says. Denial, I suppose. Or...

She stops walking. She is thinking of the kitchen of the farmhouse, filling with black smoke. Where was Anna? Making a desperate grab with a dish towel for the pot forgotten on the stove? Or lying on her marital bed upstairs, eyes closed? Waiting for the heat to tighten her skin, letting her know that flames had claimed this room as well?

Professor Swenson, are you all right?

The girl's quick touch on her arm, light as a cat's paw.

Trudy gives her head a brusque shake.

Yes, she says. I'm fine. Thank you.

They are standing in the hallway now, next to a radiator that hisses and clanks. Somewhere overhead a janitor whistles a pop-ular tune. Other than this, the building is quiet in the forlorn way busy places are when the people who normally occupy them have gone.

I haven't been particularly helpful, have I, says Trudy. Was there anything else you wanted to ask?

I guess not, the Pretty Girl says.

She hoists her backpack more firmly onto her shoulder and trots off, breaking into a run a few meters away. At the door leading to the parking lot, she turns and yells, Have a good weekend!

You too, says Trudy.

The door wheezes shut after letting in a few whirling flakes of snow. Though now free to leave, Trudy stands in the fruity synthetic wake of the girl's shampoo, looking thoughtfully after her. How she envies the young woman, not for the obvious rea-sons but because she has a family history she can talk about and be proud of. A history somebody has related to her firsthand. A history she *knows*.

A nebulae of instincts coalesce, and from the brilliant vapor of their collision an idea emerges. Takes cogent shape. Grows. For another minute Trudy is paralyzed by its logic, its persuasive simplicity—why hasn't she thought of this before? Then she pivots and jogs up the nearest stairwell. She has to find Ruth before her sudden conviction deserts her.

Ruth is not in her office nor in the teachers' lounge, but Trudy finally spots her in the cafeteria. She is sitting alone at a long wooden table, picking withered blueberries out of a muffin and wiping them on a napkin with a child's scowl of distaste.

What are you doing here? she asks Trudy.

Looking for you, Trudy says.

Well, that's flattering, but I don't get it. I'd have thought you'd be home in a hot bath by now.

Trudy pulls out a chair and sits next to her.

Listen, she says rapidly. I need to pick your brains about your Remembrance Project. How you organized it, exactly how you're going to find subjects, where you're going to get your videographers—

Does this mean I'm going to have a shiksa interviewer? Ruth interrupts.

Trudy laughs. She is shaking all over with excitement.

No, she says. I'm afraid not. But I have a proposal for you, and I'm going to need your help. Because I've got my own Project to do.

Anna and Mathilde, Weimar, 1940–1942

"Backe, backe Kuchen!"
der Bäcker hat gerufen.
"Wer will guten Kuchen backen,
Der muss haben sieben Sachen:
Butter und Salz,
Zucker und Schmalz,
Milch und Mehl,
und Eier machen den Kuchen gel'."

"Bake, bake a cake!"
the baker called out.
"Whoever wants to make a good cake,
He must have seven things:
Butter and salt,
Sugar and lard,
Milk and flour,
and eggs to make the cake gold."

12

ANNA HAS BEEN AT THE BAKERY FOR A WEEK BEFORE SHE
ventures upstairs. Or perhaps it is more than a week. She doesn't
know for certain; she has lost track of time. As she lies on the
pallet in the bakery cellar, she stares at the ragged black marks on
the damp wall next to her head. Somebody hidden here before
her has obviously charted the duration of his stay with a lump of
coal: about a month, all told. Anna could do the same. But she
rejects the idea as involving too much effort, and in any case, the
passage of time means little to her.

She curls on the cot like the embryo within her, drifting in
and out of sleep. Sometimes when she wakes, she hears the wooden
soles of the bakery's patrons clocking overhead, the meaningless
snippets of their conversations. At other times, she opens her
eyes to a darkness so complete that it seems to press on her with
the weight of a mattress. It is only then that Anna can bring herself to choke down the food Mathilde has left for her, in a covered tray at the foot of the treacherous wooden staircase.

Since Anna's arrival, mindful of Anna's delicate condition
and the cellar's lack of amenities, the baker has implored Anna to

move into her own living quarters above the storefront. But Anna cannot stomach the thought of lying beneath a braid of Mathilde's long-dead mother's hair, surrounded by dried flower arrangements and gay photographs of Mathilde's deceased husband Fritzi. The claustrophobia of the basement suits Anna much better; it is as close as she can come to the conditions Max must be enduring. Cupping her swollen breasts, Anna relishes the ropy rasp of rat tails across the floor with a penitent's zeal. She is grateful to cough in the fine black dust that the delivery of coal into the nearby chute raises each morning. The rank smell of fear from the others Mathilde has concealed here comforts Anna; with her eyes closed, she might be in the maid's staircase in the *Elternhaus*.

One evening, however, when Anna wakes from her doze, she bolts upright as if in response to an interior command: Enough. The movement is too abrupt; minnows of light dart across her vision. Anna waits for them to disperse, then climbs from the pallet and up the steps to the kitchen. Even this simple act requires enormous will; her limbs are filled with wet cement rather than blood. Anna recalls this same sensation from the days after her mother's death. Grief is heavy. Perhaps a new anguish invokes the physical symptoms of an older one.

She sways in the doorway of the kitchen, shading her eyes with a hand.

Mathilde, she says, her voice a croak. What day is it?

The baker doesn't hear her. She is attacking the vast wooden worktable with a butter knife, dislodging flour paste from its cracks. Merely watching her makes Anna tired.

Mathilde, she says again.

The baker starts, breathing hard.

Well, well, she says. Sleeping Beauty awakes.

Is tomorrow Sunday? I haven't heard churchbells. Have I been here longer than a week?

It's August, Mathilde says.

She continues her task. Her buzzing voice, trapped in layers of fat like a fly in a bottle, is punctuated with small gasps of effort when she asks, And how is our princess this evening?

Wunderbar, Anna says.

She makes her way to the sink, which is enormous and double-sided, like the laundry basin in the *Elternhaus.* She pumps water into it, then drinks some from her cupped hands. It tastes of the iron in the pipes. Her hair, hanging over her shoulders, has separated into oily ropes, and she is suddenly aware of how she must smell. She sniffs the crook of her elbow: a bit sour, salty and creamy, like buttermilk. Since conceiving the baby, Anna's own scent is strange to her.

I hope I've not been too much of a burden, she says.

Mathilde snorts. Hardly. Hardly even knew you were down there.

Anna sizes up the baker as she bustles about: the bulk constrained by an apron; the tiny doll's head, its thin dark hair combed in such severe lines that it appears painted on; the scalp shining between the furrows; the suspicious black eyes embedded in flesh.

I'm no princess, Anna tells her. I'm ready to start earning my keep.

Mathilde gives Anna an incredulous look.

Shit, she mutters, brushing past Anna to soak a rag with water. Returning to the worktable, she says as she scrubs: Your papers are still good, you know. You could still go to Switzerland, have your baby there.

No, says Anna. I'm not leaving Weimar.

Oh, you're a princess all right, used to getting your own way. Have you thought about what it'll be like for you here? Your father alone could make your life miserable.

I don't intend to have any contact with him, Anna says. He doesn't know where I am, and if he finds out, I don't care. He turned Max in to the Gestapo himself.

Of course he did. Who else? I'm surprised he didn't turn you in too. No father likes to think of his daughter rutting with anyone, let alone a Jew. But I suppose he spared you on account of the baby.

I didn't tell him about the baby, Anna says.

This earns Anna a second startled glance.

Hiding a Jew he could forgive, if he could still keep me in the house until he marries me off, Anna explains. But my condition will show soon enough, and he couldn't turn a blind eye to that. Not only would I be worthless goods, it would make him a laughingstock among his friends. They might even accuse him of condoning *Rassenschande* under his own roof. He would have to turn me in.

Mathilde gives the table a sweeping stroke.

Don't you have a nice auntie in some other city, she asks, somewhere else you could go, away from this mess?

No. And I wouldn't go if I did. I must be where I can get news of Max. Have you heard anything? Have they— taken him to the camp?

The baker nods, rubbing at a floury patch with a fingernail.

He won't last long up there, she says, skinny as he is.

Tears spring to Anna's eyes at this blunt statement. She longs so to slap Mathilde that she can see the reddening mark her hand would leave on the older woman's face. By nature, Anna is not given to anger, and the fury that has paralyzed her for days frightens her. There is an irony in it: having finally escaped Gerhard's rage, she is now enslaved by his emotional legacy. Like father, like daughter. But the feeling is now useful, steeling her spine to deal with Mathilde. If there is any belated lesson that Gerhard has taught Anna, it is that the only way to earn a bully's respect is to respond in kind.

She walks over to the table. Then I'll carry on the work Max was doing, she tells Mathilde. I'll take his place.

Mathilde doesn't bother to look up. A princess like you? she scoffs. Please! You have no idea what you're talking about.

Then tell me.

Mathilde tosses the rag into the sink and waddles into the

storefront. Anna hears the *ding!* as the register is opened, the sound of the baker removing the cash drawer. She folds her arms and waits.

Upon her return Mathilde lowers herself onto a stool and scrapes it over to the table. She separates Reichsmarks, change, and ration coupons. Counting under her breath, she enters numbers into a ledger, tongue lodged in the corner of her mouth.

You're still here? she asks, looking up in feigned surprise. Not back to bed yet? You should go. A woman in your condition needs rest.

Anna reaches over and slams the ledger shut, nearly catching the baker's stubby fingers.

Listen to me, you, she says. Don't you forget that I hid Max in my own house, right under my father's nose. I couriered information back and forth for you. I've got as much nerve as you or anyone else.

Mathilde examines Anna for a moment.

Sit, she commands.

Anna obeys.

The baker gets up and walks to the cuckoo clock on the wall. Opening one of its tiny decorative doors, she retrieves something that she sets on the worktable.

You know what this is? she asks. You should have used a couple of these.

Anna picks up the condom, gingerly.

Go on, says Mathilde, unroll it.

Inside the prophylactic Anna finds a slip of paper no longer than a finger, covered with writing the size of ants. She brings it to her eyes, squinting to decipher the minuscule code. One line in particular catches her attention: *The Good* Doktor *sends best regards.*

Max, Anna murmurs. She glances at Mathilde. You got this from him?

The baker nods, sitting back down. Not directly, she says. But we have our ways of communicating.

How?

If your lover didn't trust you enough to tell you, why should I?

Anna says nothing, but the look she bends on the baker makes the older woman suddenly fall to inspecting her hands.

All right, I'll tell you how it works, since you obviously won't give me a moment's peace otherwise, Mathilde mutters. Well... We have a deal, the SS and me. They provide me with supplies, I deliver whatever goods they order. Since 1937 I've been doing this, since that hellhole was just a muddy pit in the ground. Koch, the *Kommandant,* came to me himself. He said he'd heard about the quality of my pastries.

Mathilde preens a bit, then flushes at Anna's arched brows.

Well, they are the best, she says defensively. And if I didn't supply them, somebody else would. Why should another baker get the business? Besides, I could see the other advantages to the arrangement, ways to use it for the Resistance. Oh, yes, the network existed even then. You wouldn't know it, but there are plenty of people in this city who hate what the Nazis are doing. And what I could see during my deliveries to the camp would be priceless information to them. So I accepted Koch's contract. And I'll tell you, did I ever see some things.

She leans closer to Anna, lowering her voice to a reedy whisper.

Every week the SS have Comradeship Evenings at the Bismarck Tower, she says. You know where it is, on the hill there? Such goings-on, you wouldn't believe. Prostitutes, male and female, little boys. Orgies. Those fine officers will fuck anything that moves, don't let anybody tell you different. They wash each other in champagne afterwards. Some comradeship, don't you think?

Anna manufactures a worldly expression.

Mathilde gives Anna a caustic little smile. You won't understand, a pretty young thing like you, but when you get older, men don't really see you. To the SS, I'm just a fat old widow. That's what they call me—*die Dicke,* Fatty. But the advantage is that I'm invisible. When I'm bringing pastries to the Tower, when I deliver bread to the officers' fine Eickestrasse houses or to their mess, I might as well be a chair for how much attention they pay me. As if being fat makes you deaf and blind too. So I see everything, hear everything. And after my regular deliveries, I make a special one to the prisoners. I leave bread for them. The poor bastards, they—

Where? Anna interrupts.

What?

Where do you leave the bread?

In the forest, by the quarry the SS have them working in. There's a hollow tree where I can put the rolls and any Resistance information I can give them. And they pass camp information to me — this way.

She indicates the condom.

It's not much, what I'm doing, she says, but it gives them some hope.

Anna slips the paper back inside the rubber. Its surface is greasy and foul, and Anna can imagine all too well where a prisoner would have had to conceal it.

I want to go, she tells Mathilde. Next time you go, I go.

Mathilde takes the condom from Anna and hides it back in the clock. Then she removes an embroidered pouch from her apron. From this she produces papers and a pinch of tobacco and proceeds, with maddening slowness, to roll a cigarette.

Did you hear me? Anna shouts. I want to help, I want to leave the bread, I'm going with you!

Mathilde scrapes a match on the side of the oven and lights her cigarette. Exhaling, she watches Anna through a drifting blue membrane. Anna glares.

You've got more balls than anybody'd think just to look at you, says the baker, but no. Do you have any idea how long it took us to set up this system? One false move and we're all in the camp. You're acting from the heart, not the head. Too risky.

I'm perfectly clearheaded. I've never been more sure of anything in my life.

And the baby, Mathilde continues, tapping ashes into a tin that once, Anna observes, held corned beef. Think of the baby.

Anna waves a hand at both this argument and the smoke, which has condensed in layers.

You shouldn't smoke, she says with venom.

Suddenly I have the Reichsminister of Propaganda Goebbels in my kitchen? A good German woman never smokes, right, princess?

Anna wants to say, No, because it's making me sick. Instead, she beckons for the cigarette.

Give me that, she says.

Shrugging, Mathilde hands it to her.

Anna inhales. As she fights not to choke, she tries to come up with a statement that will persuade Mathilde she is hardy enough to be included in this venture. She thinks of *Unterscharführer* Wagner, who comes from the same social class as the baker, whose crude language Mathilde speaks and appreciates. What would he say to sway her?

If I could, Anna tells Mathilde, eyes watering, I'd blow this smoke right up the *Führer*'s ass.

Mathilde quakes with silent laughter.

All right, she says, with a wet, ashy cough. You don't have to try so hard to convince me. But no Special Deliveries for a while. You stay here, work for me, we'll see how you do. Then—

When? Anna says. When can I go with you?

Maybe after the baby, says Mathilde. She turns and spits into the sink.

But that won't be for months! Until nearly Christmas—

That's soon enough, Mathilde says, and remains implacable.

13

GINGER.

Yes, ginger, Anna. Fresh if you can get it, but I've found candied ginger to be effective too.

Why are you giving the poor child such useless advice? Ginger is for morning sickness, and Fräulein Brandt is obviously well past that stage.

But it also eases heartburn, Hilde —

Besides, where do you expect her to find ginger nowadays? It's hard enough to get the essentials, what with the rations they allow us!

Shhhhh, Hilde, watch yourself. You've always been too outspoken for your own good —

Pssht.

Garlic, then. Or onions. Those you can still get, and they'll clean your blood, increase your stamina —

Which you'll need for the birth, Fräulein Brandt, especially with the first child — hoo hoo!

(Ssst! No need to frighten her more than she already must be, poor thing.) Yes, onions, Anna —

Onions, yes—

Onions. And raspberry leaf tea, to increase and sweeten your milk.

Yes, raspberry leaf tea.

Anna, wrapping and ringing up purchases at the register, smiles politely. These fragments of advice sound to her much like the endless propaganda from the bakery's radio, which Mathilde calls the Goebbels' Snout; the women's solicitude seems as ersatz as the coffee they must all drink now, brewed from beechnuts and tasting to Anna of pencil shavings.

She hands a loaf of black bread to Monika Allendorf, who takes it without letting her fingertips touch Anna's own. As girls, Anna and Monika were particular friends, arms slung around each other's waists in the schoolyard. They were merciless, Anna recalls, in their pursuit of a boy named Geoff, with whom they were both infatuated; they circled the poor thing on their bicycles, chanting, Chicken Legs, *yoo-hoo,* Chicken Legs! Now Monika has a skinny boy of her own. She flashes Anna an overbright smile.

Can I get anyone something else? Anna asks, sliding her hands to the small of her back. Because if not, I think we're going to close a little early.

No, no, we're all settled. Thank you.

You get some rest. That's the most important thing.

Yes, rest, Anna. It shouldn't be long now?

Another month, Anna says.

That long! I'd expect it to be tomorrow. Not that you don't look the picture of health—

Yes, you're positively glowing with it. You'll have no trouble, no trouble at all, a young healthy girl like you.

As the women leave, Anna follows them to the door to lock up. She is indeed exhausted; the fantasies that once featured Max now center around sleep, endless sleep on a soft bed. But at night, rest eludes her. She hoists her nightgown to stare in horrified fascination at her belly, which seems an entity quite separate from herself, as round and hard as a moon. By day, dressed and draped in an apron, she is as large as Mathilde.

Anna throws the bolt and draws the lace curtains across the bakery's storefront window; the blackout shade will be pulled later. Thus concealed from view, she lingers in the chilly zone of air near the pane. As she suspected they would, the women have congregated in a loose knot on the street. Their faint voices reach her through the glass.

I always thought Mathilde Staudt a kind woman, but to work that poor girl so hard in her eighth month—

Come now, don't bad-mouth Mathilde. Who else would take her in? Would you, Bettina?

I don't care what you say, I never saw a pregnant woman look more peaked. Anyone can see she's inches away from collapse.

She wouldn't be if she'd get the proper rest. The way Mathilde works her is a sin.

Sin, ha! That's an appropriate word, isn't it, considering the way this baby was conceived!

For shame, Monika. I'm surprised at you. I thought you were her friend.

Well, I was, but— That was a long time ago, when I was just a girl. How could I have known what kind of person she is?

But it's not Anna's fault, you know that. She couldn't help what happened to her.

Don't tell me you believe that fish story Frau Staudt fed us.

Well, I...Not really.

Nor I.

I certainly don't.

However you want to look at it, it's broken her father's heart, I can tell you that much. Did you know he's left town?

No!

No.

Yes, I did hear something along those lines—

It's true. The last time Grete Hortschaft went out there to clean his house, she found it locked up and dark. And have you seen him going into his office lately?

Well, no, now that you mention it…

I heard he's gone to Berlin, to act as legal counsel to the Reich. Drowning his sorrows in his work, I'll wager.

Pah! Herr Brandt's not that sentimental a fellow. He's escaping the scandal, that's all.

Well, whatever way you want to look at it, it's destroyed him in Weimar.

Poor man.

Poor fellow…

The flock moves off down the street, dawdling, heads together.

Anna turns from the window, her mouth crimped in a wry smile. She has known all along that there must be some reason why Gerhard hasn't come in search of her; how could he relinquish his handmaid, his valet and laundress, his personal chef? So he has gone away, has he? Whether he has fled to Berlin or some other city, Anna knows that Bettina Borschert has come closest to the truth: Gerhard is hardly heartbroken. Either his sycophancy has finally secured him a better position or he is escaping arrest on charges of abetting race defilement. In any case, he is saving his own skin.

But there is one thing Anna doesn't know. She carries the trays from the display case into the kitchen, where Mathilde is wrapping unsold goods in brown paper and marking reduced prices on them for the next day. Anna drops the sheets of metal in the sink with a resounding clang, but the baker doesn't look up.

Anna scrubs the trays and stacks them in their racks, then rinses her mouth with water. Recently she has been plagued by a bad taste, like rancid butter coating the tongue, although she hasn't had any real butter, spoiled or otherwise, for over a year. She clears her throat, but the fatty flavor persists. Nothing will get rid of it.

Mathilde, she says, bracing her tired back against the sink. What have you told people about this baby?

The baker scribbles more busily than ever.

What do you mean? she asks, glancing at Anna with eyes so wide that Anna can see the whites all around the pupils.

Anna can't help snorting.

You'd better hope the SS never catch you and interrogate you, she says. You're a poor liar. You know what I mean. Who do they think the father is?

You shouldn't be listening to idle gossip, Mathilde tells her primly. It'll poison your milk.

She packs the markdowns in the icebox, then looks at Anna over one shoulder.

All right, you want the story?

Given that crafty expression on your face, I'm not so sure —

Mathilde lumbers over and grasps Anna's arm.

Poor Anna, she says, in a hoarse stage-whisper. Raped by a drifter, an a-social, during her morning walk! Dragged into the bushes behind the church! But thank God for the SS. They caught the bastard double-quick and put him in the camp, where they—*zzzzsht!*

Mathilde draws a finger across her throat.

And too good for him, too, she finishes, slapping her hands together.

The baby aims a kick at Anna's navel, as if in protest at this absurd tale. Anna silently agrees. She doesn't know whether to laugh or cry.

Couldn't you have come up with something a little more seemly? she asks. A soldier, for instance, killed in battle?

Mathilde turns away, her jowls quivering with obvious affront.

It's good enough, she snaps. It distracts them from the truth, doesn't it? All right, back to work. We need a big batch of dough, enough for fifty loaves. I'm making a run to the camp tomorrow. You take care of that and I'll start on the pastries.

Why must I always make bread while you decorate cakes?
Mathilde scowls.

Because you're not yet experienced enough, she retorts.

Recognizing the futility of resistance, Anna gathers the ingredients for bread: flour, yeast, water in massive quantities. She bangs an enormous mixing bowl on the worktable. Inexperienced! As if she were incapable of laying a lattice for *Linzertorte,* something any child could do! But Mathilde is right, in a fashion; nothing in Anna's years of tending to Gerhard have prepared her for this sort of labor. She rises before dawn to feed the mammoth oven its coal briquettes, dragging each pail up the steps, encumbered by her own distended body. She stokes the fire throughout the day, stocks the display case, waits on the customers, washes the trays and pans and mops the floor. She has kneaded enough bread, lifted enough loaves from the oven, to feed the entire *Wehrmacht.* Her fingertips have cracked and split from the dryness of flour. The drudgery is endless, endless.

Too much flour, Mathilde says from behind her.

Anna dips her hands in the water bowl and flings droplets onto the dough.

Shit! Not so much!

I know how to make bread, Anna mutters.

What did you say?

Anna bites the inside of her cheek to keep from replying. Because of her stomach, she must stand a meter away from the table; her outstretched arms throb as she slaps the dough into shape. Tonight, she knows, they will thrum as if the tendons in them have been electrified. The baby drums its heels against her ribs.

How long are you going to knead that? For God's sake, you stupid girl, it'll be tough as leather.

Without forethought, Anna whirls and heaves the dough at Mathilde. The heavy mass catches the baker squarely in the chest, and she emits a startled *Uff!* The bread thuds to the floor, and Anna thinks glumly that Mathilde was right again: from the sound of it, the finished product would have been much too dense.

She sinks onto a stool, waiting for the inevitable scolding. The dough, of course, is now useless, and in a time when they must cobble together even the smallest scraps of pastry to form crusts for tortes, the wasting of any ingredient whatsoever is the blackest of sins. But the baker remains as uncharacteristically silent as the child, who stops moving and drags at Anna's belly like a stone.

The consensus of the Weimarian women, from the way Anna is carrying, is that the child will be a boy. But Anna already knows this without the old wives' tales, without the wedding rings dangled on strings in front of her belly. She has so often envisioned Max's son. At night, Anna holds the baby's image before her in the cellar, adding and subtracting features, discussing them with its absent father. What a sad specimen we've created, Max, she tells him; with our blue eyes and pale skin, he'll look anemic, poor thing, especially in winter. And he'll probably have your skinny ankles to boot. I'll have to give him a strong name, then, something sturdy to compensate: Wolfgang, Hans, Günter—yes, Günter. Wishing she could shift on her back, her stomach, to entice sleep, Anna thinks that Max was wrong. Loneliness isn't corrosive. It is eviscerating.

Now, bending with difficulty, Anna retrieves the dough from the floor and sets it on the worktable. She begins working at it, punishing it, pummeling it. Then Mathilde catches her arms, trapping them at her sides.

Shhh, the baker says. Shhh. Stop. That's enough now. It's all right.

She enfolds Anna in a floury embrace. At first Anna pushes against her, weary of pity, but after a minute she droops against Mathilde's bosom, which is so large that she seems to have only one breast rather than two, like a bedroll. The baker smells of yeast, cigarettes, perspiration, and, faintly, of unwashed feet.

When Mathilde releases her, Anna reaches for her sleeve.

I'm frightened, she tries to say; so frightened that I can't sleep, so angry I could kill—

But all she can manage is, I'm— I'm—

Mathilde gazes at the floor, as if ashamed of her spontaneous show of affection and, perhaps, her inexperience in the business of comfort. Then she settles a tentative hand on Anna's hair.

I know, she says.

14

ONE NIGHT IN NOVEMBER, ANNA HAS A VIVID DREAM. Unlike Mathilde, who recounts each of her own in relentless detail, Anna is not given to dreams. She can't remember a single one from all her twenty years. She doesn't know whether she is unusual in this respect; she has simply never given it any thought, and therefore this unexpected vision etches itself in her mind with remarkable clarity, so that, when she recalls it later, it is as if she is reliving something that actually happened.

In the dream, she is standing in the vestibule of the Catholic church she attended as a child, waiting to be married. The women of Weimar brush her cheeks with their own, murmuring compliments and blessings before passing through the arched doorway to be seated, but none of them looks straight at Anna. Anna knows that this skittishness stems from the fact that her dress is pink, as garish a color as the frosting on the petits fours delivered to the camp for the SS Comradeship Evenings. She is also hugely pregnant, a giant ripe strawberry in satin and tulle.

Edging behind the doorway, Anna peers into the church. She is late; she has been standing here for some time, her entrance delayed for no fathomable reason, and the vaulted space echoes with whispered speculations as to where she is. Every pew is full. People Anna has known since childhood are scattered among SS officers and the Buchenwald prisoners in their striped rags, their shaved heads gleaming dully in the light of the tapers. Ignoring them all, remaining half-concealed, Anna cranes until she spots Max, standing by the altar.

He waits calmly in a dark suit, his profile turned to her, his hands clasped behind him like a headwaiter or a diplomat. His hair has grown too long and it curls over his high collar. The congregation's agitation increases, but nobody thinks to turn in Anna's direction except Max, who does, and suddenly, as if Anna has called to him. He quirks his eyebrows over the rims of his spectacles and sends her a small half-smile. Anna makes no move to go to him, nor he to her; they are content merely to look at one another, and she feels across the rows of rustling people his serene, wordless reassurance that all will be well.

In the world of real things, their child, a girl, is born the following day, the eleventh of November 1940, after fifteen hours of labor. Anna, unequipped with female names, seizes on the first that comes to mind, one that, like those she has chosen for a son, is serviceable rather than pleasing to the ear, selected for strength rather than grace. She bestows upon the squalling infant the name Gertrud Charlotte Brandt, but within days of her daughter's birth, Anna adopts Mathilde's habit of calling the child Trudie. Despite Mathilde's fears about the baby's immortal soul, Anna refuses to bring her to church to be baptized. She is done with churches. The two women perform the rite themselves, in an impromptu ceremony in the bakery's kitchen sink.

15

ANNA SOMETIMES SPECULATES THAT HER NEW LIFE, PAR-
ticularly given the arrival of her daughter, might actually be
pleasant but for Mathilde's gift for petty tyranny. From dawn
until dusk, the baker issues a constant stream of orders and admonitions in her girlish voice. Everything must be done immediately and exactly the way she likes it; otherwise, her red-faced
tantrums are terrible to see. During an especially bad argument
over a misshapen batch of hot-cross buns, Anna, reeling with fatigue from Trudie's nightly feedings, points out that the Reich
suffered a great loss when Mathilde became a member of the Resistance, since under different circumstances she would have
made an excellent *Feldsmarschall*. Anna expects the baker to respond with the usual threat to throw her charges out into the
street, but Mathilde takes this as a compliment and laughs.

Anna's fantasies, which have progressed from escaping her
father's reign to running off with Max to what their child might
look like and finally to hours of uninterrupted sleep, now consist
of imagining her existence without Mathilde in it. And in late
April 1941, she is granted a temporary opportunity to find out,

since Mathilde falls ill. The baker's ailment, food poisoning, is not serious, but she wallows moaning in her bed as though she has suffered a gunshot to the stomach. Anna has to race up and down the narrow staircase in answer to the bell ringing from the sickroom while simultaneously attending to the bakery's patrons and her infant daughter. She does so with great cheer. In fact, Anna is so delighted that Mathilde is confined to her quarters that she charitably refrains from saying, I told you not to eat those three tins of black market sardines.

Toward the end of the afternoon, Anna decides to close the shop a bit early. She enters the day's earnings into the ledger while sitting in Mathilde's chair, pretending the bakery is her own. Yes, life is very pleasant when Mathilde is out of the way, and Anna is just speculating as to how long this might last when the bell jingles yet again.

What is it this time? she yells, without moving.

There is no request from above, however, and Anna realizes that what she has heard is the bell over the storefront door. Startled, irritated with herself for not locking the bakery after setting the Closed sign in the window, Anna goes into the front room to send this latecomer away and finds, standing on the other side of the counter, an SS *Rottenführer*.

Anna's stomach plummets, but the apologetic smile she has summoned for the tardy patron remains fixed on her face.

Can I help you, Herr *Rottenführer*? she asks.

The man doesn't answer right away. He is examining the bakery's sole decoration, a gaudy Bavarian landscape purchased during Mathilde's long-ago honeymoon, with an air of contempt.

I've come for Frau Staudt, he says, when he has finished his inspection.

Anna conceals her shaking hands in the folds of her apron.

She's indisposed at the moment, but perhaps there is something I can do for you?

The *Rottenführer* turns his attention to Anna, who sees that he is not much older than she. If not for the Sudeten accent, he might have been someone with whom she attended *Gymnasium*. His thick neck and insolent expression mark him as one of the boys who would have been a poor student, interested only in sports, his education otherwise consisting of yelling jibes from the back of the classroom.

Frau Staudt failed to make her weekly delivery to our facility, he says.

I see, says Anna. Well, she's quite ill, unable to get out of bed. She ate something that disagreed with her—

The *Rottenführer* grimaces, apparently disgusted that he should be bothered with the intestinal problems of a fat widowed baker.

Whatever the cause, he says, it violates her contract. If Frau Staudt doesn't provide the bread by Friday, we'll have to take the appropriate measures.

I— I'm sure that won't be necessary.

Good, says the *Rottenführer*.

He looks at Anna's bosom and smirks. It is almost time for Trudie's evening meal, and Anna's breasts are leaking in anticipation. Anna straightens her spine and thrusts her chest forward, some silly vestige of female pride insulted by this boy's sneer.

I'll pass on your message, she says.

The *Rottenführer* probes a cheek with his tongue as if searching for a particle of food. Remind her that if she can't fulfill her obligations, he says, plenty of others would be grateful for the business.

I'll tell her.

Heil Hitler, the *Rottenführer* says, with a stiff-armed salute. Then he leaves.

When she hears his motorbike purring up the road, Anna locks the bakery and returns to the kitchen, where she scoops Trudie from her laundry basket under the table. The infant mewls and waves her fists, hitting Anna hard enough on the cheekbone to make her eyes water, but Anna barely notices. This may be just the opportunity she has been waiting for. She stands thoughtfully inhaling the milky scent of her daughter's scalp. Then, unbuttoning her blouse as she goes, Anna climbs the staircase to the bedroom and recounts the conversation with the *Rottenführer* for Mathilde.

The baker seems to take this news stoically enough. She listens without interrupting while Anna talks, and when Anna is done, she says only, Bring the basin, would you? I'm going to be sick again.

Anna fetches the porcelain bowl from the bureau, cradling Trudie in the crook of the other elbow. It still amazes her, after five months, how heavy the baby's head is. Trudie, undeterred by Mathilde's retching, feeds fiercely, her lips a tiny hot circle of suction. With each tug, Anna feels a simultaneous contraction of the womb, as though all of her maternal organs are connected by a delicate but tensile thread.

That gives us two days, Anna says, when Mathilde falls back onto the pillow. You won't be well enough to make the delivery by then. I'd better do it.

Mathilde hoots.

You! You don't even know how to drive the van.

I could learn, Anna argues.

Who'd teach you? Don't worry, I'll do it, if I have to get out and vomit every five meters. Those Goddamned sardines. I knew I shouldn't have trusted anything I bought from that crook Pfeffer.

Anna wipes Trudie's mouth with the hem of her apron and refrains once more from saying, I told you so.

Instead, she asks, What about the inmates?

Didn't I say I'll make the delivery?

Yes, and if you're sick by the quarry? The SS will hear you from a mile away.

The baker turns her face toward the bureau, where a portrait of her dead husband smiles shyly at her from amidst a shrine of candle stubs.

They'll have to wait, she mutters.

They can't wait, Anna counters, pressing her advantage. How many times have you told me a single roll can make the difference between life and death? You said—

Mathilde glowers at the portrait. I know what I said. What do you want me to do about it? You see what condition I'm in.

Nothing, Anna says. I've already told you. I'll make the Special Delivery myself.

Trudie digs her fingers into Anna's breast, as if in appreciation of the idea. A ragged nail scrapes the tender skin, leaving a thin red line.

Ouch, Anna murmurs. Greedy little beast!

That's why you can't go, says Mathilde. If something should happen to you, who would take care of the child?

Why, her Tante Mathilde would, Anna says.

She detaches the infant from her breast and dangles Trudie over the baker.

Look how she's smiling, she says. She wants to go to you.

That's just gas, Mathilde snaps. Don't bribe me, Anna. It won't work.

But she heaves herself into a sitting position against the headboard and takes Trudie from Anna, settling the baby on her thighs. Bouncing her, the baker sings:

> *"Backe, backe Kuchen!"*
> *der Bäcker hat gerufen.*
> *"Wer will guten Kuchen backen,*
> *Der muss haben sieben Sachen:*
> *Butter und Salz,*
> *Zucker und Schmalz,*
> *Milch und Mehl,*
> *und Eier machen den Kuchen gel'."*

Trudie belches.

You liked that, did you? the baker asks her. She sighs. *Butter und Eier*— I'd kill for some real butter, some unpowdered eggs.

I'd eat them right now, even in my sorry state...You don't even know where the drop-off point is, she adds, smoothing the dandelion fluff on the baby's head.

So tell me, says Anna. I know the woods of the Ettersberg well enough. I played there as a girl.

And this is true, for as Anna wends her way into the forest just before sunset, carrying a flour sack bulging with rolls, she can still make out the trails she hiked as an adolescent, during her mandatory participation in the League of German Girls. And although the paths don't lead there, Anna knows her way to Buchenwald. In the days before her mother's death, Gerhard often marched his small family up the Ettersberg to picnic beneath Goethe's Oak, which, according to all reports, the Nazis have left standing in the center of the camp. Sentimental fellows, these SS.

Also industrious, or at least the men in their custody are: the rumor is that the prisoners have been forced to build a five-kilometer road from the Weimar train station to the camp. Anna encounters it about a third of the way along. Naturally, rather than walking on the pavement, she threads through the dense undergrowth, keeping the road to her right as a guide. The inmates must have had a hellish time clear-cutting these trees; the hoary stands of spruce and fir, hundreds of feet tall, are so densely packed that they permit only *Pfennig*-sized blotches of light to fall on the forest floor, reminding Anna of the Grimm woodcuts in *Hansel und Gretel* that so terrified her as a child.

But oddly, she is not afraid now. Her senses are keener than they have been since Max's disappearance, and Anna notices the clumps of crocuses, the coo of mourning doves, as though she were still storing these details to bring to him in the room behind the stairs. This is ludicrous, of course; it isn't as though she is going to have tea with the man in the Buchenwald mess! But the inconsonant joy Max inspires in Anna is as strong as it ever was, and to catch sight of him, even from a distance, is all she wants. Perhaps she will be able to exchange a message with him somehow—

So thinking, Anna doesn't see the stone quarry until it yaws before her. She shrinks back among the trees, her heart thudding, a taste of iron in her mouth. Unlike what she has heard of the camp proper, the quarry isn't encircled with barbed wire, but the guards standing at regular intervals denote a sentry line. The sight turns Anna's muscles to gelatin. Mathilde has assured her that the quarry will be deserted at this hour, the prisoners having been marched back to Buchenwald for evening roll call. The baker has either forgotten about daylight saving time or underestimated the SS zeal for production.

When she has recovered herself, Anna steals around the circumference of the quarry until she spies the enormous pine Mathilde has described. The bread will go in its hollow trunk; beneath the flat stone at its base, Anna might find one of the information-bearing condoms. She will obviously have to wait, however, until the quarry is empty. Anna debates retreating to a safer distance. It is the more intelligent course of action, the wisest being to abandon the venture altogether. But Anna fears that if she does, she will never be brave enough to try again, and she can't stomach the thought of returning with her full sack of rolls to the bakery and Mathilde's derision. Besides, Max is here. So Anna conceals herself behind the tree, and waits, and watches.

The prisoners, laboring in tandem against a sunset striated the gentle lemon and orange of sherbet, are a black organism from which smaller organisms detach to carry rocks to one side. The *Kapos* who oversee them are likewise indistinguishable. But the SS who supervise the *Kapos* stand closer to Anna, and she has read enough of the prisoners' messages to discern that the taller one is the infamous *Unterscharführer* Hinkelmann. The shorter fellow, nondescript as a bank clerk, is *Unterscharführer* Blank. Or is it the other way around? In any case, they both look bored, and also quite drunk, passing a bottle of cognac back and forth between them.

Yet apparently the precious liquor isn't enough to keep them occupied, for the taller officer, Hinkelmann or Blank, levels his truncheon at a prisoner who makes the mistake of staggering too close to him with a boulder.

You, he says. Come here.

When the prisoner, trying to remain invisible, trundles onward, Blank or Hinkelmann lunges unsteadily at him, knocking the man's cap off with the club.

Pay attention when I talk to you, he says.

The prisoner, dazed, releases the boulder.

Yes, Herr *Unterscharführer,* he says. Blood trickles in a thick rivulet from his ear.

Hinkelmann or Blank fishes the cap from the mud with his truncheon, not without some difficulty, and slings it through the air. It sails past the guards.

Get your cap, he orders.

But Herr *Unterscharführer,* begging your pardon, that's beyond the sentry line.

Blank or Hinkelmann fetches the man such a blow to the head that he falls to his knees.

I *said,* get your cap. Are you fucking deaf?

The prisoner blinks up at the *Unterscharführer* through the blood sheeting down his face.

No, and I'm not fucking crazy either. Get it yourself.

Hinkelmann or Blank pivots, gaping at his SS brother in burlesque amazement.

Did you hear that? he asks. Did you hear what he said?

He delivers a kick to the prisoner's kidneys, driving the man face-first into the mud, then clubs him in the head, across the shoulders, on the back. He flips the prisoner over with his foot. He waits until the prisoner has regained consciousness, then stands on his throat and presses down with his full weight. The prisoner's limbs flail, his hands scrabbling for purchase on the officer's boot. When he has stopped gurgling, Hinkelmann or Blank bends over and peers into his face. Satisfied, he administers a last kick.

Another one shot while trying to escape, he says. Did you get that, Rippchen?

He turns to an adjutant standing a few meters away. Orating like an actor projecting to the last row, pantomiming the act of writing down the words, the *Unterscharführer* bellows: Shot— while trying— to escape.

I got it, Herr *Unterscharführer,* the adjutant reassures him.

Behind them, the prisoners continue working, with a bit more energy than before.

Jesus Christ, Blank or Hinkelmann says, frowning at the smudges the prisoner's death grip has left on his boot. Give me some of that.

His partner hands him the cognac.

Neither notices a third officer who has arrived during the beating. This fellow, whose decorations proclaim him to be of higher rank than Hinkelmann or Blank, is bigger than both, dark-haired, sober. He moves with purpose to the pair and holds a brief conference with them, his voice pitched too low for his words to carry. The *Unterscharführers* react with indignation.

Come on, Horst, Blank or Hinkelmann says. You've had this shit detail. You know how it is!

He swirls liquor from cheek to cheek and then spits it onto the ground near the corpse.

The third officer says something else, and Hinkelmann or Blank gives an extravagant salute.

Yes SIR, Herr *Obersturmführer,* SIR, he says, and gestures to the adjutant, who blows a whistle. The prisoners each pick up a rock, form columns, and run double-time to the entrance of the quarry, helped along by blows from the *Kapos*. The *Obersturm-führer* lingers behind, inspecting the dead prisoner.

Suddenly, as though he were a dog scenting the air, the *Ober-sturmführer*'s head snaps up and rotates toward Anna. He stares in her direction, and Anna thinks for a moment that he is blind. Then she realizes that this is, of course, not the case; it is simply that his eyes are so light that he appears from this distance to have no pupils. Yet even after he turns and leaves, Anna's fear of him is so great that it approaches superstitious conviction. Somehow, the *Obersturmführer* has seen her. He knows she is there.

She huddles behind the tree, her hands over her mouth to stifle the tiny, terrified hitching noises she makes as she weeps. How can human beings do such things to one another? What thoughts ran through the prisoner's mind as his life was squeezed out of him, as he looked up at a slice of Blank's or Hinkelmann's face, knowing that the foot on his throat belonged to a man with the same skin, blood, the same basic tube of meat between his legs, as his own?

Eventually, when it grows dark, Anna undoes the sack and shoves the rolls into the rotted hollow of the pine as fast as she can. Somehow she remembers to scrabble beneath the big stone for the condom. Her hands are shaking so that she tears the thin greasy membrane while excavating it. She stuffs it into her pocket nonetheless and picks up the empty flour sack and flees in the direction from which she came.

16

By December, the restrictions of rationing have tightened even further. Weimarians exist on a diet consisting almost solely of lentils and turnips. They queue in lines for hours for the privilege of purchasing meat so gristly as to be inedible; they come to blows over bones and hooves for broth. The forests of Thuringia are said to be devoid of game. The loaves Anna and Mathilde produce are heavy as rocks and in fact often contain small pebbles, as even the flour provided by the SS is substandard.

Nor is food the only thing in short supply. Gasoline and cigarettes are used in lieu of money. Thread, so necessary for mending clothes already worn for three years or more, is nowhere to be found. And the Reich has decreed that all Germans may bathe only on Saturdays, as any type of fuel for hot water, be it coal or wood, has been declared a national resource.

So it is no surprise to Anna, who has gone to the city's remaining and octogenarian doctor for medicine for Trudie's cough, that she returns to the bakery empty-handed. We have reentered the age of leeches, she remarks acidly to Mathilde; if only

I could find some! The child's croup worsens, and the baker employs an equally archaic if more violent method: Anna will never forget the sight of Mathilde reaching into Trudie's flour crate cradle in the cellar, her nightgown ripping with a flatulent sound as she hefts the choking toddler by the heels and thumps her on the back. This proves an effective temporary cure, but within a few days Trudie can no longer draw a full breath, so Anna decides to disobey one of the Reich's edicts. After securing the blackout curtains, she feeds the porcelain stove in the upstairs WC with coal, ingot upon ingot, more precious than gold. Enough to produce a full bath and a roomful of steam.

It is late at night. Anna sits on the side of the tub with Trudie in her lap, rubbing the child's back. The humidity seems to be helping; Trudie is finally dozing when Mathilde pushes the door open. She is spattered with mud that fills the room with the reek of sulfur.

How is she? the baker whispers.

A little better, thank God. But she can't go on this way. Do you think you could get some stronger medicine on the black market?

No need, says Mathilde, wheezing from her charge up the stairs. She pats her voluminous coat pockets, finds a bottle from one of them, and she hands it to Anna.

This will take care of it, she says.

Craning over her dozing daughter, Anna squints at the label but doesn't recognize the name.

You got this on the black market? she asks. From Pfeffer?

No, not that crook, he'd sell you sugarwater as soon as look at you. I bought it off Ilse, Herr *Doktor* Ellenbeck's maid, when I made the Eickestrasse deliveries this afternoon. It cost me a fortune in cigarettes, I can tell you, but she swore it would work. She has four little ones of her own.

This is an SS doctor's medicine? Anna says, aghast. It's probably cyanide!

They don't keep cyanide in their houses, Mathilde says, missing Anna's irony. Only in the hospital block.

The baker hangs her coat over the robe on the back of the door and plunges her forearms into the tub. Anna waits for her to comment on the fact that the water is a good eight inches higher than the black line painted on the porcelain.

But Mathilde only sighs.

Ach, that feels good, she says. It's a filthy night. Snowing. I almost went off the road three times.

I take it you made a Special Delivery, Anna says, nodding at the now-brown water, on which pine needles float. How did it go?

Fine. Fine. Last week's bread was gone. And I got a new message from the prisoners.

Good, says Anna.

She rouses Trudie to give her some of the medicine, which the sleepy child accepts without her usual protest. Every woman who visits the bakery comments that she has never seen a sturdier toddler, and Anna has to agree. But her pride in her daughter is somewhat tempered by a bewildered exasperation. When she is well, there is little of either her mother or her father in Trudie. She is solid and round, built like a small truck with legs sturdy as pistons, and her rages when she is thwarted, her charm when she has worn down her opponent and gotten her way, her general bullish constitution: they are exactly like Gerhard's. In a quirk of genetic hopscotch, the traits have skipped a generation.

In fact, the only similarity Anna can draw between her daughter and Max, aside from the blue of her eyes, is the light hair that grows in whorls, uncowed by any amount of brushing. Now, because of the steam, it curls in damp corkscrews that Anna smoothes from the child's flushed forehead.

Mathilde smiles as she lowers her bulk onto the closed lid of the toilet. As if catching the run of Anna's thoughts, she observes, Her hair is so like her father's.

Anna puts her hand on the small chest. The constriction within it has eased, she thinks.

Don't you want to know? the baker asks.

Know what?

Whether there's any news of your Max. You haven't asked in ages.

Anna shifts Trudie into a more comfortable position on her lap and murmurs to her.

I have to tell you, Anna, it doesn't look good. Ilse says they've finished building the crematorium. Even in this shitty weather the SS have had the poor bastards working on it night and day.

This doesn't surprise Anna. She has overheard the women discussing it in the bakery. They say that the SS have been bringing corpses in vans to Reinhard's funeral parlor in central Weimar for cremation, but that on occasion something goes wrong and the dead spill out into the street. The SS can't have this; it is bad for morale. Naturally they would devise their own methods for disposing of their victims.

Well? says Mathilde.

Well what?

Don't you have any reaction?

Anna shakes her head. A needle to the heart, dysentery, hanging, malnutrition, the murderous whims of Hinkelmann and Blank, simple overwork in the mud and snow: what good is it pretending that Max will survive? There are so many ways for him to die. When Anna thinks of him at all, which she does only when her guard is down before sleep, it is of his knowing smile over the chessboard, the narrow triangle of his freckled torso in the room behind the stairs. There have been no messages from Max since August.

He may still be all right, Mathilde says.

Angrily, Anna wipes her eyes with the back of a wrist.

Don't lie to me, she says to the baker. And please, don't be kind. I can stand anything but that.

Mathilde gets up to feed the last of the coal into the stove.

Did you love him very much? she asks shyly, her back to Anna.

Anna ducks her head. The tears Mathilde has unwittingly unleashed darken her shirtwaist in blotches and further dampen Trudie's hair.

Yes, she says. I did.

Well, at least you've had that, Mathilde says, sitting down again with a whistling sigh. At least you've got that to hold on to.

Anna looks up at the forlorn note in the baker's voice.

Why, so do you, she says. You have the memory of your Fritzi.

Oh, Fritzi, says Mathilde, shrugging. That was different.

What do you mean?

Ach, Anna, you wouldn't understand. A pretty girl like you, you must have had ten proposals before you were sixteen. But a woman who looks like me, she has to take what she can get. My Fritzi married me for the bakery, nobody ever pretended otherwise. He came from such a poor family. He never loved me, not really, not like your Max loved you.

How do you know? Anna says loyally. People who marry for convenience often grow to love one another. It happens all the time.

Mathilde gives a small rasping laugh that turns into a cough.

Not with Fritzi. He was different, she repeats.

Different how?

You know, Anna, queer! He didn't like women. He would go to Berlin on weekends and— Well, we had an understanding. He did as he pleased and I didn't end up a spinster.

The baker reaches over to take hold of Trudie's foot, which she cradles as gently as she might an egg.

The only thing I regret, she adds, aside from him getting himself blown to bits in the last war, was that because of our arrangement he never gave me a child.

Anna looks down at Mathilde's pudgy hand, thinking of the bashful young man with the pink-tinted cheeks in Mathilde's bedroom portrait. She now understands why Mathilde stares so hungrily at Trudie when she thinks Anna isn't looking, why the baker only laughs when she finds that the toddler has poked holes in the crusts of the valuable loaves to dig out and eat the soft insides.

Is that why you started feeding the prisoners? Anna asks. I've often wondered why you take the risk when everyone else turns a blind eye. Is it because some of them are...different, like Fritzi?

Mathilde blinks at Anna, startled.

I never thought of that, she says slowly. I just feel so sorry for those poor men. But...yes, I guess that could have had something to do with it.

She runs a thumb over Trudie's small foot. A silence falls between the two women, broken only by the hiss of water on the stove.

Oh, Anna, Mathilde says abruptly. Her little voice wavers. What will become of us? After the war, maybe you'll marry. The child will need a father. And me, I guess I'll go on running the bakery. But it'll never be the same, you know? The world has gone crazy. To burn people in ovens...That we talk about this the same way we used to talk about—about— whether Irene Schultz's husband was going to leave her, or the price of turnips, or the weather—

I know, says Anna, alarmed. Shhhh.

For now it is the baker who cries, her body quivering with the force of it, her small black eyes, fixed imploringly on Anna, awash with tears.

There's no use in getting yourself so upset, Anna tells her. We do what we can and that's all we can do.

Mathilde lowers her head and wipes her cheeks with her filthy skirt.

You're right, she says after a time. She heaves an enormous sigh. You're right. We won't talk of such things anymore. It's no use. I don't know what's wrong with me, bringing it up tonight of all nights.

Getting to her feet with a grunt, she bends and gives Anna a clumsy kiss on the hair.

Happy Christmas, she says.

Anna smiles at Mathilde, unable to return the gesture for fear of joggling and waking the child. War makes for strange bed-fellows, it is said; apparently it makes for strange friendships as well. The brave, unlucky baker is the only true friend Anna has ever had.

Happy Christmas to you too, she replies, and doesn't tell Mathilde that she had completely forgotten.

17

ONE MORNING IN EARLY MARCH 1942, ANNA TUCKS THE blanket around her sleeping daughter and climbs from the cellar to find Mathilde on her hands and knees in the kitchen, digging in one of the long, low cupboards that line the south wall.

Nice of you to interrupt your beauty rest, she tells Anna from within the cabinet, her voice muffled and hollow. I thought you were planning to lie in bed until noon.

Despite Mathilde's tart tone, Anna smiles in relief. Since Christmas the baker has been increasingly gloomy, falling into spells of despondency from which not even Trudie, running to her beloved Tante on fat little feet, can rouse her. Admittedly, the baker's behavior this morning is a bit bizarre, but it is better than her sitting in her rocking chair in her chamber above the bakery, staring at nothing.

What are you doing? Anna asks.

Receiving no reply, she goes to the sink, where she splashes her face with icy water. The window is a glowing sheet of gold, the frost on it lit by the first rays of the sun. It is going to be a fine day.

Her toilette complete, Anna fastens her apron around her waist and turns to watch Mathilde crawl backward from the cupboard with her fists full of pistols. Collapsing onto her haunches, the baker begins packing them in a flour sack which, by the looks of it, she has already stuffed with rolls.

Where did you get the pistols? Anna asks.

Mathilde uses the edge of the worktable to haul herself up.

Ask me no questions, she says, and I'll tell you no lies.

She buttons her tattered coat and carries the sack through the back door. Bracing herself against the cold slipstream that enters, Anna lifts the rack of loaves baked the previous night and follows Mathilde outside.

I assume you're not delivering those weapons to the SS, Anna persists, her breath coming short and smoky as she stacks the bread in the rear of the bakery van.

Mathilde snorts. She is cramming the sack into the false floor beneath the passenger's seat; once this is secured, she lets the rubber mat fall over it. Anna watches with approval. Without the most thorough search of the vehicle, nobody would ever suspect the guns were there.

Mathilde comes over and puts her mouth directly to Anna's ear.

They're for the Red Triangles, she whispers.

The Red—?

The political prisoners. They're planning a revolt.

Anna steps back, surreptitiously wiping flecks of the baker's spittle from her cheek.

Well, God bless, she says.

Mathilde hoists herself into the high driver's seat, where she rolls and lights a cigarette before starting the engine. Then she turns and looks at Anna over one shoulder, squinting through the smoke.

For shame, Anna, she calls. You're still so naive as to think there's a God?

Without waiting for an answer, she wrenches the van's stick

shift into gear and drives off, the cigarette clenched between her teeth.

Anna stands coughing in blue billows of exhaust until the flatulence of the van's muffler has diminished in the distance. Then she shrugs off Mathilde's question and hurries shivering into the kitchen. Although the pickings will be slim for the bakery's patrons today, since the SS have requisitioned their bread, there is still much to do.

In fact, the morning is so busy, the customers squabbling like pigeons over stale rolls and rock-hard rye, that Anna doesn't have a moment to herself until midafternoon, when everything has been sold. Apologizing to the last disgruntled women, she ushers them out, locks the door, and goes to tend her daughter. Thankfully, Trudie has resisted the lure of climbing the stairs, her new favorite pastime; she is still in the kitchen, from which Anna has forbidden her to move. But instead of playing with her doll, a sorry creature Mathilde has fashioned from a sock, Trudie has overturned her lunch and is happily smacking her hands in a puddle of parsnip soup.

Bad girl, Anna says, hauling Trudie to her feet and swatting her rump.

She marches the child to the corner and instructs her to stand with her face to the wall. Trudie complies until her mother is swabbing up the mess; then she whirls and scowls at Anna and slides to the floor in a heap. She kicks her wooden heels against it. She manufactures an indignant sob. Anna, trying to ignore her, wonders how it is that such an angelic-looking child should prove so intractable. She wrings her rag in the sink and starts in on the dishes.

The view from the window, so promising this morning, has turned ugly. The field is piebald with mud and snow, the dark trees beyond it lashed by wind. The sky hangs low and threatening. There will be more snow. Already the light is dimming as the sun sinks somewhere above those dense clouds. A bad afternoon for making deliveries, particularly in a temperamental van along a road treacherous even in better conditions.

So, when the last pan has been dried and put away, Anna turns to Trudie and says, Time for a nap.

Trudie, who has been digging loose plaster from a hole in the wall, shakes her head so vigorously that her fine hair escapes its braids.

No, she says. No nap.

Yes, nap, says Anna. And as a special treat, you can sleep in Tante's bed. Won't that be nice?

No, says the toddler.

But she allows herself to be persuaded upstairs, though she insists on walking up the steps instead of being carried. She breathes heavily in concentration as she lifts one small foot, then the next; to Anna, it seems to take Trudie a good half hour to reach the second-floor landing.

Once she has settled Trudie in Mathilde's bed, Anna fetches the last of the cough elixir from the WC.

Noooooooo, Trudie cries when she sees the dreaded bottle.

Anna sighs, wishing there were a neighbor she could trust to watch Trudie without asking questions.

Come now, she says, nudging the spoon against her daughter's lips. Be a good girl.

Trudie screws her mouth shut.

Mama drink it, she suggests craftily.

Despite her impatience, Anna has to laugh: Trudie is definitely Gerhard's grandchild. Anna pretends to sip from the bottle.

Mmmmm, she says, miming ecstasy with a roll of the eyes. Delicious. Now your turn.

Mollified, Trudie accepts the medicine. Anna doesn't dare give the child more than two teaspoons, but this should be enough to put Trudie out for a few hours. The elixir has a codeine base.

Sitting on the edge of the bed, Anna waits, stroking the child's slippery hair, until she is sure Trudie is fast asleep. Then Anna layers a sweater over her dress, wraps a dark shawl around her head, bundles herself into her coat, and leaves the bakery through the back door. She crosses the field to the Ettersberg.

The woods are not welcoming this time of year. As the birds have fled in search of kinder climes and the deer and rabbits have become stew, the only sound Anna hears is the ice crunching like thin glass beneath her boots. It begins to snow. Anna catches a few flakes and rubs her fingertips beneath her nostrils to test whether it is precipitation or ash from the crematorium, but she is not really conscious of doing so. She creeps alongside the road, closer to it than is advisable, but she is straining for any sign that something bad has happened to the delivery van: the black swerve of tires marks on the tar, for instance, or broken branches that would indicate the vehicle's plunge into a gully.

This is foolishness, really. The baker has handled deliveries in far worse weather than this. And Anna is going the wrong way now, following the road as it branches toward the quarry, which Mathilde would not take unless she were making a Special Delivery, which in turn she would never attempt in daylight. Yet Anna's unease has reached such a pitch that she is shocked but not surprised when her suspicions of disaster are confirmed by the sight of the van canted off the roadside, not a quarter kilometer from the quarry. A hot filament, like that in an electric bulb, glows for a moment in Anna's stomach, then is extinguished. That is all.

She wends through the underbrush, branches snapping back across her face, until she is almost to the pavement. Then she sees the foot lying on it, shod in a sturdy black boot laced to the ankle. Anna has often poked fun at these boots, teasing Mathilde that they are for old ladies. A meter to the right and the rest of the baker comes into view. She is splayed half-on, half-off the road like a big pallid doll, her eyes staring at the sky. There is a neat hole in her forehead, its edges charred black with gunpowder, and all around her the blood has turned the snow into a slushy red soup.

No, Anna whispers. No.

She takes another step toward the baker, though some vestigial instinct warns her that this is unwise. The blood is still spreading from the body, and the snow falling into Mathilde's eyes melts and trickles down her cheeks. The execution is recent, then, and whoever has done it is most likely still in the vicinity. Yet Anna doesn't conceal herself until she sees the SS noncom stumble around the side of the van. Then, trapped on her stomach in the undergrowth, she has no choice but to watch him. He is young, and obviously a newcomer to the business of killing, for his greatcoat is spattered with vomit, his expression both horrified and sheepish. But he recovers quickly: when he has finished swabbing his mouth on his sleeve, he walks a slow circle around Mathilde, squatting to peer curiously into her face. He withdraws the truncheon from his belt and uses it to push up the baker's coat and skirt. He prods one of her legs. He lifts the limb and lets it fall. The boot thumps on the paving.

Forgetting herself in her outrage — is it not enough that he has murdered the baker, he has to play with her too? — Anna reacts before she thinks.

Stop that! she says.

The noncom's head jerks up. He fumbles his pistol from its holster. His hands are shaking so hard that any shot he fires will go high and wild.

Who's there? he yells, his voice cracking. Show yourself!

He starts toward the thicket in which Anna lies, her hand belatedly clamped over her mouth.

Then he whips around. From the direction of the camp comes the noise of an approaching convoy: the growl of engines, the waspish buzz of motorbikes. Replacing his pistol, the noncom adjusts his cap and checks his reflection in the van's wing mirror. Thus satisfied, he stands at attention over the corpse, thrusting his chest out, a hunter posing with his kill.

Anna uses the opportunity to begin wriggling backward, still on her belly, pushing herself along with her hands. Thirty meters into the forest, she jumps up, turns, and runs, heedless of noise. Nor does she make any effort to cover her tracks, though the snow sifting through the pines may soon hide them. It doesn't matter. The SS are thorough. They will know. They will investigate. A long black car will pull up in front of the bakery and officers will emerge and pound on the door. By this evening, Anna will be in a basement cell at Gestapo headquarters. Or, more likely, she and Trudie will have been shot where they stand.

She crashes through the undergrowth, her breath tearing in her lungs, her eyes stinging with tears not of grief but of rage. Were Mathilde alive, Anna would shake her until the baker's teeth rattle. How dare Mathilde do this? How could she have been so selfish? There are better ways to commit suicide than making a Special Delivery in broad daylight; she could have done it without endangering anyone else. She has left Anna with nothing, not even information as to how to contact other members of the Resistance. There is nowhere for Anna and Trudie to go where the SS will not find them. Anna has no choice but to return to the bakery and change her clothes and give the appearance that everything is normal. She will feed her daughter, who should at least die on a full stomach, and she will keep the child close to her, and she will try not to think of her dead friend. And through all of this she will wait. She will wait until they come for her.

Trudy, December 1996

18

TRUDY IS WAITING FOR THE GERMANS TO COME TO HER. While the rest of Minneapolis throngs the malls and swarms the supermarkets in a pre-Christmas frenzy, while Trudy's colleagues gripe about balancing holiday obligations with grading their final exams, Trudy has been huddled in conference with Ruth, trying to get her German Project off the ground. It is true that the Director of Holocaust Studies has to be prodded out of initial reluctance — stemming more, Trudy suspects, from Ruth's having to share her hard-earned funding than her objections about giving the perpetrators of the Nazi regime as much airtime as its Jewish victims. But Trudy persists, coaxing and wheedling. Put the History Department's needs above your own, she pleads, and finally she sees Ruth kindle.

I suppose you're right, Ruth says thoughtfully, one dreary December afternoon when, exhausted from wrangling, the pair are picking at dispirited sandwiches in the university cafeteria. There never *has* been a really extensive study of the reactions of German civilians — not live sources recorded on tape...

Her sputtering enthusiasm sparks, then catches fire; she begins to wave her small freckled hands about, scattering crumbs. Forget Yale; this double-headed Project would put us on the international map! All right, Trudy, you've got it. I'll give you access to my videographers and equipment and some of the money—*with* the proviso that *you* apply for more when we need it. Why should I have to do all the work? Deal?

Deal, says Trudy, and pats her lips with a napkin to hide a smile of victorious relief.

But now, as she sits in her office just before Christmas, praying for her prospective subjects to call, Trudy thinks that her triumph may have been a bit premature. She has done all she can to lure the Germans from their foxholes. She has gone to their restaurants, the Black Forest Inn on Nicollet Avenue and the *Gasthof zur Gemütlichkeit* in North Minneapolis, where pilsner is drunk from life-size glass boots and men in lederhosen wander among the tables, forcing from wheezing accordions nostalgic folk tunes that get stuck in Trudy's head for days. *Ich mein Harz in Heidelburg veloren*... She has ventured to the local chapter of the German-American Society, where a moth-eaten stag's head presides over the door and polka parties are listed on the bulletin board, where beer-bellied old fellows give her glances of cursory interest before returning to their cards. She has visited *Die Bäckerei* on Lyndale, where she waited warily for a déjà vu that never came: the lights and appliances too modern, the display case crowded with cupcakes and reindeer-shaped cookies instead of the *Lebkuchen* and *Stollen* Trudy had anticipated. And in each of these places, Trudy has posted flyers that say this:

> *Wanted: Germans of native descent to participate in study conducted by University of Minnesota history professor. I am seeking any and all recollections you have about living through the war in Germany. Interviews will be filmed on camera but used for university research purposes only. Female subjects of partic-*

ular interest but males also encouraged to apply. You will be re-
imbursed for your time.

This is a chance for you to tell your story, which contemporary
history has largely ignored. If interested, please contact Dr.
Trudy Swenson, Department of History, University of Min-
nesota, extension...

Trudy has also run this advertisement in the German papers, the *Minneapolis Star Tribune* and the *St. Paul Pioneer Press,* placing them—after some bemused consideration—in the Personals section as well as the Classifieds.

Because of the holiday tumult, Trudy has anticipated not getting many responses before the turn of the year, but she hasn't expected to receive none. She lurks in her office, gripped by the superstitious conviction that if she stays by the phone her potential subjects will call, in the same way that leaving milk and cookies for Santa guarantees his visit. She grades papers and reads journals and draws up next semester's lesson plans, meanwhile trying to feign unawareness of the silent phone at her elbow as if she were waiting for nothing at all.

December 20, a day whose blinding sun and hard blue sky provide the illusion of warmth while really signifying that it is too cold to snow. The campus is eerily quiet, the students long since fled to their homes and the professors, after turning final grades in to the registrar, having followed suit. Trudy has nothing to do. She sits canted back in her desk chair, gazing through the windows at the empty pathways of the quad, noting without conscious thought the sharp contrast of light and lengthening shadow. In one hand she holds the little gold case that contains the incriminating photograph. She runs her thumb over the swastika and art deco design.

Come on, Trudy thinks. Come on, Germans. I know you're out there.

The only reply is snow falling, with a gentle *whump,* from an overhead cornice to the ground.

Trudy sighs and gets to her feet. She reminds herself that her subjects have other things to do right now—gifts to buy and wrap, Christmas dinners to cook, arriving grandchildren to spoil. All Trudy has to do is be patient. But as she pulls on her coat, she worries that this entire endeavor is doomed, a waste of money and energy and hope. Anna has never talked. Why should her compatriots be any different?

Trudy is in the hallway, sorting through her keys to find the one that locks the door, when her phone rings.

She steps back into her office and stares at the blinking red light on the console. It's probably just Ruth, Trudy tells herself, checking in to see if there has been any progress—or to boast, in the subtlest of fashions, about the number of Jewish subjects' testimonies she has already recorded.

Professor Swenson, Trudy says into the phone.

Hello?

It is a woman's voice. Not Ruth's. Containing the quaver of the elderly.

Ja, und with whom am I speaking? Have I reached the Department of History?

Trudy's pulse quickens and flutters in her throat. The woman's accent is more Bavarian than Anna's, but some similarities exist: the broadening of the vowels, the clipped consonants, the emphasis on the *ff*'s in *of. Department uff History.*

Yes, ma'am, this is the History Department, Trudy says. Are you calling about the advertisement? The German Project?

There is a clunk, as if the caller has dropped the receiver, and some scuffling in the background. Trudy braces herself for the buzz of a severed connection, but then she hears the woman breathing.

What is your name, ma'am? Trudy asks. Are you still with me?

Kluge. *Frau* Kluge. First name Petra.

Trudy grabs a pen.

Danke, Frau Kluge, she says. Now, I assume you're volunteering for—

You want to know about the war, the woman says.

Yes, that's right.

Why is this?

Well, says Trudy, as I said in my ad, I'm doing some research—

What kind of research? You will not make me look bad? *You vill nutt mekk me look bett?*

Of course not, says Trudy. I'm just trying to collect some stories—

Gut, the woman says. Because I can tell you a little something...But! You said volunteer?

What's that? says Trudy.

Volunteer, you have said this. But your advertisement said I will be paid. How much, exactly?

Um, says Trudy, annoyed with herself; she has forgotten to ask Ruth the amount of the stipend she is offering her own subjects. Fif— A hundred dollars?

Gut. That is agreeable.

I'm glad, Trudy says. So, when would you—

I live at 1043 North Thirtieth Street, apartment B. You will come tomorrow.

Oh, says Trudy, scribbling madly. Well, thank you, Frau Kluge, but are you sure you want to do it so soon? We won't have much time to prep—

Three o'clock, the woman says.

Okay then, says Trudy. Now, there are a few other things you should know, Frau Kluge: I'll have a cameraman with me to record the interview, and—

But Frau Kluge has hung up.

Trudy removes the receiver from between shoulder and ear

and regards it for a moment. Then she wedges it back into place and sifts through her German Project paperwork for the number of Ruth's videographer. It seems too much to hope that he will be available this close to Christmas. But if he is not, Trudy is prepared to beg.

Her luck holds, at least until the following afternoon, when it seems to abruptly run out: the cameraman, while cheerfully acquiescent on the phone, is late. Trudy waits for him in her car on Frau Kluge's street, feeling like a burglar. This would be nothing new in this neighborhood, she thinks; the residents here are probably on perpetual alert for thieves. Frau Kluge lives in a two-story brick building in a grid of five identical others, all surrounded by chain-link fencing into which garbage has blown. In the parking lot, a few old cars are nosed up to dirty drifts of snow. Somehow this surprises Trudy. She doesn't know what she has expected, but it was certainly not to find her first subject in the projects.

She is trying to focus on the questions she has spent all night preparing when a white truck turns the corner, cruises slowly down the street, and parks at the curb a few yards away. A man in an army jacket jumps from the driver's side and jogs around to the tailgate, which he yanks up with a rattle. Thank God, Trudy thinks. She grabs the bakery box of cookies she has bought for Frau Kluge and gets out of her car to greet him, her boots gritting on the sanded ice.

Hello in there, she calls, for the man has disappeared inside his truck, from which a ramp protrudes like a corrugated steel tongue. Are you my videographer?

The man pokes his head out, and Trudy sees that his eyes are so light as to be nearly colorless. Her stomach drops. She has always been uneasy around light-eyed men.

She reaches up to shake his proffered hand.

Trudy Swenson, she says.

Thomas Kroger, replies the man. Sorry to have kept you

waiting, the damned tailgate was frozen shut...Just give me one more minute.

Again he vanishes from view, and a cart loaded with bulky equipment in padded blankets begins descending the ramp. The man follows, clinging to its handle. As more and more of him emerges, it becomes apparent that he is very tall, perhaps six-five. Once on solid ground, he smiles down at Trudy; he is about her age, a throwback to the hippie era. His face is so round that it is unlined except for the eyes, but he wears a red bandanna around his forehead beneath his shaggy graying hair.

Trudy imagines Anna's disdain over the bandanna and wishes she could ask him to take it off. Instead, she looks doubtfully at the cart.

I didn't expect you to bring all this, she says. This Project is a relatively modest operation—

Thomas laughs.

You did want this interview filmed, right? he says. I'm a professional, you know, Dr. Swenson, not a tourist. I don't work with a handheld camcorder.

Oh, I guess not, says Trudy, though she is a bit startled by the protruding tripods and sound booms after all Ruth's talk about operating on a shoestring budget. Forgive me; I didn't mean to offend. And please, call me Trudy.

Thomas shuts the tailgate and secures it with a padlock.

No offense taken, he says. Okay, Trudy, I'm all set. Lead the way.

Trudy does, Thomas and his cart trailing her through the chain-link fence to the proper building. The outer door is heavy steel and covered with graffiti; next to it is a security panel. Trudy presses B and waits. Nothing happens. Thomas reaches past her and pushes the door open.

It's broken, he says.

Trudy ventures into a hallway so dimly lit that she has to pause to let her eyes adjust. The building smells of mildew and urine and industrial-strength floor cleaner. Trudy approaches the nearest apartment, squinting to make out its number, and leaps away from the ferocious barking and snarling inside.

God in heaven, she says, putting a hand over her galloping heart.

Thomas chuckles again.

Somebody's got a rottweiler, he says. But not the somebody we want, thank goodness. Over here, Trudy.

She follows his voice down a few steps to a basement apartment near a stairwell and knocks on the door. No response. Trudy tries again, more emphatically this time.

Ja, ja, calls a voice, somewhat peevishly, from within.

Trudy hears a chair being scraped back and the scuff of slippers, but the door doesn't open. She gives Thomas a pained smile.

Sorry about all this, she says. I had no idea—

I've worked in worse places, Thomas says.

Well, I appreciate it. Especially that you were able to do this so close to Christmas.

Thomas shrugs, as best he is able. He is hunched in the triangulated space beneath the stairwell, his head bent so as not to bang it on the risers.

Christmas doesn't mean much to me, he says. I'm Jewish.

Trudy cranes to discern his expression, but it is impossible in the hallway's jaundiced gloom.

Ruth did tell you I'm interviewing Germans? she asks.

Of course, says Thomas. That's why I'm here. I'm dying to hear how these people could possibly justify what they did.

Trudy's queasiness increases. She should have known that Ruth's videographer would be Jewish. But this is the last thing Trudy needs, a cameraman who is not impartial. What if he disrupts the interview, interjects indignant questions or snorts in disbelief?

She has no time to envision how to handle this, though, for she hears a series of bolts being drawn and then Frau Kluge opens the door. An inch, anyway.

What do you want, she says.

Vhat do you vant. Trudy steps to the side so Frau Kluge can see her, trying her best to produce an ingratiating smile.

Frau Kluge? she says. I'm Trudy Swenson—

I am not interested in anything you are peddling, the woman says.

No, no, I'm from the university. We spoke yesterday on the phone, remember? About the German Project. You agreed to let me interview you? About the war?

There is a pause, and then the woman says, *Ach, ja.* This slipped from my mind.

The door opens halfway.

Trudy squares her shoulders and steps into Frau Kluge's studio, a little box of an apartment redolent of mothballs and tomato soup. The blinds are half-drawn, and beneath them through the window Trudy sees the fender of a car. Frau Kluge is lowering herself, with some difficulty, into a chair at a Formica table, the only place, with the exception of a second chair and a sagging daybed, where it is possible to sit.

You have a, um, a cozy home here, Trudy says.

Frau Kluge dismisses this with the wave of an arthritis-bunched hand.

It is a dump, she says.

Trudy looks somewhat desperately at Thomas, who is inspecting the room with narrow-eyed concentration.

Is it all right if I set up over here? he asks, indicating the daybed.

Ja, Frau Kluge says, shrugging.

Trudy refreshes her smile and sets the bakery box on the table.

What is this? Frau Kluge asks.

Cookies.

Frau Kluge picks at the striped string. Trudy reaches over to help, but Frau Kluge whisks the box away and gets up to fetch a knife from the sideboard. She slashes the lid open and peers inside.

Ach, Makronen, she says. My favorite.

She fishes out a macaroon and begins to eat, scattering crumbs on her cardigan. Trudy takes advantage of the conversational lull by sitting and consulting her notes, stealing glances at Frau Kluge all the while. She is approximately Anna's age, Trudy guesses, in her late seventies, but the resemblance ends there. Frau Kluge is a small squat woman, her face pouched and creased, her eyes hidden behind large square drugstore glasses. Her hair is a mushroom cap of such uniform gray that it can only be a wig. One real hair, long and white, grows from her chin.

Frau Kluge roots through the box in search of more macaroons; then, having apparently consumed them all, she pushes it toward Trudy.

No, thanks, says Trudy. I'm glad you enjoyed them, though.

They were stale, Frau Kluge says.

Trudy inhales deeply and looks down at her portfolio.

Frau Kluge, I thought we might talk about the interview—

Where is the money?

Excuse me?

The hundred dollars. Where is it?

From her purse Trudy extracts a check embossed with the university logo and slides it across the table. Frau Kluge fumbles it up and holds it close to her eyes, then folds it and makes it vanish into a pocket.

Ja, she says. *Gut.*

She struggles to her feet to stow the bakery box string in a drawer. Then she removes something from the refrigerator door and scuffs back to the table with it.

My grandchildren, she says, holding it out.

Trudy takes it from her and looks obediently at two children encased in magnetized Lucite. From against the marbled suede backdrop favored by school photographers, they grin up at Trudy, the girl's hair so tightly bound in ribboned barrettes that her eyes are pulled in a painful squint, the boy's mouth brash with braces. They appear to Trudy deeply ordinary children. She turns the photograph over and through the yellowing plastic reads the inscription: *Andi und Teddy, 1989.* Seven years ago.

Trudy looks up at Frau Kluge with new interest.

Your grandson must be quite a young man by now, she says.

Frau Kluge mumbles and tugs at a loop of yarn on her sweater.

Trudy hesitates, then presses her advantage: Are you going to see them at Christmas? she asks.

Frau Kluge snatches the photograph.

Ja, of course I am, she snaps. Why should I not? Do you have grandchildren?

No, I—

Children?

No—

You have at least a husband?

I was married once, but—

Frau Kluge nods in satisfaction. He is dead, she says.

Trudy laughs.

No, he's very much alive. Runs an extremely successful French restaurant, in fact. Le P'tit Lapin, maybe you've heard of it? It—

I do not eat French food, Frau Kluge announces. Rich sauces rot the bowels.

She glares triumphantly at Trudy. A small silence occurs, during which Trudy hears water dripping and dripping in the woman's sink.

Then Frau Kluge, perhaps mollified by her victory, thaws somewhat, for she tells Trudy, You remind me a little of my daughter. Of course, you are several years older. But you are something like her, through *hier.*

She pats the air near her cheeks. Trudy nods.

You are German? Frau Kluge asks.

Yes.

A true German? Not a *Mischling*?

Trudy makes a mental note of Frau Kluge's use of the Nazi

term for *half-breed,* but she is not about to spurn this peculiar olive branch the woman is offering. She decides to go a step further.

Nein, Trudy answers. *Ich bin keine Mischling, Frau Kluge. Ich bin Deustche.*

Frau Kluge scrutinizes Trudy from behind her glasses, which a beam of weak light has transformed into opaque white squares. Then she slowly lowers them and gives Trudy a smile of complicity.

So, she says. *Sehr gut.* I should have known you were pure of blood. From your pretty blond hair.

Trudy's hand involuntarily rises to her bangs.

Excuse me, Thomas calls.

Trudy turns toward him with dread, anticipating what he might say, but his face is benign. Behind him the area around Frau Kluge's daybed is now a movie set of sorts: light screens and big lamps, a camera mounted on a tripod, a sound boom the shape of an enormous peanut dangling in midair. Thomas holds up two microphones, their wires trailing into a tangle on the tired carpet.

Let's get you ladies miked and bring those chairs over here, he says. Then we'll be ready to begin.

19

THE GERMAN PROJECT
Interview 1

SUBJECT: Mrs. Petra Kluge (*née* Petra Rauschning)
DATE/LOCATION: December 21, 1996; North Minneapolis, MN

Q: Let's start with a few simple questions, Frau Kluge. When and where were you born?

A: I was born 14 August 1919, in Munich, Germany.

Q: Did you remain in Munich throughout your childhood?

A: Ja, I lived there until I came to this country.

Q: So you were in Munich at the beginning of the war, in September 1939?

A: Where else would I be?

Q: You were how old then—twenty? No, excuse me, twenty-one.

A: Ja, just turned.

Q: So you were a young woman when Hitler invaded Poland. What was your reaction to that?

A: [*subject shrugs*] Whatever the *Führer* wanted to do, this was fine by me.

Q: So you approved.

A: Approved, disapproved, it made no difference. Who was I to question such things?

Q: Were you frightened?

A: There was no cause for fear. Everybody knew the Poles were no match for us. And the *Führer* was recovering only what belonged to Germany. He was thinking of his people, of *Lebensraum*—

Q: Living space. He invaded Poland for more living space.

A: Ja, for Aryans, that is correct.

Q: So you agreed with the war in principle.

A: Ja, I already have said this. *Natürlich,* if I had known what would then happen, I might not have...But I was only young.

Q: What did you think of Hit— of the *Führer*'s other theories?

A: What do you mean by this?

Q: About the Jews. About making Germany, um, free of Jews.

A: Judenrein.

Q: That's right.

A: I was too busy to pay attention to such things. It did not concern me.

Q: What was happening to the Jews did not concern you?

A: Ja, it held no meaning for me personally. I did not know any Jews.

Q: None?

A: Ja, well, perhaps in *Gymnasium,* there were...But they soon had to go to their own schools. They kept to themselves. You know how they do, in their temples and their...their what-have-you.

Q: But surely you must have encountered Jews in the course of your daily life. On public transportation, in cafés, on the street—

A: Nein, nein. Very little. Very little. At first perhaps I encountered some without knowing it. But when they had to wear the Star, *nein,* they were no longer in the parks and trains and such.

Q: And what did you think of this?

A: I thought nothing of it. As I have said, it had little to do with me. Perhaps it made some things easier—

Q: What things? In what way?

A: [*shrugs*] *Ach,* you know. Not so crowded. In the stores, more space, more food for us Germans, once they had to go to their own stores where they belonged.

Q: I see. Did you think this was fair?

A: Fair, unfair, it made things easier. You knew who belonged with who.

Q: It didn't bother you that Jews were no longer allowed to buy things in Aryan stores, to visit Aryan doctors, to attend the theater—

A: Nein. And it did not bother them either. They like to stick to their own kind. And they did not suffer, believe me. They could still buy whatever they wanted.

Q: How is that?

A: They had their ways. They always had their ways.

Q: They had money, you mean?

A: Ja, ja, this is exactly right. Before the war, when Germans were starving, when we had to wait hours for a loaf of bread... when there was looting, windows being broken, people being killed for a few *Pfennigs*...they could just waltz in and buy whatever they pleased. Their pockets clinked with money. Their coats were lined with fur.

Q: And during the war?

A: Ach, this made no difference to them. They still had the money. They hid it. Buried it in their cellars, in their homes, under the floors. You know how they are.

Q: How they—

A: Sneaky. The Jews were sneaky. They no longer flashed their money about under our noses, but they had it. They had diamonds sewed into the linings of their coats.

Q: But, Frau Kluge— Not to contradict you, but you said you had no contact with Jews. How did you know they were hiding money?

A: Everybody knew.

Q: Everybody?

A: Ja, everybody.

Q: Well, how did everybody know?

A: They just did. It was a fact.

Q: By everybody, I assume you mean Aryan Germans.

A: Ja, Germans.

Q: Did the Germans— Did you know what would happen to the Jews when they were deported?

A: Nein, nein. We were told nothing. That was government business.

Q: So you knew nothing about the camps?

A: Camps?

Q: The concentration camps. To which the Jews were deported.

A: That is all propaganda.

Q: Propaganda!

A: That is right, propaganda. *Ach,* I am sure some Jews did die. But from the war. From bombs and cold and sickness and hunger. Just like the Germans did.

Q: But— But Frau Kluge, what about the photographs, the—

A: Propaganda. As I have said. Falsehoods spread by the Allies after the war.

Q: I see…Now, um, now, Frau Kluge, perhaps you could tell me a little more about what your life was like during the war. What do you remember most?

A: The rations. At first. Then no food anywhere. We were starving. The cold. The air raids. Terrible.

Q: What were you doing during the war? Did you have a job? A family?

A: Nein, no family. My mother died in 1936 of tuberculosis.

When everybody but the Jews was starving. She had no medicine while they pranced about in fur.

Q: And your father?

A: [*shrugs*] I never knew him. He died in the first war.

Q: You had no family of your own? No husband, no—

A: Nein. Ja, there was a man. We were to be engaged. But he was in the *Wehrmacht* and he died in Russia. On the Volga.

Q: So you were alone during the war.

A: Ja, ja, I had to fend completely for myself. To stand on my own two feet during this time, it was very difficult.

Q: What did you do? What kind of work?

A: I was a switchboard operator.

Q: And this paid well enough for you to get along?

A: Nein. Nein. I had barely enough to survive. And with the rations— *Ach,* it was so bad. The things I had to do to get by.

Q: What sort of things?

A: Nothing. Nothing. Just…to get by. That is all.

Q: How did you get by, exactly?

A: I— What do you think? Waited in lines with everybody else. Sometimes stole. When there is nothing to put in the stomach…

Q: It must have made you desperate.

A: Ja, ja, desperate, that is right, now you understand me. What I did I had to do.

Q: Which was?

A: I have already told you. Nothing. But. Some others. Some other people…

Q: What other people?

A: They were terrible times.

Q: Desperate.

A: Ja, desperate. And this one woman I knew…

Q: She was your friend?

A: Nein, nein. Not a friend. An acquaintance. Somebody I knew from work. Not very well. Sometimes we shared a little lunch. Not very often. You understand?

Q: Yes. What was her name?

A: I do not remember. I do not remember.

Q: That's fine, Frau Kluge. But you were telling me…She also was desperate?

A: Ja. And she, so she had to do something…

Q: What was it? What did she do?

A: She…This woman, she did not mean to do anything bad. But she was desperate, as you have said, *nicht?* And so hungry while the Jews, they still had the money. And she, this woman, she thought, what would be the harm in it, you understand? She knew there still were some of them around. Hiding. Like they hid their money. She—

Q: Forgive me for interrupting, Frau Kluge, but where was this? Where the Jews were hiding?

A: All over. The city was riddled with them. And this woman, she knew of some in the building next to hers. In the cellar. So she—

Q: This was in Munich?

A: Ja. Very near to where I lived. On the, the outer ring, the—

Q: The suburbs?

A: Ja, that is correct, the suburbs. On the outer ring there were still some hiding. So she, the woman, she went to them.

Q: To the Jews?

A: Ja, ja, to the Jews. I was just— You know, *she,* she said to me, Petra, I know where some are. In this cellar. Under a staircase, in a room for holding potatoes, and they once owned a store, a very big shoe store, many of them around Munich so they must still have money and also there was a reward—

Q: A reward for turning in the Jews?

A: Ja, ja, that is right, to the Gestapo. A big cash reward. So this desperate woman, she went into that basement and she said to them, Jews, I do not want to turn you in. I have nothing against Jews. So you will give me the same amount of money as the reward, and I will say nothing.

Q: And they gave her the money?

A: Ja. They had diamonds. Small ones. Not very good quality. It was a little disappointing. But some rings. Also earrings. Sewed into the linings of their coats.

Q: So she took their diamonds.

A: Ja, natürlich. She was desperate.

Q: I see. And she didn't turn them in?

A: Nein. She did not turn those Jews in. She said to me, Petra, you see, now I have a little something, at least enough to eat. Now I can provide for myself. She had no family, nobody to look after her—

Q: So she took their diamonds and she didn't turn them in.

A: Ja. Nein. Not right away.

Q: Not right away.

A: That is correct. Not immediately. But you know, money goes only so far, and soon, soon they had nothing left to give her, at least that is what they said, although of course there probably was more. So she had to turn them in.

Q: For the reward.

A: Ja, that is right. She went to the Gestapo and she got that reward. And do you know what he said?

Q: Who?

A: The Gestapo man. A little fat man with no hair on his head— This is what she told me.

Q: Right. So what did he say?

A: He said, Fräulein whatever-her-name-was, I do not remember, Fräulein, he said, you have done a very good thing. For your country. For your *Führer* and *Vaterland.* I am very happy to give you this money. And if you know of more Jews, I will be happy to reward you again in this way. If you bring them to my attention.

Q: And— Did she?

A: Did she what?

Q: Did she know of more Jews?

A: Well, *ja,* they were everywhere. All over, as I have said.

Hiding in the woodwork. Like lice. Like, what do you call it, termites.

Q: Did she turn them in too?

A: I— I— *Ach,* well. Who knows. I did not want to know about such things. As I have said, they did not concern me, *nicht?* And I did not know her, you remember. I did not know her very well at all.

Q: But what do you think? Do you think she turned in other Jews?

A: I do not— Well, *ja. Ja.* I did. I mean, what I mean to say is, I think she did. *Ja.*

Q: For the money.

A: Ja, that is correct. She, she might have felt sorry for them. A little. But she had to do it anyway.

Q: I see.

A: She was desperate.

Q: Yes, so you said…Frau Kluge, how do you feel now about what she did?

A: Me? Why should I feel anything? I feel nothing. I did nothing to be ashamed of!

Q: But I said…Excuse me. Let me ask again: How do you think *she* feels?

A: [*shrugs*] How should I know? She probably is dead.

Q: But if she were alive and you could ask her, what do you think she would say? Do you think she would feel guilty?

A: Nein. Nein. Not guilty. Why should she feel guilty? Why should she have had to starve while those Jews still had money? She had to get by.

Q: Yes, but—

A: She had nobody. Nobody to look after her. Nobody to take care of her. They had each other. They had the money. While she was a woman alone. To be a woman on her own is a terrible thing.

Q: Yes, but—

A: You should know this. You know what I mean.

Q: Well, I do to some degree, but—

A: And in those times. Such terrible times. You cannot imagine. You know nothing of what it is like to be cold. To be hungry. To be sick with hunger. You do not understand that.

Q: That's true, but—

A: Und so. Das ist alles. That is all I have to say.

Q: One more thing, Frau Kluge, with your permission... You've told me what you think your, um, acquaintance, might have felt. But do you, you personally, ever feel bad about what happened to those Jews?

A: I? I did not even know them. I knew no Jews. And I do not feel bad about doing only what I had to do either. Because a woman alone has to watch out for herself in this world.

20

As soon as Frau Kluge's interview is done, Trudy and Thomas flee her apartment as quickly as the dismantling of Thomas's equipment will allow. In fact they are so fast about it that Trudy fears, watching Thomas coil cables and fold tripods with a speed almost comical, that Frau Kluge will notice their haste and take offense. Not that Trudy is particularly concerned about Frau Kluge's feelings, but if the woman senses what they think of her, she might be insulted enough to demand that her testimony not be used. Yet Trudy shouldn't have worried, for Frau Kluge seems to wish them out of her apartment as much as they want to go. When they leave, the woman is still sitting in her chair, watching a game show on a small black-and-white TV and indifferent to their departure.

Trudy stays near the truck while Thomas loads the contents of his cart into it, ostensibly keeping a lookout for muggers but really rehearsing apologies to him about what they have just heard. When he is done, however, and they are standing face-to-face on the curb, all Trudy can say is: Wow.

Yes, says Thomas. Wow.

They stand awkwardly in the cold, chuffing vaporous breath like racehorses, Trudy prodding with one foot at a dirty chunk of ice. While they have been engaged with Frau Kluge, the world has turned from day to night—something that always startles Trudy no matter how she tries to prepare for it. She squints at Thomas, trying to gauge his expression in the sickly orange flicker of the streetlights, but he is gazing over her head toward Frau Kluge's apartment. His jowly face is stern, remote.

I'm sorry, Thomas, Trudy says. That was rough.

That's all right, he says. It was about what I expected.

Trudy frowns down at her boots. But we're not all like that, she wants to tell him. Really we're not. There are some good Germans. Instead, she gives the ice a good kick, sending it skittering across the street.

I could use a stiff drink right about now, she says.

Thomas laughs. Me too.

Trudy looks hopefully up at him. Do you want to go get one? I know this place not far from here, in Dinkytown, that has great margaritas—

I would, says Thomas, but I already have plans. Sorry.

Oh. Okay. Maybe next time.

Sure, he says. Next time.

Trudy tarries a minute longer, wanting to say something to confirm that there will *be* a next time, that Thomas will give her another chance, that lets him know she truly is sorry. But she can't think of how to phrase it, so finally she just flutters a hand in the air near his elbow, half rescinded touch, half wave.

Thanks again, she says. I'll talk to you soon.

Bye, says Thomas.

Trudy sits in her car while her engine warms up and watches Thomas climb into his truck and speed off. He honks as he turns the corner—shave-and-a-haircut, two-bits. Maybe he actually does have somewhere else to be. On the other hand, maybe he just wants to get away from Trudy and her German Project as fast as possible. Trudy doesn't blame him. She sighs and shifts into gear.

She really does want a drink, not so much for the alcohol as to wash the bad taste of her sycophancy to Frau Kluge out of her mouth, to return to the world of normal things. She is not ready to go home to a solitary brandy—she craves company— yet she is not about to go to a bar by herself to seek it. There is little in the world more pathetic, Trudy believes, than a middle-aged woman sitting alone on a bar stool. She runs over her list of possible drinking companions: there is Ruth, but this being her short day at the university, she is probably home preparing dinner with her husband. There are a couple of colleagues Trudy could call, but they are more acquaintances than friends, and casual conversation with them—invariably consisting of campus gossip—seems both irrelevant at the moment and too much work. And aside from this, there is...Trudy gnaws her lip and makes a decision on impulse. Perhaps it is because her pre-interview sparring with Frau Kluge has made Trudy think of him for the first time in a while; whatever the cause, she will pay her ex-husband Roger a little visit.

She gets off 394 at Fifth Street, where Roger's restaurant, Le P'tit Lapin, is still located despite the girders of the highway, a dream in some city councilman's head when Roger and Trudy first bought the place, that now eclipse it in permanent darkness. Trudy smiles a little as she parks and picks her way over the ice to the door. Given the restaurant's success, Roger could certainly afford to move it to a more upscale neighborhood, but it is typical of him that he has not. Such an act would smack of pretension, which Roger claims to despise above all else. He has always thumbed his nose at trend; whereas the city's newer establishments boast imported light sconces and marble-painted walls reminiscent of Italian villas, Le P'tit is as plain as ever. It is a tiny place, seating only forty at its fullest capacity, with sooty tricolored awnings flapping over the windows. Inside, the brick walls are whitewashed, the lights bright so as to be able to see the food. A Vivaldi string quartet plays quietly from somewhere overhead; when Roger is feeling wild and crazy, he will slip an Edith Piaf CD into the sound system, but normally the music is as muted as the decor. Nothing that will distract from *la cuisine*.

The dining room is empty at this hour, although in the kitchen, Trudy knows, the line and *sous* chefs will be sweating and swearing in an ill-tempered frenzy of dinner preparation. She finds a spindly server wedging napkins into wineglasses and asks the boy to let Roger know she is here. Then she waits by the hostess stand, looking around a bit sadly. Imagine, a whole decade of her adult life spent in this place as Roger's helpmeet! Trudy can almost see a translucent version of her younger self, hair parted in the middle and tied back with a hank of yarn, moving among the tables to set tealights on them. These have been replaced, she notices now, by fat tapers sparkling with embedded glitter. Tinsel twines about their bases. A Christmas tree bedecked with gingham bows presides in the window. Trudy is startled by this display of seasonal kitsch, which—certainly not Roger's idea—must be the doing of Roger's current wife, Kimberly. Who at the moment is clacking quickly toward Trudy from the swinging doors to the kitchen.

Well, hi there, calls Kimberly. What a surprise!

I hope you don't mind my dropping in like this—

Don't be *silly*. Not at *all*.

Kimberly leans in to bestow air kisses on either side of Trudy's face. She is a well-coiffed blond in her midthirties, her porcelain complexion and china-blue eyes so making her resemble a doll that Trudy fancies she can hear the click of lids when Kimberly blinks. She does so now, rapidly: *click click click*. But it is a mistake to underestimate the brain beneath that fashionably tousled hair; it is, Trudy knows from the post-divorce division of property, as relentless and practical as an adding machine.

Roger's in the wine cellar, Kimberly says. Some mix-up with the Merlot delivery...But you know how *that* goes.

She winks, twinkling.

So I thought I'd keep you company until he comes up. Can I offer you a drink?

Please, says Trudy.

The pair cross the hall to the bar, a dark-paneled little room whose draperies exhale the breath of decades' worth of cigars. Trudy settles onto a stool and watches in the leaded mirror while the younger woman sets out glasses. If not for the twenty-year gap in age, Trudy and Kimberly might be mistaken for sisters.

Red or white? Kimberly asks. Oh, silly me, did you want something stronger? A vodka tonic, or a Scotch—

Red's great, thanks, Trudy says.

She samples the Bordeaux Kimberly pours for her. Chateau Souverain, an excellent vineyard, a vintage year. Unlike most restaurateurs, Roger has not hired a sommelier, preferring to select his wines himself. His taste has not slipped.

Kimberly fills Trudy's glass to within a half inch of the brim and prepares her own drink, a Perrier with lime. She glances at the mirror and scrapes the lacquered nails of thumb and forefinger over the corners of her mouth to remove any crumbs of dried lipstick collected there. Then she comes around the bar to perch on the stool nearest Trudy.

So, she says, crossing her legs to exhibit a thoroughbred's thighs encased in glittery hose. How *are* you?

Trudy nods, glancing at the haunches while taking a long swallow of her wine. Maybe it wasn't such a bright idea to come here.

I'm fine, she says. Busy as always. You know.

Oh, I sure do. This time of year, it's *crazy,* isn't it?

Kimberly sighs deeply and pulls at the wisps of her bangs. I could just yank it all *out,* she says, laughing. You know, Trudy, I was just thinking about you the other day.

You were?

I sure was. Thinking how I envy you. You single gals have *all* the fun. No family to cook for—Roger's *whole* family coming for Christmas, even that ancient aunt, can you believe it? And no grouchy old bear of a husband to put up with...So *tell* me, since I have to live through you. Any new men in your life?

Not really, Trudy says.

Kimberly pouts and leans closer, providing Trudy with a view of the admirable and freckled cleavage nestled in the salmon satin of her blouse.

Oh, now, she says. It's not *nice* to keep all the good stuff to yourself. There must be *somebody*.

She smiles expectantly at Trudy, who gulps her wine.

Well..., she says, thinking of Thomas.

I *knew* it! You couldn't fool me for a *second* with that poker face. I could tell by just looking at you!

Kimberly gives Trudy's arm a playful just-between-us-girls tap. So who is he, she says.

Oh, it's nothing serious, says Trudy. We just met, really.

There you go again, not playing fair. Come on, *tell* me. Tell me all *about* him.

Well—

Trudy is saved by Roger choosing this moment to make his entrance. She gives him a huge smile. She hasn't been so happy to see him since their wedding day.

Whoopsie! Kimberly says brightly and zips the air near her lips.

Roger strides to Trudy and kisses her on both cheeks, the rasp of his mustache raising its usual prickle on the nape of her neck.

I should have known I'd find you two ladies in the bar, he says.

Kimberly vacates her stool and Roger slides onto it.

I'll have a glass of whatever she's having, hon, he says to his wife. Thanks.

Then he turns back to Trudy and slaps his knees.

So! he says. This is an unexpected pleasure. How long has it been?

I don't know, says Trudy. Too long?

I think we saw her about eight months ago, hon, says Kimberly from behind the bar. Remember, when we ran into each other at Lunds?

Oh, that's right...Well, that's still too long. Roger smiles at Trudy. You look great, though.

So do you, Trudy tells him, although this is something of a lie. Like his restaurant, Roger is both as familiar to Trudy as her own skin and subtly, disconcertingly changed. He is still a big fellow—the female servers, their ranks once including Kimberly, ever prone to remarking this, to squeezing his biceps and cooing over Roger's resemblance to the Brawny paper towel man—but now his center of gravity has shifted from his chest to the spare tire around his waist. His face, in the past a healthy pink leading Trudy to tease him that he looked as though he were made of marzipan, is now the red that signifies high blood pressure. And there is more than the suggestion of a double chin.

I see business is good, Trudy can't help saying.

Roger gives her a look and sips his wine.

Can't complain, thanks, he replies, and swabs his mustache on the sleeve of his chef's whites. So! How's the teaching? How, as they say, are kids these days?

Apathetic as tree sloths, says Trudy. But one can always hope that something one says is penetrating the ether.

Oh, I'm sure it is...And what else is going on? Any ventures outside the academic realm?

Not really, says Trudy. I am doing a research project that's of personal interest, but I got funding through the university, so I guess you'd consider that academic.

Well, that depends. What's it about?

Trudy takes a larger gulp of Bordeaux than intended and spills some of it. She licks the side of her hand.

Germans, she says. I'm interviewing Germans of my mother's generation. To see how they're dealing with what they did during the war.

Really, says Roger.

Yes, well, it's still very much in the beginning stages. I just came from my first interview, in fact. And it was...difficult. But I thought it would be interesting—I mean, necessary—to hear about the war from live sources. There's not much documentation of the German reaction, especially straight from the horse as it were, and it'll be invaluable to the study of this time period to add—

Well, here's where I leave you two, Kimberly interrupts. Trudy, *super* to see you again. Give me a call and we'll do lunch, okay? So we can talk about— *you* know. What we were talking about before *this* big lug came in.

She drops a kiss on Roger's hair, sends Trudy a final wink, and leaves.

Trudy glances at the antique railway clock over the bar.

I should probably let you go too, she says.

No, that's all right, replies Roger. I still have a few minutes, assuming there're no brush fires in the kitchen...So. Difficult, you said. In what way?

What?

Your interview.

Trudy raises her eyebrows at Roger. Is he just being polite? But he appears genuinely interested, so she gets up, goes behind the bar, refreshes her wine at Roger's go-ahead nod, and returns to her stool, where she recounts Frau Kluge's interview for him in detail.

And that's it, Trudy says when she has finished, with a flourish that sends a tongue of Bordeaux leaping onto the floor. Interview *ein. Kaputt.*

She sets her glass carefully on its napkin. She is getting a little drunk.

So she never admitted she was the one turning in the Jews, Roger says.

Not outright.

And you didn't confront her with it.

Well, no. But. It was obvious she was talking about herself.

Yes, of course, says Roger. Mmmmm. Interesting.

He props an elbow on the bar and tugs his mustache, examining Trudy with the heavy-lidded, deceptively sleepy gaze that she knows masks his keenest curiosity.

What, Trudy says.

Nothing. It's nothing.

What *it's nothing*. It's not nothing. Not when you're giving me the Look. What is it?

I really don't want to get into this, Trudy.

Into what? Come on, Roger. Out with it.

It's just still amazing to me, that's all.

What is?

The lengths you'll go to to avoid therapy.

What? says Trudy. What are you talking about?

Roger gazes at the ceiling as if beseeching the skies above for patience.

It is beyond me, he says, why you would waste all this time and energy on this project of yours when you could just get counseling to deal with your issues in a normal way and move on.

I am doing, says Trudy, biting off each word, empirical research.

For whom? Tell me honestly. For the academic realm? Or for yourself?

What difference does that make, Trudy snaps.

A smile spreads Roger's mustache, and Trudy bristles. She knows exactly what he is thinking of: their single session of marriage counseling, after which Trudy had a fit of hysterical giggles in the car over the therapist's earnest, sweating attempts to foster rapport—*Now, Roger, hold Trudy's hands, that's right, and look deep into her soul and tell her exactly how you feel about her*—and bulging froglike eyes. She refused to go back.

Counseling is not the answer to everything, Roger, she says now. Just because you and Kimberly go to, to encounter groups and retreats and sweat lodges to, to discover your inner animal spirit guides or God knows what—

Roger's smile curls further.

Oh, Trudy, he says.

Don't you take that pitying tone with me.

I don't pity you, says Roger gently. I'm trying to help you. Don't you see, Trudy? It's all about your mother. I still don't know what your particular beef with her is, but any Psych 101 student could tell you the underlying pathology: you're just like her.

Trudy is so enraged that she can't speak. She sputters incoherently for a minute, then finally manages to come out with, Oh yeah?

Absolutely.

Trudy slides off her stool. Well, that's exactly what I'd expect from Psych 101, she says.

She reaches for her wine to polish it off in a show of bravado, but her hand is shaking so hard that she has to put the glass down. She decides not to give Roger the satisfaction of watching her try to button her coat.

Besides, she says, snatching her purse from the floor, what would you know about it? You've hardly even met my mother.

Of course not, says Roger smoothly. You wouldn't let me. But from the rare occasions I did meet her, I'd say the similarity is obvious. More than obvious. Striking.

Is that so.

Yes, it's so.

Well, it is not. I am not remotely like my mother.

Now there's an interesting Freudian slip, says Roger. She *is* remote. And so are you. You always have been. Remote. Formal. Cold. Compulsive about cleaning. All those good German traits. You know.

I do not know, says Trudy, storming toward the door to the street. I do not know anything of the kind. All I know is that you're still a pompous ass. You haven't changed a bit.

Nor have you, says Roger, following her. Sadly.

He opens the door for her with a sardonic little bow, denying Trudy the chance to slam it in his face.

Always a pleasure, he says.

Go to hell.

Trudy brushes past him and stalks down the sidewalk, cursing the ice for making her watch her step and foiling her grand exit.

And Roger ruins it further, for as Trudy reaches her car she hears him call, And hey, Trudy, about your German Project? I don't know why you're even bothering. Of course all those old Krauts are Nazis! What else did you expect?

21

BY THE TIME TRUDY GETS HOME, IT IS FULL DARK AND snowing a little—a few flurries spinning uncertainly in the motion-sensitive light over her garage—and the large round thermometer affixed to the neighbors' deck shows the temperature to be fifteen below zero. But Trudy doesn't notice the cold. She steams up her walk with her coat still unbuttoned, and as she shakes out her keys to unlock the door she tells the indifferent yard all the things she should have said to Roger back at Le P'tit.

Just like my mother, she mutters. Typically German. Krauts! What would *he* know about it? Big ox. Stupid Scandinavian. Big— dumb— woodenheaded— Viking!

She flings the door open and steps inside, pulling off her gloves, finger by finger, with small angry yanks.

No wonder I never remarried! she says.

Then she hits the light switch and stands looking around her kitchen, as she always does when returning home, to ensure that everything is in place. And it is. The room is exactly as Trudy left it—no surprise, since she is the last person, the only person, to have been here. The floor boasts the snail trails of a recent waxing. The counters gleam. The teakettle—which Trudy scours with a steel wool pad every Sunday—is so shiny that she can see her face in it, elongated and miniature, from across the room. Normally this would please Trudy, to find her home and the things in it in such perfect order.

So nice and clean.

So *nett und sauber.*

Trudy frowns and folds her arms. Knocks the heel of her boot on the linoleum a couple of times.

Then, deliberately, she tosses her keys onto the counter instead of hanging them on the hook by the door.

She wriggles out of her coat and slings it on a chair. Her gloves follow, one landing on the table, the other on the floor. Stepping daintily over it, Trudy crosses to the stove, where she puts water on to boil. While she waits, she leans against the refrigerator, eyeing the muddy tracks her boots have left on the tiles, and when the kettle sings, she makes herself a messy cup of tea, flinging the used bag toward the sink without looking to see where it lands, carefully ignoring the sugar granules she scatters. She leaves the spoon on the stove top and the sugar jar next to it with its lid off, for the mice—were there any—to plunder.

She steps back, surveying the room over the rim of her mug.

There, she says.

Then she retreats to her study with her tea before she can give in and tidy everything up. From down the hall the disorder tugs at Trudy, the coat and gloves and canister and muddy floor reproaching her: *But what have we done to deserve this?* Trudy shuts her study door and turns to her stereo.

A Brahms symphony thunders forth when she presses the PLAY button. Grimacing, Trudy sets her mug on the desk and crouches to canvass her stack of CDs. Bach, Beethoven, more Brahms, Mahler, Wagner—God in heaven, has she nobody but German composers? Finally Trudy finds an Austrian buried among the rest, and a sprightly Mozart concerto replaces the symphony on the turntable. This accomplished, Trudy walks over to her couch and collapses on it, digging the heels of her hands into her eyes.

What did you expect? It is, perhaps, a fair question Roger has asked. Trudy doesn't know. She feels stupid for having not anticipated what Frau Kluge might say. Naive in her hope—unarticulated even to herself before the interview—that the woman would confirm that not all Germans are as bad as people think; they can't all be Nazis at heart, can they? It is as though Trudy has reached under a rock and touched something covered with slime. And now she too is coated with it, always has been; it can't be washed off; it comes from somewhere within.

Trudy tells herself not to be so childish. She lies back and gazes blearily through the semidark to the window and the house beyond. All along its gutters colored lights are strung, or rather tubing in which tiny bulbs light up in frenetic sequence and at insane speed, like running ants, before stopping to blink and blink in agitated rhythm. Trudy wishes she could lie to her neighbors, tell them that she is epileptic and their decorations are causing seizures and have to be taken down. Why must people make such a hoopla of Christmas? It is a wretched holiday, really, one that Trudy has always spent at the farmhouse, sitting straight an as exclamation point in her black clothes while Anna serves more goose and stuffing than the two women could ever hope to eat. And this year Trudy's Christmas will consist of a visit to the New Heidelburg Good Samaritan Center, where she will spoon up Jello cubes in the face of her mother's eternal silence.

Trudy closes her eyes. Maybe she should abandon her Project altogether. Why invite additional punishment when she already has Anna to deal with? Perhaps it is best not to stir up this particular nest of snakes. To leave well enough alone.

The past is dead. The past is dead, and better it remain so.

The lights pulse in frenzied patterns on Trudy's lids. She slings an arm across her face. The concerto comes to an end, and in its absence the house is so quiet that Trudy can hear a clock ticking in another room, reminiscent of the water dripping in Frau Kluge's sink.

After a time Trudy gets up, takes her mug from the desk, and returns wearily to the kitchen. She pours the cold tea down the drain. Washes the cup and spoon and sets them in the dish rack. Throws out the teabag and screws the lid tight on the sugar canister and puts it in the cupboard. Sponges the stove and countertops. Hangs her keys and coat and tucks the gloves in the pockets.

When everything is in place, Trudy turns off the lights and climbs the stairs to her bedroom, where she removes her boots and curls on her side, wedging her clasped hands between her thighs. Her last conscious thought, conjured by the pale parallelogram on the far wall, is that she has forgotten to draw the curtains. But at least the neighbors' crazed lights can't be seen from here.

Trudy drifts into an uneasy sleep. And dreams.

SHE IS IN HER LIVING ROOM, CROSS-LEGGED ON THE FLOOR, wrapping Christmas presents. This is a peculiar and pointless endeavor, for aside from Ruth and Anna, Trudy has nobody to bestow gifts upon. Yet she is surrounded by children's toys: a hobbyhorse, a waist-high nutcracker, an army of tin soldiers; there is an endless amount, and if Trudy does not wrap them they will multiply further and take over her house. She sips from a snifter of schnapps and reaches for the next item, a rifle so realistic in appearance that Trudy is surprised it doesn't leave oil on her hands.

She is struggling to disentangle a piece of tape that has stuck her thumb and forefinger together when she sits upright, suddenly alert. Something is wrong. Her Brahms, the Second Concerto, sounds scratchy, as though emanating from a record turntable instead of her CD player. In the corner is a Christmas tree draped with tinsel and garish bulbs from the forties. And beneath Trudy is not a careworn Oriental rug but her mother's deep-pile carpet. Trudy sinks back on her heels and shakes her head over her stupidity: she is not in Minneapolis at all. She is in the farmhouse. But...if Jack is dead and Anna is at the Good Samaritan Center, who is in the kitchen? For Trudy hears somebody walking about in there, and the creak of the refrigerator door as it opens.

Brushing snippets of paper and curling ribbon from her knees, Trudy walks into the kitchen to investigate. And there, his back to her, she finds Santa Claus. He is hunched in front of the old Frigidaire, digging through its contents and tossing those he doesn't like to the floor, wolfing down those he does with such gusto that his shoulders shake.

Trudy is indignant.

You aren't supposed to be here, she says. Santa is supposed to come only at night, when people are sleeping, don't you remember?

Santa turns. He is drinking milk straight from the bottle, a habit both Trudy and Anna deplore as unhygienic. His red sleeve, trimmed with jolly fur, blocks his face from view, but Trudy sees his Adam's apple working beneath it.

When he has drained the milk, he throws the bottle across the room in the direction of the sink. It misses and shatters on Anna's linoleum, spraying glass and droplets.

You get out, Trudy tells him, her voice shaking. Get out of my mother's house.

Santa laughs heartily.

My dear child, he says, your mother won't mind. Why, she's the one who invited me.

Then, to the forlorn horns of the concerto's second movement, Santa begins an incongruous burlesque. He slowly undoes the buttons of his jacket, and it pops open to reveal not the pillow or cotton stuffing one might expect, but food: a netted ham, a tin of sardines, several loaves of black bread. He sets these one by one with great ceremony on Anna's Formica table. Then he unbuckles his belt and starts to unzip his trousers.

Stop that, Trudy cries.

But Santa ignores her. Humming the Brahms, which now plays at the wrong speed so that the strings drone and shriek, he pushes down his trousers and kicks them free of his feet. He has to do an awkward little dance to do this, since he hasn't removed his shining black boots, but Trudy soon understands why: beneath the Santa suit, he is wearing the gray uniform of the *Schutzstaffeln,* the SS.

He swings a chair out from the table and sits, his face hidden now by the brim of his peaked cap. The light splinters off the double-eagle insignia.

He pats his knee.

Come, sit down, he says, and tell me: Have you been a good girl this year?

No, says Trudy. No, no, no —

He cocks his head. Yes? he says, as if he hasn't heard her. Good. Then I will show you a little something.

He rises from the chair and starts to undo the buttons of these trousers as well.

Stop it, Trudy shouts. I don't want to see!

He parts the cloth and holds it open, standing at attention. He wears nothing underneath, and his stomach and pubic hair are smeared with dark blood.

You see, I am not Santa, he says. I am Saint Nikolaus, and I come whenever I please.

Anna and the *Obersturmführer*,
Weimar, 1942

22

HE COMES FOR ANNA ON THE DAY OF MATHILDE'S DEATH, in the late afternoon, wasting no time. This is always a quiet hour in the bakery, but now it seems abnormally so, as if the citizens of Weimar have sensed the danger and stayed home with their doors locked and blackout curtains drawn. It is so still, in fact, that Anna fancies she can hear the small noises of her eyes rolling in their wet beds as she looks this way and that, at the door and away. Her every instinct screams to grab Trudie from the pile of sacking at her feet and run. But surely the child will howl if so roughly awakened, and beyond the dooryard, of course, there is nowhere to go.

So Anna forces herself to the door, on which somebody is again pounding so violently that the bell above it jingles. After she undoes the bolt, she retreats behind the counter, gripping her elbows in her hands in an attempt to hide their shaking. Maybe they will assume she is simply cold, a logical mistake. She has not stoked the ovens since the morning, and even within the meter-thick bakery walls her breath is visible.

But when the officer enters, Anna's trembling stops. The shock of recognition renders her too terrified to move: he is the one she glimpsed in the quarry with Hinkelmann and Blank during her first delivery of bread, the pale-eyed officer whom she initially mistook to be blind. His decorations indeed proclaim him to be an *Obersturmführer* rather than a *Hauptsturmführer* or *Sturmbannführer;* thanks to Gerhard's attempted matchmaking, Anna is able to make such distinctions. Oddly, this *Obersturmführer* seems to be alone. At least, Anna hears no commotion outside, no desultory talk or laughter from where his brethren would be lounging against a car, waiting, perhaps smoking.

The *Obersturmführer* crosses the room. He is an enormous man, projecting an air of complete solidity except for a weakness of the jaw; his face disintegrates into his neck. He moves with the same purpose Anna recalls witnessing at the quarry, but his gait is odd, almost mincing. Anna will later discover that this is because his feet are disproportionately small for his body, barely bigger than hers, sometimes causing him to trip over his own toes.

He plants his gloved hands on the counter and leans forward.

Do you always lock the door in the afternoon, Fräulein? he asks. Hardly an astute business practice.

Then he grins as if he were any man flirting with a pretty girl, teasing her into giving him a free sweet from the display case. The expression transforms his face into one nearly handsome, the upward movement of his cheek muscles lifting the flesh from his doughy jawline. There is something wrong about it, however, that Anna can't put a finger on.

She attempts a return smile. I was just about to close up, she says; I'm afraid we've sold out of nearly everything. This time of day, you know. But—

I haven't come for bread, the *Obersturmführer* says.

Oh, of course! Forgive me. For a special customer such as yourself, I'm sure I can find something more appealing. There's a *Linzertorte* in the back, and some poppy-seed cake, very fresh.

The *Obersturmführer* examines Anna for a moment. At this

close range, his eyes are like those of a sled dog, the pinprick pupils set in an absence of color ringed with black. Anna feels them on her flushed cheeks like small cold weights.

Your business partner, Frau Staudt—

Anna twists her hands in her apron. My boss, you mean? she babbles. She's not here, she's delivering the afternoon orders—

The *Obersturmführer* makes an impatient noise and strides behind the counter, passing close enough to Anna that she can smell the wind in the folds of his greatcoat, cold air, promising more snow. He glances into the kitchen.

She's been executed, he says.

Executed! Anna gasps.

She has been rehearsing this moment for hours, knowing how important it is to appear shocked, and now that it has arrived she finds she hardly has to pretend. She braces herself against the display case, her breath materializing in white gusts. She is nearly panting.

That can't be true, Herr *Obersturmführer*; begging your pardon, but you must have made a mistake!

The *Obersturmführer*'s gaze alights on Trudie, still sleeping in her pile of makeshift blankets. He bends for a closer look, bracing his hands on his knees.

A pretty girl, he says. Yours?

Please, Herr *Obersturmführer*, Frau Staudt is a good woman, absolutely loyal; I haven't heard her say or do the slightest thing against the *Partei* since I've been working here! Why on earth should she have been executed?

Why don't you tell me? the *Obersturmführer* says absently.

Tell you—? I'm sorry, I don't understand.

He removes his gloves and places a finger on Trudie's cheek. The toddler stirs.

How old is the child? he asks. One, one and a half?

One and four months, Anna whispers.

The *Obersturmführer* nods. Then he stands and beams at Anna, who realizes why his grin seems ersatz: he waits a beat too long before delivering it, like a bad actor reminded to perform by a director's hissed cue from backstage.

Now then, says the *Obersturmführer,* slapping his hands together as if about to tackle a difficult task. Let's not waste any more time, shall we? Why don't you tell me how long this has been going on?

What? says Anna. I don't know what you mean.

The *Obersturmführer* makes a moue of exaggerated surprise. You don't? he asks. Really?

The tendons in Anna's neck creak as she tries to shake her head.

You don't know, Fräulein, that your boss was feeding the prisoners in our correctional facility, leaving bread for politicals, a-socials, murderers?

No, I didn't know—

I suppose your ignorance also extends to the weapons we found in the bakery truck, beneath the bread.

Weapons? Of all the— Where would Frau Staudt get weapons?

Why, I haven't the slightest idea, the *Obersturmführer* says, taking a step toward Anna. But you do, don't you, Fräulein? Just as you helped load them into the truck yourself; just as you worked all night, every night, to make that extra bread. Come now, don't look at me that way. Don't insult my intelligence by pretending you didn't know where it was going.

I knew it was going to the camp, but Frau Staudt told me it was for you, for the officers. She acted so proud, saying it was such an honor to supply you—

Anna starts to cry. She lied to me! she says, weeping.

The *Obersturmführer* watches her.

Enough, he says.

Anna continues to sob. She took advantage of me. She thought I was an idiot! she wails, spraying spittle.

The *Obersturmführer* stalks to Anna and grabs her by the chin, forcing her to look up at him as though she were a naughty child.

Then his thumb is in her mouth, callused and tasting of cigarettes. Anna gags, her eyes tearing afresh. When he withdraws it,
she tries to see his face, to gauge his intentions. The *Obersturmführer* is breathing hard through his nose. He clamps his hands to
Anna's cheeks, kneading the skin, rolling his tongue in her mouth.

Anna struggles free. Please, she says.

The *Obersturmführer* raises an eyebrow.

I don't want to wake the child, Anna whispers.

Nor does she want to take him to her bed in the cellar, where
Mathilde has hidden so many enemies of the Reich, so Anna begins walking toward the staircase. She is thinking of all the rewards she has reaped from being a pretty girl, things she has
come to accept as a matter of course: compliments, catcalls, men
turning to watch her on the streets, smiling, offering her seats on
trams, setting aside the best produce for her at market, imminent
marriage proposals, flowers. She would trade every last one of
them if only this *Obersturmführer* would now follow her up the
stairs. Anna acts with a primitive cunning she didn't know she
possessed, an innate knowledge of an ancient system of barter;
she wordlessly urges the *Obersturmführer* onward as she mounts
the first step, the second, her breath trembling in her lungs.

Her prayer is granted. Mathilde's old bed is not meant for
such punishment: the mattress spills them toward the middle,
and the frame cracks beneath their combined weight. The *Obersturmführer* doesn't bother to remove his clothes; he merely
shrugs off his greatcoat and yanks open the buttons of his
trousers. He grunts and heaves on top of her, and Anna tries to
stifle her own noises by biting the inside of her cheek. Max too
was often rough, taking her by surprise and sometimes using his
teeth, but he was at least quick. Nothing has schooled Anna for
this burning, this prolonged internal abrasion. She concentrates
on widening her eyes at the ceiling, knowing that if she permits
herself to blink, the tears welling in them will spill over.

When the *Obersturmführer* is finally done, he says, You like to
watch.

Pardon? Anna whispers.

You kept your eyes open. I like that.

The *Obersturmführer* sits on the side of the bed for a minute, staring at the floor, a man making a weighty decision. Then he sighs and says, I will come once a week to inventory the bread. I will come myself; I won't send anybody else. Do you understand?

Anna bows her head over her woolen stockings, which she rolls slowly up her legs.

Yes, she says. I understand.

23

THE *OBERSTURMFÜHRER* PROVES TO BE A MAN OF HIS WORD, a punctual man. He comes every Thursday evening, after the bakery is closed, often bearing some trinket: a bar of Belgian chocolate, a scarf, a tube of lipstick too bright for Anna. She stows these in a drawer of Mathilde's bureau after he leaves. But the gifts for Trudie she uses, the blue blanket of softest lamb's wool with sateen border, the warm red dress, the only spots of color in the bakery.

They have developed a routine. The *Obersturmführer* makes a cursory inventory of the bakery's output, which is now picked up by a noncom on Friday mornings; he prowls about the kitchen while Anna gives Trudie the fresh milk he brings. She suspects that it is laced with a mild opiate to make the child sleep, but at least it is real, fatty and nourishing, not like the powdered stuff Anna must use now in her patrons' bread. When Trudie's eyelids begin to flutter, Anna leads her to her bed in the cellar. Then she and the *Obersturmführer* proceed upstairs. The heaviness of the silence is like being underwater.

Beneath him on Mathilde's bed, lying completely still so as not to give offense, Anna makes a game of envisioning the lives she might have had if not for the war. She is in the sunny back garden of a house on the Rhine, the child squatting to watch a glittering line of ants in the dirt while Anna hangs laundry, the sheets snapping and fresh in the wind. Or: Curtains ripple at the window of a breakfast room, city traffic purrs on the street below; her husband stuffs an extra roll in his pocket and kisses Anna before rushing out the door. Perhaps these are her real lives, after all. The gray walls of the bakery, the cracks Anna traces in the ceiling beyond the *Obersturmführer*'s shoulders: perhaps she is really asleep in a warm safe bed somewhere, twitching through the details of this recurring nightmare, this grinding existence that has become such a bad joke that she sometimes thinks she will laugh until she rips out her throat with her nails.

Often, afterward, the *Obersturmführer* talks. He is irritated by his small, stuffy office, by the amount of paperwork he must cope with, by the pressure of forcing constant production from the munitions factory and the quarry. He is frustrated by the fact that, living at the camp, it's impossible for one to ever feel quite clean. It's not that I have direct contact with them, you understand, he explains, but the constant mud, and the Jews just have this dirty air about them; I swear it impregnates one's clothes, one's skin. Anna knows about the latter. The *Obersturmführer*'s sweat emanates an odor much like woodsmoke except fattier, richer, as if he eats nothing but bacon; a smell that, despite herself, makes her stomach growl.

But he rarely seems to expect a response, so when he first asks her a direct question, Anna is startled. It is a muggy August evening, the air tired and stale; Mathilde's bedroom is musty with the *Obersturmführer*'s exertions and dust from the rugs. It smells like an attic unopened for years, and perhaps because of this Anna has been thinking not of her whitewashed breakfast room nor the sun of a summer garden but something cooler: strolling down a broad avenue lined with rows of linden trees, her toes hot and pinched in her shoes, strands of her damp hair clinging to the nape of her neck; spying a café, she sits in the shade at a wrought-iron table, eases her feet from her pumps and orders an icy drink, something with a slice of lemon in it. She sips it while gazing at the passersby, her mind blank.

The *Obersturmführer* repeats his question, not without a note of impatience.

Pardon? says Anna.

He sighs in exasperation and runs a thumb over the stretch marks on Anna's soft belly.

I said, how did you come to be in this position? You've no husband; you don't wear a ring.

The war, Anna says. There wasn't time.

The *Obersturmführer* nods. But you're from a good family; that's obvious from your breeding. They didn't take you in?

My father didn't think much of the match, Anna tells him. He drove me from the house. Frau Staudt gave me room and board in exchange for labor.

Ach, fathers, the *Obersturmführer* says. He crosses his arms behind his head and smiles at the ceiling, which is lost in the darkening room. I know about fathers. Did I ever tell you about mine?

It is as if they are real lovers, sharing pillow talk. Next he will offer her a cigarette. For a vertiginous moment, Anna thinks she might laugh.

The *Obersturmführer* digs in his ear and absently examines his finger. A stupid little man, he says, a nothing really, a weak-spined dilettante who never did a day's honest work in his life, but always throwing his weight around as if he were God. Horst, bring me the newspaper! Horst, where are my cigars? He used to beat my brother and me with a belt if we didn't move fast enough to suit him.

Horst? Anna moves her lips, silently tasting the *Obersturmführer*'s Christian name. It has a dark feel in the mouth, a little thorny. Then she realizes he is waiting for her to say something. She makes a noise in her throat.

One day I took the belt from him, the *Obersturmführer* continues. I must have been fifteen, sixteen—he didn't realize until then how big I'd become. I threw it across the room and said, Let's go, then, let's fight. But I promise you only one of us will get up, and it won't be you. He never touched me after that.

Anna glances sideways at him.

He still had egg in his mustache from breakfast, the *Obersturmführer* says reflectively.

Then he pushes her legs apart again.

Maybe we shouldn't, Anna ventures. My— monthly flow is beginning.

And this is true: she feels the cramps, her womb a big dumb fist clenching and easing in slow waves, ignorant as to what goes on outside.

The *Obersturmführer* pauses for a second before flashing Anna his ersatz grin.

Then I'll remove my clothes, he says.

Without the chafe of worsted trousers against Anna's thighs, without the *Obersturmführer*'s shirt buttons branding her face, the ordeal isn't as painful as it usually is. The slippery sensation of skin on skin, the unexpected breezes, shock Anna. She blinks in an effort to summon the café of her daydream, the leaves on the linden trees turning up their silvery undersides, but the *Obersturmführer,* watching her, thrusts a hand between her legs. He works diligently at a kernel of sensitive flesh, and Anna's interior muscles clutch in spasms. She can't prevent herself from letting out a yelp. This is not supposed to happen, this has never happened to her before.

From the doorway, there is an answering cry: Mama?

Still pinioned, Anna rolls her head to the right and sees Trudie standing there, arms and braids akimbo. In Anna's impatience to get this over with, she has been careless in ensuring that the child finish her milk. She should have known Trudie would disobey and climb the steps.

Go downstairs! Anna tries to call.

But before she can draw the necessary breath, the *Ober-sturmführer* says, Shit! Without withdrawing, he leans halfway off the bed and grabs one of his boots from the floor. He hurls it at Trudie; it thuds against the wall near the door, leaving a black mark. Anna hears the child's wooden soles clopping quickly, unevenly, down the risers. The *Obersturmführer* continues his business. When he levers himself up and out of Anna, she sees her blood clotted in his pubic hair, smeared on his stomach.

In ominous silence, the *Obersturmführer* cleans himself with a handkerchief and then offers it to Anna. She shakes her head. He departs quickly, slamming the door, leaving Anna to collect his boots before she too descends to the bakery.

She looks for her daughter in the kitchen while fetching the brush and boot polish the *Obersturmführer* has brought her, but Trudie isn't in any of her usual hiding places. Anna finds her instead in the storefront, wedged behind the display case. The *Obersturmführer* stands in front of the child, fists on hips; when he bends over her, she shrinks farther into her corner, staring.

Why are you hiding back there? he asks. Don't you want to see what I've got for you?

Anna, buffing the boots, watches Trudie shake her head.

From his briefcase, the *Obersturmführer* produces a pair of red child's shoes, actual leather. He sighs.

What a shame, he says. I suppose I'll have to find another little girl to give these to.

The child says nothing, but she extends a hand toward the shoes. Then she draws it back as if they might burn her.

I wonder if these would fit you, the *Obersturmführer* says, dangling the shoes by the straps at Trudie's eye level. What do you think?

The child nods. The *Obersturmführer* sets the shoes on the floor and ruffles Trudie's hair. Then he turns to Anna, beckoning with two fingers. She hands his boots over in silence. They are three sizes too big for him, Anna knows. His masculine vanity won't permit public display of his childlike feet.

Next week, he says, standing.

After Anna unlocks the door and latches it behind him, she draws the curtain aside to watch him go. She can barely make him out, a dark shape in the dark. Whenever he leaves, the night seems blacker than it is, a solid thing pressing against the windows.

She lets the curtain fall.

You must never come upstairs when the man is here, do you understand? she says to Trudie.

But Mama—

Never! Because...Anna gropes at sudden inspiration. He's Saint Nikolaus; do you remember what I told you about Saint Nikolaus? He doesn't like to be seen.

Trudie frowns.

But it's not Christmas, she says.

That doesn't matter. Saint Nikolaus has magical powers; he can do whatever he wants. He travels the world year-round, looking for good little girls. And if you're a bad girl and try to see him, do you know what will happen?

No more red shoes? Trudie whispers, gazing at them.

A rotten taste thickens Anna's saliva to the consistency of aspic. This has always happened to her, periodically and for no apparent reason. No amount of throat-clearing can get rid of it; if she waits, it will usually disappear on its own. Yet now this feeling isn't just in her mouth. Tainted gray jelly clings to her like a membrane. It is beneath her skin, inside and out, invisible and foul.

That's right, she says to her daughter. She scrubs her arms with both hands, shivering, although there isn't a hint of a breeze. No more milk. No more red shoes.

24

ANNA LEARNS A GREAT DEAL FROM THE *OBERSTURM-führer,* the first thing being that, postcoitus, he talks talks talks talks talks, a broken faucet from which words pour instead of water. From this, she conjectures that either superior rank precludes private conversation or that the *Obersturmführer*'s peers do not like him well enough to listen.

She learns the difference between Hinkelmann and Blank, although she will never truly be able to separate them: in her mind, they remain a single murderous demigod, vaudevillian and double-faced, blithely dispensing death. In actuality, however, Hinkelmann is the taller fellow, while Blank is the squat bureaucrat, and the former has been considered so effective at his job that he has been awarded promotional transfer to a camp called Mauthausen, where there is a bigger stone quarry.

She learns that the quarry is considered the worst work detail, and that for this reason, to avoid mutinous dissatisfaction, the guards are rotated fortnightly. The prisoners refer to one of the current crop as Gretel because of his feminine prettiness, while another is known as Lard Ass, for equally obvious reasons;

it is said that they have a particular friendship, though nothing of the sort can be proven. In any case, the *Obersturmführer* adds, one never takes such rumors seriously, as they are either fairy tales or downright malicious. He turns a deaf ear to the prisoners' nicknaming the guards, though in other camps their doing so might be considered treason. It is good for them to feel that they have some modicum of power, he explains; this allows them to blow off steam and keeps them from perpetuating other, more serious mischief.

Anna further learns that the *Obersturmführer* was, before the war, a telegram delivery boy and then a police officer. That during the war, he served first at the front, during which he earned decorations for bravery and the craterlike wound in his right shoulder, and secondly in the *Einsatzgruppen,* the SS mobile death units in Poland. From his description of these glorious but trying days, she learns that the Jews there went meekly to their liquidation. How, the *Obersturmführer* asks rhetorically, can one respect a race such as that? We Germans, he says, we place a high premium on obedience, of course, but not at the expense of bravery.

She learns that the *Obersturmführer*'s mother, unable to stomach his father's tyranny or perhaps simply faithless, ran off with a traveling salesman of wigs; that the *Obersturmführer* reported his father, his childhood nemesis, to the Gestapo as having had repeated sexual congress with a Jewish woman, which, although untrue, earned the man a prolonged stay in KZ Dachau. That the *Kommandant* of KZ Buchenwald, Koch, *does* have a Jewish mistress, but nobody dares say a word, of course. That the *Obersturmführer* sometimes suffers wretchedly from insomnia brought on by the stresses and contradictions of his work, and at these times, nothing but hot milk with pepper in it will soothe him.

Much of this information Anna discards, for it is useless stuff. The prisoners will not benefit from it, and as for herself, whom would she tell, and to what purpose? However, she does remember the SS designation for the crime she and Mathilde have committed: *füttern den Feind,* feeding the enemy, punishable, as has been made all too obvious, by death. Anna thinks of the phrase every time she delivers bread to the quarry, which she does every Wednesday evening. It is madness, of course, given her liaison with the *Obersturmführer.* Why, then, Anna asks herself, as she stuffs rolls into the trunk of the tree, does she continue to do it? Unlike Mathilde, it can't be a subliminal urge toward suicide. If it were just her, Anna, the option might seem appealing, but there is Trudie to consider; everything Anna does, including yielding to the *Obersturmführer*'s demands, is for Trudie. Except for these Special Deliveries: they are less for the prisoners than a way for Anna to convince herself that she is more than a whore, a whim, a plaything; they forge a link with the recent past, during which, though it was unpleasant in many respects, she at least felt human.

So, on Wednesdays, Anna gives Trudie some of the *Obersturmführer*'s narcotic milk, which she has been careful to store in the icebox from the week before, and she makes the Special Delivery to the quarry and hurries back to the bakery to cook the drowsy child's dinner. Thus far, everything has gone like clockwork, but on this particular Wednesday, Anna is late. She has lingered overlong at the quarry, hypnotized into stupid reverie by the sight of the prisoners, hoping against hope to find Max among them. Her flight back through the woods thus takes place in the dark, and as Anna runs, the phrase plays over and over in her mind: *füttern den Feind, füttern den Feind,* like the opening bars of a catchy waltz, *The Blue Danube* perhaps. Clumsy in her haste, she snags a foot on a root, wrenches her right ankle, and falls headlong into the dirt.

And when she finally limps through the back door of the bakery, calling reassurance to her daughter, Anna sees to her horror that the *Obersturmführer* is there. He stands with his arms crossed in the center of the kitchen, a monolith, while Trudie sits red-faced and crying in the corner. Anna hobbles to the child and lifts her. My God, is it Thursday already? How could she have made such a fatal mistake? It can't be; Frau Buchholtz came for her weekly bread this morning, as she does on Wednesdays, always on Wednesdays, or has she altered her schedule? Or has the *Obersturmführer* acted on uncharacteristic impulse and changed his instead? If it is indeed Wednesday, what is he doing here?

Not that this matters: he *is* here, impassively watching the maternal scene.

Where were you? he asks, when Trudie's squalling has trailed off into snuffles and hitches.

I? says Anna idiotically. I was— Well, the child is sick, you see, with stomach pains, she's been complaining of them all week, so I— I ran to the doctor for medicine.

The *Obersturmführer* eyes her from head to toe, his scrutiny doing a much more eloquent job of indicating Anna's torn dress, her scratched and dirt-stained hands, than if he had pointed at or touched them.

Flushing, Anna turns away to help Trudie climb onto her chair.

I tripped and fell, she says; I was in such a hurry that I caught my heel in a grate, and I—

Because her back is to him, Anna doesn't know the *Obersturmführer* has crossed the room until she feels his gloved hand on her neck. His kidskin fingers dig into the soft troughs behind her ears, making Anna's arms instantly numb. She gasps.

I won't stand being lied to, the *Obersturmführer* says, shaking Anna by the nape as though she were a puppy. Her teeth clack painfully together. I won't tolerate falsehoods, Anna, do you hear?

I—wasn't—lying— Anna stutters between shakes. She pulls at his hands, but his grip is like a manacle. I went—to the doctor— I swear!

In her peripheral vision, Anna sees Trudie watching quietly from the table, which upsets her more than if the child had been screaming.

The *Obersturmführer* releases Anna and she stumbles, the wounded ankle sending up a flare of pain.

Get upstairs, he says.

Please — can I at least give her the medicine — some milk —

Now.

The *Obersturmführer* seizes Anna by the arm and half propels, half drags her toward the staircase.

It's all right, little rabbit, she calls gaily to Trudie over her shoulder. You stay here. I'll be down soon —

In Mathilde's bedroom, Anna backs to the window. Despite the time of year, the weather is still deceptively hot; the curtains hang limp as bandaging, and Anna wishes like a child that she could hide behind them. The *Obersturmführer* closes the door quietly, with finality.

Get undressed, he says.

Please, Herr *Obersturmführer,* the child truly is sick, you heard her crying when you came in, she —

I don't have time for this, the *Obersturmführer* says. Your clothes.

He flicks a finger and sits on the bed, watching as Anna obeys. Inept with fear, she has trouble undoing her garters. When she dares glance up, the *Obersturmführer* is leaning forward, the familiar greedy look in his ghostly eyes.

He gazes at the red indentations the garters have left on her thighs. He likes these.

I'm a busy man, he says petulantly. It's hard enough for me to take time from my schedule to come here. If you should require something in the future, you ask me first, understand? I expect you to be here at all times, whenever I need you.

Anna nods.

The *Obersturmführer* gives her a grin: all is forgiven, for now. He draws her to him; he cups her breasts and lets them fall, cups them and lets them fall.

Lovely, he says, such delicious bouncy breasts, the very ideal of breasts.

He pinches a nipple, then rubs his fingertips together, blinking at them.

What's this? he says.

Anna flushes. Downstairs, Trudie is crying. Although the child has been weaned for months, Anna's body still responds to her pleas for food.

It's milk, she mumbles.

What?

Milk! snaps Anna, humiliated past caring whether his tone is one of surprise or disgust. Perhaps, if it is the latter, he will take himself away.

The *Obersturmführer* laughs.

Really? he says. And the girl nearly two. Well, Anna, you've just made my evening easier: I can have my dinner here. Kill two birds with one stone, as they say.

He takes her nipple into his mouth, drawing milk through the aureole in thin threads. Anna closes her eyes, pretending that it is the child, only the child, but the sensation is wrong, he uses his tongue rather than his lips, and his stubble prickles against her skin. Her hands, rising in instinctive quest to his dark head, encounter coarse, close-cropped hair; she knots them together behind her back, swaying for balance on her painful ankle, staring at the wall. She has learned another lesson from the *Obersturmführer* this evening: she will no longer make deliveries to the quarry. It is too dangerous to even contemplate. She has other mouths to feed.

25

COME HERE, ANNA, THE *OBERSTURMFÜHRER* SAYS.

Anna complies. She stands before him, as usual, as he sits on the side of Mathilde's bed. This is how the game always begins. What Anna can never guess at are the middles or the endings. He will bring a phonograph player from the camp, place a forbidden jazz record on its turntable, and order her to strip to it. *Ach,* never mind, he will say, laughing at her artless burlesque. Or he will command her to stand on a chair, naked and blindfolded, while he circles her, touching her here and there with teeth or tongue or baton. He has poured bourbon onto her shirtwaist and suckled her through the whiskey-soaked cloth. Yes, the *Obersturmführer* is endlessly inventive in this wearisome schoolboy fashion. Has he gleaned these scenarios from the forbidden books in his father's bedside drawer? Anna pictures the *Obersturmführer* as an adolescent, hunched over such a manual in the WC, the door barred, his shorts around his ankles, eyes bulging, and she feels the same cold revulsion as she would for worms writhing on the sidewalk after a rain. She waits now for some indication as to what he has devised this time.

Tonight he wants her passive, to remain still so he can mold her in his hands like bread. His breathing thickens as he undoes Anna's blouse, unbuttons her skirt, rolls the silk stockings he has brought her down her legs. Anna moves only to kick them free of her ankles. Perhaps he will bind her with them, as he once did, then removing a straight razor from his pocket and shaving her all over: legs, arms, armpits, pubic bone. The hair grew back rough, in sharp bristles that reminded Anna of those on a pig's hide. It itched for days.

Raise your arms above your head, the *Obersturmführer* commands. Then turn around. Like a ballerina. As a girl, did you want to be a ballerina? Of course you did; all little girls do. Yes, like that. So I can see you.

The *Obersturmführer's* voice, while engaged in such play, drops to a deeper register; normally crisp, his consonants soften like chocolate melted in the pan. The tone makes Anna think of rich, dark cake, a too-sweet dessert that she would cram into her mouth, helpless to stop, until she vomited it up.

He pulls her to him by the hips, positioning her between his knees. Anna can't contain a gasp: his hands are, as always, cold. He lightly bites the flesh above her bellybutton, shaking his head like a dog. Anna feels him grin against her stomach. But when he slides a finger into her, clinically, like a doctor, and pushes her away a few inches so he can watch her face, his expression is grave.

You are the most willing woman I've ever known, he says. It's as though you have some eternal wellspring inside you— here.

He crooks the finger. Anna strains not to react with a sound, a blink, an arch of the back, a moan. She stiffens her spine against her head's instinctive loll.

But the *Obersturmführer* knows. Yes, here, he says, this one spot, rough as a cat's tongue. You like that, don't you?

He wiggles his finger, as though beckoning to an adjutant, a prisoner, to her: *Come.*

How very strange to be a woman, he muses, springing himself free of his regulation briefs and pulling Anna onto the bed; poor women, everything hidden from them, on the inside. You see, he adds as he rolls grinning on top of her, I know you better than you know yourself.

Anna thinks that this is true. And that perhaps it is at these moments that she hates him the most, for robbing her of her own familiar flesh by making it respond in such a way, as though it is no longer hers to command.

Every time he leaves, after Trudie is safely in bed, Anna punishes her traitorous body with lye soap and a pumice stone. She fills the bath with water so hot that her skin, that white sheath with its dark freckles that the *Obersturmführer* finds so appealing, will surely peel off like that of a boiled tomato. Standing nude in the bedroom, she slaps her face, stomach, thighs, but this only reminds her of other activities the *Obersturmführer* enjoys. She digs her nails into her lower lip, drawing blood. She touches herself between the legs and examines her fingertips: dry when she does it.

One night Anna fetches the sewing bag from Mathilde's bureau and sits naked on the toilet, a hand mirror placed between her feet. She licks the thread and slides it through the needle, her eyes already watering as she imagines pressing it against that tenderest of flesh: how sharp it will be, how cold. Despite her rehearsal, the reality is more painful than she imagines; tears spurt, and she drops the needle, hearing it land with a tiny *clink*! on the mirror. She is too cowardly; she can't go through with it. Instead, she contents herself by picturing the *Obersturmführer*'s reaction to finding her sewn shut, the stitches black and clumsy against the dark pink folds.

But he steals even this poor comfort from her through a story he tells her one December evening, after returning from a trip that has prevented him from visiting the bakery for two weeks. Anna doesn't know where he has been, but he is particularly insatiable, having been deprived of his pleasures for so long.

Dispensing with the scarves and razors, the whiskey and the gimmicks, he takes her three times, always from behind. Anna wonders, as she braces her palms against the wall to keep her head from being bashed into it, whether this predilection is peculiar to the *Obersturmführer* or if all men have a secret fondness for this position, the woman anonymous, merely a back and jiggling buttocks and a hank of hair, the man pumping like a dog.

When he has finished with her physically, the *Obersturmführer* again begins speaking, as though resuming a conversation. Anna has become accustomed to this; she should even welcome it, as nothing more is required of her than that she nestle against him with her head pillowed on his chest. But dear God, he is so boring! Complaints about the starchy food; the trivia of his domestic routine — particularly laundry, the *Obersturmführer* has a fetish about the whiteness of his shirts; indignant analysis of whether his adjutant's smile is insolent; on and on. When Anna envisions hell, she suspects it will look just like this: a gray box of a room in which she is trapped with this man while he talks and talks and talks for all eternity.

Sometimes, if the *Obersturmführer* appears sufficiently caught up in what he is saying, Anna dozes. At other times, such as now, she mentally lists the maternal chores that have yet to be fulfilled: Trudie must be fed, bathed, tucked in, and lied to. Every night the child poses the same question, making a sort of game out of it. Where is Tante Mathilde? she asks, and Anna patiently repeats a version of the same story she has told the bakery's patrons: Mathilde has been placed by the Work Bureau in an officers' dining hall in Hamburg. Some men needed her to come and make bread for them by the sea, Anna explains to Trudie, and each time the child gazes at the ceiling, says Oh, rubs her blanket against her cheek, and falls asleep. Just like that.

But this evening, Anna's list of tasks is interrupted by a word the *Obersturmführer* utters an inch from her ear. *Auschwitz*. So he has been in Poland, then. The *Obersturmführer* has mentioned

Auschwitz before, since he has been arranging transports of
Jewish prisoners from Buchenwald to this bigger camp. (The
time this takes, which could be spent on other, more worthy dis-
ciplinary causes! The hours of maintaining the camp records!)
Anna also knows about Auschwitz from the rumors contained
in the prisoners' condoms. And rumors they must be, of course;
it is beyond belief, what the prisoners say. Marching the Jews
straight from the trains to gas chambers, the crematoria? Even
the SS wouldn't be so insane as to squander such a massive labor
force in the middle of a war, particularly given the invasion of
Mother Russia. No, this must be the invention of a mind deranged from overwork and starvation. Such tales grow from
such conditions, even as mushrooms will sprout from a pile of
dung.

Nonetheless, the repetition of the word makes Anna pay attention, for once, to the *Obersturmführer*'s monologue.

I'm sorry, I didn't catch what you just said, she murmurs.

The *Obersturmführer* blinks at her as if one of the pillows has
spoken; then, looking pleased, he rotates his damaged shoulder
beneath Anna's head, joggling her a bit closer. The smell of him,
meat and smoke and his *Kölnischwasser, 4711*, drifts from beneath
his arm.

I was just remarking what a help it will be to us in our own
experiments, he repeats, the chance to watch Mengele at work.
Of course, our chaps mostly prevent outbreaks, preserve the
healthy, instead of making great scientific strides. We don't have
the equipment for it, for one thing. But we do the best we can;
we do our part with what limited resources we have.

And what is it you do? Anna asks.

Oh, the usual. We're trying to develop an inoculation against
typhus, for instance—though that hasn't been quite successful
yet, as most of the specimens die. But we have made some
progress in curing the homosexual disease—you know what
this is? You do? You are a constant surprise to me, Anna! Well,

as I said, the advances are very small but perhaps significant in the long run, involving castration, that kind of thing. Which is why, as I was saying, it was so instructive to observe Mengele, since on the day we were allowed into his laboratory, he was performing surgery on the reproductive organs.

On a homosexual? Anna whispers.

The *Obersturmführer* laughs. No, that's nothing to Mengele; that's for pikers like us. He was working on a Jewess, a former prostitute. He was sewing up her—

The *Obersturmführer* glances sideways at Anna and clears his throat.

—her feminine opening. What happens when she is not permitted her monthly flow? Do the internal organs wither, stop functioning? Fascinating prospect. Impractical for use on the general population, but scientifically...

Anna feels her stomach muscles convulsing. Cold sweat breaks out beneath her arms, on her neck. She puts a hand to her mouth as if stifling a belch.

Excuse me, she says.

Certainly. In any case, that's what Mengele is, first and foremost, a scientist, perhaps the Reich's most valuable. Though what a surgeon he must have been as a civilian! We stood in the balcony with a hundred others, mirrors placed all about the table so we could see. He must have been under enormous pressure. And the Jewess kept moving. But did Mengele's hands falter? Not once! Golden hands, as swift as hummingbirds.

Anna knows she is going to be sick. She sits up, breathing shallowly and staring into the hallway; she focuses on the lamplight, lying in a skewed rectangle on the floor. Then a shadow moves, eclipsing it.

Trudie? she calls. Go downstairs.

The shadow doesn't move.

Anna squints at it. Behind her, the *Obersturmführer* has fallen silent, a bad sign. Anna sinks back onto his damaged shoulder, as he has not yet signaled that he wishes her to do otherwise.

She is coming apart, imagining things, seeing shadows that aren't there.

Even the way Anna sleeps now is unfamiliar to her: each morning she wakes with a stiff neck, unable to turn her head more than a few degrees to either side. She has slept on her back, her arms flung above her head, in a position of abject surrender.

Trudy, January 1997

26

SLEEP DEPRIVATION, TRUDY HAS COME TO REALIZE, IS A form of torture. The Nazis knew this, of course: one of the Gestapo's favored interrogation methods, quieter and less messy than the extraction of fingernails or breaking bones, was to isolate subjects in a room where the lights were never extinguished, shocking them with a low dosage of electricity whenever they started to doze off. Trudy thinks she can now understand, to some degree, why people were so forthcoming with information after only a few days of this treatment. Since the continuation of her Project she sleeps little, and when she does her dreams are frequent and bad. She is lost in a forest, diminished to child-size, the hoary trunks of trees towering on all sides: calling out and searching for something she is doomed never to find. Or she is a Berlin *hausfrau,* wandering from room to room in an endless, unheated flat, rubbing her arms and stooping to peer through windows for something dreadful that never comes. Trudy is ever hungry and always cold; she thrashes awake to find she has kicked the covers onto the floor. And although he hasn't made another appearance per se, Trudy senses that she has also dreamed of Saint Nikolaus; he is somewhere nearby, the officer, engineering bureaucratic destruction at his desk or eating a leg of chicken, wiping on the sleeve of his tunic a mouth glistening with grease.

Actively afraid of the dreams, Trudy takes to swallowing sleeping pills to ward them off. But the drugs don't work; they keep her perversely alert, sweating and twitchy, staring owl-eyed at the ceiling until, just before dawn, she succumbs to a soupy doze from which she jerks violently awake with the sensation of falling. As Trudy slumps sour-stomached over the kitchen table with her first coffee of the day, watching the sky turn from black to gray to white, she debates over and over the wisdom of proceeding with this Project. She vows each time that this afternoon's interview will be her last. Then she gets up and goes into her study, where she listens to a recording of Thomas Mann reading *Lotte in Weimar* in German while she memorizes the day's questions. She can't give it up now. Whether because of word-of-mouth—Frau Kluge spreading the news of Trudy's sympathetic ear and access to the university's checkbook—or because they have seen her advertisements, Trudy has more subjects than she can handle.

At first deciding to continue her interviews simply to overcome her fear of doing so, Trudy has discovered her anxiety unfounded: none of them has been as shocking as Frau Kluge's. The women profess relative ignorance of the Nazi regime and regret over its consequences; they speak of bombs, of hunger, of husbands killed or returning terribly changed, disfigured or missing limbs or wraithlike and prone to strange tempers. Of cold and illness and privation. The garden-variety grim tales. So Trudy, far from having her confidence further eroded, feels it growing with each interview. She has a talent, it seems, for interrogation. And although Trudy despises her trust-invoking methods—widening her blue eyes, touching her blond hair, wearing her high black boots, her *Stiefel*—she also takes acerbic satisfaction from their success. There is more than that, too: sometimes, when lying awake and waiting with dread for sleep to overtake her, Trudy has to admit to a certain comfort, the relief of accepting her genetic predisposition—to her odd sense, in those neat houses, of coming home. Sitting in tidy kitchens much like hers, Trudy rediscovers things she didn't know she had lost: the tang of *Teewurst* on the tongue, the delicious sibilance of a forgotten German word. And as much as she hates herself for it, Trudy finds she is hungry for her subjects' praise, for their delighted clapping over her fluency, for their compliments on her appearance and their treating her—though they are sometimes not much older than she—like one of their own *Kinder,* their children.

Mrs. Rose-Grete Fischer, Trudy's seventh subject, is a case in point. She welcomes Trudy and Thomas—who has mercifully agreed to film more interviews, even sounding a bit startled at Trudy's assumption that he wouldn't—into her bungalow with a flutter of hands. While Thomas sets up his equipment in the living room, mumbling happily to himself about the open space and comfortable armchairs, Trudy sits with Rose-Grete in the kitchen, nibbling a slice of *Kaffeekuchen.* This, too, Trudy has come to expect; most of her subjects have proven more hospitable than Frau Kluge, and although in her current state Trudy doesn't dare eat much for fear of nodding off under Thomas's hot lights, she always takes a little something so as not to offend her hosts.

Rose-Grete watches Trudy appreciatively from the corner of her eye.

You are a good girl, she says, to take the time to visit an old lady. To be interested in what she has to say.

Trudy smiles at her, a trifle uncomfortably. Rose-Grete is a tiny woman, all delicate bones poking at skin the texture of an old peach, and at sixty-eight is still lovely but for the eye patch she wears, which lends her something of a piratical air. Trudy longs to know why she wears it, but as Rose-Grete hasn't brought the subject up, Trudy is determined to act as if she hasn't noticed it either. It is difficult not to stare at the black triangle of cloth, though, and when Trudy concentrates on Rose-Grete's remaining eye, she feels as though her gaze is unnaturally and insultingly forced.

She takes a bite of cake and evades Rose-Grete's lopsided appraisal by looking around the woman's kitchen. It is small but cheerful, the walls yellow, the table cluttered with the detritus of widowhood: a wicker basket containing fruit and prescription bottles, a magnifying glass, a litter of Social Security check stubs on the sunflowered oilcloth. The heat from the radiator beneath the window creates a shimmering distortion through which Trudy sees birds hopping around a backyard feeder.

She glances at the refrigerator, anticipating the ubiquitous family photographs, but there is only a stainless steel sheet with a few dents in the center.

Do you have children? Trudy asks—one of the best questions, she has discovered, for fostering rapport.

But Rose-Grete has turned her head so as to be able to see the yard.

You like my little friends? she says. Look there, that cardinal, the big fat fellow. He is my favorite. He is greedy to a fault, pushing aside the others to get the seed. But every morning he visits, without fail. Often he comes to the windowsill and sits there, like so. I sometimes think he knows what I am thinking.

She leans over and taps the pane. The birds scatter, with a flurry of wings, into the air.

Oop-la! says Rose-Grete, laughing. Then she turns to Trudy.

You must think me foolish, she says. But they are good company, my little friends, if fickle. It is not easy to grow old alone.

She draws a napkin toward her and smoothes it with the flat of her palm. Trudy waits.

I do have children, Rose-Grete says to the napkin. Two sons. But they live far away, and they cannot be bothered to come and see their old mother anymore.

That's a shame, says Trudy, thinking guiltily of Anna, whom she has not visited since the Christmas ordeal at the Good Samaritan Center two weeks ago.

Yes, it is, isn't it?...Rose-Grete sighs and begins folding the napkin into squares. My firstborn son telephones every so often:

Mother, how are you feeling? Have you been to the doctor? What does the doctor say? But I know he does this only out of duty. And the other, Friedrich—Freddy—lives now in England, and I do not hear much from him at all.

I'm sorry.

Rose-Grete looks shyly at Trudy and smiles.

I always wished I had a girl, she says softly. It is different with mothers and daughters, yes? There is a closeness that is not possible with sons. You and your mother, you are close, I am sure.

Trudy busies herself with the remains of her cake, using the tines of her fork to push the crumbs into a pile.

Um, she says.

She can feel Rose-Grete's eye fixed upon her. After a moment the older woman touches Trudy's hand. It is like being brushed with a small bundle of sticks.

I have embarrassed you, Rose-Grete says. But there is no need to answer. I can tell you are a good daughter. You will take more cake?

Trudy shakes her head.

I couldn't eat another thing, she says—truthfully, as her throat is suddenly tight.

Rose-Grete nudges the pan of *Kaffeekuchen* toward Trudy.

Please, she says. It will only go to waste otherwise.

Please, she repeats.

Trudy obediently cuts a second slice of cake.

THE GERMAN PROJECT
Interview 7

SUBJECT: Mrs. Rose-Grete Fischer (*née* Rosalinde Margarethe Guertner)

DATE/LOCATION: January 11, 1997; Edina, MN

Q: Rose-Grete, I'm going to start by asking you a few simple questions, all right?

A: Yes, fine.

Q: Where and when were you born?

A: I was born in 1928, in a town called Lübben. Although to call it a town is to give it high praise, since really it was a village, a tiny speck of a place near the Polish border. Located in the Spreewald, with perhaps only five hundred population, very poor. Farmers and lumbermen mostly, though my parents owned a small shop, what Americans would call a general store... You have said your own father was a farmer?

Q: Yes, that's right... Rose-Grete, were you and your family living in Lübben when the war began?

A: Yes, we were there for the duration. I stayed in Lübben until I came to this country.

Q: Can you tell me what you remember about the start of the war?

A: Well, it was not for us how it was for the rest of Europe. Or at least in the big cities. For us there was no immediate — how do you say it, impact? It trickled through to us in bits and pieces. Some of the young men were called up to serve, of course. And the Jews of the village... But most of what was happening, because we were such a small place, we found out from newspapers brought in from other towns, sometimes a week or two old. And rumors.

Q: Rose-Grete, you mentioned the Jews of your village. What happened to them?

A: In the beginning — Well, I was only eleven when the war began, you know; I didn't understand much of anything. Most of what I know was learned from listening at doors.

Q: Do you remember anything you heard, specifically?

A: Only that my parents were always fighting during this time. Quietly, and when they thought we children were asleep, but still we knew what they were quarreling about. They had heard the rumors too, about the Nazis and especially the *Einsatzgruppen,* the special units whose job it was to come and take away all the Jews. Nobody knew what would happen to them after, and nobody asked questions. Everyone was scared, you see. But we knew it could not be anything good. So some of the people in the town hid the Jews or helped them escape to the forest, where there were Partisan bands.

My father wanted to help in this fashion. He was a religious man and he thought it was a sin, what the Nazis were doing. But my mother begged him not to get involved. No, Peder, please, the children, you must think of them — that is what I remember her saying.

Q: So he didn't hide any Jews or help them escape.

A: If he could have seen what would happen when the *Einsatzgruppen* came, I am sure he would have — But no. In the end he did not.

Q: When did the *Einsatzgruppen* come to Lübben?

A: In... 1944, I believe. I was sixteen years then, so it must have been 1944.

Q: Can you tell me what you remember about that?

A: I — One moment, please. It is not so easy for me to talk about this.

Q: Take your time. All the time you need.

A: Thank you. You are very kind.

[*long pause*]

A: What I remember first is that many people rejoiced when the *Einsatzgruppen* came. I remember them standing by the main road and cheering and giving the Nazi salute, like so! I think this is because there were plenty of native Poles in Lübben, and the Poles hate Jews as much or more than we Germans did. Not many people know this, but it is true.

In any case, come they did, and a few days later I... Well, my parents sent me on an errand. It was very hot, that I remember; it was then late June, a beautiful summer day. I remember the heat especially well because I had to walk many kilometers to a farm to barter some of our eggs for raspberries. For my mother.

She was pregnant, and craving them, and we did not stock any fruit in our grocery. But we did keep hens, and so I went to trade eggs for the berries and some fresh bread. And I...

On the way back I decided to take a shortcut through the forest. Because it was cooler. I didn't know it was forbidden to be there. I didn't know what they were doing. I wanted only to get out of the sun, the road was so hot and so dusty.

So I was walking through the woods with the berries and the bread for my mother, and all of the sudden I heard *pop-pop-pop-pop-pop,* just like...like firecrackers. But it was not firecrackers, it was gunshots. And I was so young and so stupid, I followed the sound to a clearing, and there I saw them. The Jews and the *Einsatzgruppen.* The Jews had been made to undress and were standing at the edge of a pit. And the *Einsatzgruppen* were shooting them in groups of four or five.

Well, I was absolutely horrified. I remember being more shocked at first that they were naked than that they were being... slaughtered in this way. I had never before seen anyone naked except my mother, and I was...I was just so shocked and so confused. I remember thinking, Why don't they run? Better to be shot in the back while running than waiting for it, and perhaps one or two could get away to the Partisans...And the shame of it, the women and the children naked with the men, I had never seen such a thing. How I wanted to hide my face. But I could not. I stood and watched while they prayed, some of them, and held hands and begged and cried and were shot. The women and babies along with the men. Nobody was spared.

And then I saw a girl I knew. Oh, I didn't know her very well, but when we were little we had played together. Rebecca was her name, and although I had not spoken to her in some time I recognized her by this gesture she had. She had very curly hair, beautiful dark curls, and when she was nervous she would twirl one curl, like so, around her finger. I remembered this from school, how when she was called on and didn't know the answer she would twist her curl around her finger in just this way.

She was standing a little apart from the rest, close to me and very calm, although tears were running down her face and she was twirling her hair. And I remember thinking, oh, you think such stupid things at times like that, thinking something like, I should have played with her more or gotten to know her better and now it's too late, or something like this, I don't know what I was thinking. But then she turned and looked at me, just as if she had heard me, and I was so stupid, I don't know what came over me, but I was thinking, It is so hot, so hot to be standing there like that with no clothes, no hat, nothing, and I held out the basket of berries. As if, I don't know, I could give them to her and they would ease her thirst a bit before— I don't know what I was thinking.

But she started walking toward me, very slowly, so as not to be seen.

But she was seen. One of the *Einsatzgruppen,* this officer, saw her and yelled, Halt! And she did. Just froze there. Everybody did, for this officer called, Halt! again and held up his hand. The rest of them stopped shooting and the officer looked at Rebecca and saw what she was looking at and he came walking toward me. Strolling, really, as if he were on a city street or had all the time in the world.

Well, I would have turned and ran, but I was frozen too. I had no feeling in my legs or the rest of me either. I remember that I dropped the basket and that the bread fell out on the ground and the berries too, and they rolled to a stop next to his feet in front of me, and that his boots were very shiny like mirrors so I could almost see my face in them.

What is your name? he asked.

Well, of course I could not say a word.

What is your name? he asked again.

I looked up at him then. He was very big and tall with eyes like a wolf, and very fine he thought he was too. While the rest of them were in their shirtsleeves, he was wearing his full uniform, even his hat, and it was cocked at a certain angle, like so.

But I could see him sweating, big big drops rolling down the side of his face.

What are you doing here, little girl? he asked me. Don't you know you're not supposed to be here? Or are you on a mission of mercy, a little Jew-loving *Rotkäppchen,* Red Riding Hood bringing food to the Jews?

Some of the other *Einsatzgruppen* laughed then, *ha ha ha ha ha,* like this was the funniest thing they had ever heard. And this didn't please the officer at all. He was not a man who was used to being laughed at, I suppose, even if he invited it. He took his pistol from his belt and yelled, Shut up! and fired it into the air. Some of the women screamed, I remember. But still they did not try to run away.

The officer put his gun under my chin—I still remember how it felt there, how cold it was when everything else was so hot.

What is your name, little Jew-lover? he asked a third time.

And when I still could not answer, he made a disgusted sound and waved over one of his men who was standing near the car. He called something to him that I to this day do not remember, he said it maybe too fast or I was not thinking clearly. But he must have said something like, Bring the medical kit, for that is what the man brought over and the officer took something from it and I couldn't see what it was except that it was shiny, and he did it so quickly I didn't have time to react.

But anyway, what he took from the kit was a pin, and before I could do anything he pushed it into my right eye. Which popped just like a grape, except that unlike a grape it deflated and there was all this liquid running down my face, blood and whatnot. And of course there was pain, the worst pain you can imagine, and I threw my hands over my eye and screamed. And the officer turned to Rebecca and shot her, and some other women too, *bang bang bang bang bang,* except I didn't realize it until a minute later because all I felt was the pain and I couldn't believe this had happened to me — it was so quick — that in one second this strange man had blinded me and destroyed my face.

Ja, I heard him say, there, that will teach you not to be so nosy, my little Jew-lover. Now run along home. And I heard his feet gritting in the dust as he turned and walked back to the car.

So I did. I ran and ran and didn't stop until I got home, where as you can imagine my mother screamed at the sight of me and she and my father cried and sent my younger brother Günter for the doctor...But of course it was too late. There was nothing he could do. And you know, this is strange, but after this day we never referred to what had happened. We were still so scared. Even more than before. Scared of what the Nazis could do, for no rhyme or reason, whenever they wanted.

So now you know what happened to my eye. This is something I have never told anyone...Because I am still so ashamed, you see. I often think it is fitting punishment for all the times I could have helped that girl before that terrible day, or helped others get into the woods, or hidden them in the barn without my parents knowing. But I did not. I turned a blind eye, yes? And as the Bible says...Well, I just think it is appropriate.

27

LATER THAT EVENING TRUDY IS IN THE SHOWER, WITH THE hot water turned up as high as it can go. She scrubs herself all over with a stiff-bristled brush, then stands letting the spray needle her skin. This routine has become her post-interview necessity—this, and the consumption of a large snifter of brandy. Maybe tonight she will permit herself two, Trudy thinks, for Rose-Grete's tale has been an especially grim one. Perhaps the combination of liquor and a pill will finally have the desired effect.

Sleep that knits up the ravell'd sleeve of care, Trudy mumbles as she wrenches the faucets off and climbs from the tub. She wishes it would come and knit her up. She is feeling distinctly unraveled.

She whisks a towel from the rack and begins to briskly rub herself dry. Then she catches sight of movement in her peripheral vision, the pumping of her elbows in the full-length mirror hung on the door. She turns to it; she reaches out and wipes a clear swath in the steam. Then she lets the towel drop.

She has not seen her naked body in its entirety for some time—nor has anybody else, for that matter. She is used to seeing herself in bits and pieces, those demanding the most attention: her face, when she cold-creams it. Her calves, when she bothers to shave. Her hair, which she wears in a short no-nonsense style that requires only a cursory combing before she leaves the house. It's true that Trudy has never had to watch her weight, that people have always told her, *I bet you're one of those who can eat whatever she wants and not gain an ounce.* She has escaped the hammock of soft flesh that wobbles from the undersides of her contemporaries' arms, the fat bulging over their waistbands and the bra straps bisecting their backs. Trudy rarely bothers with a bra at all. But there is a downside to this: she is starting, Trudy thinks, to get the tendony look particular to thin women of a certain age. Stringy. Like an underfed chicken. And Trudy has always thought of herself as a poor, skinny excuse for a woman. Women are meant to be soft. Like Anna. Like Anna in the bath, the gleaming white skin and floating freckled breasts. Anna rolling a stocking up one sturdy thigh. Anna in her slip, the deep generous curves of hip and bosom. Verboten images, gleaned by a younger Trudy from behind various doors, of enduring femininity.

These memories still induce in Trudy, as does her nudity, a distinct shame. For Anna has schooled her—by implication, as she would never speak directly of such things—that nice people are not supposed to loiter about in states of undress. Baths should be taken solely for the sake of cleanliness and washcloths always used, to prevent skin touching skin. Once out of the tub, clothes should be donned as quickly as possible. Lovemaking should occur for procreative purposes only and always in the dark, and one's female functions must be referred to only when necessary, for medical reasons, and then in code: *The Monthly Visitor. The Curse. The Change.* It is a messy, humiliating, secretive business, this being a woman. Slippery creams and sanitary pads, rituals conducted in closets and behind bathroom doors and never, God forbid, mentioned in front of one's husband. Trudy can't imagine Anna ever lingering before a mirror for this length of time. Or letting anyone else see her nude.

The shame of it.

The shame of it, the women and the children naked with the men, I had never seen such a thing.

Trudy looks at herself and tries to imagine her various imperfections exposed in broad daylight, in front of all those others. Those *men*. But of course, Trudy would not have been in this position. She would have been safely home in the village with the rest of the Germans, moving quietly behind shuttered windows and locked doors.

A mottled flush rises on her chest and neck, on skin already pink from vigorous scrubbing.

Her pale flesh. Her father's flesh. Her milk-white, translucent, Aryan skin.

Trudy makes a little noise in her throat.

Then from down the hall the phone shrills, and Trudy starts and grabs her robe. God in heaven, what is she doing, standing around staring at herself? She is even more unraveled than she thought. Trudy pictures Anna's reaction to this foolishness, and then Ruth's, and then her students', and she is still smiling over this last as she runs toward her bedroom, leaving evaporating footprints.

She scoops up the receiver on the fifth ring; it is probably Rose-Grete, whom Trudy has asked to call and check in if the aftermath of her interview proves traumatic.

Hello, says Trudy, shrugging on her bathrobe. Rose-Grete? How are you doing?

But it is not Rose-Grete. It is Ancy Heligson, the manager from the New Heidelburg Good Samaritan Center. She ignores small-town pleasantries and gets straight to the point, speaking with urgency. And to Trudy, cinching her robe tight as if the woman were in the room and could see her, it seems as though what is happening is her fault, as if she has somehow conjured Anna up merely by thinking of her. Or is being punished for having disobeyed Anna's dictates about modesty. For the manager's news is not good. Listening, Trudy leans against the bureau for support. She closes her eyes.

28

AND SO IT IS THAT THE NEXT MORNING, A SUNDAY WHILE most good Minnesotans are in church, Trudy is making another pilgrimage to the New Heidelburg Good Samaritan Center. She arrives at the nursing home in record time and parks beneath the billboard on the far side of its lot. LET US ALL REMEMBER THE AGED, it commands. YES, EVEN *YOU* ARE GET-TING OLD!!! Normally Trudy can't help a wry smile at this; it is as though the staff wants to ensure that visiting a loved one here is as depressing an experience as possible. But at the moment she is in no mood to find anything funny.

Trudy bursts through the sliding doors at a near-run, the tails of her black wool coat belling behind her, and skids across the slick linoleum to the reception desk.

Excuse me, she says to the aide behind it. I'm here to see Mrs. Heligson.

The aide, who is on the phone, shows no sign of interrupting her conversation. Trudy draws herself up to her full height and gives the girl her most imperious look, the one she uses in class to quell obstreperous students. This has little effect. The aide, who is about the same age as Trudy's pupils, with a sweet, puddingy face, flashes her an apologetic smile but keeps on talking.

Trudy leans over the desk and joggles the phone's cutoff button.

Hey! the aide says, her mouth dropping open in protest. Then her nail-bitten hand flies to cover it.

Oh, Mrs. Swenson, I'm sorry, I didn't recognize you—

Get Mrs. Heligson, says Trudy. Right. Now.

The aide jumps up.

Sure. You bet.

She backs toward a door bearing a plaque marked MAN-AGER and bolts inside. Through the thin plywood Trudy hears the aide's high excited voice and Mrs. Heligson's lower, slower responses. Trudy waits, breathing shallowly through her mouth to avoid taking in too much of the Center's smell of Lysol and urine and bland mashed food. The Center's more ambulatory residents are here, slipping sideways on mismatched couches or locked into wheelchairs behind metal trays. Under ordinary cir-cumstances, Anna, more compos mentis than these poor husks, would be among them, picking at her lunch or staring with a faded lack of interest through the picture window at the two-lane road. But she is nowhere to be seen.

Eventually the door to the manager's office flies open and Mrs. Heligson hurries out. The aide, trailing behind her, resumes her position behind the desk and begins dividing pills into Dixie cups with a vindicated, businesslike air. This doesn't fool Trudy for a second. She knows the girl will be straining to catch every last word of this encounter, which will be discussed and analyzed among the nurses with great relish for months to come.

Trudy walks a few feet away into a corridor, leaving the man-ager no choice but to switch direction and follow her. She folds her arms and watches the woman's waddling progress, gimlet-eyed.

Where is my mother? she asks when Mrs. Heligson reaches her.

Now, I know you're angry, Mrs. Swenson, and I don't blame
you. But let's stay calm here. Your mom's in her room, and she's
doing just fine.

Trudy lets out a snort.

I find it hard to believe she's *just fine*. How could you let her
get away like that? What were you people doing, watching talk
shows while my seventy-six-year-old mother was wandering
down the highway in her nightgown?

Mrs. Heligson's mouth compresses into a hot-pink line.

Well, it wasn't just her nightie, she says. She had her coat on
over it...Then, as Trudy boggles at her in astonishment, she
adds hastily, Of *course* we were keeping a close eye on her. We do
our best to monitor all our old folks. But you have to understand
something: Your mom's still got it up here —

Mrs. Heligson taps her temple.

—and whenever she makes up her mind to get out, she gets
out. There's really not much we can —

Wait, says Trudy. Wait just a minute. Am I to understand
from what you've just said that this isn't the first time she's run
away?

Well. Well, no. It's the third. But —

And you didn't see fit to inform me of this?

Trudy is so aghast that she waves her hands about as though
fighting off a swarm of bees. You couldn't have called? Or when
I was here at Christmastime —

Mrs. Heligson holds up a fat palm.

Now just a minute, she says. I *did* call you. I called a bunch of
times.

Trudy is belatedly reminded of the blinking red light on her
answering machine and how she hit Save without listening to the
messages, vowing to return them when she had fewer interviews
and more sleep.

And as for Christmas...Mrs. Heligson shakes her head. We
did try our best to contain her, she says.

Mrs. Heligson, says Trudy, then stops to regain control of

her voice. Mrs. Heligson, are you familiar with the phrase *criminally negligent*?

The manager bridles and crosses her arms beneath her prodigious bosom.

We are not at fault here, she says stiffly, and you won't find a single judge in the country who'll think otherwise. Your mother has been trouble from the start. Not eating, not talking, running away...Well. Like I said on the phone, we just can't be responsible for her anymore. I'm so sorry.

Trudy glares at her. Mrs. Heligson looks anything but sorry. In fact, she appears decidedly smug. There is a subtext here: Trudy knows that Mrs. Heligson knows that Trudy remembers when Mrs. Heligson was still Ancy Fladager, one of nine Fladagers living in a trailer down by Deer Creek—*those no-account Fladagers,* everyone called them; *those shanty Irish.* And Trudy also recalls all too well when Ancy, only a grade ahead of her but a foot taller, pushed Trudy into the dirt on the playground and ripped off her skirt, to see if Trudy really had a swastika birthmark, as rumored; and how, finding none, she spat on Trudy and raced off, yelling, *Stupid Kraut!* Perhaps Anna hasn't really run away at all. Perhaps Ancy Heligson, now the buxom embodiment of New Heidelburg respectability, has contrived a way to finally eject Anna from the town, even as the body will try to rid itself of any foreign object.

I wouldn't let my mother stay here if you paid me, Trudy tells Mrs. Heligson coolly. In fact, I'll be taking her with me right now. Today.

Well, I think that's best.

And before you get too relieved, Mrs. Heligson, let me tell you that I'll be lodging a complaint with the county health board. And the state. The way you run this place is a disgrace. Now, you said my mother is in her room?

Mrs. Heligson manages to nod, her chins quivering with affront.

Thank you.

Trudy turns on her heel and stalks off to the Alzheimer's wing. Anna doesn't have the disease, of course, but this was the only single Trudy could procure for her. It is the caboose of the ward, the very last room, and the only one whose door is bare of Hallmark cards, Bible verses, fuzzy and unflattering Polaroids of its inhabitant. There is just an oaktag name card: MRS. JACK SCHLEMMER (ANNA). Trudy knocks, waits a polite interval for a response she knows is not forthcoming, and enters.

That the first thing Trudy sees is her mother's back comes as no surprise to her; she sometimes thinks that after Anna dies the most enduring memory Trudy will have of her will be this pose. She takes off her coat and lays it on the hospital bed. The room is a small gray box with cinderblock walls, its reek of disinfectant not doing much to disguise the urine of its previous occupant. Anna is sitting in a plastic chair by the window, looking out at the view: a field scoured bare by the insistent wind from the Dakotas. Corn husks protruding from frozen clods of earth. Anna appears to be studying the sole demarcation line, a fence. She gives no indication that she has heard Trudy come in.

Trudy walks to her mother and crouches beside the chair, putting her hand on it.

Hi, Mama, she says. How are you feeling?

No answer.

I hear you've had some adventures lately, Trudy says. Gave the folks here quite a scare. The manager says you've run away three times — is that true?

Anna continues to stare through the window. Only the slight flare of her nostrils shows that she is alive at all.

Trudy sighs. Come on, Mama, talk to me, she persists. Have they been mistreating you? Why did you do it? Such a stupid thing to do — don't you know you could have frozen to death? Or...

Trudy pauses.

Or perhaps that was your intent, she says.

This is apparently worthy of response, for Anna twists to bestow a pale glare of indignation on her.

Of course it was not, she says, and faces forward again.

Then she adds, *Du bist keine gute Tochter.*

Trudy blinks. What? What did you say?

You heard. You are not a good daughter.

Anna clears her throat. Her voice is rough, from lack of use, Trudy assumes.

Only a bad daughter would put her mother into such a place as this, Anna says.

Trudy watches her for a minute, then stands.

How unfortunate you feel this way, she says dryly, since you're coming to live with me.

She turns her back on Anna and crosses to the closet, from which she retrieves Anna's battered maroon suitcase. Behind her she hears a scrape as Anna rises from the chair.

Is this true? Anna asks. We will leave right now? Today?

As soon as I can pack your things, says Trudy, tossing dresses and blouses and skirts into the case. I called around last night to find another place for you where you might be happier, but nobody has space on such short notice. So for now you're stuck with me.

Oh, says Anna. Oh, I...I mean to say, that is quite acceptable.

Trudy sets two pairs of pumps atop the clothes and hands Anna her boots. She is trying to stuff Anna's robe into the case when Mrs. Heligson, perhaps no longer confident that she would win a lawsuit, appears at the door to make amends.

So, Anna, she says, looking a little flustered at the speed with which Trudy is dismantling the room. So I hear you're going to live with your daughter for a while then. Won't that be nice!

Anna gives the woman a long, chilly stare but says nothing. Mrs. Heligson flushes the red of the pantsuit she is wearing, the color rising into her doughy cheeks.

Come, Mama, says Trudy, helping Anna into her coat. Button up. It's cold out there.

She refrains from adding, *As you already know,* as she takes

Anna's elbow to guide her down the hall. She has no wish to needle Anna further; in fact, Trudy is feeling quite kindly toward Anna at the moment, since there is a distinct triumph in rescuing her, in mother and daughter promenading past the goggle-eyed aides, in shielding Anna from the shaking old hands that reach out to touch them as they pass. Indeed, the relief of departure is so great that it is not until the two women are in the car, the sign for the New Heidelburg town limits dwindling in the rearview mirror, that Trudy realizes she has won a Pyrrhic victory: her mother is really coming to live with her.

Trudy glances sidelong at her passenger. Perhaps Anna too is nervous about such an arrangement, for she is looking anxiously about her at the scenery. Not that there is much to see. Everything is white, the sky, the fields. After the tiny town of Coates, the land opens up into acre upon acre so relentlessly flat that Trudy fancies she can see the curvature of the earth at the horizon. It is, she thinks, like driving on the surface of an eye. What is the joke about emigrating Scandinavians? That they searched the globe until they found a place as miserable as that they left behind. Trudy envisions Anna trudging along the roadside in only her coat and nightgown, her feet purple with cold, and shakes her head.

The wind pushes snaking, hypnotic waves of snow across the highway, the joins thudding rhythmically beneath the tires with a sound as though the car is swallowing the road. Other than this, the miles pass in silence. Trudy can think of nothing to say but inanities, and every time she attempts one of these her mouth seems to dry up, her lips parting with a soft rip as though she has been sleeping for hours. She doesn't, of course, expect Anna to say anything, so Trudy is startled when Anna suddenly bursts out, as though resuming a conversation: Pay it no mind.

Trudy struggles to right the course of the car, which she has steered into the oncoming lane.

What are you talking about, Mama? she asks.

What I have said back there. That you are a bad daughter. I did not mean it.

It's all right.

It is not right, Anna insists. It was only anger talking. That place. It was unspeakable.

Trudy takes her attention from the road for a second to give Anna a strained smile.

It's fine, Mama, she says. Forget it.

Anna looks uncertain, but after a moment she nods and leans back against the headrest. The shadows in her sockets have the density of bruises, as though somebody has gouged his thumbs into the tender skin there.

She dozes until they reach Trudy's house. Then, apparently rejuvenated, Anna snaps to attention and climbs from the car and—spurning Trudy's outstretched hand—marches up the porch steps by herself. Following with the suitcase, Trudy finds her mother in the living room, gazing around with wide-eyed interest. She has been in Trudy's house only once before, for the small reception following Trudy and Roger's wedding over three decades ago; since then, mother-daughter visits have always—at Trudy's insistence—taken place at the farmhouse. Now Trudy stands like a stranger by her own front door, watching uneasily as Anna wanders about, skating her fingertips over the surfaces of the furniture as if checking for dust.

You must be tired, Mama, Trudy says, although Anna has slept for the past hour. Why don't we go up and get you settled?

No, thank you, I am fine, Anna replies, bending to peer at Trudy's asparagus fern. She blows on one of the waving fronds.

Trudy feels herself flushing. She is a good housekeeper, of course, but next to Anna, hausfrau extraordinaire, she is nothing, and she notices for the first time that the plant's soil is parched and that it needs to be repotted, that a pair of dust mice—stirred into life by the gust of wind from the door—are tumbling animatedly in a corner. And then there are the idiosyncrasies of the house that Trudy, accustomed to them, keeps intending to repair but hasn't gotten around to: she will have to warn Anna about the stove burner that clicks but doesn't light, emitting dangerous gas; about the fact that the taps on the bathroom sink are reversed, so hot water gushes from the cold faucet and vice versa.

Yet if Anna notices anything amiss, she doesn't comment. Instead, she drifts through the house, pausing here to examine a lithograph, there to rub the fabric of drapes between thumb and forefinger. And still she says nothing, until Trudy—who has tired of trailing her and decided to bring the suitcase upstairs—hears Anna exclaim, What is all of this?

Trudy drops the case and runs down the steps toward her study.

Oh, that's nothing, Mama, she says, don't look at those—

But she is too late, for Anna is standing over Trudy's desk, peering at the titles of the books there, her lips moving as she translates the long English words. *Frauen: German Women Recall the Third Reich; The Nazi Officer's Wife; Tales of the Master Race; Hitler's Willing Executioners: Ordinary Germans and the Holocaust.*

Anna looks up at Trudy, who tries a smile that seems suspiciously large and fishy, even to herself.

Teaching materials, she explains, for one of my classes.

Anna's expression is unreadable.

Come on out of there now, Mama, says Trudy, and let me show you to your room.

But Anna has turned again to the texts, and Trudy knows from the set of Anna's shoulders that she is not about to move. Trudy shrugs and feigns nonchalance.

Fine, she tells Anna's back, you can find me upstairs when you're ready.

Then Trudy saunters from the room, as if her books and what Anna thinks of them means nothing to her at all. She takes the suitcase to the guest bedroom and sets about unpacking Anna's clothes. Every now and then she stops to listen, silencing the jangling hangers. For a long while the house is as still as if Trudy were alone, but eventually she hears the slow thump of Anna's rubber boots ascending the risers.

Trudy turns to the bed and smoothes sheets already pulled tight, plumps pillows already fat.

Well, Mama, she says, when Anna comes in. What do you think of the room?

Anna takes a few tentative steps forward, gazing at the white walls, the uncarpeted hardwood floor, the yellow tulips on the bureau and afghan of the same color that Trudy has draped over the rocking chair to brighten the otherwise monastic space.

It is very nice, Anna says.

Then she makes her way to the rocker and lowers herself into its creaking cane seat. Drawing the curtain aside, she looks through the window at the house next door, from which, Trudy suddenly remembers, one can often hear the neighbors—they of the offensive Christmas lights—making love with great grunting gusto. It is possible to see them, too, as they are careless about lowering their blinds. Trudy has sometimes found herself viewing this floor show—a flailing leg here, a bobbing head there—with amusement and repugnance and an odd, uncomfortable sense of déjà vu. She is disgusted with herself afterward, of course. But there is something comforting about glimpsing this little sliver of boisterous life, as well as the fact that the woman's jiggling breasts and belly are no more attractive, if much fleshier, than Trudy's own.

Trudy stows the empty suitcase on the closet floor and slaps her hands together in a workmanlike fashion.

Well! she says. You're all set. Make yourself comfortable, Mama. If you need anything, just ask. I'll let you rest now.

She is almost out of the room when behind her Anna says, Trudy.

Trudy stops. Then turns. Anna has let the curtain drop and is staring at her.

Yes?

Those books, says Anna. Those books downstairs—

I already told you, Mama, Trudy says. They're teaching materials. For my seminar.

I see, says Anna. And what is its name, this seminar?

Trudy steps back into the room and shuts the door.

It's called Women's Roles in Nazi Germany, she says.

I see, Anna repeats.

She says nothing further, but the way she looks at Trudy causes Trudy to feel a scalding, primal shame the likes of which she has not experienced since childhood, as though she has been caught watching Anna in the bath or rifling through her drawers.

Yet she faces Anna's inspection squarely, and her voice is level when she says, I take it you don't approve.

Anna gives a little shrug, as if the matter is of no consequence to her. But the skin around her nostrils has blanched, as it always does when she is angry or upset.

You know my view on such things, she says.

Yes, of course, says Trudy, and recites: The past is dead, *nicht*? The past is dead, and better it remain so.

Anna folds her hands in her lap.

Just so, she says.

Trudy looks at her. Something about the way she is sitting is familiar. And after a moment it comes to Trudy: if Anna were fifty years younger and holding the child Trudy in her lap, if not for the cheerful yellow blanket behind her, Anna could be posing for the photograph in the gold case, which is now hidden down the hall in Trudy's own sock drawer. Not only is the past not dead, it has come home to roost.

Trudy exhales and rubs her tired eyes.

Well, Mama, she says, if you'll excuse me, I have a lot of work to do.

She leaves without waiting for Anna's response, if any, and— resisting the compulsion to have a peek at the photograph—she goes instead to the bathroom, where she wets a washcloth and presses it to her face. It seems, thinks Trudy, sinking onto the toilet lid, as though her entire adult life has been a hallucination, a long hallway through which she has walked only to find that it is circular, leading her back to a door that when unbolted reveals Anna standing there. But this won't last, Trudy reminds herself, cold water trickling from her compress toward her ears. Anna's stay here is temporary. Sooner or later, one of the nursing homes to whose waiting list Trudy has added Anna's name is bound to have a room for her. Trudy peels the cloth from her forehead and tosses it toward the sink.

The door opens.

Oh, I am sorry, says Anna, backing away as rapidly as though she has come upon Trudy with her pants bunched around her ankles.

That's all right, Trudy replies.

Without getting up, she reaches past her mother's embarrassed face to shut the door. Another home repair Trudy will have to make. She will have to put a lock on it.

29

THAT EVENING, WANTING TO BE ESPECIALLY HOSPITABLE ON Anna's first night in the house, Trudy emerges from her study early to cook dinner. It is rather more extravagant than her usual solitary supper: an omelet with herbs and cheese, a clear soup, a salad, a slender baguette that Trudy cuts into pretty coins to camouflage the fact that it is two days old. And instead of hastily consuming this standing at the kitchen counter or at her desk—all the better to get back to work—Trudy sets the table in the dining room and, once Anna has been summoned and seated, brings everything in on a tray. She knows her mother will notice and appreciate this latter touch; Anna has always been adamant about adhering to the niceties of dining even in the farmhouse, cloth napkins and place mats and bread in a basket and dainty dishes of pickles placed just so. And indeed, although Anna doesn't offer praise—this etiquette being standard, after all; hasn't she raised Trudy in this tradition?—her silvery eyes gleam at the sight of the food and she tucks into her portion with relish.

The two women eat in silence, Anna speaking only to murmur approval of the meal. Trudy observes her covertly. At least

Anna seems to have regained her appetite, which is a relief. Maybe she was never really ailing at all; given the fare at the New Heidelburg Good Samaritan Center, Trudy thinks, she might choose to be fed through an IV herself. But what is she going to *do* with Anna? The atmosphere over the table is airless in a way that is all too familiar, as though the candles Trudy has lit are sucking the oxygen from the room. Anna mops her plate with a slice of bread and reaches for another, and Trudy, watching her, reflects that even the most ordinary acts performed by the beautiful seem blessed with grace, simply because they look so good doing them. She also thinks of Frau Kluge and Rose-Grete and the others she has interviewed, and of the photograph in its gold case upstairs and all the subsequent evenings she will have to endure in which there is nothing to say, or rather so much to say that neither she nor Anna will ever say it, and her omelet clogs, congealed and nasty, in her throat.

When Anna is done she stands and begins to clear the table with the efficiency of long habit.

No, Mama, let me, says Trudy. You don't have to do that.

I do not mind, says Anna. Then she looks down. Oh, forgive me, Trudy. You are not yet finished.

Yes I am, Trudy says, getting up too. She holds out her hands for the silverware Anna has collected.

Anna clutches it to her waist.

But you have barely touched your food, she says. Are you not well?

I am fine, Trudy says, then shakes her head; Anna's formal sentence structure is contagious.

I'm *fine,* she repeats. Just not all that hungry.

Anna deposits the cutlery onto the tray with a clatter and sweeps Trudy's full plate next to it.

Still, you must eat, she says. It is not good for you to eat so little. This is why you are so thin, Trudy. And so pale.

She lifts the tray with some effort and carries it off to the kitchen. Trudy, looking after her, starts to call, Leave the dishes,

Mama! Then she reconsiders. If Anna wants to wash them, let her. It will make her feel useful to have something to do. And with Anna thus engaged, she, Trudy, is free to return to her study.

Which she does, promptly, shutting the door behind her. She pulls her chair up to the desk with a resolute air, and then she realizes she has little to do. It is true that the new semester begins tomorrow, but since it is the first day, all Trudy will do is greet her students and distribute the syllabus. And this she has already prepared this afternoon. Trudy glances at the tape of Rose-Grete's interview, lying a few inches away on the blotter. She could transcribe it. She gets up and slots it into her VCR and plugs the headset in. Then she sits at her computer with the earphones slung around her neck like a stethoscope, listening not to Rose-Grete's faint voice but to the water running in the kitchen sink, the grind of the garbage disposal. Trudy shuts her eyes and tries to deduce from Anna's footsteps and the opening and closing of cupboard doors whether she is putting everything away in the right places.

Then Trudy's chin touches her breastbone and bounces back with a jerk. She has dozed off in her chair. She consults her watch and untangles herself from the headphones. It is ten o'clock; she can go to bed; this first difficult night with Anna in the house is over. And maybe, Trudy thinks hopefully, maybe things will get easier from here, as they get more used to each other.

Trudy opens the door and pokes her head out. The house is quiet. She investigates the kitchen. It is dark save for the fluorescent light bar humming over the stove; the countertops are shining; the dish towel is folded in thirds on the sink. Trudy smiles a little wryly at this and stumbles upstairs, yawning and grateful. She will not even bother to brush her teeth; she will go directly to bed and burrow into the comfort of sheets and blankets that smell of her own hair. And sleep.

But once she is there, sleep deserts her.

No, Trudy groans. No, no —

She turns on her left side. Then her right. Rolls onto her stomach and buries her face in the pillow, though she knows this will result in a stiff neck. No matter, for it is to no avail: Trudy eventually finds herself in her usual insomniac position, lying flat with her hands buckled across her stomach like a seat belt, staring at the ceiling. She tries not to look at the digital clock on the bedside table, but she can't help it: 12:13, 1:46, 2:03, 3:01. Why is it that losing a night's sleep should induce such panic, as if Trudy is squandering precious currency she will never get back?

Finally Trudy throws off the covers and pads down to the kitchen, where she takes the bottle of pills from the spice rack—alphabetized under *S* for *sleep,* between sage and thyme. She pours herself a large tumbler of brandy and washes down a caplet, grimacing at the burning, chalky residue in her windpipe. She has not wanted to do this, to dare this combination with a class tomorrow—particularly the first day. Despite all the years she has taught, Trudy still suffers stage fright at the thought of walking into that basement room with all those wary and curious eyes fixed on her. *Good morning, folks, and welcome to our lovely Bunker.* Standing by the window over the kitchen sink, staring at houses and garages black against a sky the pink of undercooked meat, Trudy forces herself to drink the rest of the liquor.

When the glass is empty, Trudy rinses it and sets it in the drainer, then steals back upstairs. As she passes the guest bedroom she pauses. There is no sound from within, no stripe of light under the door. Of course not; why should there be? But then Trudy hears it again, the noise that has arrested her: a stealthy creak, and then another, as if somebody sitting in a canebottomed rocking chair is moving it very slowly so as not to wake others in the household.

Trudy raises an eyebrow. Then she tiptoes down the hall to her room. So Anna, too, has her troubles sleeping. Trudy isn't really surprised—like mother, like daughter. And since the daughter can't help even herself, apparently, best to leave the mother alone.

Trudy climbs into her own bed and pulls the duvet up over her face. In the tented dark she measures her heartbeat, hushed and hammering. There is something familiar about this, too: a flash of memory, of lying very still beneath some rough fabric—burlap? flour sacking?—of the humidity of her own trapped breath; of her mother saying as if from a distance, bright and false, *That's right, little rabbit, go to sleep, I will fetch you when he is gone.* Then the recollection is also gone, swimming away like a minnow with an insolent flick of its tail.

Trudy stares at the cotton she knows is an inch from her face, although she can't see it. In the other room, the chair creaks back and forth.

Creak. Silence. *Creak.*

I will never get to sleep, Trudy thinks.

She falls into unconsciousness as suddenly as if she has been dealt a blow to the head.

SHE IS PLAYING IN THE REAR DOORYARD, BEHIND THE house that houses the bakery. She has been banished there. Her mother has told her to go outside and amuse herself until called. Why don't you clean your *Trog,* little rabbit? Anna suggests, urging a glass of milk on Trudy before guiding her to the door. Trudy dutifully fetches the broom from behind it and walks to the stand of lilac bushes that conceals her *Trog,* her rabbit hutch, a child-sized play space in which she serves tea and *Brötchen* to imaginary companions. When she is sure her mother isn't watching, she pours the milk into the grass; she doesn't like the taste of it, fatty and cloying. Then she sets about sweeping the dirt floor of the *Trog,* which she and Anna have industriously tamped down. This she usually enjoys. But today, though it is spring, the weather is raw and damp; the *Trog* is muddy so that soil clings to the broom, and really it is not much fun being outside.

After a quarter hour spent drawing bristles through the mud, trying to create orderly swirls, Trudy parts the bushes and abandons her *Trog.* She stands in front of it, watching the house. It is a gray house made of gray plaster, its steeply canted roof jutting into a gray sky. A light rain starts to fall, mist condensing in droplets. Trudy chews a finger and wiggles her bottom back and forth; surely her mother doesn't intend for her to remain out in this wet! Dragging the broom behind her, Trudy marches toward the door.

But on the stoop she hesitates. An upstairs window is cracked open, the one in Tante Mathilde's bedroom; Anna keeps it this way for air, Trudy knows. From behind the blackout curtain comes her mother's voice, forming not words but sounds: *nnnnff, nff, uff, nnnff!,* like the whimpers of a dog asleep and dreaming of an owner who kicks it.

Mama? Trudy calls.

The noises stop. Trudy slings the broom aside and, without removing her shoes as Anna has always admonished her to, she runs into the kitchen.

There she finds not her mother but Saint Nikolaus. He is wearing trousers and a white shirt, Anna's ruffled apron knotted about his waist. When Trudy bursts in, he is bent over the oven, taking something from it.

Why, hello, he says, turning to her with a sheet cake pan in his hand. He sets it on the wooden worktable and perches on a stool.

I've just finished baking, he says. Would you like a slice of delicious cake?

Trudy stares.

Come now, says Saint Nikolaus; don't be shy. Clapping, he starts to sing:

> *"Backe, backe Kuchen!"*
> *der Bäcker hat gerufen.*
> *"Wer will guten Kuchen backen*
> *Der muss haben sieben Sachen:*
> *Butter und Salz,*
> *Zucker und Schmalz,*
> *Milch und Mehl,*
> *und Eier—"*

He breaks off, smiling.

It's got all those good things, he says, butter and milk and eggs. Won't you try even a little piece?

Trudy shakes her head.

Saint Nikolaus makes a *tsch tsch tsch* noise with his tongue and pulls the other stool over next to him. He pats it.

I'm not accustomed to having my invitations rejected, he says. You've hurt my feelings.

He splays a hand over his heart and inclines his head toward Trudy with an expression of exaggerated sorrow. His eyes are like quartz with two black flaws dead center, the pinprick pupils, floating black specks.

Trudy tries to back away in the direction of the door, but her legs will not obey her. They carry her to Saint Nikolaus.

That's better, he says. That's much better.

From the pocket of Anna's apron he removes a straight razor and shears away a square of cake. It is golden and spongy, and Trudy salivates helplessly over the unfamiliar sugary fragrance. Saint Nikolaus extends the slice in his bare hand.

Take it, he says.

Trudy reaches for it. As she does, she sees a single blue eyeball embedded in the sponge. Saint Nikolaus has put her mother in the oven and baked her. Trudy wants to scream; the skin around her mouth hurts from being stretched so wide, but she can't make a sound.

Poor appetite? Saint Nikolaus asks. A shame.

He shrugs, then folds the cake in half and pops it into his mouth.

Delicious! he says, and claps his hands to dust off her mother's crumbs.

Anna and the *Obersturmführer*,
Berchtesgaden, 1943

30

Anna has never given much thought to the *Obersturmführer*'s mode of transport to and from the camp. In her mind, he simply appears in the bakery, not there one moment and demanding all attention the next. She would not be that surprised if told that he drops out of the clouds, ejected from the doors of some dark carriage, or that he materializes from the ground itself, drawn up from the bowels beneath it like an emissary from the Brothers Grimm.

In actuality, his chariot is a Mercedes, a sleek black staff car that seems to Anna to be as long as the bakery's front room. Its ornaments gleam even in the muted light of this overcast April morning; two Nazi flags flutter on the hood. As the *Obersturmführer* hands Anna into the cave of the backseat, she allows herself the small pleasure of inhaling the smell of well-tended leather, boot polish, hair pomade, smoke. She thinks for a moment of Gerhard.

Then the *Obersturmführer* lowers himself in beside her with a grunt, the seat squeaking under his weight. The young driver closes Anna's door and races around to attend to the *Obersturm-führer*. Anna can't see the chauffeur's hair beneath the peaked uniform cap, but his face has the naked, lashless look of the red-head. Anna wonders whether he was driving the first afternoon the *Obersturmführer* came for her. And has he been idling within this steel cocoon throughout subsequent evenings, smoking and peering at the bakery windows, picturing his master's activities within? He looks through the windshield, expressionless, but Anna thinks she has glimpsed a gleam of prurient interest. She stares with hatred at the vulnerable hollow between the tendons of his neck, just below the skull.

The driver starts the engine and maneuvers the staff car around the holes in the road. Anna turns to watch the bakery's thick gray walls and darkened storefront recede from view. For a moment she is terrified. Then they are passing the villas on the outskirts of the city, and Anna cranes at her neighbors' houses. Like the bakery, they are in glum disrepair. The Weisbadens' home looks as though it hasn't been inhabited for months; star-lings swoop in and out of a nest beneath the eaves. Anna is seized by the sudden certainty that the townsfolk have all been evacuated, that she and the *Obersturmführer* and the driver are the only people left in Germany. She begins to feel carsick.

The *Obersturmführer* pays little attention to her. He is in something of a temper. His briefcase acting as a surrogate desk on his knees, he shuffles through documents, tossing some aside and scratching his signature on others so viciously that the nib of his pen tears the paper. He purses his lips, emitting *pfffff*s of irri-tation. He glares through the side window, then pinches the bridge of his nose between thumb and forefinger. He mutters phrases under his breath. He unbuttons his uniform tunic and shrugs it off. Then he swears.

Ach, look at this, he says.

Anna isn't certain whether he is addressing her or the driver, but she looks anyway. One of the *Obersturmführer*'s shirt cuffs bears a brown scorchmark.

It's a disgrace, the *Obersturmführer* says. After Koch assured me she possessed impeccable credentials. What kind of laundress can't even handle an iron? What do you think, Karl?

I don't know, sir, the driver says. His voice is surprisingly froggy.

I think she falsified her papers, that's what, says the *Obersturmführer*. I think she was a Jew. A Jewish laundress who can't iron a shirt—the joke's on me, eh, Karl?

I suppose so, sir, the driver says.

The *Obersturmführer* raises his cuff to eye level, squinting at it.

Jew or not, she's ruined her last shirt, he says. It should be enough that I have to cope with this endless paperwork—everything in duplicate, triplicate—I have to be bothered with these petty domestic details too? Where am I to find time to find another laundress?

I don't know, sir, the driver says.

The *Obersturmführer* rolls up his sleeve with short, jerky movements, hiding the scorchmark.

Maybe she was a Pole, he muses.

The driver says nothing. Except for the rattle of the *Obersturmführer*'s papers, the car is silent. Anna pictures the *Obersturmführer*'s office, reconstructing it from details she has gleaned. He is a man of Spartan tastes: the room contains his desk, a chair, a bank of file cabinets, and a portrait of the *Führer*. There is also the window from which he surveys the inmates. On bright days, he can see beyond them to the patchwork fields and hills in which Weimar nestles. The hapless laundress would stand in front of his desk, her head covered with a neat white cloth.

But here Anna's imagination falters. Does the laundress sink to her knees, her hands grasping at the *Obersturmführer*'s boots; does she babble pleas for clemency? Or does she stand hollow-eyed, silently accepting her punishment? Does the *Obersturmführer* take her around the side of the building himself, or does he summon an underling? Perhaps the laundress never saw the inside of his office; perhaps she was pulled from a cot in the basement of the *Obersturmführer*'s lodgings, her eyes grainy with sleep, stumbling as she was led outside.

Suddenly conscious of the eely speed of the car, Anna gropes at the inside of her door for the window crank.

What is it now? the *Obersturmführer* asks, frowning over at her.

I'd like some air, says Anna. Please.

The *Obersturmführer* sighs.

Karl, he snaps, and the glass glides down a few inches.

Anna tilts her face into the rush of wind, which loosens her hair from its careful roll. The breeze is cold but sweet, its smell of damp earth heralding the advent of spring. This reminds Anna of something, but what? After a moment it comes to her: she remembers wresting her hand from her mother's to run ahead, skipping through the puddles on the flagstone walk, delighting in the flutter of the ribbons on her braids. She can hear her mother calling, *Anchen, slow down! Little girls never run in the churchyard.*

Anna has not regularly attended church since her mother's death, over a decade ago. The *Partei,* as Gerhard often reminded her, frowns on such activities, such blind obedience to the antiquated dictates of Catholicism. And so it has come to pass that now, Anna has no opportunity to tie her own daughter's hair in ribbons: at the *Obersturmführer*'s request, Anna has placed the child in the care of Frau Buchholtz, the butcher's widow, and on this Good Friday, Anna is accompanying the *Obersturmführer* to Berchtesgaden for the weekend.

Her nausea slides away, replaced by an emptiness at the pit of her stomach. Initially, Anna mistakes it for hunger; then she recognizes it as an uneasy anticipation. She has not been to the Alps since she herself was a child. It is Easter 1943, and she has not left Weimar in five years.

31

THE CESSATION OF MOVEMENT JOLTS ANNA AWAKE. FOR hours, it seems, she has been dreaming of being in a lift, rising and falling in an iron cage. Now she climbs from the car with the discombobulated sense of having traveled back four months as well as south, because Berchtesgaden presents the impression of permanent Christmas. The frigid Alpine air, more reminiscent of December than April, seeps through Anna's coat and tweed suit. Candles glow in the windows of the houses. Anna imagines breaking a piece from one of the stepladdered Bavarian roofs and biting it to find the taste of gingerbread. She yawns, coughs in the thin air, then yawns again, shivering.

Anna, the *Obersturmführer* says. Is it your intention that I stand in the cold all night?

His glacial tone signifies extreme displeasure, his sour humor exacerbated by the flat tire they suffered in the foothills. As the driver unloads the bags from the trunk, the *Obersturmführer* propels Anna toward the entrance of the hotel, his hand iron against her spine.

The reception room is more opulent than one would guess from the Gasthof's storybook exterior. The walls are draped with hunting tapestries in red and gold and forest green; Anna's feet whisper over Oriental rugs. Two men wearing the gray tunics of the SS lounge in carved wooden chairs before a snapping fire. They examine the new arrivals before turning back to their schnapps. The woman with them, a stunning brunette Anna's age, doesn't bother to look up at all.

The *Obersturmführer* stalks to the front desk and summons the innkeeper, a middle-aged Brunhilde with coiled braids and a chest on which one could balance a plate of *Schnitzel*. Anna feels drunk with color and sudden warmth. Yawning convulsively, she watches a little drama unfold by the door: yet another officer, young and with flat Ukrainian features, has just stumbled in, clinging to a girl whose tongue is in his ear. When he notices the other guests, he pushes her away, saying, Shh. Shh. But flecks of spittle fly from his lips with each Shh, and he begins to laugh.

The girl can't be more than sixteen; the sharp planes of her face are blurred with drink, and she wears no coat. The ruffled neckline of her tea-party dress, far too flimsy for the altitude and season, slips from her shoulder. She claps a hand to the young officer's behind.

Stop that, you shameless slut, he slurs; behave yourself or you'll get a spanking.

Bitte, she says, and cups his crotch, looking around with drunken craft. Then she spots Anna.

Well? she says. What are you staring at?

Pulling a long face of prudish dismay, she sways toward Anna. I didn't know we were in a convent, she says. Something smell bad to you, Sister? Or do you just have a spindle up your ass?

Really, Gitta, you are incorrigible, the young officer says, and sniggers.

The *Obersturmführer* crosses the room in three strides and seizes the girl by the nape of the neck, forcing her into a chair. She sputters, struggling to rise, but he shoves her back down.

Then he takes the younger officer's elbow and murmurs something too low for Anna to hear. The group by the fire watches intently.

Whatever the *Obersturmführer* says, it has the desired effect: a blush suffuses the young officer's face, starting at his neck and climbing upward like wine filling a glass. When the *Obersturmführer* releases him, he sketches a salute, staggering a little. Then he drags the complaining girl out into the night.

One of the officers by the fire sets his schnapps on the table and applauds. You have preserved the spotless reputation of the *Schutzstaffeln* single-handedly, he calls. Well done.

Shut up, Dieter, the other says amicably. He smiles at the *Obersturmführer*. Pay my friend no mind; he has so few opportunities to be gallant himself, you know.

For a moment, the *Obersturmführer* looks uncertain, as though trying to decide whether these comments are genuine or sardonic. Then his colorless gaze sweeps past his brethren and alights on the innkeeper.

What kind of establishment are you running here? he barks. Have you no discernment in your clientele?

No, sir, she says, wheezing. Yes, sir. We cater exclusively to officers—

And to their whores as well, apparently, the *Obersturmführer* snaps. I have been a visitor here since 1933, and I have never seen such behavior. It is a disgrace to the Reich.

Yes, Herr *Obersturmführer,* sir, the innkeeper says. *Bitte*—

I am mortified, says the *Obersturmführer,* that my wife should have witnessed such a scene.

He turns his back on the innkeeper.

Heil Hitler, he says to the other officers, and then, Come, Anna.

Dutifully, her head lowered like a good wife, Anna walks behind the *Obersturmführer* to the staircase. Only when she has gauged from his pace that he will not turn and catch her does she make a wide-eyed face of amazement at his broad gray back.

32

IF THE RECEPTION AREA OF THE GASTHOF MIMICS A BARO-
nial castle, its sleeping quarters are undeniably *gemütlich*. When
the innkeeper unlocks their brightly painted door, there is another behind it, reminding Anna of an Advent calendar. Since
she is in the *Obersturmführer*'s world now, Anna half expects this
second door to reveal a scene of dismemberment rather than the
chocolate she found as a child. Instead, it opens into a little room
that could belong to a maiden aunt: the furniture is sturdy pine,
the bed heaped with a white eiderdown, the only wall decoration
a sampler featuring a boy in lederhosen and a girl in a dirndl,
holding hands.

Anna moves to the window and pushes aside the lace curtains. Downstairs, the SS strut in pomp and circumstance, but
here they clearly prefer the plainer comforts of childhood. Max
would have borrowed a term from Herr *Doktor* Freud to describe it, Anna thinks, staring toward the mountains she knows
are there but cannot see; what is the word? Schizophrenic. Or
perhaps Mathilde's explanation is more apt: *At heart, Anna, men
are all babies, wanting nothing more than to suckle at the tit.*

A pity about that flat tire, the *Obersturmführer* says from behind her; we would have arrived in daylight otherwise. The view
is stupendous.

I can imagine, Anna says, without turning.

Have you everything you need? he asks. I would order dinner
brought to us, but at this hour—

No, it's perfectly all right, Anna says. Having not eaten since
morning, she has arrived at the stage beyond hunger, in which
the stomach feels like a rock.

We'll have a fine breakfast, the *Obersturmführer* assures her.
They provide quite a repast, if memory serves.

His footsteps creak on the floorboards and Anna braces herself for his touch, but then she hears the snick of a latch and understands that he has gone instead to the WC. She releases her
breath and fetches her bag, which has been deposited with the
Obersturmführer's by the bureau. Anna digs through her daytime
clothes to the lingerie beneath. What is the *Obersturmführer*'s
current inclination? Which would he prefer, the diaphanous red
negligee, the garters? Although the tags are missing from every
item he brings her, their cut indicates that they are French. She
has long stopped trying to picture whom they belonged to before. The embroidered children smile at her from the wall.

The door to the WC opens and Anna turns, straps dangling
from her hands. Which—, she begins, and then words fail her:
the *Obersturmführer* has emerged in yellow paisley pajamas.

Anna's face works madly. She bites her lip, but it is no use.
Laughter explodes from her, and the more she tries to choke it
back, the more helpless she becomes. She laughs and laughs, and
the muscles of her diaphragm, unaccustomed to such exercise,
ache as though she has just been sick. It is a delicious feeling.

Eventually she regains control and lowers her hands. The
Obersturmführer is climbing into bed with great dignity, wearing a
wounded expression.

I'm sorry, Anna says. Really, I apologize. I don't know what
came over me.

Perhaps the altitude, the *Obersturmführer* suggests.

That must be it, says Anna. She coughs into a fist to conceal a final giggle.

Please, could you— The *Obersturmführer* jerks his chin toward the lamp.

Oh, of course, Anna says. But do you want me to —?

She holds up the lingerie.

No, it's— No.

Bemused, Anna shuts off the light. She strips to her brassiere and slip, modest garments designed for comfort rather than seduction; then she settles into the bed, pulling the eiderdown to her chin. The *Obersturmführer* lies stiffly on his portion of the mattress, his limbs not touching hers. Between them, there is a zone of cool air.

He shifts toward her and again Anna tenses, but he merely places a kiss on her cheek.

Good night, he says.

Good night.

Anna's vision has adjusted; she can discern the window's outline, a faint gray rectangle on the wall. If the *Obersturmführer* is watching her, he will see her smiling, so she turns on her side to hide it. She fights to stay awake, for it is heavenly to be lying in this wide bed, revered as a wife, unmolested. She must not waste it. It must be too good to be true.

It is: an indeterminate time later, Anna is yanked to consciousness by the *Obersturmführer* thrusting against her from behind, pushing her insistently across the mattress. Anna has to grab the edge of the bed to keep from tumbling to the floor. At some point he must have removed the pajamas, for his hair grates against her skin. He entangles one hand in Anna's braids and pulls; with the other, he tugs up her slip.

Anna remains in a fetal position. She feels like a snail who, believing the outside world to be safe, pokes its soft head from its shell only to be prodded once again; she curls inward both mentally and physically. As the *Obersturmführer* wedges a knee between hers, she thinks how very unpleasant it is to be awakened this way, worse almost than the *Obersturmführer*'s regular visits by dint of its being unexpected. She thinks, Let him get on with it and then we can go back to sleep. She twists onto her back and makes noises to encourage him, scissoring her legs around his waist. The *Obersturmführer*'s breath steepens. He cups Anna's buttocks and lifts her against him, and then her cries become involuntary.

It is nearly dawn. A tinny churchbell begins to clang just outside the window, tolling the hour. The *Obersturmführer* thrusts in perfect, solemn rhythm. *Bong. Bong. Bong. Bong. Bong.* He hisses like a goose in Anna's ear, as he always does near climax, but this time he says, Anna!...Then she feels the telltale trickle, as though she is being tickled internally. The *Obersturmführer* collapses, trembling.

Anna turns her head toward the window and receives her first visual confirmation that they are in the Alps: gray and white peaks rear sawtoothed into the sky. She waits for the *Obersturmführer* to roll off her, but he stays as he is, lying on her like a dead thing, his weight pressing her into the mattress. His sweat slicks them, or is it Anna's? Anna is unable to take a full breath; she can't tell whether the heartbeat that thuds against her ribs is the *Obersturmführer*'s or her own.

33

BY MIDMORNING, THE WEATHER HAS TAKEN A TURN FOR the worse. From the dining room, Anna watches a fog roll across the mountains, first snagging on the peaks and then cloaking all Berchtesgaden in a dense shroud. The *Obersturmführer* is disappointed; he has envisioned a rigorous hike in the foothills, lunching like Tristan and Isolde beneath the trees. But the conditions permit neither picnicking nor perambulation, so after their breakfast, they return to their room.

Anna sits astride the *Obersturmführer* on the bed, straddling his buttocks; he lies on his stomach, his dark head turned sideways on the pillow. He wears only his briefs. His wounded shoulder, he tells Anna, reacts poorly to the cold and damp; it often troubles him in the camp, but it is a misery to him here. I am a human barometer, he says ruefully, his voice muffled. Anna doesn't have the breath to answer. Massaging the muscles around the wound, as he has instructed her to do, is a vigorous business.

The *Obersturmführer* gazes sadly toward the window. The fog, a swirling gray mass, is so heavy that one cannot see the church opposite.

The Gods conspire against us, Anna, he sighs. And I so wished to show you the trails. The excursion up the Höhe Göll is especially magnificent.

Hummm, Anna murmurs. She is drugged, gravid with food. As the *Obersturmführer* promised, breakfast here is a veritable feast: eggs! cheese! yogurt with muesli, and, a small miracle, jam! Her overladen stomach groans. Even the *Obersturmführer's* back reminds her of unbaked bread. His wound is a saucer-sized crater near the right shoulderblade, the scar tissue stiff and shiny, but the flesh around it is elastic as dough. Anna plucks it between thumb and forefinger, watching fascinated as it slowly sinks, reddened, back into place. The *Obersturmführer* is getting fat.

And the Berghof, the *Obersturmführer* adds. The Berghof and the Kehlsteinhaus, the *Führer's* private retreat—a marvel, truly!

As Anna probes an obstinate tendon, he grunts and closes his eyes.

I was there only once, in 1938, when Koch and I were summoned, he continues. We SS stayed in the Hotel zum Türken, of course; only the biggest wheels slept at the Kehlsteinhaus. But I never forgot the view—one could see into Austria!—nor the grounds. Just think, Anna. Among those inhospitable peaks, Bormann has created Utopia as a gift for the *Führer*: a greenhouse, a mushroom farm, beehives, and birdhouses. Salt licks for the *Führer's* deer.

It sounds quite opulent, Anna says, unable to prevent a note of sarcasm.

Oh, yes, you can't imagine...The *Obersturmführer* chuckles. Just reaching the place is an engineering exhibition. First the drive up the mountain, a nightmare of a road, hairpin turns every hundred meters or so. And when the road stops, one drives straight into the heart of the Höhe Göll and then is whisked to the top by a lift. I have never been fond of heights, but Koch's face—it was absolutely green, I can tell you.

He laughs again.

One can drive into the mountain? Anna asks, intrigued despite herself.

Bormann ordered a tunnel blasted through the rock with dynamite. Ingenious...

The *Obersturmführer* grows pensive. The laborers were all criminals, of course, he says; rapists and murderers. But I must admit, I felt some sympathy for them, clinging to the mountainside like goats. The explosives and exposure did away with quite a few. And to look down from that height is to see oneself falling into the abyss, to envision one's own death...However, they were well-treated. There was even a cinema where they could watch films once the day's work was done.

Suddenly the *Obersturmführer* stiffens, drawing air through gritted teeth.

Achhh, he says, not so hard!

Anna forces her hands to unclench.

I think it's revolting, she hears herself say.

After a pause, the *Obersturmführer* replies thoughtfully, Yes, I suppose you're right. Such decadence when even gasoline was declared a national resource—yes, it shows poor judgment.

Anna resumes her work, pummeling harder than necessary, her hair swinging on either side of her face.

Between us, says the *Obersturmführer,* this sort of thing is rampant within the higher levels of the Reich, this...corrosive decadence. It troubles me. It corrupted Koch, you know.

The *Obersturmführer* flexes his arms backward. His spine cracks. I myself am no angel, he says; at the front, I...In any case, some adolescent behavior is to be expected, given our demanding work. One seeks spiritual release in the physical. But one would think the *Kommandant,* at least, to be above such behavior— More on the left shoulder, please.

Anna obliges. The *Obersturmführer* groans: Koch, what a *Dummkopf*! That he contracted syphilis—stupid, but understandable. To want to hide it—who wouldn't, in his shoes? Ha!

Frau Koch would have had his head on a platter had she known. To order the extermination of the doctors who treated him— just covering his tracks. But to record the whole business in writing! Unpardonable stupidity! The decadence dimmed his thought processes, you see. The incessant parties, the orgies; exactly the sort of degenerate behavior that riddled the Weimar Republic, which one was led to believe the Reich would stamp out.

Anna tries to picture the *Obersturmführer* participating in an orgy and fails. It seems more likely that he has learned his dexterity from whores. In a group activity, she imagines, he would have stood to one side, watching.

The *Obersturmführer* sighs. *Kommandant* Pister runs a tighter ship, which is a relief. But he has given me Section II duties, whereas Koch never would have wasted a deputy *Kommandant*'s time with paperwork! I haven't much nostalgia for the early days, but...without Koch, you see, I'll never be...more than a small cog in a big machine. I don't have the...the stand-out quality; I do my job well, but...I don't possess the...the requisite...

As he struggles for the words to express his inadequacies, a man unacquainted with introspection, Anna thinks she can almost hear the dirt gritting between the gears of his own strange clock-work. She has never seen him this preoccupied, vulnerable, dreamy. How many camp inmates, how many members of the Resistance, would give their lives to catch the *Obersturmführer* in such a state? Anna's hands tremble on the whorl of moles between his shoulderblades. How many people could she save by shooting him in the center of this natural target? His pistol lies within reach, on the bureau with his dagger. All she has to do is cross the room.

Instantly, Anna thinks of all the reasons why this is impossible. She would be arrested. There would be reprisals, not only her own death and Trudie's but within the camp. And even if, as in a fairy tale, she could escape undetected, another officer would take the *Obersturmführer*'s place. The rations and provisions for bread, the lifeline upon which she and her daughter depend, would be cut off. On a simpler, pragmatic level, Anna has never fired a gun, nor so much as held one.

Yet beneath these concerns exists another. It revolts Anna to feel any understanding for this creature. How is it possible? But that morning, the *Obersturmführer* hesitated in the doorway of the breakfast room. He must have heard, as Anna did, the sarcastic stage whisper of the officer who applauded his actions the night before: *Look, it's the hero with his little...wife.* For a moment, watching the *Obersturmführer's* face sag, Anna glimpsed him as a small boy: wary, ridiculed by his peers, never quite comprehending why. Then, nodding icily, he guided her to a table on the opposite side of the room.

The despair within Anna over her own cowardice, her instant of fellow feeling for this man, is so great that it seems to have an accompanying sound, a desolate internal whistle. She lowers her forehead and touches it briefly to the blotch of dark spots on the *Obersturmführer's* back.

The *Obersturmführer* heaves galvanically beneath her, turning over. He takes her hands in his.

My masseuse, he says. Such strong hands, like those of a pianist, or a farm girl.

It's from working with bread, Anna tells him.

He catches one of her fingers between his teeth and nibbles.

And what astounding things you do with these demure little hands, he murmurs, mouth full. You—

Without any forethought whatsoever, shocking herself, Anna asks, *Do* you have a wife?

The *Obersturmführer* thrusts her hand aside and swears. He frowns in the direction of the sampler. Anna doesn't dare look at him. She stares instead at her lap, split in a Y because she is still straddling his waist.

After a time he snaps, Yes, I have a wife. She's a spoiled, fat, wretched woman who suffers agoraphobia; she hasn't left the house in years. She lives with her mother in Wartburg. Does that answer your question?

Yes, Anna whispers.

She senses rather than sees the *Obersturmführer*'s gaze on her. Then his index finger is on her chin, forcing her to look at him. He has mistaken her surprise for heartbreak, for he bestows a smile upon her, rich and reassuring.

But I never expected to meet somebody like you, the *Obersturmführer* says. Do you know, you alone save me. Your purity, your values—our shared values—they elevate me above the filth that surrounds me every day.

He grasps Anna's hands again and gives them a small shake.

You are my savior, he says. After all, if not for you, I might have been pulled into Koch's decadence, and then I too would have been removed from my post. We might never have met, Anna! I often think of that.

As do I, says Anna. As do I.

34

THE *OBERSTURMFÜHRER* DEPOSITS ANNA AT THE BAKERY late Sunday afternoon. She stands watching his car pull away, realizing belatedly that she could have asked for transport to collect Trudie. The thought never so much as crossed her mind; the less people know about her arrangement with the *Obersturm-führer,* the better for all concerned.

No matter; it is a fine, mild evening, and the sun now holds some warmth even as it sets. Yet Anna wants to grizzle like a child as she trudges along. She is exhausted from the *Obersturm-führer's* revelations and nocturnal demands. How much faster this journey could be in the *Obersturmführer's* car! Anna finds that she would like to slap herself for such a thought, but it persists nonetheless. She vows not to look away if she encounters a labor detachment; she will give the pastries in her handbag to anyone wearing the yellow star. But the streets are deserted. And no wonder: it is dinner hour on Easter Sunday.

Indeed, when Anna knocks on the door of the butcher shop, Mother Buchholtz and her flock are just sitting down to eat. The butcher's widow leads Anna behind the store into the kitchen, where her children are gathered around the table. All sounds of slurping and chewing cease as Anna enters; the children inspect her traveling suit, its warm nubbly tweed, with awe.

Mama! Trudie calls. She has been stuffed into a highchair far too small for her, and she struggles to escape.

Just a minute, little one, Anna says.

She makes a face of chagrin at Frau Buchholtz. I'm sorry to have interrupted your meal, she says.

Frau Buchholtz averts her eyes.

That's all right, she says to the corner.

Her hands wander to the Mother's Cross pinned to her shirtwaist, her reward for having produced six children for the Reich. Its silver glints as though she polishes it every day. Perhaps she does.

Anna unfastens Trudie from the chair, planting a kiss on the child's head where the parting divides into the fair braids. In preparation for Trudie's stay here, Anna has carefully selected the child's shabbiest clothes, only those of the *Obersturmführer*'s gifts that have stood the most wear. Even so, the difference between Anna's daughter and the Buchholtz children is all too evident: Trudie, though spindly for a girl of two and a half, has good color and a shine to her hair, while the wrist bones of the Buchholtz brood look as if they will soon break the skin. Their eyes, staring at Anna over plates of bread spread with lard, appear simultaneously sunken and too large.

Anna hoists Trudie on her hip. What do you say to Frau Buchholtz? Anna prompts her.

Thank you, says the child, uncharacteristically dutiful.

Frau Buchholtz smiles and sticks out her tongue. Leaning from Anna's arms, Trudie touches it with the tip of her own.

I hope she's been no trouble, Anna says.

No, not at all, says Frau Buchholtz. As she guides Anna back through the hallway, the widow's hands are again drawn to her decoration, caressing it.

And did you have a good journey? she asks.

Oh, yes, says Anna, brightly reeling out the tale she has rehearsed all the way from Berchtesgaden. My Tante Hilde was in fine spirits, though she complained about the lack of food. I thought in Leipzig one might be able to procure more rations, but apparently it's the same as here. Too much to die, too little to live, as they say.

Frau Buchholtz shakes her head in commiseration.

Anna, knowing she is embroidering too much but helpless to stop, continues, And the train! A hellish journey. Though I was lucky to get a spot at all, since it's all *Wehrmacht* these days. It would have been impossible with the child. I stood the entire time, crammed in with the others like sardines...

She trails off. It is peculiar: in the *Obersturmführer*'s presence Anna lies with impunity; yet in front of this woman, she flushes. Does Frau Buchholtz, who has provided meat to Anna's family for years, know that Anna has no Tante Hilde? Anna wonders how many others have seen the *Obersturmführer*'s car idling in front of the bakery. Frau Buchholtz continues to finger the Mother's Cross. Her fidgeting suddenly irritates Anna beyond endurance. She stands as tall as she can and squares her jaw.

But when Frau Buchholtz, perhaps perplexed by Anna's silence, looks directly at Anna for the first time, Anna understands that not only does the woman know, she is terrified. There is no condemnation in Frau Buchholtz's glance, only the fear that Anna might have spied some infraction that she will certainly report, well connected as she is. Apparently disdain is a luxury, like sugar or real coffee, that one cannot afford in wartime.

Anna wonders what small crimes this good mother might have committed: trading on the black market, perhaps, to feed that multitude of hungry mouths, or listening to the BBC broadcasts. She puts a hand on the other woman's arm. Frau Buchholtz's flesh wobbles loosely from the bone, like chicken skin.

Thank you for watching Trudie, Anna says. There will be extra bread for you this week.

My pleasure, truly, Frau Buchholtz replies. She is again looking anywhere but at Anna. She opens the door, her relief at Anna's imminent exit as palpable as sweat.

As Anna, feeling much the same, steps over the jamb, Trudie uncorks her thumb from her mouth.

Mama, she pipes, did you see Saint Nikolaus? What did he bring for us?

Shush, says Anna. If you're a good quiet girl, you'll get a story before bed.

I don't want a story, insists the child. I want a rabbit. Saint Nikolaus said I could have a rabbit.

Quiet now, Anna says. Shhh.

She glances back at Frau Buchholtz, who has withdrawn into the shadowy interior of her shop. Though she can no longer see the butcher's widow, Anna can feel her watching, listening.

Mama, let go, you're hurting me, Trudie says, pushing against Anna. She drums her feet on Anna's thighs.

I want Saint Nikolaus, she wails.

Anna presses the child's face into her shoulder. She has often told herself that she is not so badly off, really. Men of power have had mistresses since time out of mind, and it doesn't matter that none of the gaunt women who visit the bakery will look directly at Anna. At least she and Trudie are safe in a warm place with access to food, and she is earning her keep in ways both legal and illicit while at this very moment others are dead, dying, starving, having their eyeballs lanced and toenails pulled by the Gestapo, laboring with heavy machinery that crushes their fingers to nubs, standing naked in the rain, their children wrenched shrieking from their arms, being shorn, shot, tumbling into pits. It is really very enviable, Anna's prosaic little arrangement with the *Obersturmführer*.

But Anna has overlooked something. She has not foreseen that his contamination of her would spread to the child.

Saint Nikolaus won't come if you're bad, she whispers to Trudie. Remember?

She embraces the girl more tightly. The door to the butcher shop slams behind them.

Trudy, February 1997

35

ONE MORNING IN MID-FEBRUARY TRUDY JERKS AWAKE TO FIND the reek of meat and something more acrid filling her room. Anna, she thinks. Anna is at it again, up since dawn, cooking and cleaning. Today, from the smell of it, Anna has fried sausages and is now wiping down the windows with vinegar, which she insists is more effective on glass than store-bought solutions. Trudy pulls the sheets over her face and lies quietly, waiting for her dream to release her. It is dissolving now in the matter-of-fact light of day, but a shard remains: Anna standing in the bakery storefront, polishing—how strange, Trudy thinks—a boot sitting atop the display case, her eyes dark as they always are when she is wary or sorrowful.

After a time Trudy swings her legs over the side of the mattress and sits up, blinking dully at nothing, stomach roiling from the smell wafting up the stairs. To the outside observer, it might seem that this arrangement of having Anna in the house isn't so bad. Anna has taken great pains to stay out of Trudy's way. She goes for walks each afternoon, trudging a determined circuit around Lake Harriet even in the most dismal weather. Sometimes she makes longer trips and returns with groceries for dinner, purchased with her widow's pension checks. And she keeps to herself when Trudy is home, sequestered in her room most of the time, reading or looking out the window or listening to the small radio Trudy has bought her. Passing with an armful of laundry or en route to her own bedroom, Trudy hears nothing from behind Anna's door but the constant, mellifluous murmur of the announcers on MPR.

Yet if Anna has rendered herself largely invisible, her presence is felt in other ways. The odors of the cooking and cleaning she does when Trudy is out, for instance: they pervade the house like a contagion, subtle and stealthy as gas, and Trudy is often mortified to find, once in the open air, that they have contaminated her hair and clothes too. She now reflects with weary resignation that, given how Anna has infiltrated her home, it is little surprise she should have invaded Trudy's dreams as well.

But there is nothing to be done about it, since the local nursing homes are all still full—which puzzles Trudy; aren't the elderly more prone to going to their Great Reward during this dreary winter season? She gets up, makes the bed, dresses, and washes her face in a bathroom so strongly redolent of bleach that she succumbs to a sneezing fit. She has no time for a shower, much as she longs for one; she is running late, slated to meet Thomas in half an hour for an interview. And she has a class to teach after that. But Trudy is in dire need of coffee, so she runs down to the kitchen and starts rummaging through the cupboards. Of course, the canister is not in its usual place on the shelf. Anna, of the firm opinion that too much caffeine erodes the intestines, has hidden it somewhere and replaced it, rather pointedly, with a box of chamomile tea.

Trudy searches the lower cabinets—this being where Anna concealed the coffee last week—and bangs her head in the process. *Ow,* she mutters, standing and casting a baleful eye at the sausages, which lie fatly in congealed grease on the stove.

Mama, she yells. Where did you put the coffee?

When there is no answer, Trudy bangs through the swinging door into the dining room. No Anna there. Nor in the living room. Has she already gone for her walk? But Anna's boots are neatly aligned on a rectangle of newspaper near the coat closet, toes facing the wall.

Trudy checks the pantry, the downstairs bathroom. Where is she?

Mama? she calls.

She cocks her head, listening. There are voices, but they are coming from the wrong direction. Trudy marches down the hall to her study.

Ah ha, she says, flinging open the door.

Anna jumps, flustered and guilty. She is holding a can of Pledge and a rag—one of Trudy's favorite T-shirts, Trudy sees, scissored into a square—with which she has been ostensibly dusting Trudy's desk. And perhaps Anna did start out doing this, for Trudy's books have been piled on the carpet, and the leather blotter is streaked with cleaning fluid, and the air is syrupy with synthetic lemon. But somewhere along the way Anna has gotten distracted, and then curious enough to brave the complicated mechanism of the VCR, for behind her on the television Rose-Grete is reciting the tale of her encounter with the *Einsatzgruppen*.

Trudy is astonished.

What are you doing, Mama? she asks, so flabbergasted that she can think of nothing else to say.

Anna fumbles for the remote control, pointing it toward the set and pressing buttons and shaking it when nothing happens.

Here, let me, says Trudy, and takes it from her. She hits Pause, and Rose-Grete freezes in the midst of saying, *And the officer turned to Rebecca and shot her, and some other women too.*

Anna gives Trudy a sheepish look.

I am sorry, Trudy, she says. I know I am not meant to be in here. I was just—

Cleaning? says Trudy.

Anna tucks the rag into a pocket with trembling little jabs.

Trudy watches her, heart pounding, her mind suddenly crystal sharp. She would never in a million years have anticipated this opportunity, and now that it is here she is not going to let it pass. But she must be very careful; she must approach Anna with as much caution as any hunter who has sighted unexpected prize prey at a watering hole.

She kneels and makes a show of going through the books on the floor for her portfolio.

So you've seen one of my subjects, she says. What do you think?

Subjects? Anna repeats.

Trudy extracts the binder from the middle of the stack.

For my Project, she explains. I'm interviewing Germans of your generation as to what they did during the war. And how they feel about it now. Here are the questions—you see?

She opens the portfolio and holds it out to show Anna the list penned on the legal pad.

Anna takes a step backward and bumps up against the desk.

This Project is for your class? she asks.

No, it was my own idea. I put up flyers and ran newspaper ads, and all these people came forth to tell their stories. It's amazing, how many of them want to talk about it.

She smiles at Anna and slides the binder into her briefcase.

You know, she adds, as if the thought had just occurred to her, maybe you'd like to do it too.

Anna glances at Rose-Grete and lifts a hand to her throat.

Me? she says. Oh, no. I could never.

Why, sure you could, Mama, Trudy says, standing. It would be good for you. So many people tell me what a relief it is to finally talk about what happened back then. It's cleansing, they say, like confession.

This is not strictly the case; in fact, Trudy can only guess as to her subjects' motives. Yet she suspects that for some of them—Rose-Grete, for one—this may be true.

But Anna is shaking her head.

Such a thing is not for me, Trudy, she says. I have nothing to say.

Oh, but I think you do, Mama, says Trudy. I think you have a lot to say.

She takes a small breath.

About the officer, for instance, she adds softly.

Anna is dead quiet. Trudy steals a glance at her. She has gone bright pink but for the white area around her flaring nostrils, which stands out like a rash.

I do not know what you mean, she says.

Trudy fights to appear neutral, but she feels her eyebrows rising.

Don't you? she asks.

Nein. I have not the slightest idea.

The two women lock stares. Trudy's eyes narrow. Anna is kneading the belt of the apron, but her chin is high. Neither will look away.

Then Trudy's watch beeps, signaling the turn of the hour. She swears silently.

She makes one last effort.

Please, Mama, she says. I know you know what I'm talking about. Please tell me about him. It would mean the world to me.

But the opportunity has passed, if ever there was one, for Anna turns to run a hand over the blotter, then frowns at her palm as if it had come up black with grime.

There is nothing to tell, she says.

Trudy bites her lip and bends to pick up her briefcase.

All right, Mama, she says. You win for now. I have to go. But please. Think about what I've said.

She leaves Anna in the study and hurries through the house to the front closet, where she pulls on quilted vest and coat and hat and scarf and gloves. It will be such a relief—though it is impossible to believe that such a day will ever come—when Trudy can venture outside without feeling as though she is girding up for battle. And these preparations are doubly uncomfortable at the moment, since Trudy is as hot as if with fever. She has some difficulty with her boots. She is shaking all over.

A noise — the crack of a floorboard — makes her look toward the study.

Mama? Trudy calls, abruptly and absurdly hopeful: maybe Anna has changed her mind.

But of course she has not. Trudy yanks savagely on her laces, snapping one. She thinks of Anna creeping about the house in her absence and feels the burn of angry tears behind her eyes. Yet she is really more irritated with herself than Anna, for she has wasted this chance given to her. She has tried to crack her most important subject, and she has failed.

For a moment Trudy considers abandoning her interview and returning to the study and making another attempt. But her work ethic won't permit it. And she is so very late. Trying to remember the subject's name — Ralph? Rolf? Rudolph? something along those lines — Trudy steps out onto the porch and has to grab the railing to keep from falling on her tailbone. The world has been transformed overnight into an ice rink. The sidewalks are sheeted with it; stalactites hang from branches and dangerously low telephone wires; the road is a blinding plane. Shielding her eyes against the glare, Trudy skates down the walk to her car only to find that its doors are frozen shut. She will have to force the trunk and climb in through the hatchback. Which means another fifteen minutes lost, at least.

Trudy kicks the solid chunk of snow in the rear tire well and yelps in pain. Then, clutching at the hedge as she pulls herself along, she scuffs back toward the house for a screwdriver with which to break into her own car. The morning has gotten off to a fine start.

36

THE SUBJECT'S HOUSE IS IN TANGLEWOOD, A NEIGHBOR-hood about fifteen blocks from Trudy's own, and by the time Trudy pulls up in front of it, her car has thawed enough that she is spared the embarrassment of exiting the same way she got in. Trudy glances at the dashboard clock as she cuts the engine: twenty minutes late. Not good, but it could be worse. Indeed, considering how treacherous the roads are — radio announcers imploring people to stay home if they don't have to drive, accidents at nearly every intersection — it is something of a miracle, Trudy thinks, that she is here at all.

Thomas's white van is at the curb, and Trudy sees that he has already loaded his equipment and is waiting for her. She makes her way toward him as quickly as she can, which isn't very fast given the ice and the fact that her snapped lace forces her to do a clumsy shuffle just to keep the wretched boot on her foot. Trudy rolls her eyes and throws out her arms in a pantomime of haplessness, mistaking Thomas's grimace for a suppressed grin at the sorry picture she presents.

But when she reaches him, slipping a little, Thomas grips her elbow both to stabilize her and to draw her behind the truck where they can't be seen from the subject's house. His round face is set in lines of uncharacteristic anxiety.

Whoa, he says, steady there. You all right?

Well, it's been a hectic morning, as you can tell, but I'm fine. What's the matter?

Maybe nothing, Thomas says, adjusting his bandanna. Maybe it's just me. Still...

What?

Thomas lowers his voice, although the subject cannot possibly hear him from here.

I think you might have some trouble handling this guy, he says. He seems a bit...angry.

Trudy glances automatically over her shoulder and sees only the truck blocking the house from view. This will not be her first male subject; there was a Mr. Pohl, a butcher exempted from fighting in the *Wehrmacht* because of a hand lost to a cleaver. And some of her subjects, of course, have been difficult. But...

Angry? she asks. Angry how? Because I'm late?

Thomas nods.

He's come out four times to ask where you were. Look, I'll show you.

The pair edge around the truck. Sure enough, the subject pops out onto his porch and stands with his arms crossed, breath chuffing in the frosty air.

See? says Thomas from the side of his mouth.

He points to Trudy.

She made it, he yells. She had trouble with the ice. We'll be right in.

Trudy waves and smiles at the man, then turns and rubs her eyes.

Wunderbar, she mutters. This is all I need.

Thomas glances down at her with concern.

Are you sure you're up to this? You look a little...

He trails off tactfully, and Trudy laughs.

I know how I look, Thomas. Thank you for being too polite to say it. No, let's do it. If— Oh God, what's this guy's name again?

Goldmann, says Thomas.

That's it, Goldmann. It completely slipped my mind...Well, we've kept Mr. Goldmann waiting long enough, don't you think? Let's get started.

Yes ma'am, Thomas says.

The two of them pick their way up the icy path to the house. Mr. Goldmann has disappeared inside but left the door open a crack, which Trudy interprets as an invitation to enter. She walks tentatively into the foyer and stops there, disoriented; after the glitter outside, she is blind as a mole.

Hello? Trudy calls. Mr. Goldmann? I apologize for having kept you waiting. But at least you've already met my camera-man—

Indeed, I have had ample opportunity, a deep voice rumbles from somewhere in the dim hall. You are twenty-seven minutes late, Dr. Swenson.

Mr. Goldmann looms suddenly in front of her, and Trudy blinks up at him—and up and up, for he is very tall, taller even than Thomas, and heavyset, with a large, square, rather magnificent head topped with thick pewter-colored hair. He would be intimidating even if he were not impatient; his face is ruddy, his expression stern; he fixes Trudy with a penetrating glare over gold-rimmed bifocals. All he needs, Trudy thinks, assessing his pressed slacks and fine Scottish cardigan, is a tumbler of Scotch in one hand to complete the impression that he is a lawyer relaxing at home after a long day of bullying witnesses.

Yet in fact Mr. Goldmann is, Trudy remembers from their brief phone conversation, a teacher. She decides to use this as a bargaining chip to win back rapport as she follows him farther into the house.

As I recall, you said you teach history? she says, trotting to keep up with him, her unlaced boot slapping against the floor. So, you know, that's something we have in common. What's your field of interest? It's probably much broader than mine, since I specialize in —

Mr. Goldmann stops and turns.

I am well aware of your credentials, he booms. I telephoned the university to establish their validity, Dr. Swenson. Or perhaps I should say Frau *Doktor*?

Trudy smiles weakly at him.

Trudy would be fine, she says.

Mr. Goldmann raises an eyebrow.

To answer your question, Dr. Swenson, I no longer teach anything, he says. I retired last year.

Oh, says Trudy.

Mr. Goldmann stalks into a living room of Hitchcockian gloom and proportion, its high ceiling and dark wainscoting muffling sound. He picks up a teacup and saucer from a low table — the delicately flowered china incongruous, surprisingly fussy for such a large man — and gestures with his free hand at the space.

I trust this will be sufficient for your cameraman's purposes? he asks.

Oh, yes, says Trudy, although she hears Thomas muttering about the lack of light and knows he will have to set up extra lamps.

Mr. Goldmann nods but keeps a weather eye on Thomas as he sips his tea. Trudy's empty stomach growls at this reminder of the coffee she hasn't had. She wouldn't mind a cup of something hot with cream and sugar in it. And perhaps a sweet roll or two. However, Mr. Goldmann, unlike her previous subjects, does not appear to be about to offer her anything to drink, let alone food.

How long did you teach? Trudy asks.

Thirty-eight years. In the Minneapolis public school system.

That's quite a stint. And you're newly retired, you said? You must miss it.

For the first time Mr. Goldmann smiles, if a bit acerbically. Rainer, Trudy remembers; his name is Rainer.

As a matter of fact, I don't miss it at all, he replies. I found my students to be a profound disappointment. Their lack of intellectual curiosity was staggering, whatever native intelligence they might have possessed destroyed by their preference for pop culture. Their brains have been turned to mush by a steady diet of television, on which they have been fed from the womb.

Trudy strives to maintain a polite expression, but she can feel her jaw slotting out in defense of her students. It is true that she has had the same thoughts on occasion, that the majority of faculty conversations consists of woe-is-us hand-wringing over pupils' lack of preparedness, their laziness and apathy. *Kids these days!* But Trudy has always secretly granted her students the benefit of the doubt, as she is convinced that their indifference is a facade, cultivated in answer to the American aversion to overt shows of intelligence. And behind this self-involvement, they have such rich inner lives! One only need tap into that energy; they are not stupid; they are simply in need of proper stimulation. How Trudy pities the students of this mean and terrifying man! God in heaven, who let him into a classroom? Why be a teacher at all, if one doesn't like kids?

Mr. Goldmann is watching Trudy's struggle for control with some amusement.

I gather you don't agree with my assessment, Dr. Swenson, he says. You are ruffling like a hen.

Well, says Trudy. Well, with all due respect—

Trudy.

She whips around. Thomas gazes benignly at her.

We're set to go, he says.

Oh. Right. So I see. Thank you.

Trudy and Mr. Goldmann take their places at two chairs set catty-corner at a broad dining-room table, which Thomas has bracketed with screens to retain light and create the illusion of intimate space. Trudy is grateful for the heat of the lamps, which provide an excuse for her flushed cheeks. Also, it is otherwise cold in this big old house, a fact to which Mr. Goldmann, in his cardigan, seems impervious.

Trudy forces a smile as Thomas stoops to affix a grass-hopper-sized microphone to Mr. Goldmann's tie.

Very good, she says briskly. Are you ready, Mr. Goldmann?

Whenever you are.

Thomas?

We're...rolling.

Trudy leans forward.

Can you state your name for me, please?

My name is Rainer Josef Goldmann, it was Rainer Josef Goldmann at birth, I am sixty-six years old, I was born in Berlin, and, with permission, I have prepared a statement I wish to read in lieu of answering the usual questions.

Trudy senses Thomas shifting, detaching his head for a moment from the camera. She wishes he were not behind her so she could exchange a meaningful glance with him: *What now?*

Instead, she knots her chilly hands beneath the table and—with resigned foreboding—says, By all means. Go ahead.

From the breast pocket of his cardigan, Mr. Goldmann extracts a sheet of paper. He places it on the table and irons out its creases with several thumps of his fist. He settles his gold-rimmed bifocals more firmly on his nose and glances over them at Trudy. Then, in a voice resonant from decades of classroom training, he begins to read.

THE GERMAN PROJECT
Interview 10

SUBJECT: Mr. Rainer Josef Goldmann
DATE/LOCATION: February 14, 1997; Minneapolis, MN
* subject reading prepared statement, per request *

Subject:

You will be forced to wear a badge. You will bring your little girl, dressed in red, hair bouncing in curls on her shoulders and tied with a ribbon, to another child's birthday party. When you take off your coat to enter the Gentile home, your badge will be hung in the closet along with it. Later, holding your child on your hip, you will back toward the door. You know the birthday girl means no harm; she is herself only a child. But you will not be able to keep your face from crumpling when she cries, Where's her Star? Where's her yellow Star? I saw her wearing it yesterday! She has to wear it; all Jews have to wear the Star! Mama, make her put it on!

You will trade your dead father's watch and your dead mother's rings for a crust of bread, for a few parsnips, a potato. To do this, you will venture into dark and filthy streets that terrified you before they became part of the ghetto, and they still do. You will have to deal with men to whom you would never have spoken before they became black-market dealers, men you would cross the street to avoid, whose jeers you would self-consciously try to ignore. You will feel stupid approaching these men, you who hated to haggle over the price of vegetables in the prewar market. You will beg these men to accept your family heirlooms, and when they toss them on the ground and sneer you will cry, and you will, in the end, let one of them have sex with you against a back wall, your coat still on, his coat smelling of dirt and sweat and his breath of herring and cheap wine, because after all he is right when he points out that your father's watch is not gold but only gold-plated and therefore not worth an entire loaf. Then you will have no jewelry left to barter, and as you wonder where the other family who lives in your room got their diamonds, you will watch your daughter grow emaciated and die of malnutrition. Sometimes you will eat rats. You will dream of eating the dead.

You will drink your own urine in the dark from your cupped hands. You will smell excrement and feel it splashing on your legs and not know whether it is your neighbor's or your own or perhaps comes from the single bucket the Germans have provided, which started overflowing two days ago. You will feel your tongue grow fat with thirst and your breath will become sour and your dress soiled and your hair matted, and as you wait for the doors of the cattle car to roll open, you will know that your chance of making a good impression and thus your sole chance for survival is shrinking with every passing stinking moment.

But you will not be given that chance. You will not be permitted to plead with your executioners. You will not be allowed to visit the latrines, even though your stomach burns with dysentery. You will not be able to clean yourself properly after the train journey. You will not be granted the dignity of keeping your hair, the hair you have washed, pomaded, styled, cut, brushed, and fretted over on days when it rained or snowed. They will shave it with a blunt razor, so as you march to the gas chamber your scalp will sting and you will be unrecognizable to yourself, as strange and ugly as the people you see around you, and you will have a dim understanding of why the SS see you as so ugly, as dispensable and interchangeable as sticks of wood, and you will feel ashamed of being so ugly and long to hide your head.

You will not know how to act as they shove you naked through the doors with slivers of soap and mouthfuls of lies and blows from their clubs if you do not move toward your death fast enough; it will not matter whether you laugh or cry or pray or sing or grab a stranger's hand for comfort as you watch the nozzles overhead in terror. You will not be prepared for the milling panic nor the screams nor the punches of people pushing you down and trying to stand on top of you in an instinctive effort to get more air, even though they are really climbing toward the gas. You will not know what you want your last thought to be, nor be able to fix one in your head, and in the end it will not matter: you will be one of a pyramid of anonymous corpses that they will remove from the chamber with rakes, entangled so tightly with strangers that they will have to walk among you and separate you forcibly.

And then they will burn you. They will burn you: you, your body, your own beloved and maddening body with its quirks and birthmarks, its trick knee or double-jointed thumb, its scars each with its own story; the body that you and others have nursed through colds and fevers; the body whose digestive processes have provided the visceral rhythm for your days; the body that it has been your goal in life to feed and clothe and shelter; the body that only your mother and your lovers know better than you. They will burn your brain with its magnificent network of neurons, in which are stored memories and hard-earned philosophies, books you have read and sights you have seen, the endearments you used for others and the concept of yourself as an individual being, that inviolable essence of yourself so deeply personal that it can never be articulated. They will put you in the oven and they will burn you, and the only thing that distinguishes them from the monsters of the Grimm tales is that they will not eat you afterward. In all other respects, they are monsters, with the faces of businessmen and bullies, monsters literal and insane; they will yawn as you go up the chimney.

[*Subject pauses to refold statement.*]

This is not what happened to me, obviously. This is what happened to my aunt Sarah, whom I loved dearly. Or rather, this is what I imagine happened to her. There is, of course, no way of knowing for certain. There is no way to know what they felt, those millions who were given no chance at survival. I can only speculate. And even I, a Jew—yes, I am a Jew, Dr. Swenson, and my entire family was murdered by the Nazis—even I can only imagine a pale facsimile of what it must have been like.

But I do know that there is no justification. No possible rationalization for what the Nazis did, for what civilian Germans permitted and encouraged to happen.

And yet: you. Here you are. You have the temerity to sit in my home, at my table, with your lights and your cameras and your questions and your historical credentials. You dare to seek some explanation. You dare to record the stories of the butchers and those who abetted them. You dare to seek some exoneration of a people who committed wholesale slaughter of an entire race!

Take your things and get out of my house.

I said, get out. Now.

Get out, I said! Get out of my house!

37

AFTER THIS UTTER DISASTER, TRUDY WANTS NOTHING more than to go lie down in a very dark room for a very long time. But of course this is impossible: she has a seminar to teach, and even though Mr. Goldmann's interview has been, to put it politely, truncated, Trudy must still scramble if she is to make it to the university for her class. So she leaves Mr. Goldmann's house immediately as ordered, waiting on the porch for Thomas to pack his equipment. She hangs her head when she hears him coming outside; she can't bear to look at his face, to find even a trace of triumph there.

Thomas touches her shoulder.

Are you all right? he asks.

I'm fine, says Trudy, staring over at her car. Just late.

She starts to walk down the steps. Thomas's cart bumps along the risers behind her.

God, that was terrible, he says. I never would have expected—

I'm sorry, Thomas, but I really have to go.

Trudy.

Yes?

Try not to take it too much to heart, what he said. It wasn't your fault.

Trudy feels the treacherous sting of tears behind her eyes. She quickens her pace until she is nearly running toward her car. As she opens its door, she raises a backward hand in farewell and calls, I'll be in touch later, okay?

She pulls away from the curb with a rattle of salt. The temperature has risen during her sojourn at Mr. Goldmann's house and the roads are safer now, but they are also clogged with lunch-hour commuters and people getting a belated start on their day. Trudy drives like a maniac, weaving in and out of lanes, cutting off trucks, smacking her horn whenever she encounters somebody making too slow a turn or lingering at a four-way stop.

Come on, come on! she yells when she hits the snarled traffic on the bridge over the Mississippi.

She parks aslant in her space in the faculty lot and runs clumsily through the basement hallway of the History building, *thump-slap, thump-slap,* her unlaced boot threatening to come off her foot with each step. She hears her students chattering as she nears her classroom, their voices louder and more lively than they ever are during lecture. No doubt they are hopefully analyzing the likelihood of her not showing up. Trudy frowns and plunges through the door.

Sorry to disappoint you, folks, she says, but here I am.

There are a few good-natured groans, and then the room quiets as Trudy grimly *thump-slap*s toward the podium. She struggles out of her coat and scarf and throws them onto an empty chair in the front row—somebody is absent; who has decided not to bother with class today? She bends to her briefcase and unzips it, and only then does she realize she has forgotten her notes. All she has with her is her interview portfolio.

Trudy runs her hands through her hair and looks into the briefcase again as if this would cause her lesson plan to magically appear. When it does not, she props the portfolio on the lectern. She can at least give the impression of being prepared.

As she opens the leather binder she hears whispering and what sounds suspiciously like a snicker, and then some wit calls, Tough morning, Professor?

Indeed, says Trudy. Thank you, Mr. Phillips, for once again exercising your gift of stating the obvious.

She turns and limps to the board to take from the trough a fresh stick of chalk, which she snaps in half. She rubs her thumb over the rough edge as she returns to the podium, trying to remember what lecture she is meant to give.

Today—, she says.

Tiny fragments of chalk patter to the floor. Trudy clears her throat and looks down at her legal pad. *Goldmann, Rainer Josef,* is written there, in her own rather cramped handwriting. *Subject b. 1931, Berlin…*

Goldmann. Of course. It seems so obvious in hindsight. Trudy should have known he was Jewish. But he responded to her ad— He knew what the Project was about— She even spoke with him on the phone! How could she possibly have guessed?

Sneaky. The Jews were sneaky.

Trudy slaps the portfolio shut.

Today, as indicated by the material you've read since we last met, she says, we're going to discuss, um, the roles German women played in the Resistance—

There it is again. A definite snigger. Trudy's head whips up. In the last row—why must fraternity boys always sit in the back? Do they think this renders them invisible?—this semester's version of Frick and Frack are sharing some private joke, most likely at Trudy's expense.

Excuse me, Trudy says. Do you gentlemen find something amusing?

The pair glance up and around as if Trudy might be speaking to somebody else. Then they blink innocently at her: *Who, us?*

Yes, you, says Trudy. If you think something is funny, I'd really like to know what it is.

The boys smirk and shift and stare past their desks at their enormous sneakers.

So, what is it?

The rest of the students hunch frozen in their seats, not daring to look at the offenders. Trudy folds her arms and waits.

Finally, Frick or Frack mutters, Nothing.

Nothing, repeats Trudy. Nothing. I see. I'm glad to hear that. Because I personally don't find anything funny about the content of today's lecture. But perhaps you do? Or perhaps it means so little to you that you can giggle over some fraternity prank while we're discussing the fact that people once died trying to fight a regime of monstrous tyranny. Gave their lives for the freedom you so blithely take for granted. Is that it? It means so little to you?

Trudy looks out over the room. Not a single student will meet her eye. Some are doodling in their notebooks, lounging and slack-mouthed, the living embodiment of Mr. Goldmann's theory that they are intellectually void. The possibility that he might be right makes Trudy angrier than ever.

Well? she says.

She turns again to Frick and Frack, who grin with embarrassment.

Then one of them winks at Trudy and says, Hey, Professor, lighten up. It's Valentine's Day, you know? Where's the love?

There are some stifled giggles at this. Valentine's Day. This would explain the preponderance of red sweaters in the classroom, the teddy bear holding a satin heart on one girl's desk, the Hershey's Kisses the students are mouthing. Trudy grips the edges of the lectern.

Ah, yes, she says. Valentine's Day. So it is. And do any of you happen to know what was happening on Valentine's Day in, say, 1943? In Germany? I can assure you it was somewhat different. People your age were not sitting in a classroom with their stuffed

animals and little hearts. They were dying. Some because they
had been caught performing Resistance activities and were
strung up by the Gestapo. With piano wire. From meat hooks.
Others were dying in air raids and from the flu that all of you can
just run to the infirmary and get shots for. Can you believe that?
Dying from the *flu*? Or how about dying of cold? Or starvation,
perhaps you can imagine that. What would it be like not to have
even bread, let alone chocolate? Do you know that in 1943 in
Germany there were children who had never *tasted* chocolate?
Who didn't even know what chocolate *was*?

She glares at the class.

Well? Do you?

Total silence. Then somebody mumbles, You don't have to,
like, yell.

Oh, don't I? Trudy asks. Thank you. Thank you for that sage
piece of advice. But it seems to me that there is no other way to
shake you out of your self-indulgent stupor, to make you realize
that this isn't just something I make you read about in history
books. This is real. This is something that happened to *real
people*. And let's forget about the Germans for a second. Let's
think about the Jews. Oh, what the Germans did to the Jews.
Did you know that when the Americans and Russians liberated
the concentration camps, there were people your size who
weighed under seventy pounds? *Seventy pounds*. Half of what
some of you weigh. And their stomachs were so shrunken, so
decimated from years of starvation, that when the soldiers tried
to be kind to them and fed them meat and soup and cheese and,
yes, chocolate, they died. Died from eating a Hershey bar. Can
you imagine that? Any of you? You think about that next time
you go to the dining hall— to the *gym*— when you're trying to
decide between yogurt or salad because you're sticking to your
little *diets*—

Trudy breaks off. A small choked noise has come from just
beyond the podium, from a nice assiduous girl who always sits in
the front row. She is staring at Trudy, tears in her eyes. The other

students are either boggling at her too, thunderstruck, or looking at the floor.

Trudy turns and puts the chalk, by now a stub, back in the trough. Then she picks up her portfolio and coat and scarf.

That's all for today, she says.

She walks with as much dignity as her boot will permit her from the room, conscious of being watched in stunned disbelief, and shuts the door quietly behind her.

38

IT IS EARLY EVENING WHEN TRUDY RETURNS TO MR. Goldmann's house. The sky is a deep navy overhead, shading in the west to a lighter blue so pure it seems to vibrate: a gift of a color peculiar to midwinter Minnesota nights, compensating in clarity for what it lacks in warmth. To Trudy, standing by her car, it is reminiscent of a Maxfield Parrish painting; like a Parrish, too, is the yellow of the windows in the neighboring houses. Trudy eyes Mr. Goldmann's, which are dark. Perhaps he is not home. She feels such relief at this prospect that she forces herself up the front walk and onto the porch without thinking about it further.

She is carrying a casserole of latkes, the recipe for which she wheedled from the owner of Murray's Deli and that she has spent the entire afternoon making. The latkes look like potato pancakes to Trudy—or their German cousins, *Kartoffelkuchen*—but what does she know. In any case, they seem to have turned out all right: crisp and brown, rich with onions and butter and flecks of parsley. She has even included a side of sour cream.

She holds the Pyrex dish awkwardly under one arm while she turns the iron key that rings the bell. The ensuing tinny clatter is loud enough to send the dog in the house next door into a frenzy, but Mr. Goldmann does not appear. Trudy starts to try again, then draws her hand back. Once is enough. She sets the latkes on the welcome mat and is rummaging through her purse for paper and pen to write a note to go with them when she hears the *whish-whish* of approaching slippered feet.

Yes, Mr. Goldmann rumbles. What do you want?...Oh. It's you.

Trudy tries to smile.

It's me, she agrees.

For a long moment Mr. Goldmann merely looks at her.

Then he says, You have interrupted my dinner, and starts to shut the door.

Wait, says Trudy. Please.

She shifts her pocketbook onto her shoulder so she can stoop and pick up the latkes. The bag sags open and disgorges its contents onto the floorboards: pens, Chapstick, a rattling bottle of Motrin, nickels bouncing and rolling into the corners.

Oh, God, Trudy says.

Dropping to her hands and knees, she scrabbles to sweep the mess back into her purse. She doesn't dare glance up at Mr. Goldmann; she can feel his displeasure as surely as if it were cold air emanating from an icebox. His slippers, which are leather and embossed with his monogram, remain in exactly the same position in the doorway as Trudy crawls past them.

When she has finished retrieving her things, Trudy stands and picks up the casserole dish. She holds it out.

For you, she says.

Mr. Goldmann lifts an eyebrow. There is something different about him, Trudy thinks. He is not wearing his bifocals. He is marginally less intimidating without them. But his silence is daunting enough.

Please, Trudy says again. I made them for you. Though I should warn you, they're not kosher. I didn't have the proper cooking equipment—

That is irrelevant, Dr. Swenson, says Mr. Goldmann, as I am not observant. I am Jewish in name only.

Oh, says Trudy.

Mr. Goldmann squints at Trudy's offering.

What are they?

Latkes.

He leans forward over the pan and sniffs suspiciously.

They look like potato pancakes, he says.

Well, they are, essentially. That's what latkes are.

Ah.

Mr. Goldmann straightens, his hands in the pockets of his cardigan. Trudy shifts from foot to foot, waiting for him to say something else or at least take the pan. When he doesn't, she bends to put it on the mat.

I'm sorry to have disturbed you, she says. I'll just leave these here. You can keep the dish.

Dr. Swenson.

Yes?

Mr. Goldmann sighs.

You might as well come in, he says. And bring those—

He gestures to the pancakes.

Latkes.

Yes, the latkes. Since my dinner will no doubt be cold by now, I suppose there is no harm in adding a side of cold potatoes to it.

He turns and walks into the house, again merely leaving the door open in brusque implication that Trudy should follow.

So she does, hurrying to catch up with him as he strides through the dining room, the scene of the earlier debacle, and through a long narrow throat of a hallway that opens into a kitchen. It is somewhat warmer in here, but only a little; the drafts, the room's large and chilly proportions, the high tin ceiling remind Trudy of the farmhouse. Like those in the farmhouse, too, are the old gas range from the fifties and the gigantic refrigerator with its rounded corners, the walls painted their original Depression green. A Beethoven symphony plays quietly and incongruously from some other room.

Trudy looks around for a place to put the latkes.

On the table is fine, Mr. Goldmann says.

Trudy sets the casserole next to a glass of milk and a half-eaten slab of roast. There is also a candle in a pewter holder, though unlit, and photographs spilling from an envelope, in disarray on the checked oilcloth as though Mr. Goldmann has just been sifting through them.

Trudy can't help glancing at them.

Are these of your family?

My daughter and granddaughter.

May I?

Mr. Goldmann says nothing, which Trudy takes as tacit permission to examine the top snapshot. Against a backdrop of palms, a small woman with dark curly hair laughs into the camera, hugging a pretty child to her waist. Mr. Goldmann stands slightly to one side. They are all wearing Mickey Mouse ears, Mr. Goldmann included. He looks uncomfortable.

Disney World, he explains from behind Trudy, somewhat unnecessarily. A recent vacation. They live nearby. A hideous place, but my granddaughter loves it.

I can see that. She's a beautiful little girl. What's her name?

Hannah, after my late wife. Who died twelve years ago of cancer, a miserable agonizing death I wouldn't wish on an SS dog. The irony being that at the end she was as thin as she was in the camps, skin and bones, all her hair gone. Dr. Swenson—

Trudy looks up. Mr. Goldmann is standing stiffly next to his chair, one hand on its laddered back as though he is posing for a portrait.

Yes?

Why are you here?

Mr. Goldmann—

Rainer. Since you have for some unknown reason seen fit to invade my home a second time, you might as well use my first name, don't you think?

Trudy's face burns.

All right. Rainer. And please, call me Trudy. Anyway, I just came...

She shakes her head.

Go on.

It seemed like a good idea at the time. To bring the latkes, I mean. I somehow had the misguided notion that they might work as a sort of peace offering, you know, to make amends for what happened earlier today, to — Well. It was stupid, really. Nobody could ever compensate for what was done to you and your family. Least of all me.

Trudy hitches her purse more securely onto her shoulder.

But thank you for inviting me in, she says. I'll leave you in peace now.

She walks quickly from the kitchen, leaving Mr. Goldmann still gripping his chair. She is nearly to the front door, cursing herself for being a fool, when she hears him call: Dr. Swenson.

Trudy turns. Mr. Goldmann is standing at the mouth of the hallway.

Trudy, she says. Please.

Very well. Trudy. Have you eaten?

Well, no, but—

In that case, perhaps you would join me.

Why, I— Yes, that would be lovely. I'd be honored, in fact.

Mr. Goldmann looks startled. Then he nods.

Sit, he says. I will bring the food out here.

Oh, no, says Trudy. Don't go to any trouble. The kitchen is fine—

But he is already striding away, so Trudy removes her coat and unwinds her scarf and lays them on a chair next to the dining-room table. She pulls out another and settles cautiously on its edge. As she had no chance to take note of her surroundings earlier, she does so now: dark wallpaper with small tasteful wreaths, a sideboard displaying the flowered china, faded Oriental rugs. In an alcove next to the bay window is another, smaller table with a chess set on it, the pieces arranged in midbattle configuration. There are no curtains; on pleasant days, sunlight would stream over the board. Trudy pictures Mr. Goldmann playing himself, angling forward to move a knight and then sitting back to contemplate its position, the light glinting on the gray hair of his wrist and glancing off his watch.

He returns with a tray, from which he doles two plates of meat, carrots and peas, and Trudy's latkes. Their lacy edges look fussy, she thinks, next to Mr. Goldmann's simple bachelor fare.

He sits opposite Trudy and picks up his knife and fork.

Gut essen, he says.

Trudy eyes him warily. Is there a faint irony to his smile?

Bon appétit, she replies, and toasts him with her milk.

Mr. Goldmann begins to eat. His complete concentration on his food does not encourage conversation, so Trudy takes her cue from him. She saws at her meat, trying to keep the plate from moving on the table, and brings a forkful to her mouth. Halfway there, her hand pauses: the Beethoven, which Trudy has almost forgotten, stops and starts again, the same piece. It is the second movement of the Seventh Symphony, which to Trudy has always been, with its clever, tortured minor-key strings, the very essence of grief. Mr. Goldmann has programmed it to repeat.

He looks up and levels his knife at Trudy, who notices that his watch is exactly as she has imagined it. Plain, durable. And his large square hand is indeed thatched with silvering hair as thick as that on his head.

Is there something wrong with your food? he asks.

Trudy finishes her bite, chewing and swallowing with difficulty. The roast is in fact overcooked, so tough and stringy as to be nearly inedible.

No, not at all, she says. It's delicious.

Mr. Goldmann grunts and returns to his meal.

Then eat your dinner, he says.

Trudy does. The cutlery clinks and scrapes on the plates.

Anna and the *Obersturmführer*,
Weimar, 1943–1945

39

But Horst, where are you taking us?

Don't ask questions. Just get in.

Anna balks, refusing to relinquish the safety of the bakery's shadow for the *Obersturmführer*'s car, which idles a few meters away. She is so terrified that the blood vessels in her brain must have constricted to threads, for she sees the swastika-draped Mercedes and the grim-faced *Obersturmführer* as a two-dimensional trompe l'oeil, a trick of the eye.

But Horst—

She glances at Karl the chauffeur, who holds the door open, deaf to this unseemly little scene between his master and his master's mistress.

But Herr *Obersturmführer,* it's the middle of the day. The bakery—

The bakery is now closed. I hereby declare it closed. You're trying my patience, Anna.

But—

Get in.

Anna helps Trudie climb into the *Obersturmführer*'s car. What could Anna have done to cause offense? Has she been less than enthusiastic in bed, has she polished the *Obersturmführer*'s boots incorrectly, has Trudie irritated him, has he somehow confirmed her past feeding of the prisoners? Has he simply tired of her and found somebody else? This is not the way it is supposed to happen; people disappear at midnight, not at noon. *Nacht und Nebel.* The antennae of Anna's instincts, delicately calibrated as tripwires to anticipate any change in the *Obersturmführer*'s moods, quiver with effort but pick up nothing. His bearing is military, his face impassive.

Anna would like to pray, but as she is so long out of practice, the only words she can find are *dear God.* She shifts in her seat for a last look at the bakery. It now seems a shimmering mecca, *dear God dear God,* an oasis of everything precious, *dear God dear God please,* cracked walls and all. The car slides away.

Trudie goggles about the interior with intense curiosity. She bounces, kicking her heels against the leather.

Mama, what's this? she asks. Is it for laundry?

It is not, the *Obersturmführer* tells her gravely. It contains food, and it is a surprise for your mother.

He presents Anna with a picnic hamper, a wicker relic from another, more carefree age.

Surprise, he says. Are you surprised?

Anna closes her eyes.

You could say that, she tells him.

Happy birthday, says the *Obersturmführer.* After a moment, he remembers to grin.

Happy birthday, Mama! Is it really your birthday?

Why, yes, says Anna. I suppose so.

I thought you might enjoy a picnic, the *Obersturmführer* says.

Anna tallies the days: it is indeed the second of August. She is twenty-three years old. She manufactures a weak smile for the *Obersturmführer,* who pats her knee with a self-satisfied air. Has she ever told him when her birthday is? If so, it is a remark she made long ago, in passing. Either his memory is preternaturally keen or he has gone to some trouble to look up her birth record. Having seen him at his most vulnerable, having grown accustomed to viewing him through a lens of ridicule, Anna has gotten sloppy. She must remember always how smart he is. She must never underestimate him.

Karl drives through Weimar, negotiating potholes. Trudie is silent and round-eyed, awed by the speed of the vehicle. In all the child's three years, Anna realizes, it is her first experience of travel by car. Yet as they near the Park an der Ilm, Trudie recovers. She jumps on the seat, pressing her face to the window glass.

Mama, she says, pointing at a work detail repaving a road. Why are those funny men wearing pajamas?

Be quiet, Trudie, Anna hisses. Sit down!

She glances at the *Obersturmführer,* who has recently taken to commenting on the child's lack of discipline. He is staring straight ahead, his eyes blank with reflected light. He often falls into these peculiar trances now, and at such times he looks much as he did in the breakfast room in Berchtesgaden: his shoulders slump, his mouth sags at the corners. He is an appliance unplugged. But he comes back to life without warning and usually angry, as though suspecting he may have missed something important while gone.

Today, however, he seems calm enough; when he reanimates he merely hoists the picnic hamper and a satchel and marches into the park. Trudie scrambles after him. Anna follows the pair at a more sedate pace. Karl, the faithful mannequin, remains with the Mercedes. As soon as the *Obersturmführer*'s back is to the car, a stream of gray smoke shoots from the driver's window.

The sky is white with haze and the air smells sticky, of running sap and milkweed pods burst open to spill their seeds in the heat. The tall grasses whir with insects. Anna expects the *Obersturmführer* to seek the shade of Goethe's *Gartenhaus* or one of the pavilions, but he forges on toward the water. She exchanges a quizzical glance with the statue of Shakespeare, which the

Nazis have doused in black paint. Once upon a time the Bard would have beheld sheep grazing here in the park, but they have long since metamorphosed into stringy mutton on the dinner tables of Weimar.

The *Obersturmführer* and his flock, in contrast, dine well. The hamper, opened beneath a tree on the river's edge, reveals champagne, ham, currant jelly, sweating brown bottles of the heavy beer the *Obersturmführer* favors, sardines, pickles, bread. Anna marvels anew at the innocence of the plaid fabric, the clever pockets for cutlery and wineglasses. She has little appetite, but the *Obersturmführer* and Trudie eat with hearty appreciation. The smacking of lips and licking of fingers is accompanied by Brahms' Second Concerto, emitted from the phonograph the *Obersturmführer* has thoughtfully packed in the satchel. The record player is a portable antique from which music is coaxed by turning a crank. The proud horns of the opening movement emerge scratchily from its throat.

After the meal, the *Obersturmführer* walks stretching to the riverbank, where he sits and dangles his feet in the current. Anna pictures the black hair on them undulating underwater, an odd form of seagrass. The *Obersturmführer* turns his face toward the sun and twitches a hand in time to the Brahms. As the music swells, he sings along; he leaps up to conduct, waving his arms wildly. Trudie stares at him, mouth open. The *Obersturmführer* pretends not to see her. When the movement reaches its crescendo, he falls solemnly, face-first, into the river; he surfaces snorting and blowing like a horse. Trudie screams with laughter. The *Obersturmführer* crawls toward her. The child climbs onto his back and he carries her into the river, pawing the water and whinnying.

As she watches, Anna shreds blades of grass in her lap. On occasion, she still finds herself drifting into the solace of her simple daydream, the walk along the broad city avenue, the sojourn at the café for a cool drink beneath the trees. And during the long evening sessions with the *Obersturmführer* in Mathilde's bedroom, the fantasy has evolved: After the café, Anna and her husband push their daughter in her pram back to their hotel. Theirs is a modest room, paneled in dark wood, heavy drapes layered over curtains of lace. The girl is bathed and settled for a nap; they will rest for an hour and wake refreshed for dinner. Anna will linger by the window in her slip, shaking talcum powder onto her skin. She will gaze at the linden trees outside, the quiet street, as her husband sheds his clothes and pulls back the coverlet for sleep.

The dim little room is so real to Anna that she wonders if she stayed in a similar place as a girl, if she might once have been the child, listening to her parents going about a pre-evening routine. Either way, memory or invention, the vision has always been there for her whenever she needs it, comforting and mundane. Now, however, she realizes that the husband has at some point become the *Obersturmführer*. His face remains obscure, but she knows his grunt as he sinks into the mattress, that the clothing discarded on the room's chair includes an SS tunic, that it is his small feet that twitch against the cool sheets as he dreams.

Anna presses her fingers to her mouth. The willows weep into the grass. The *Obersturmführer* shouts and Trudie splashes and shrieks. The child flails in the river, the *Obersturmführer*'s palm balanced beneath her round stomach.

Take her out of there, please, Horst, Anna calls. She's too young to learn to swim.

Nonsense, he says. Children are born swimmers. They're like tadpoles. They learn in the womb.

As if for emphasis, he swings the child by the arms and releases her into the Ilm. She paddles wildly, spitting water.

Please! Anna says.

All right, all right.

The *Obersturmführer* wades to the bank. Come out, he orders the child. You heard your mother.

Trudie splashes into the reeds, yelling for him to catch her, but when she realizes she has lost his attention, she stands in the shallows, staring entranced at her submerged feet. Perhaps there are minnows at her toes.

The *Obersturmführer,* his white shirt transparent, stands over Anna and rubs his hands through his hair, showering droplets onto her dress.

Don't, she says.

He flops down beside her, grinning.

Why such a sour face on my birthday girl? he asks. Is it because I didn't get you a cake? I could hardly have had you bake your own, you know. It would have spoiled the surprise.

I'm quite content without cake, Anna tells him.

The *Obersturmführer* reclines, crossing his arms behind his head and squinting into the crown of the tree. Shadows dapple his face.

Listen to that, he says, that beautiful andante. I've always preferred Brahms to Bach; Bach is so mathematical...Well, there must be something else you want, then. What is it, Anna?

He plucks playfully at her skirt. Come now, don't be too shy to tell me. A diamond? Perfume, perhaps? A string of pearls for that lovely neck?

He presses a finger to the pulse in Anna's throat.

Anna swallows. During the afterlife, if there is such a thing, she will have to pay a heavy penalty for her intimacy with this man. During this life, then, she might as well try to make it count.

There is something, she murmurs.

I knew it!

Horst, she says, and puts a hand on his. It's a bit strange, but what I really want—

Tell me.

Could you— I wish you would spare the lives of twenty-three prisoners. That's not so many, is it? One for each year I've been alive.

The *Obersturmführer*'s grin widens; then he laughs. You have such a quirky sense of humor!

Anna rips at another stem of grass.

The *Obersturmführer* sits up. You're serious, he says.

Anna says nothing.

Look at this, the *Obersturmführer* says. Feel this.

He pulls Anna's hand to his right bicep. The muscles bulge beneath the skin, thick as a mature rattlesnake coiled around the bone.

You know how I became so strong? he asks. Manning the machine gun. In the *Einsatzgruppen*. Shooting Jews.

Anna wrenches her hand from him and wipes her green-stained fingers on her skirt.

Like this, the *Obersturmführer* says.

He lunges for his pistol so suddenly that Anna feels the breeze of his movement against her skin. The report of the shot makes Anna's ears ring. She covers them and screams. The *Obersturmführer* empties the chamber into the Ilm, five bullets in all. Blue smoke hangs in an acrid haze over the water.

You see? says the *Obersturmführer,* tossing his pistol onto the grass.

Anna jumps to her feet, crying her daughter's name. Trudie runs toward them and Anna stoops to catch her. He fired without even a preliminary glance; the child could be drifting lifelessly downstream—

She turns to say as much to the *Obersturmführer,* but he has gone away again. He stares blankly at the river, mouth drooping. Then he scowls.

What else can I offer you? he asks, with cold formality. Perhaps you would like me to resign? To denounce myself as a traitor? No, I have it: We could go to England. We could vacation on the white cliffs of Dover. Would that please you better, Anna?

Anna clutches Trudie to her midsection.

No, she says. No, no. This is fine, Horst. This is fine.

The *Obersturmführer* raises an eyebrow, his chest heaving. The Brahms is in its final movement, legato as a lullaby.

40

THE *OBERSTURMFÜHRER* FOUNDERS. HE SWEARS. HE SPEEDS
up in compensation, hammering away. Anna, gripping the
sheets, locks her legs around his buttocks: sometimes this en-
courages him enough to finish. Not this time. She feels him wilt-
ing. After a moment, he slips out. He slumps atop her, his breath
a gale in her ear. Then, with a sudden shove, he propels himself
from the bed.

He storms naked around the room, his flaccid penis flapping. Under other circumstances, this might be a comic sight,
but not now. Anna can barely see him in any case; the blackout
curtain he insists on pulling even in the daytime screens out
most of the light. The room is dim, stifling. No matter how
often Anna washes the bedclothes, which are now more hole
than fabric, they retain the sour yellow smell of nightmares and
copulation. She takes small sips of air through her mouth. The
odor reminds her of the juice in a jar of pickles. Her stomach
gurgles.

She knows what will come next, but she still flinches when
the *Obersturmführer* punches the wall. He has hurt himself; he

flexes his hand and shakes it, staring at it in mild indignation as though it has insulted him. Yet this doesn't stop him from pivoting to slam the same fist down on the bureau. The washbasin and pitcher shudder against one another, affrighted.

What is it? Anna asks softly.

Nothing, the *Obersturmführer* mutters.

Nothing! he yells.

But Anna knows better. This has happened before. It occurs more and more frequently as things worsen for the *Wehrmacht*. In fact, Anna has noticed a direct correlation between Nazi impotencies and the *Obersturmführer*'s personal ones. The first incident was in January, just after the bombing of the Schweinfurt ball-bearing factory. The Allied landing at Normandy spawned further inadequacy and fits of rage. In July, when France started to topple, the *Obersturmführer* was unable to perform for three full weeks. And Anna has anticipated that he would be bad today, for she has spent the last two nights huddled in the cellar with Trudie while the unlit ceiling bulb swings on its wire and cement patters from overhead. It is not the city of Weimar the Spitfires are after.

Although she knows it will make the *Obersturmführer* angrier, Anna shrinks from him as he stamps back to the bed. She has learned to dread his failings. Not only does he grow violent at such times, but he must degrade her to achieve his satisfaction, subjecting her to ever-greater perversions. Her muscles clench against the memory of outraged tissue, his brusque exploration of orifices never meant to be invaded, the humiliating sensation of fullness and the need to move her bowels.

The *Obersturmführer* throws himself onto the bed.

Let's get back to business, he says. I haven't much time.

Is it the air raid? Anna ventures. If she can only keep him talking. Did they hit the camp?

Hit! Destroyed would be a better word. The prisoners running for the forest even though it was in flames, the idiotic little trolls. And the fucking Ukrainian guards shooting every which way, hitting my own men, a bunch of hysterical schoolgirls. You'd think they'd never held a gun before. The Slavs are imbeciles, worse than the Poles. Why we don't liquidate the lot of them is beyond me.

He grabs Anna by the shoulder.

Was there much other damage? Anna persists.

The *Obersturmführer* snorts. Oh, no, not much, if you don't count the Gustloff armament works, the radio factory, the stone quarry, the political department. The records, the years of paperwork! I don't know where the bombers got their information, but it was all too fucking accurate.

Anna thinks of the rolls of film waiting in their prophylactic packaging beneath the flat rock near the quarry.

That's awful, she tells the *Obersturmführer,* making a long face. But surely you can set things to rights. You're so clever, you—

Don't be a nuisance, Anna, the *Obersturmführer* snaps. When I want sprightly conversation, I'll ask for it.

He pushes Anna's head down.

She expels a sigh of relief: so this is what it's to be. It could be worse. Mechanically she takes him into her mouth. She is dull with lack of sleep. Her vision grays out. She stands in front of the silverware drawer, unable to remember why she has opened it. When she speaks to Trudie, she often forgets what she is saying mid-sentence. And she is delirious with hunger. Last year's birthday picnic: how could she have wasted the jam, the bread, even the beer? That ham, a fat pink haunch. What she wouldn't do for even a shred of it! She wouldn't chew and swallow, heedlessly. She would wedge it into her cheek like tobacco, sucking the meat until the last of its salty flavor had gone.

The *Obersturmführer*'s hands fall to his sides. As usual, he has propped himself up against the pillows to watch, his eyes agleam in the false dusk. His face is empty; he might be waiting in a queue at the bank. His chin, a hanging bladder of fat, folds into dewlaps and wattles. He is not wanting for nourishment, not he.

Where is he getting the food, all the food, now that even the black market is defunct? And why doesn't he bring her any? Anna has a constant low-level headache. Her eye sockets throb with hunger. She is cold no matter how warm the weather. At night she runs her hands over her body, taking stock of the new concavities and protrusions. Her stomach is a depression ringed by ribs and hips and pelvic bone. The squares of sponge she once inserted before the *Obersturmführer*'s visits are no longer necessary; her flow dried up months ago. What if it never returns? Anna eyes the roll of white flesh above the *Obersturmführer*'s pubic hair with hatred.

The *Obersturmführer* is still at half-mast, sticky and malleable. Even the smell of him makes Anna's stomach growl: the bacon-smoke sweat, the damp globes loamy as mushrooms. She frees her hands to pull at him like a milkmaid, forcing him deeper into her throat. She has learned not to gag. When she does, he corrects her with a sharp rap of knuckles to the skull. She envisions pork chops. Lamb chops. Veal. One morning this week, Anna discovered the front lock forced, the bakery window shattered. The burglars found nothing, of course; there is nothing to be found. When the noncom from the camp brings her supplies, an increasingly rare event nowadays, they are of the poorest quality: scant salt, no yeast, government-issue flour wriggling with maggots. What do they think, these women Anna must turn away, their hands empty but for their useless ration booklets? Can they not see that Anna too is starving, that any bread she makes now goes to the child? Which one of them broke in?

The *Obersturmführer* groans. His eyes are closed now, his breath harsh. Good. Good. Perhaps it is almost done, then. Anna shakes her arm to relieve the cramp in her elbow and re-applies herself to her chore. She hears Trudie singing in the dooryard: *Backe backe Kuchen, der Bäcker hat gerufen...Butter und Salz, Zucker und Schmalz...* She chants this all the time. The only way Anna can keep from slapping the child is to remind herself that poor Trudie doesn't even know what sugar and lard are, let alone cake. *Milch und Mehl, und Eier machen den Kuchen gel'*. Yes, milk and eggs, Anna thinks. *Sauerbraten*. Liverwurst. Bratwurst. Rabbit. Trudie's pet, a longhaired angora that the *Obersturm-führer* brought her last month from the camp's breeding hutch, was the only thing taken during the burglary. And Anna is grateful; a few more days and she might not have been able to resist eating it herself.

The *Obersturmführer* finally begins to thrust. Anna's jaws ache from the effort of not clamping down. *Mettwurst. Bock-wurst.* Don't bite, don't bite! Her cheeks are wet with tears, her chin with spittle. She swipes it with a wrist before continuing.

A little faster, the *Obersturmführer* is saying, *Ach,* you've got me right there, right there right there —

He digs his nails into Anna's scalp and hisses.

Weisswurst, thinks Anna. Or better yet, *Blutwurst.* Ah, yes, *Blutwurst:* blood sausage.

41

OCTOBER 1944. A CRISP FALL, THE NIGHTS SEARINGLY cold. From the east and from the west, the Russians and the Americans are closing in, squeezing the *Vaterland* between them like the pincers of a gigantic crab, and Anna is watching the *Obersturmführer*. She is always watching the *Obersturmführer*, whenever he is in close proximity, and when he is not, she thinks of him incessantly. She is as helpless to stop analyzing his every word, nuance, flick of the wrist, as a schoolgirl with her first crush. It is part survival tactic, of course; the more Anna knows about him and how he perceives her, the safer she will be. Yet she would like to take a circular saw to the top of her skull, scoop out her brains, and hurl them against the wall.

She has been his mistress for two and a half years now, longer than her friendship with Mathilde, more than twice the time she was allotted with Max, and in some ways Anna knows the *Obersturmführer* better than she has ever known anyone. She knows his vanity: how fanatic he is about his boots, his uniform; how he curries his dark hair with Mathilde's brushes while practicing his smile in the mirror over the bedroom bureau. She knows that his appearance is crucial to him because his immaculate facade has carried him further than any true leadership ability. She knows that he doesn't see himself as monstrous, that were he to be called before the Throne of Judgment to account for his infinite misdeeds, he would be honestly perplexed. To the *Obersturmführer,* his murderous work is merely a job, taxing at times but affording power and advancement. Not that he considers the issue much. When faced with self-reflection he shrugs his shoulders, giving it up as being too difficult a task altogether.

Yet in other aspects the *Obersturmführer* is an enigma to Anna, a study in contradictions. For instance, his zealous adherence to the twisted principles of *Partei* purity: a sham. He is married, as all top-echelon SS must be, and yet he keeps her, Anna, and seems to care for her. Or does he? This is what Anna puzzles over as she watches him, trying to slot the disparate pieces of him into place. Is she cherished or a convenience? Would the *Obersturmführer* put a foot on her neck and shoot her in the head if she gave enough cause for offense? Will he do this anyway, when the end comes? Anna tries to envision herself from the *Obersturmführer's* height, from behind the cage of bone and pale windows through which he surveys the world. Perhaps, confronted with the matter of his own survival, the imperative of not leaving any evidence for the advancing armies, the *Obersturmführer* could quench his fondness for Anna as easily as turning off a faucet.

Tonight, All Hallows' Eve, Anna is watching the *Obersturmführer* from across the table in the bakery kitchen, at which she and he and Trudie are having dinner. These are, perhaps, more humble surroundings than the ones in which the *Obersturmführer* is used to dining, but Anna has tried to make it as nice as possible by spreading a sheet over the floury wooden boards in lieu of a lace cloth, using blackout candles as a centerpiece. She has done all of this to show her appreciation of the food the *Obersturmführer* has provided in response to her pleas that she and the child are virtually starving. And Anna is genuinely grateful for the venison, more gristle than meat but substantial enough to bring tears to her eyes; for the potatoes, the beetroot she has boiled and sliced into a dish, the lentils and—a marvel—the handful of desiccated peas.

Her appetite finally satisfied, Anna tries to shake off the stupor of unaccustomed satiation to resume observing the *Obersturmführer*. Despite being twice her size, he has eaten somewhat less than she; he has actually left a few small potatoes on his plate. His uniform jacket hanging on a peg near the door, he sits with his shirtsleeves rolled to his elbows, tipping his chair back on two legs and conversing with the child. He and Trudie are spinning a tale between them, some fable that seems to involve a family of rabbits living in a nearby *Trog*. The *Obersturmführer* nods quite seriously as Trudie chatters on, interrupting her only to insert the occasional question, and Anna imagines what the three of them would look like to somebody peering in from outside: a happy little family—indeed, happier than most in these times, given the unusual presence of the patriarch—enjoying the end of a meal.

…But you have left the father rabbit out entirely, the *Obersturmführer* is saying. And that will never do. What is his name?

Guess, says Trudie.

Ach, I am not smart enough. You'll have to tell me.

No, guess, you have to guess, the child insists.

Peder.

No.

Dieter, says the *Obersturmführer*.

Trudie whips her head from side to side, braids flying.

The *Obersturmführer* throws out his hands.

I give up, he says. What is it?

Horst! Trudie shouts.

She giggles wildly as the *Obersturmführer*'s chair thumps to the floor.

Horst? he says, feigning great astonishment.

Yes, yells Trudie; yes, yes, your name, what Mama calls you!

She squeals and squirms as the *Obersturmführer* plucks her from her chair and slings her over his shoulder in much the same way he carried the side of venison in earlier.

That's very clever, he tells her, very clever indeed. And do you know what becomes of clever little girls who steal other people's names?

No, what?

They must go straight to bed, says the *Obersturmführer*.

Nooooooooooo, Trudie cries. Please, let me stay up just a few minutes longer, I'll be good, please —

The *Obersturmführer* dumps her unceremoniously on her feet.

That's enough. It's late. You'll go to sleep so fast you won't know what happened.

He swats Trudie's rump and turns.

Anna, he says.

Anna rises and takes Trudie by the hand.

Can I have a story? the girl begs.

You have already had one, Anna tells her. Come along now.

The *Obersturmführer* stretches mightily, canvassing the table, and releases a belch.

You may leave the dishes, he says to Anna, sotto voce, as she passes. I will be upstairs.

Anna lingers as long as she can putting Trudie to bed, washing the child's face and unbraiding and brushing her hair, checking beneath her nails for dirt and even behind her ears, but eventually Trudie is settled yawning on her basement cot and there is nothing more to be done. Anna brushes her lips over Trudie's forehead before pulling the string that turns off the light.

That's right, little rabbit, she says. Go to sleep.

Then, her stomach heavy with food and dread, Anna walks slowly up the two flights to Mathilde's room. The *Obersturmführer* is standing by the window, although there is nothing to see as he has drawn the blackout shade. He has also lit the flame under the kerosene lamp on the nightstand.

He says nothing but turns his head to stare at Anna, which she takes as her cue to undress. When she is naked she lies down, teeth chattering. She has not kindled the fire in the WC stove, and the heat from the kitchen has done nothing to warm this room. Her breath is visible in the frosty air.

She waits, but the *Obersturmführer* remains silent, merely watching her over one shoulder, so Anna reaches for the threadbare blanket near the footboard.

Don't, the *Obersturmführer* says.

He turns to face her, and Anna sees that his fly is unbuttoned. She glimpses a tuft of dark hair through the slit of his briefs, the sadly hanging flesh. He has been handling himself, to no avail.

As if unaware of the potential embarrassment of this, the *Obersturmführer* walks casually to the bed. He stands by Anna's side, looking down at her.

Did you get enough to eat? he asks.

Anna nods.

Are you sure? No more complaints?

Anna shakes her head.

Good, says the *Obersturmführer*. Very good. For I should hate to think I was failing you in some way, Anna.

He starts to remove his belt and pauses. He takes his pistol from its holster and holds it thoughtfully in his hand.

Then he begins to trace Anna's ribs with it. The muzzle bumps down the bones one by one as though he is playing a xylophone.

You *are* quite thin, he comments. I suppose that is why you also complain of the cold; you have too little fat…Are you cold, Anna?

Anna keeps her eyes fixed on his. His expression is polite, concerned. He is at his most dangerous when he is like this. She shakes her head again.

The *Obersturmführer* smiles, his eyes crinkling at the corners.

You must not lie to me, he says. I can tell you are.

He trails the Luger up Anna's arms, across her breastbone, around her nipples, beneath the curve of her breasts, over her belly. The metal leaves gooseflesh in its wake.

You see? says the *Obersturmführer,* bending to blow on the tiny bumps. You *are* cold. But I will forgive you the lie. I know you said it only to please me. Didn't you?

The pistol pauses at the top of Anna's thighs, nuzzling, moving back and forth, a cat's tail switching.

You are so unlike any other woman I have ever known in this respect, adds the *Obersturmführer.* Always. Wanting. Only. To please. Me.

His tone is dreamy, distracted. He is for once not looking at Anna's face. Instead he gazes at the Luger, which with each word he is wedging further between her legs. Anna feels nothing. She has come untethered from herself now, so separate that she is unable to summon any of her usual comforting fantasies. She floats above the bed like a bride in a painting she once saw, long since classified as the degenerate work of a Jew: Chagall, the artist's name was.

And I know what pleases you, the *Obersturmführer* continues, still sounding as though he is speaking to himself. This. This. There. You like that, do you? No, don't answer. I can tell you do. I'm going to keep using it until you come. And don't fake it, either. You know I can tell when you do.

A few minutes pass in complete silence but for the *Obersturmführer*'s increasingly labored breathing and the quicker rhythm of Anna's own.

There, he says, working at her with his free hand. There. There—

At the moment of climax he pulls the trigger.

Bang! he says.

Anna gives a small shriek and lies shuddering, staring at the ceiling.

The *Obersturmführer* slips the pistol from her and tosses it across the room. He climbs onto the bed to kneel above Anna.

Bang, he repeats, this time cocking a thumb and forefinger in imitation of the gun. He bends over Anna and studies her. Then he throws his head back and roars with laughter.

Your face, he gasps, when he is capable of speech. The look on your face!

He wipes tears from his eyes. Did you really think it was loaded? You really did, didn't you? My poor silly girl.

And somehow this or Anna's expression or the business with the pistol or a combination of the factors must have excited him, for the *Obersturmführer* is now at the ready. He becomes abruptly solemn and scrabbles to yank his trousers down.

I would never—, he says, pushing into Anna, —never use— a loaded gun— with you— of all people— the way— you go off— like a pistol— yourself— three, four times— in a row— like a rocket. It makes— a man— feel— like a god. If only Eisele knew— that smug— prick— with— all his bragging— about enforced— impotence— if he only knew— about you— Anna— he'd know— something— much! more! important!—

The *Obersturmführer* shouts and pulls Anna's hair. He falls forward, panting. When he has regained his breath, he clambers off her and reaches for his trousers.

You are my cure, he mutters, you have cured me...*Ach,* what's this?

Something has fallen with a clatter from his pocket. The *Obersturmführer* comes back to the bed and presses it into Anna's stomach, and she hisses in a breath: whatever it is, it is made of metal, and cold.

I have been meaning to give this to you for months now, says the *Obersturmführer.* Stupid of me to have forgotten.

He retrieves his Luger from the corner and walks to the door.

I suppose I am growing forgetful in my old age, eh, Anna? he adds, and laughs as he leaves, high good humor restored.

When she hears him clanking plates about in the kitchen, his appetite postcoitally stimulated, Anna sits up gingerly, wincing and sore. She examines the sheet beneath her, streaked with oil from the *Obersturmführer*'s pistol. She will boil and scrub, wring and scour, but she suspects nothing will get it out, not lye nor salt nor bleach. No household manual, no exchange of feminine wisdom, has prepared her to vanquish this kind of stain.

From the thin torn cotton, Anna picks up the object the *Obersturmführer* has left on her belly and turns it over in her hands. It is a small gold case with the symbol of the Reich on its cover, the sort of container that might hold cigarettes. But when Anna opens it, she finds instead a photograph, a portrait of herself and Trudie and the *Obersturmführer*. Taken, Anna recalls now, during her surprise twenty-third birthday expedition, in the Park an der Ilm. After they had eaten and returned to the Mercedes.

Still naked, shivering convulsively, Anna huddles over the photograph. She brings it close to her eyes, squinting in the weak light of the kerosene lamp. In the portrait the *Obersturmführer* is standing behind her as she sits with the child in her lap, his hand on Anna's shoulder. Is this pose casual? Possessive? Proud? The brim of his cap hides his face so that she cannot read it.

What does it mean, this gift? Does the *Obersturmführer* truly care for her after all? Or is it merely a bauble, the sort of thing he might give to any girl he had taken as a mistress? His cure; he has said Anna is his cure. He has said he will never harm her. Or has he? Anna tries to remember his monologue of a few minutes earlier. No; he has said he would never use a loaded gun on her. A different matter entirely. He has made no promises, and Anna is no better off; she is no closer to understanding him than she was when he arrived for dinner nor even a few months before.

Pulling a blanket around her shoulders, Anna hobbles painfully to the bureau, on which she sets the case — propped open in the event that the *Obersturmführer* should return to the room. She stares at his image. Does she exist for him at all outside of bed? away from the bakery? The stiff little uniformed figure tells her nothing. Perhaps, Anna thinks, if one were able to open the *Obersturmführer* the same way one can this hinged frame in which his likeness is contained, undoing a latch to swing his face aside, one would find only a dark space. Nothing behind it. Nothing at all.

42

WERE MATHILDE STILL ALIVE, SHE WOULD BE AGHAST over the condition of her beloved bakery. The lathing is exposed where plaster has fallen from the walls during the air raids, the shattered window covered with the boards of a dismantled crate. The portrait of the *Führer* that the *Obersturmführer* brought for Anna to hang behind the register has likewise suffered: a diagonal crack in the glass bisects the leader's face, so that he appears to be looking in two directions at once. The pages of the calendar have long since been conscripted for service as toilet paper, the beginning of 1945 swirling down the pipes of the WC.

The refugees are in worse shape than their temporary haven. When the cellar and the kitchen are occupied, they sleep on the floor in their threadbare coats amid puddles of snowmelt, filling the bakery with the stench of wet wool and unwashed bodies. Anna spends her days catering to the visitors and keeping Trudie from them. At first it is a relief to have the girl entertained; an elderly gentleman, a former schoolmaster, begins teaching Trudie her ABC's. But one afternoon Trudie does not respond when called, and a frantic search finds her halfway down the road, struggling in the clutches of a woman who screams, She's mine! You stole her from me! and fights with the strength of dementia when Anna pries Trudie away. The refugees from Dresden are the worst, however, with their staring eyes and hair burned in piebald patches. Sometimes Anna sweeps up the shreds of themselves they have left like discarded snakeskins on the floor.

Yet Anna is grateful for this miserable company. These people know nothing about her; they don't sneer or dart fearful looks in her direction; they view her solely as a source of bread, bandaging, or shelter. Anna much prefers the role of hostess to that of the *Obersturmführer*'s whore. She misses the refugees when the *Obersturmführer* appears and orders them out, sending them into the frigid February nights. He hates to seem hardhearted, he explains to Anna, but he simply cannot relax amid such chaos. He prefers the company of his little adopted family.

Anna stands in the storefront one evening, sorting the refugees' goods into piles. It is astonishing, what they have been willing to trade for accommodation. The display case and the floor are heaped with offerings. All gold jewelry is stashed in one of the *Obersturmführer*'s trunks. Another is reserved for silver. Into a *Wehrmacht* footlocker go miscellaneous items of value, such as pots, pans, furs, and the occasional Oriental rug. The *Obersturmführer* has unsentimentally requested that Anna remove photographs from their valuable frames, but he hasn't ordered her to dispose of them. Sometimes, when sleep evades her, Anna squanders a candle in order to flip through the couples posing stiffly on their wedding day, the groupings of children, the spinster with her cat on her lap.

What about this? she asks now, holding up a tapestry for the *Obersturmführer*'s inspection. The brocade looks like gold, but I can't tell in this light.

He shrugs. Use your best judgment, he says. He is distracted by Trudie, whom he is teaching to march.

Hup-one, he says. Hup-two. Hup-two-three-four.

Anna runs her fingers over the material. It glitters even in the stingy light shed by the hurricane lantern the *Obersturmführer* has bought from the camp. She folds the cloth and places it in the footlocker atop a length of silk, in which she has wrapped a crystal decanter. The *Obersturmführer* is partial to crystal. Again Anna wonders what he does with these spoils. What good are they when the only true currency is the food that is in such short supply? One can't eat heirlooms, after all.

Hup, hup, hup, the *Obersturmführer* says to Trudie. Now turn. No, not like that. Here, watch.

He marches across the room, his boots thudding on the floor. He pivots, goose-steps back to Trudie, and clicks his heels.

Heil Hitler! he says, saluting.

Heil Hitler, says the girl, mimicking the gesture.

The *Obersturmführer* bends to touch her nose with a finger. Very good, he says. Now you do it.

Hup, hup, hup, says Trudie, stamping around the bakery. Despite the lack of rations, she continues to grow rapidly; her legs, as skinny as her father's, look like those of a stork.

Watching her, Anna is reminded of the sorcerer and his apprentice. She can't abide this game any longer.

Do you know, Horst, people will trade the strangest things for food, she says loudly. Just this week a woman tried to give me her pet schnauzer. What did she think I would do with it?

She laughs. I could always have eaten it, I suppose.

Her gambit doesn't work. The *Obersturmführer* is not listening.

Lift your feet, he commands. Bend your arm at the elbow. Hup! Hup! Hup!

Trudie shuttles back and forth in front of the *Obersturmführer*. That's better, he says, that's much better; there's a good little soldier.

Clapping, he bursts into the Horst Wessel song:

> *Raise high the flags!*
> *Stand rank on rank together.*
> *Storm troopers march with quiet, steady tread.*
> *Millions, full of hope, look toward the swastika;*
> *The day breaks for freedom and for bread.*

I think that's enough for one evening, Anna calls. It's past the child's bedtime.

But the *Obersturmführer* is truly carried away now. He taps time with a foot, singing in his faulty baritone. His voice cracks; his face contorts as though he is suppressing gas, and Anna sees to her amazement that he is about to cry. His colorless eyes brim with tears.

> *Raise high the knife!*
> *Sharpen the blade to cut the Jewish flesh.*
> *Jewish blood will run in the gutters;*
> *On every corner the Hitler flag will flutter—*

Horst, Anna says, I really don't think—

The *Obersturmführer* rounds on her.

WILL you be quiet! he roars. WILL you for once in your Godforsaken life just! shut! up!

Trudie, shocked into sudden immobility, stares at him and then begins to howl.

Stop that! the *Obersturmführer* screams.

He raises a hand and clouts the girl across the face. She goes spinning to the floor. The *Obersturmführer* rakes the same hand through his hair and paces, muttering.

Anna pushes past him and drops to her knees beside her daughter. Trudie is silent, and Anna is certain that the *Obersturmführer* has snapped the fragile little neck. But then the girl sucks air into her lungs and lets it out in a wail. Anna gathers her onto her lap and rocks her.

And shut that brat up, the *Obersturmführer* shouts from above. Wheeling, he sweeps an arm across the display case. Anna huddles over Trudie, trying to shield her from the shower of jewelry and silverware and candlesticks and china.

Jesus Christ, she's worse than an air-raid siren, the *Obersturm-führer* rants. Of all the spoiled— disobedient— What does a man have to do nowadays for some peace and quiet? Just a second's worth of order!

Shhh, Anna says to Trudie, cupping the girl's face to feel for damage. One cheek is already puffy, blood welling from a cut in-flicted by the *Obersturmführer*'s death's-head ring. But he doesn't seem to have broken any bones, and the teeth are still intact. Shhh. Be quiet now.

Trudie tries to swallow her sobs. The *Obersturmführer*'s boots pass back and forth a few centimeters from Anna's nose. Glass crunches and grinds beneath them. A young bride, still in her frame, smiles at Anna from the shards.

Things fall apart, Anna thinks, remembering a poem Max once read to her; the center cannot hold. She is unaware that she has uttered the words aloud until the *Obersturmführer* lunges at her.

What? he says. He grabs the braided coil at the back of her neck and yanks Anna to her feet. What did you say? Why did you say that?

Anna cries out. She bats at his hands; an ounce more pres-sure and her hair will come out by the roots.

Nothing, she gasps, it was nothing, a foolish poem, it doesn't mean anything!

The *Obersturmführer*'s grip slackens somewhat, but he keeps a firm hold on the braid while he draws his pistol from its hol-ster. He tries to fumble the safety catch off. This is an awkward maneuver one-handed; he nearly drops the revolver; he swears.

For all our sakes, he is saying, maybe it would be cleaner, bet-ter, the best solution for all of us if I—

Time slows to the sludgy pace of dream. Over the roar in her ears, Anna hears the click of the safety being drawn back. She won't make it easy for him, she will put up a fight, she will bite his arm as hard as she can—

But then the *Obersturmführer* drops her hair. He gazes bewildered around the bakery. His mouth hangs down as though he has suffered a stroke. He is once again unplugged.

No, he says. It may be all right. It may still come all right.

Anna shuts her eyes.

Of course it will, she whispers, and touches his sleeve.

The *Obersturmführer* looks down at her hand, his lips thinning in disgust.

Clean this place up, he snaps, sliding his pistol back into its holster. He straightens his uniform tunic and yanks his greatcoat on. In the glare of the lamp, his shadow bulks to monstrous proportions on the wall. It's a disgrace. You're a disgrace. I've had it with the pair of you. Puling, whining, ungrateful! I've half a mind not to come back at all.

Please, Anna says, though she is not sure what she is begging for. Part of her rejoices, exulting, Good riddance, thank God! But if the *Obersturmführer* abandons them, she and Trudie will have no choice but to join the ranks of the dispossessed.

Please, Horst, don't go away angry—

He casts a pallid glance in her direction. The door slams behind him.

Anna looks about for Trudie, who is standing in the corner, her thumb in her mouth.

Come, little rabbit, Anna says. Hop upstairs and get ready for bed. I'll be up in a minute with some ice for your face; won't that feel good?

The girl gives no indication that she has heard. Anna reaches for her shoulders to turn her around. Trudie flinches from her touch.

I'm sorry, Anna whispers. I'm sorry, little one.

Trudie slips away from her and walks toward the staircase.

Anna watches her go. Then she kneels to salvage what she can from the debris of the *Obersturmführer*'s tantrum, raking the stuff into a pile. Her uncoiled braid swings over one shoulder like a hangman's rope; her scalp smarts; the tine of a fork pierces her forefinger. Anna rocks back on her heels, sucking the wounded finger. She relishes the salt of her own blood. She has not eaten in two days.

What is to become of us? she asks aloud.

As if in response, there is a rap on the door. Anna gets to her feet to answer it. Then she bends and rummages through the refugees' plunder until she finds a brass candlestick, big enough to have adorned a cathedral's altar. Perhaps it once did. She conceals this in the folds of her skirt as she lifts the latch. She has not endured the indignities of the past three years to die at the *Obersturmführer*'s hands. If she opens the door to find the cold circle of his pistol's muzzle pressed against her forehead, she will bash his head in. Though maybe he is returning to apologize, to give her another chance?

He is not: when Anna opens the door, holding the candlestick in a death grip, she hears only a timid voice. Begging Anna's pardon, it says, they are sorry to disturb her at this hour, but can she spare any food for a mother and her four starving children? Or, lacking that, a room for the night…

43

As March 1945 goes out like a lion, the remaining townsfolk of Weimar resign themselves to meeting their enemy face-to-face. We're finished, they whisper; everything is lost, the end will come any day now. The American infantry, it is said, has seized control of cities as close as Eisenach and Ehrfurt, ransacking and burning the houses, raping the women, worse than the Russians. German citizens have been forbidden to leave their homes. The percussive rumble of artillery shakes more plaster from the bakery ceilings. The SS, wall-eyed and jittery, march columns of prisoners through the streets, bound for the train station. But Anna would have known without these harbingers that things are crumbling around the edges. She hasn't seen the *Obersturmführer,* her personal wartime barometer, for a month and a half.

Yet even Anna doesn't suspect how near the end is until the first of April, which also happens to be Easter Sunday, falling abnormally early this year to coincide with the Day of Fools. Anna finds this appropriate. She has little patience with people who still believe in the possibility of resurrection. She is mopping the floor of the bakery, the first chance she has had to do so since the last sad handful of refugees, when she hears the drone of engines overhead.

Trudie, run to the cellar, Anna calls, swabbing another clean arc on the cement. She isn't overly concerned; she has learned to distinguish the sound of light reconnaissance aircraft from the heavier throb of bombers, and these sound like spy planes. The attacks have become a regular occurrence, the days and nights turned topsy-turvy by the wail of air-raid sirens: Air raid, all clear. Air raid, all clear. Anna listens for the clip-clop of Trudie's soles, indicating that the girl has obeyed her. Satisfied, she bends to wring the mop into the pail. Then she straightens, dripping dirty water onto the floor. Something is wrong. The sirens have not sounded at all.

Anna is approaching the door to see what is happening when it flies open, nearly knocking her backward. One of her former customers, Frau Hochmeier, charges into the bakery. She is wearing an absurd hat, no doubt for the Easter service, its bunch of silk violets askew and dangling.

Frau Hochmeier bends double, catching her breath, and then shakes a piece of paper in Anna's face.

What is this? she screams. These messages from the sky, what do they mean?

Anna takes the leaflet from the woman and flattens it on the display case. Her command of English, learned so long ago in *Gymnasium,* is shaky at best. But she can decipher the basic meaning of the words, and when she flips the paper over, she finds a German translation. Scholarly fellows, these Americans.

Citizens of Thuringia, Anna reads aloud. Due to atrocities perpetuated at concentration camp Buchenwald and by the Nazi regime in general, hostilities are imminent in your area. Be prepared to surrender peacefully to the Army of the United States of America.

Frau Hochmeier stares.

Is that all? she asks.

Anna folds the paper. Somewhere nearby, gunfire rattles like popping corn. The announcement of imminent hostilities, Anna thinks, is a bit belated.

Yes, she answers. That's all it says.

Frau Hochmeier nods stoically. Then she shrieks, We're done for! They're going to kill us, they'll shoot every last one of us!

Anna has never been fond of Frau Hochmeier, who in recent years is one of those who has leveled at Anna the flat stare of condemnation, as though Anna were the bearer of contagious immorality. But at the moment Anna feels some pity for her. Deeply religious, once pretty, the woman now looks mad, the sleepless nights carved in creases on her face. Then again, they all look different now.

Get hold of yourself, Anna tells her, voice low. My daughter is downstairs.

But what should we do, Anna? Frau Hochmeier asks. What will you do?

Anna shrugs. Wait, I suppose, she replies. What else is there?

Frau Hochmeier backs away.

I'm going to run, she says. I'd run if I were you. Especially if I were you.

When she has gone, Anna bolts the door and draws the blackout curtains. After a moment's thought, she carries a chair in from the kitchen and props it under the knob. Then, surveying these flimsy precautions, Anna laughs at herself: she is behaving like an idiot, like Frau Hochmeier. If the Americans want to come in, they will come in. And it is useless to run from them, for there is nowhere to go.

But the waiting is a strain on the nerves, for there is nothing to be done in the meantime. By midafternoon, Anna finds herself with no way to occupy the hours. The bakery is clean, the child napping in the cellar next to the sole remaining refugee, a manicurist from Wiesbaden with a convulsive cough. The woman has assured Anna that her throat is irritated from smoke inhaled during a bombing, that she doesn't have the highly infectious typhoid or pneumonia. Anna isn't convinced that her guest is telling the truth, but her proximity to the child can't be helped. Trudie needs her rest; she has adopted a silent, unblinking stare that Anna doesn't much like the looks of, and aside from the hiding space Anna has outfitted for the girl in one of the kitchen cupboards for when the enemy tanks arrive, the cellar is the safest place for Trudie to be.

Anna has resorted to distracting herself by making tea, coaxing it from sodden leaves already steeped three times, when a knock on the door startles her into dropping the pot. She upbraids herself as she stoops to gather the pieces: stupid Anna, to be so jumpy over the arrival of another refugee! Or perhaps it is a *Wehrmacht* deserter, one of the boys, pitifully young, who creep shamefaced from the Ettersberg forest to beg from Anna anything she can spare them: salt-and-flour soup, a crust of bread. Whoever her visitor is, he is a persistent fellow. The knob beneath the bolt swivels back and forth. Anna takes a rolling pin to the door with her, hoping she will not be forced to use it.

Coming, coming, she calls.

When she sees that her impatient guest is the *Obersturmführer,* Anna utters an exasperated *pfft!* and turns her back. Fetching the broom, she begins sweeping up the smaller fragments of china.

I thought you'd abandoned us, she says. Do you have any food? Anything—flour, lentils?

No, says the *Obersturmführer.* Stop that now. I haven't time to watch you do your housework.

Anna hurls the shards into the rubbish bin.

But I suppose you have time to go upstairs, she says, in a shaking, scolding tone. Oh yes, there's always time for that. Well, I've news for you: you'll have to carry me. I haven't the energy to climb the steps. Do you know how long it's been since I've eaten? Do you? The whole city is under siege, we're starving and terrified, while you sit up there safe as a king, gorging yourself on— on God knows what— you—

When you've finished your tantrum, Anna, the *Obersturm-führer* interrupts, perhaps you'd be so kind as to listen to what I've come to say?

His overly courteous tone, his use of the formal *Sie,* frightens Anna into composure. She grips the lip of the sink until her knuckles are as white as the porcelain. Then she looks at him as if to say, Go on, and what she sees startles her further: the *Obersturmführer* is in civilian clothes. He wears patched trousers and an ill-fitting jacket, the garb of a peddler or dockworker. His jowls are blue with stubble. For a moment Anna is amused by this pathetic dirty costume, this affront to his vanity. How it must gall him! Then her attention is riveted by a brown stain on his shirt. It looks like sauce of some sort, gravy or mustard. She longs to lick it.

It is nearly over now, the *Obersturmführer* tells her. Pister has given orders that the camp be completely evacuated. Once this is done, it will be destroyed...

He snaps his fingers beneath Anna's nose. Are you listening, Anna? Pay attention.

Anna arranges her features into an expression of polite inquiry.

I am meant to travel south with the other deputies, to ensure that the largest shipment arrives at KZ Dachau, the *Obersturm-führer* continues. They have bigger containment facilities there. We're scheduled to leave tomorrow, before dawn.

But what about us, Anna starts to protest, myself, the child —

The *Obersturmführer* makes a silencing slash with a forefinger. However, I have decided to leave sooner, he says. Now, in fact. And instead of going to Dachau, I will travel to Munich and from there to Portugal, where I will board a ship for Argentina.

Anna's gaze returns to the sauce on his shirt. Argentina. The very concept is as remote to her as the schoolroom in which she once studied it.

You're thinking me a coward, the *Obersturmführer* says peevishly. But there's no good in hanging on, Anna. The war is lost, our cause in ruins. You were right when you said things fall apart, and in such situations, it's every man for himself, no?

The *Obersturmführer* pauses for her response. Receiving none, he continues, You will come with me, traveling as my wife. I already have the documents.

He pats the breast pocket of his threadbare jacket. After a moment, he produces a semblance of his former grin.

But there is one other matter, he says. We can't take the girl.

Anna's head snaps up.

What are you talking about?

I couldn't get papers for her. But it's impossible in any case. Use your brain, Anna! We have to be careful. There are borders to cross, there will be questions; she would give us away. I've arranged for her to be transferred into the *Lebensborn* program in Munich. The fellow in charge there is an old friend who owes me a favor. He'll watch out for her. She'll be perfectly safe.

They lock glances, Anna's disbelieving, the *Obersturmführer*'s beseeching. The kitchen is silent but for the tick of rain, the manicurist's cough, a distant rumble that might be thunder or the thud of artillery.

We haven't time to dawdle, the *Obersturmführer* says, taking Anna's silence for agreement. You've a few minutes to pack. One small bag for each of you—

No, Anna says.

What?

No.

I admit it's not an ideal solution, Anna. But she'll be safer than if both of you stay here.

No, I said.

The *Obersturmführer* advances toward her and Anna backs away, wincing in anticipation of a blow. But he kneels at her feet, taking her hands in a grotesque parody of proposal.

Be reasonable, he pleads. What will you do when the Americans get here? It will happen any moment now, I promise you. Do you know what Americans do to children? They drive their tanks over them, run them through with bayonets. I know, I've seen the reports firsthand. Come now, go upstairs and pack—

No, Anna shouts. No, no!

She slaps him. He makes no effort to protect himself other than lowering his head. Anna rains blows on it, pounding his skull with her fists. She grips his dark hair, coarse as steel wool, and pulls with all her might.

The *Obersturmführer* clasps Anna about the waist. She can feel his face working, hot and wet, through her dress. She beats at his head, trying to push it away. He endures it.

After a time, Anna stops as suddenly as she began, simply running out of strength. She stands with her eyes shut, swaying in the *Obersturmführer*'s embrace, her hands resting on his hair.

Slowly, the *Obersturmführer* withdraws his arms and rises to his feet. Sweat runnels down his face from temples to jaw.

For the final time, he says, are you coming with me or not.

Anna shakes her head: no.

After all I've done for you, the *Obersturmführer* says. After all the gifts I brought you and the child. I fed you; I protected you when I should have shot you the first moment I saw you. I should have finished you off long ago—

He pats his hip, where his holster usually rests; not finding it, he yanks his shirt from his waistband.

Perhaps I should do it now, he says.

Go ahead then, Anna shouts. Go on.

But they both know the *Obersturmführer* is bluffing. His hand trembles so badly that he can't extract the weapon from beneath his belt. He lets the shirt fall over the hairy bulge of his stomach, hiding the small scimitar of a scar resulting from a childhood dog bite, this flesh more familiar to Anna than her own.

I thought I knew you, the *Obersturmführer* says. I even loved you. Now I find that I don't know you at all.

But I know you, Anna tells him. I've always known you for exactly what you are.

The *Obersturmführer* gazes at Anna for some time with his

ghostly eyes. Then he clicks his heels, executes a military turn, and walks to the door. En route, he stumbles over his own small feet, pitching forward. It is the first and only time Anna will see the *Obersturmführer* wearing civilian shoes.

He catches himself on the jamb.

Very well, he says. So be it. I wish you luck. You'll need it, I assure you.

He opens the door and pauses, his hand on the knob.

But we would have had a good life together, he adds. I would have provided handsomely for you, you know.

Anna stands watching him grow smaller through the fly-specked window over the sink. The evening is green and watery, the trees dripping condensation on the *Obersturmführer*'s bare head. As he climbs into a truck much like the delivery van, he stops and looks at the bakery for a long moment. Then he starts the engine and drives away.

Trudy, March 1997

44

EVER SINCE THE BEGINNING OF MARCH, ANNA HAS BEEN acting strangely, although Trudy doesn't notice it at first. It is only in retrospect that she realizes her mother's walks around the lake are growing longer; that Anna returns somewhat disheveled, her hair mussed from her plastic rain scarf and with a blank staring look about the eyes; that she cleans the house obsessively and with astonishing thoroughness: beating the rugs, scrubbing the walls with watered-down Clorox, endlessly washing the sheets and—as she disdains Trudy's dryer but lacks a clothesline in the yard—hanging them from her bedroom window like flags of surrender. It is true that Trudy is a bit taken aback by Anna's ferocity, but she shrugs it off as spring cleaning, to which Anna annually subjected the farmhouse as well. At least Anna is keeping busy.

But then toward the end of the month, as Easter decorations appear in the neighbors' windows and crocuses thrust purple heads through dirty crusts of snow, Anna begins to bake.

She bakes in earnest and with a vengeance, starting early in the morning before it is light and continuing until well after dark. She bakes with fierce and silent concentration. She bakes as if being forced to do so at gunpoint, as if her life depends upon how much she produces, and she begins with bread. Black bread, white bread, marble bread, rye; loaf after loaf pulled from the oven and set to cool on the counters, the table, the windowsills. Trays of dinner rolls. Batches of *Brötchen,* enough to feed an army. And then the pastries start. *Eissplittertorte* and *Erdbeertorte,* ice-chip and strawberry tarts. *Honigkuchen, Käsekuchen, Napfkuchen, Pflaumenkuchen*: honey, sweet cheese, pound, and plum, respectively. Buttercream cake. *Windbeutel*—cream horns. They flow from the kitchen as if on an assembly line, so quickly overwhelming the refrigerator and cupboards that Trudy takes to leaving them wrapped on her neighbors' doorsteps in the middle of the night. Yet the floury Anna continues to bustle about the kitchen, bits of dough stuck to her cheeks and crusted in her hair. She shows no sign of stopping. And Trudy, dizzy from sugar and a nonsense jingle she cannot get out of her head—*Backe backe Kuchen! der Bäcker hat gerufen. Backe backe Kuchen! der Bäcker hat gerufen*—starts to wonder if Anna's ulterior motive isn't really to drive her from the house. Or to drive her mad.

She complains as much to Rainer one night in his dining room, where they are lingering over Anna's latest confection, a *Kirschentorte.* They have already decimated a chicken dinner purchased—at Trudy's suggestion, since she recalls all too well the tough roast of her first night here—from the Lunds on Fiftieth Street. This was a meal Trudy was more than ready for, as prior to it she and Rainer walked three times around Lake Harriet. Rainer insists upon these bracing constitutionals: Human beings are animals, after all, he booms over Trudy's objections, and to deny oneself exercise is to ignore a basic need. So while he forges stolidly ahead, she scurries after him on the sleety paths, breathless and panting and keeping his fedora in her line of sight as a focal point. It is a shame, she thinks, that more men don't wear hats these days.

Now Rainer reaches for the decanter of Grand Marnier and poises its lip over Trudy's tumbler.

No thanks, Trudy says.

Rainer refills her glass and helps himself to a second slice of torte.

Perhaps you are overreacting, he says, returning to the subject at hand; perhaps your mother simply likes to bake.

Well, yes, she does...Trudy huddles in her chair. But this is different. It has a—a frantic quality, as if she's preparing for a disaster. She's clearly disturbed by something.

Rainer shrugs.

If that is the case, you should let her alone. The activity is no doubt soothing to her. She is coping with her troubles in the Old World way, denial and physical labor; would you rather she vegetate in her room, as so many elderly do?

No, says Trudy.

There you are.

But—

At least we are being well fed as a result, Rainer says.

He attacks his dessert, savaging the pastry with a fork. Trudy looks down at her own. Cherry filling pools beneath the crust like clotting blood. Trudy closes her eyes and focuses instead on the music Rainer has selected: Brahms' Second Concerto, her favorite. But tonight the solemn horns, instead of producing an ache in the throat, raise a chill in Trudy, along with the odd nagging feeling that she has forgotten something vitally important.

Rainer sets down his silverware in surprise.

What is the matter with you? he asks. You usually have the appetite of a horse.

Trudy rubs her arms, which have rashed in gooseflesh beneath her sweater.

I guess I'm just not that hungry, she says.

What a shame, says Rainer, and pulls Trudy's plate toward him. He spears a cherry, which bursts in a spray of juice. Trudy looks away.

Did you have a difficult day? Rainer asks.

No more so than any other. I taught this morning, of course.

The kids are all sick, coughing and sneezing and spraying germs everywhere—Oh, I'm sorry, I forgot your allergy to students. You don't want to hear about that.

You're right. I don't. Could you please pass the sugar?

Trudy obliges, and Rainer pours a neat pyramid of crystals on the remains of Trudy's appropriated torte.

Then I had a faculty lunch, and after that an interview. With a native of your hometown, in fact. A Mrs. Appelkind, from Berlin.

Rainer merely grunts and keeps shoveling in his food. It is naturally something of a touchy topic between them, Trudy's Project. But she doesn't see why she should have to hide it. It is important to her, after all. And he has asked about her day.

So Trudy continues, You should have seen this woman, Rainer. Three hundred pounds if she weighed an ounce. She ate the entire time we were talking, even on camera. She was so red in the face I was afraid she would have a stroke. And she did have high blood pressure, she told me, but she said that ever since the war she can't seem to get enough to eat...Are you listening to me?

Rainer doesn't answer. He hunches over his pastry, chewing quickly as a rabbit, the grape-sized muscles along his jawline appearing and disappearing as they clench.

When he is done, he pushes the plate aside and regards Trudy through narrowed eyes. Trudy braces herself for a disparaging remark, or at least for Rainer to ask her why on earth she keeps bringing up her little Project, as it holds absolutely no interest for him.

But instead Rainer says, Why do you always wear black?

Trudy plucks at the sleeve of her turtleneck.

This? You need to clean your glasses. This is navy blue.

Navy blue, black, gray, it is all the same. You look like a walking bruise.

I like dark colors, Trudy retorts. They lend me a certain sophistication.

Rainer snorts and refreshes his drink.

Women should wear bright clothes, he pronounces. Pink, for instance. Or fuchsia. You are not entirely unattractive, despite being mulish and argumentative, and it does not suit you to appear to be constantly in mourning.

Is this Rainer's idea of a compliment? Trudy raises her eyebrows and takes a sip of her liqueur.

Rainer settles back in his chair and laces his hands across his stomach, studying her.

I'm curious, he adds. What has caused you to be this way?

Now what are you talking about?

Your demeanor, your clothing, the way you carry yourself. It is as if you are ashamed of something and wish to be invisible.

Stung, Trudy laughs again and jerks her chin toward the window, beyond which, although they can't see it in the dark, it is snowing.

If that were true and I really wanted to blend in, she says cleverly, I would wear white.

Rainer impatiently waves this away.

What is it you are ashamed of? he asks.

Trudy's smile slips.

This is an absurd conversation, she tells him. Also boring.

I don't think so, says Rainer. I find it exceedingly interesting. You strike me as being representative of that large segment of the population who believes that there is no nobler achievement than self-awareness. So I repeat, Dr. Swenson. Tell me. What has made you this way?

Trudy rolls her eyes.

That is a question unworthy of a man of your intelligence, she says. You know it's impossible to answer. The variables are infinite: upbringing, genetics, defining incidents in childhood and adulthood, God knows what—

Rainer salutes her with his glass.

A valiant effort to dodge the question, he says, and perhaps acceptable in certain circles. But quite untrue. Psychological pablum. I do not buy it for a second. Nor do you, in fact; it contradicts your own theory, or at least your avowal as to why you conduct these interviews: trying to determine what factors made the Germans act in the ways they did. This, of course, does not interest me. What does is why you are so interested in them.

I've *told* you, Trudy says sharply, exasperated. Do you think I have as little intellectual curiosity as my students? What I'm doing will be an invaluable addition to the study of contemporary German history—

Again, untrue. Or rather, I don't doubt the validity of your eventual contribution, but you are being slippery, Dr. Swenson. What is the real reason behind your compulsion? This project is so dear to you that it surely must be a personal one. Perhaps it is somehow connected to the German mother whose excellent pastries we devour...?

Trudy pushes away from the table.

I'm going home now, she says. Thank you for a lovely evening.

Rainer smiles at her.

I see. So you can come into a stranger's home and expect him to regurgitate his secrets, but it is beneath you to do the same, is that it?

I have had quite enough, snaps Trudy, and stands to leave.

But Rainer leans forward and grabs her wrist, pinioning it to the table.

Wait, Dr. Swenson, he says, eyes glinting. Don't go just yet. Please, be seated.

Trudy glowers at him.

Please, Rainer repeats, and indicates her chair.

Trudy sits.

That is better, Rainer says, releasing her arm. You must not be so quick to take offense.

He lifts his tumbler, cupping it in his palm and thoughtfully swirling the amber liquid.

It is true, he says, that I consider this project of yours misguided on many levels. First, that the Germans should be allowed to speak of what they did: this is wrong. Why should they be permitted the cleansing of conscience that accompanies confession? It is analogous to adultery: the guilty party, far from spilling out his misdeeds and easing his mind while injuring the innocent other, should have to live with the knowledge of what he has done. A very particular kind of torture, subtle but ongoing. Let the punishment fit the crime—although, of course, if we were to take that as an absolute, so many Germans would deserve so much worse.

Trudy shifts in her chair.

Yes, but—

Rainer holds out a large palm. *Furthermore,* he booms, even if I thought it morally right to invite such confessions, I would find your project offensive on the level of its naïveté. It is an offshoot of the American concept that it is somehow attractive to air one's dirty laundry in public. It is everywhere, this ideology: your talk shows, your radio hosts encouraging people to call in and whine and gripe and pick their little scabs. You are such a young and childish country, believing that one can better understand the injuries of the past by wallowing in them and analyzing their causes. You do not know enough to understand that the only way to heal a wound is to leave it alone. To let sleeping dogs lie, as it were, rather than enthusiastically kicking them as you do.

Trudy, enraged, would like to point out that this is not only unfair but ridiculous: Rainer is just as assimilated as anyone else. He has lived in this country for decades; he has made a living here, taught its children, raised a family—

You drive a Buick, for God's sake! she bursts out.

Rainer ignores this. He frowns at his glass, which he is rotating on its coaster.

Yet I must admit, he tells it, that I admired your courage when you first bludgeoned your way in here. Thoughtless and headstrong, yes, but brave. For I have never been able to tell my own story to anyone. Not my wife nor my daughter nor even a stranger in a bar. Not a soul. And when the university contacted me to ask whether I would participate in your sister study, the Remembrance Project...

He smiles tightly at the tumbler.

Other Jews are telling their stories, I told myself; why not you? But...I could not. I simply could not bring myself to do it. Then I saw your flyer and thought, Now even the Germans are talking.

Rainer drains his glass and sets it down with a bang.

So I called you, he says, and I played a nasty trick on you. Cruel and cowardly. I am ashamed of that now.

Trudy looks at him. He sits tall and rigid, his posture Prussian.

And yet you came back, Rainer says. I have often wondered why. The only conclusion I can draw is that you are a true masochist, a glutton for punishment.

He glares at Trudy over his bifocals.

Trudy bends her head to inspect her wrist, which she has been rubbing against her trousers under the table. The skin Rainer's fingers have braceleted is tingling, as though it has been asleep and is just starting to wake up. She smiles secretly down at it.

I suppose I am, she tells him.

45

WHEN TRUDY LATER LETS HERSELF IN HER BACK DOOR, humming the opening bars of the Brahms, she is agreeably surprised to find that Anna is not in the kitchen. What a pleasant night this has turned out to be! True, the results of Anna's afternoon labors crowd the counters, cakes and pies exquisitely decorated and suffocating beneath airless shrouds of Saran Wrap. A more recent product, a *Schwarzwalder Kirschtorte,* awaits similar treatment on the stove. But Anna has apparently succumbed to either exhaustion or sanity, for there is no sign of her. She must have hung up the apron at a decent hour, Trudy thinks, and gone to bed like a normal person for a change.

The *Schwarzwalder Kirschtorte* will go stale if left out until morning, so Trudy rips off an arm's length of plastic wrap and drapes it over the cake. The smell of chocolate frosting drifts up to her, rich and nauseating, reminding Trudy of skin that has been licked. Yet even this cannot spoil her good mood. The cake duly protected, Trudy shuts off the lights and walks down the hall to her study, still humming under her breath. She wants to watch Rainer's interview. Or rather, not to play the whole thing, but just insert the tape and put it on Pause, so she can see him once more before bed and say good night.

But somebody has beaten her to it, for in Trudy's study Anna is huddled on the couch, staring across the room at Rainer on the television. Her expression is one of unadulterated horror. And because of this, and her long white nightgown, and the fact that her hair is in a single braid down her back, she reminds Trudy both of Bluebeard's wife—how that new bride must have looked when she opened the forbidden door to discover the severed heads of her husband's former curious spouses—and a child listening to the tale, too terrifying to be believed.

Trudy sags against the jamb, suddenly bone-tired. Then she walks into the room and sits quietly next to her mother on the sofa.

Oh, Mama, she says, closing her eyes. What are we going to do with you?

She feels Anna reach past her for the remote. This Anna must have been practicing with, for abruptly, as Rainer is saying, *They will burn your brain with its magnificent network of neurons,* his voice cuts out. Trudy opens her eyes and looks at his large, square, rather florid face on the screen. His bifocals are slipping down his nose, his mouth open. He might be yawning, or reading a menu.

Anna clutches the couch cushions for leverage as she starts to get up.

Once more I am sorry, Trudy, she says. I will go to bed.

No, that's all right, Mama. Sit if you want to.

Trudy sighs and massages her eyes. Then she says, Don't you think it's time we stopped all this? Aren't you tired of it, Mama? Aren't you sick to death of it? I know I am. Why don't you just tell me about him.

In her peripheral vision she sees Anna's hands—small, rough, hard-knuckled, the only parts of her that are not beautiful—tighten on the sofa.

Who? I do not know what you—

Oh, come on, Mama. Don't feed me that same old party line...Trudy waves toward the frozen Rainer. You're obviously drawn to watch these tapes for a reason. And I don't think it's just because you want to know what happened to others during the war. It's a kind of expiation, isn't it? A penance. But the guilt is never going to go away unless you talk about it. So tell me, Mama. Tell me about the officer.

Anna pushes herself off the couch and heads toward the dim safety of the hall.

Not this again, Trudy, she says. It is absurd. I will not hear this. I am going to bed.

Trudy leaps up and rushes past Anna, blocking her path. She pulls the door closed and leans against it.

Not yet, you're not, Trudy says. Not until you tell me something about him.

Anna folds her arms, and in the muted light from the television Trudy sees the stubborn set of her jaw.

But Trudy persists, Because I remember him, Mama. I *remember* him, don't you get it?...Her voice, an octave lower than usual, quavers; she is close to tears. I *dream* about him, she says. A big huge guy with jowls and dark hair and very light eyes. Calls himself Saint Nikolaus. And he's always in uniform—he holds a fairly high rank, I think. A *Hauptsturmführer? Sturmbannführer?* Maybe an *Obersturmführer*—

You shut your mouth, Anna says. You know nothing.

Well, that's certainly true, retorts Trudy. And whose fault is that? You never would tell me. All my life I've asked you about him and you've given me nothing in return. So who was he, Mama? Who was this man whose mistress you were?

Shut your mouth, Anna repeats, more loudly. As it always does when she is upset, her accent has thickened: the A's broadening to E's, the S's slurring to Z's. I do not know how you have gotten such ideas into your head, but—

Because I was *there*, Mama. I *saw* things. I *remember*. And what I want to know is: How could you do it?

Anna is breathing hard now, snorting air through her nose like a bull. Trudy can feel it, warm and damp, on her cheeks.

Oh, I understand intellectually, Trudy continues. The old adage about desperate times calling for desperate measures—I know that was true. I've studied it for decades, read all the case histories—

Case histories, Anna scoffs. You would never understand. *Du kannst nicht.*

But I *would,* if you'd explain it to me. *Help* me understand, Mama! Did he force you? What were the circumstances? Tell me how it was so I can *understand,* in my heart of hearts, how you could have been with such a man!

I will not discuss this, says Anna.

She reaches past Trudy for the doorknob. Trudy puts her own hand over it.

Or maybe he didn't force you after all, she continues. Or maybe he did in the beginning, but then you grew...fond of him. Is that why you never talk about it, Mama? Is that why you kept the photograph all these years?

Anna's arm drops to her side.

What photograph, she says.

Of you and him, Trudy says triumphantly. And me, on your lap. It was in your dresser at the farmhouse. And now I have it upstairs in my sock drawer.

Anna looks horrified.

That, she whispers.

Yes, that. I've known about it since I was a little girl. And why else would you have kept it all this time if you didn't care for him? If you didn't love him—

Anna leans forward and slaps Trudy across the face with all her might.

Trudy, stunned, gasps to regain her breath. But before she can, Anna takes a step closer and grabs her by the chin, forcing Trudy to look at her, even as she did when Trudy was a child.

How dare you say such a thing, Anna says. Now you will listen to me. I will tell you this once, and once only: I did it for you, Trudy. Anything I ever did, it was all for you.

Anna stares steadily at Trudy for another long moment. Then she releases her.

And that is all I will say about such things, she says. I have closed the door on that time and I will never open it. Not even for you. Now you will excuse me. I am going to bed.

Anna reaches for the knob again and this time the dazed Trudy moves aside to let her pass. She stands rubbing the tender spots Anna's fingers have left, listening to Anna ascend the stairs, as slowly as a queen.

Anything I ever did, it was all for you.

Right, says Trudy.

She looks around the darkened study and gives a hopeless little laugh. For how can one argue with that?

Then guilt rushes in to fill the vacuum of shock, a crushing thing whose tangible weight takes Trudy's breath away. She runs up the stairs after her mother and stands in front of Anna's closed door. All is quiet behind it.

Mama, Trudy calls. She taps on the door. Mama?

No response.

I'm sorry, Mama, says Trudy.

Silence.

Trudy hugs herself, waiting.

Did you hear me, Mama? I said I was sorry…

Eventually Trudy trails down the hall to her own room, where she sits on the edge of the bed. Tentatively, she brings her hands to her face in the dark. Her cheeks are bruised and swelling where Anna has gripped them. And wet.

46

AND AT SOME POINT TRUDY MUST SLEEP, FOR AS SHE LIES first on her back, then curled and flinching like a dog, she sees this:

She is sitting cross-legged on the floor of the bakery, which has been turned into a refugee center of sorts. There are mountains of suitcases, carpetbags, and heaped coats; some of the latter have people rolled up in them, resting. Others sit nearby, rocking themselves or staring at the devastated walls or whispering to children with whom Trudy has been forbidden to play. Still more are in the kitchen with Anna, helping her boil bandages or dole out cups of water. Trudy isn't frightened by the strangers or the odd sight of adults lying on the floor; the visitors lend the bakery a holiday feel. Even the dust they raise, which spins in the thin columns of light allowed by the boards over the window, seems to have a festive air.

Then the old bald schoolteacher snaps his fingers in front of Trudy's face.

Pay attention, child, he commands. Repeat after me: *ein, zwei, drei*.

Trudy wriggles, trying to find a comfortable position. The

cement is damp and unkind to childish buttocks, and she has been sitting for a long time.

Ein, zwei, drei, she says.

No, no, no. *Ein, zwei, drei. Vier, fünf, sechs.*

Ein, zwei, drei, vier, fünf, sechs, Trudy repeats. She looks expectantly at the old schoolteacher, waiting for praise. She wants to please this strange man.

But his lips purse in disgust.

You are not concentrating, he tells her. You had better learn to do it right, child. Otherwise —

He rotates his head slowly to the left, and the scourged flesh, a raw and weeping pink that has sealed one of his eyes shut, comes into view like a ruined moon.

Do you want to end up like this? he asks. No? Then do it again, correctly this time. *Ein, zwei, drei, vier—*

Trudy, her chest hitching in a prelude to tears, begins once again to recite the numerals. But the old schoolteacher is no longer listening. He scrambles to his feet, his blasted face blank. All around Trudy there is a kinetic movement and murmur as the other refugees do the same. For Saint Nikolaus has arrived. He stands at attention in the doorway, surveying the ragged bunch.

Trudy doesn't jump up like the rest. Instead she backpedals on her rump, scrabbling her heels against the floor, trying to hide among the forest of legs as Saint Nikolaus strides into the bakery. She knows it is her he is looking for.

Up! up, he calls. March.

Obediently, their eyes on the feet, their refugees form a circle with Saint Nikolaus at its center. They parade past him as he claps and chants:

> *Backe, backe Kuchen!*
> *der Bäcker hat gerufen.*
> *Wer will guten Kuchen backen,*
> *Der muss haben sieben Sachen:*
> *Butter und Salz, Zucker und Schmalz...*

Trudy finds herself walking along with the refugees. They plod past Saint Nikolaus in despairing rhythm, as dull and stolid as circus elephants. Then, suddenly, they are all gone and Trudy is marching alone. This does not surprise her: of course this lies well within the scope of Saint Nikolaus's many and peculiar powers. He makes people disappear.

...und Eier machen den Kuchen gel', he sings, tapping time with the toe of a gleaming boot. *Backe, backe Kuchen! der Bäcker hat gerufen.* Hup! Hup! Hup! Raise high the flags! Stand rank on rank together. Storm troopers march with quiet, steady tread—

I think that's enough for one evening, Trudy hears her mother call. It's past the child's bedtime.

Trudy's head swivels in her mother's direction. Anna is standing behind the display case, rubbing her arms.

Saint Nikolaus ignores her.

No, not like that, he scolds Trudy. Here. Watch.

He goose-steps across the room, his boots thudding on the floor. He pivots and comes back toward Trudy. He is as tall as a tree; she tips her head up as he approaches and sees his worsted crotch, the muscles of his thighs pumping beneath the cloth.

Now you, he says, and begins to mark time again.

> *Raise high the knife!*
> *Sharpen the blade to cut Jewish flesh.*
> *Jewish blood will run in the gutters;*
> *On every corner the Hitler flag will flutter—*

Horst, says Anna. I really don't think—

Trudy looks in her mother's direction. Anna is standing behind the display case, watching the scene with dark and sorrowful eyes.

Saint Nikolaus rounds on her.

WILL you be quiet! he roars. WILL you for once in your Godforsaken life just! shut! up!

Then he spins and deals Trudy a backhanded blow to the face. She reels to the floor, her ears ringing. She doesn't feel the impact of his hand. Her right cheek is numb from forehead to chin.

Saint Nikolaus's shining boots pass a few centimeters from her nose. Trudy hears him yelling something unintelligible overhead and hears Anna's answering cry. She tries to move, but the cement beneath her exerts a pull stronger than gravity.

You're a disgrace, I've had it with the pair of you, Saint Nikolaus is screaming. Puling, whining, ungrateful! I've half a mind not to come back at all.

And then the strangest thing happens: the ceiling must open up, or perhaps the sky, for treasures rain down, forks and watches and rings and brooches. They shower around Trudy in a crashing, clanging cacophony. Not a one touches her, however, for Anna is there, crouched over her, shielding Trudy in her arms.

Yet terrified as she is, Trudy struggles to squirm free of her mother's protective embrace. The press of Anna's flesh turns her stomach, as does her smell. For Anna doesn't smell like herself, sharp like celery beneath flour and honest sweat. She smells of bacon fat, of fish starting to go off. She smells like Saint Nikolaus. She smells like the man.

47

RAINER COMES TO THE DOOR MORE QUICKLY THAN ONE might expect, considering that it is nearly three in the morning. Trudy, however, is not surprised; she knows that he, like she, is prone to insomnia. He is as fully clothed as a man can be at this hour without being actually dressed, in pajamas and robe and his monogrammed slippers. He is even wearing his bifocals, as though he has been expecting just such an intrusion. The only signs that Trudy has disturbed him are his hair, which stands up in a cock's comb at the crown, and a somewhat wild look about the eyes, and Trudy realizes belatedly that, given his past, Rainer will be even more alarmed than most by a pounding on the door in the middle of the night.

Why, Trudy, he says.

He lowers his chin to peer at her over his glasses, as if to confirm that she is truly there, then slides them off and slips them into a pocket of his robe. In his other hand is a paperback, a John Le Carré thriller.

My God, he says. What has happened to your face?

Trudy shakes her head.

It's nothing.

It does not look like nothing, Rainer says, frowning. You really should have some ice on those bruises. Who has done this to you? What is wrong?

His concern makes Trudy shy. She digs her toe into the weave of the welcome mat.

I'm sorry to bother you at this hour, she mumbles.

Don't be stupid. Come in. Whatever has happened, you can tell me just as well inside.

When Trudy doesn't move, staring at her boots, Rainer takes her by the arm.

You are letting all the heat out, he tells her.

He walks Trudy into the living room and indicates that she should sit on the couch. But Trudy remains on her feet. She is panting a little, from the cold and her rush over here and the fear of what she has come to say.

And the only way to say it is to say it. Rainer is waiting, watching her. Trudy puts an icy hand on her breastbone.

I'm not who you think I am, she says rapidly. I'm not just an ordinary German. I'm the daughter of a Nazi officer. An SS officer. There. Now you know.

Rainer looks down at the book he is still holding.

I've never told that to anyone, says Trudy. Not even my ex-husband knew. And —

She buries her face in her hands.

I'm so ashamed, she cries. So ashamed. My entire life I've felt so — stained.

Rainer says nothing, but after a long moment Trudy feels him grasp her shoulder. He steers her to a chair.

Stay there, he says.

He disappears down the hall. Trudy leans back, drained. The armchair, though cold, emits a comfortingly masculine smell, of chilled leather and polish and a whiff of Rainer's citrus aftershave.

Rainer returns with a tea set on a tray. He sets it on an end table and switches on a floor lamp. The shadows leap and retreat a few yards, leaving a small ring of buttery light.

Rainer taps Trudy's knee and passes her a cup and two aspirin.

Take those, he says. They should reduce the swelling somewhat.

Trudy complies, washing down the caplets with a mouthful of Darjeeling that burns, not only because it is hot but because Rainer has put in it, along with honey and lemon, something much stronger. The alcohol has no taste, but Trudy can feel it searing a path through her throat and into her gullet. She coughs and starts to lower the cup.

All of it, Rainer commands.

Trudy braves another swallow and sits up a bit straighter.

What *is* that? she asks. Schnapps?

Rainer makes a twirling come-on gesture. When Trudy has drained her tea, he reaches over with the pot and refills it, then pours one for himself. But instead of drinking it, he sits with his feet firmly planted on the rug, turning the cup this way and that, frowning at it.

I am going to tell you a little story, he says, and then pauses.

Trudy waits. This is the first time she has been here without music in the background, and without it the house is deeply, sadly quiet. There is a *whummmm* and a rush of air from the floor vents as the furnace kicks on.

As if prompted by this, Rainer sighs and takes a sip of tea.

In November 1938, he says, when I was seven years old, my father was arrested. I do not know why. This happened during *Kristallnacht,* the Night of Broken Glass, so it is entirely possible that there was no reason. Perhaps he was simply in the wrong place at the wrong time. What I do know is that he was deported to Buchenwald, like many of the other unfortunates who were rounded up, and held as an enemy of the state. My mother received a notice to this effect. She clung to the hope, as did many in similar circumstances, that my father would soon return. And indeed some prisoners were released, though not in quite the same condition as they were going in. My father was not one of them. In 1940 my mother received another notice, this one stating that he had died of typhus and that there was no need for her to make funeral arrangements, for the body was highly contagious and had been disposed of by the state.

By this point, of course, anybody with any common sense could tell which way things were going for the Jews, so my mother decided that we, my younger brother Hansi and I, should go into hiding. She sat us down and explained to us that we would become U-boats, Jews living on Aryan papers, and that we would pretend to be the orphaned nephews of a Christian lady who lived near the Kurfürstendamm. This was in the heart of Berlin, so we would be big-city boys for a while; we should act like little men and not be afraid. She did her best to make this sound like an adventure and I, being nine at the time and fond of cloak-and-dagger stories, found it indeed an exciting prospect, particularly as Mutti assured us the situation would be only temporary.

The reality, of course, was quite different. My mother, for whatever reason, was not able to stay with us. She had to work to pay our benefactress, and perhaps she had to live in workers' lodgings in another sector of the city; I do not know. In any case, one morning in 1940 Hansi and I were taken from the house in the Grünewald where we had been born and brought to the apartment of Frau Potz, an elderly retired schoolmarm whom we had to call Auntie. There my mother left us, with tearful promises to visit as soon as she was able. I will leave you to imagine how difficult this parting was. I did not cry, mindful of Mutti's admonition to be a model for my brother, but Hansi, who was four, sobbed and clung to her legs. Nonetheless, she took her leave of us, and Frau Potz tried to comfort us as best she could. As she knew children only through teaching them, however, having had none of her own, she was not very affectionate; she did not hug or kiss us as we were accustomed to, and

Hansi and I had to draw whatever solace we could from one another.

I must grant that we were always well provided for. In addition to whatever money my mother could contribute, Frau Potz was a widow from the Great War and received a hefty pension, and the flat was, in retrospect, quite luxurious. But I saw it with a child's eye, and much of our surroundings frightened me in the illogical way children are often frightened. I retain the impression of big chilly rooms and highly waxed floors on which we were forbidden to run. The furniture was heavy and dark and upholstered with unwelcoming material such as horsehair, and everything smelled of mothballs, and there was a clock in the hallway presided over by a yellow-eyed mechanical owl that would flap its wings and hoot when the hour was struck. Things such as this gave me nightmares.

Nor was there any respite from the flat, for Hansi and I were no longer allowed to attend school nor even walk in the Tiergarten. Berlin at that time was rife with Jew-catchers, venal people who made it their business to ferret out the remaining Jews and turn them over to the Gestapo for a monetary reward, or extra rations, or travel stamps on their *Ausweis,* their passport. So Frau Potz would not take the risk of allowing us to leave the flat. We read our lessons to her in the mornings, and in the afternoons, when she went out to stand in the interminable lines for food, Hansi and I were left to our own devices. We were forbidden to run or sing or talk or make any noise whatsoever; we were not permitted even to look out the windows. We were meant to sit quietly with our books and drawing paper until she returned.

Naturally, this was an impossibility for two active little boys who missed their garden in the Grünewald and had once had their own ponies, and naturally, as soon as Frau Potz left on her errands, we disobeyed her. The moment I heard the descent of the lift, I would drag one of the hideous horsehair chairs to the window and help Hansi climb up beside me so we could watch the street. And there was always something of interest to see: the flat fronted directly onto the Ku'damm, which is the main shopping avenue in Berlin, and I remember ladies wearing everything from the latest fashions to *Zellwolle* coats and wooden shoes that made a noise like horses' hooves; there were boys my age running and jumping onto the streetcars like monkeys until the conductors chased them off; there were Brownshirts and soldiers with rifles; always some commotion. We were terrified of the soldiers, of course, and would duck whenever one of them glanced in our direction, but I must confess I was also fascinated by their gleaming guns and boots, and sometimes, until Frau Potz returned, I would run about the flat with a broomstick shooting imaginary invaders.

In any case, the afternoon street-watching became a ritual, and so it was that one winter day in 1942 while we were standing at the window, Hansi and I saw our mother across the street. She was shuffling forward in a long line of Jews, some wearing the yellow Star and some not. She was not. But she had obviously been caught and her papers declared invalid, for she was being herded with the rest toward the train station.

It was the first time we had seen her in two years.

And Hansi, then only six, became quite agitated. Mutti, he shouted, pointing; there's Mutti! And he slid off the armchair and raced from the flat.

I followed him, taking the stairs instead of the lift, which was old and slow. But by the time I reached the building's exit, Hansi was already running across the street. Cars screeched to a halt; everyone on the sidewalk turned to look. Mutti, he was shouting, Mutti! And he ran alongside her as she walked, tugging on her dress—she was not wearing a coat despite the cold—and holding his arms out to be picked up and held.

And at first my mother pretended not to hear. She swatted at his hands and kept walking, facing straight ahead. But this of course had no effect, so eventually she stopped and said to Hansi, Go inside, little boy. You'll catch your death of cold.

Mutti, said Hansi again, and threw his arms around her, burrowing his face into her stomach. I stood and watched from the doorway as my mother looked about in desperation, whispering to Hansi and trying to disengage him. But she had no luck in doing so, and she was holding up the line of deportees, and one of the soldiers came over, a big fat fellow in a greatcoat, and said to her, Is this your child?

No, my mother said, no, he is not mine, and she finally succeeded in thrusting Hansi away from her and started walking again.

But he trotted next to her, wailing, Mutti, look at me, Mutti, pick me up! until the soldier pulled him away. He took my mother's arm, too, and turned her to face my brother.

He certainly seems to know you, this soldier said. Are you sure he's not yours?

Yes, yes, said my mother, trying to smile, although by this point she was weeping as well. He must have confused me with somebody else.

The soldier appeared to consider this. He stood with his legs far apart and—this I will never forget—digging in his mouth with one finger as if there were some food lodged there.

Then he said, I understand. These matters of mistaken identity happen all the time, especially among Jews. Well, then, if he is not yours, you won't mind if I do this—

And he unholstered his Luger and shot Hansi in the head.

Of course there was screaming, my mother loudest of all, and people scattered to try and get away from my brother's body, which was lying in the street with a pool of blood spreading from it, and my mother on her knees beside him. But I, I...

Rainer looks at his cup of tea, then sets it on the floor.

I just stood and watched. I stood while the soldier kicked my mother and then while he pulled her to the feet by the hair and dragged her off, and I stood there while the Jews started walking again and the rest of the people on the street went about their business as though nothing had happened, with my brother's little body in the gutter with the horse dung and old newspapers. I stood there, you understand, not just because of the shock and disbelief of what I had seen, but because I knew for the first time in my life what it means to be so ashamed that you wish to die.

For I had had ample time to stop Hansi from running from the flat. And even afterward, I could have gone into the street and coaxed him away from our mother. He worshiped me; he would have listened to me. But I did nothing, and I had made a conscious decision to do nothing while all this was happening. Because I was angry with my mother. I was angry that she had broken her promise and had not come to visit us and had abandoned us to Frau Potz. So I deliberately did nothing and in this way caused both of their deaths...

Rainer bows his head. He sits that way for a moment, staring at the carpet. Then he turns to Trudy.

So you see, he says softly, we are all ashamed in one way or another. Who among us is not stained by the past?

Without waiting for a response, he stands. Trudy stares at his slippers, wiping her tears with the back of a wrist. Then she looks up at Rainer. His face is in shadow, but his eyes shine like mercury. The silence hums between them, tensile with understanding.

Rainer holds out his hands.

Come, he says.

Trudy puts her hands in his and he pulls her to her feet. Then the two of them, joined this way and by mutual and unspoken accord, go up the stairs to his bedroom and shut the door behind them.

Anna and Jack, Weimar, 1945

48

ALTHOUGH NULL HOUR HAS DESCENDED UPON THE GER-
mans, shifting the tectonic plates of their lives into new and unrecognizable shapes, Nature proceeds with her spring pageantry
just the same. In fact, Anna has to admit that she has never seen
a more glorious May. The kitchen window of the bakery affords
a view of cherry and lilac trees so heavily laden with blossoms
that their boughs graze the ground; the sky above them is so
blue it looks enameled; a crisp and steady breeze tosses the new
leaves with a sound like the boiling hiss of surf. A fanciful observer might suggest that the world has been washed clean
overnight, that even the weather is showing its approval of the
events of the past few weeks: the *Führer*'s suicide, the German
surrender, the end of the war.

But Anna has lost all trace of whimsy, if ever she had any, and
to her this beautiful afternoon is a personal insult, a dirty trick
sent to lull her into thinking that everything will be fine now. She
knows better. She has seen so many atrocious things happen on
radiant days. Is she supposed to forget the first evening she went
to the quarry, the mild air, that sky with its glowing stained-glass

striations? Or a more recent incident, a prisoner being marched
past the storefront window en route to the train station. Clubbed
in the mouth for not moving fast enough, he squatted to furtively
collect his teeth from among a growth of new tulips. That occurred on a lovely afternoon much like this one.

Anna is not alone in being plagued by such images, these insistent apparitions elbowing reality aside in their constant bid for
attention. She has glimpsed others, Weimarians and American
soldiers alike, standing in the middle of the road like stopped
clocks, staring not at what is in front of them but at visions presented by the mind's eye. However, the knowledge that her misery has company is little comfort, and this jubilant springtime
display is not to be trusted. Life is a frosted cake made of worms.

She turns to wash her hands of the clinging remnants of
doughy sponge. At least the Americans, disproving rumors of
rape and disemboweled children, have proven to be decent, even
generous captors. They are also ravenous. After years of living
on food from tins, they have an unappeasable appetite for anything fresh. Hence the sacks of flour piled against the south wall
of the kitchen like trench fortifications, U.S. ARMY NINTH
INFANTRY stamped on their bulging burlap. And what flour it
is! Fine as dust on the fingertips, no need to sieve it for insects or
rocks. Anna has been baking for days, ever since the first private
arrived at the bakery, ducking beneath the white sheet Anna had
hung from Mathilde's bedroom window. *Hey, we've got bread!*
Anna heard from where she and the child were crouched in the
cellar. *We're dying for bread,* Fräulein; *make us some fresh bread!*
Even forgoing sleep, Anna has been unable to keep up with the
demand.

Now Anna levers a batch of loaves from the oven with the
wooden paddle and slides them onto the worktable. Her nose
wrinkles at their smell of yeast, that hot rich fermentation so reminiscent of the whiffs rising from her flesh in the WC after the
Obersturmführer's visits. But her stomach's commands are stronger
than her repugnance, and her mouth is suddenly full of bitter

juice. Unable to wait for the bread to cool, Anna rips open a loaf and begins devouring steaming dough by the handful.

She doesn't immediately notice the soldier standing in the doorway to the storefront, watching her. Then, catching movement in her side vision, she sputters, Oh! and chokes down the bread with effort.

She wipes her face with her apron, smiling apologetically. You startled me, she says in her own language. She pats her breastbone to denote the rapid beating of a heart.

Can I help you? she then asks in English, a phrase she has perfected since the Americans' arrival.

The Ami advances into the kitchen, head swiveling like a gun turret. Anna tries to place him. Has she seen him before? Yes: although all the Amis are enchanted by Trudie, the girl's looped braids and storybook clothes, Anna recalls this fellow as being particularly smitten. He has brought Trudie chocolate, which Anna hides from her for fear that it is too rich for the child's shrunken stomach. Once he gave Trudie a stick of the chewing gum to which all Americans seem addicted. This Trudie promptly grabbed and swallowed, causing Anna to worry that the girl's innards would be permanently glued together.

Can I help you? Anna repeats, wondering if he has come to play with the girl. *I have fresh bread...*

The soldier continues walking toward her. His hip thuds against the worktable, and Anna understands that he is reeling drunk. The rotten-sweet smell of whiskey, half meat and half fruit, hangs around him in a vapor. Anna looks about for something she might use as a weapon—a pot, the rolling pin. Then she sees that the Ami is crying, a muscle beneath one eye jumping in a tic that makes him look as though he is winking at her. He is only a boy, poor thing, too young to have coped with the carnage of Europe's battlefields. He is merely seeking comfort, a female touch, soothing words spoken in a woman's voice.

So thinking, Anna is caught off guard when the soldier lurches into her, driving her against the worktable. He fumbles at her blouse, the worn material purring as it rips. Buttons pop off and bounce to the floor.

Anna tries to scream, but the Ami, even intoxicated, is too swift for her. Wrenching her arm behind her back, he forces her flat on her stomach on the table, one hand clamped around her throat. Anna's head knocks against the wood. Through a drift of flickering confetti she sees a loaf not an inch away, still letting off its warm yeasty smell.

The Ami is pushing up her skirt now. *Kraut bitch,* he is saying, *Kraut bitch, you want this, huh? You want this? Huh? Huh?*

The bright spots in Anna's vision spread and grow dark. Her hands, pinned beneath her, are numb and tingling. Even if they weren't, however, she would not move them. Why bother to fight? Whether this boy or the *Obersturmführer,* it all comes down to the same thing in the end. She hears the liquid trill of a bird in the tree beyond the window, growing ever fainter. She too is waning, starting to lose consciousness. She is grateful. It will be better this way—

Then the Ami's weight is hauled off Anna and air rushes into her burning throat. She chokes on it, taking great rasping lungfuls. There is shouting behind her, swelling and retreating like the oscillation of waves. Anna grips the table, waiting for the dizziness to either claim her or pass.

It passes. Anna straightens and turns to find her attacker being restrained by another, older soldier. He, too, Anna has seen before. Unlike the others, who throng around her to flirt and tease, this Ami is made of more timid stuff, standing to one side until it is his turn to accept bread. A quiet man, a man apart. Now, though, he is quite voluble, shaking Anna's assailant by the shoulders and yelling into his face. The younger Ami is drooling a little, and Anna realizes that throughout the entire encounter he has been chewing gum.

He is also determined to have his say; when the older soldier releases him, he wipes his mouth and mutters. Anna, straining for comprehension, hears him say...Buchenwald. He points at her with hatred.

They asked for it, he says.

The older Ami, unmoved by this argument, shoves the younger toward the door. Anna's attacker gives her a last poisonous look but slinks from the kitchen. Obviously he is of subordinate rank and must follow orders.

The remaining soldier turns to Anna. To her surprise, he speaks in her own language, albeit with a strangely mushy accent that makes him sound as though he has a cleft palate, and as loudly as if she were deaf.

Are you all right? he shouts.

He puts his face quite close to Anna's. It is kind, but it is not handsome. His skin is terrible, oddly lumpy as if there were porridge lodged beneath it, and his eyes are small and dark and blink like a turtle's. Anna looks away.

Do you need a doctor? he yells.

This Ami reminds her of somebody, but who? After a moment it comes to Anna: of course, *Hauptsturmführer* von Schoener. The American has the same wistful air about him as Gerhard's old friend, the kicked-dog hopelessness of a man whose looks have condemned him to watching pretty women from afar. Still, Anna can feel the Ami's interest pulsing from him as surely as she can see the corresponding beat of blood in the hollow of his throat. Another one! She would like to claw at her face with her cracked nails, all the better never to elicit this kind of attention in a man's eyes ever again.

Yet he has saved her, so Anna supposes she must act grateful. Painfully, she swallows and shakes her head.

No doctor, she croaks.

Are you sure?

The Ami raises a hand as if to touch the bruises ringing Anna's neck. Anna shies away.

I will not hurt you, he shouts. He thumps himself on the chest.

I'm Jack, he continues; Lieutenant Jack Schlemmer. Don't worry about that kid, Fräulein. I took care of him. He won't get fresh with you again. Do you understand?

The Ami nods vigorously, trying to elicit a positive response via encouragement. His small muddy eyes are as anxious as a boy's.

You're sure you're all right?

Anna attempts to say *Yes* and *Thank you,* but her outraged throat, swelling now, will not permit it, so she nods as well. They bob their heads in tandem for a moment. The Ami seems to want to say something more, but at last he settles for patting the air near Anna's shoulder and turns to leave.

When the bell over the storefront has signified his departure, Anna drops to her knees to rescue the loaves that have fallen to the floor during the scuffle. She brushes them off with her apron and lines them up on the worktable like a regiment. Then she rises and staggers through the back door into the grass. Reaction is setting in; her legs shake, threatening collapse. Her neck throbs. She puts a hand to it and leans on the bakery wall for support, gazing across the yard. The bird has fallen silent. The afternoon sun is tangled like a gold net in the trees.

Fresh, this Ami has said; he won't get fresh with you. What an extraordinary expression! Bread can be fresh, as can vegetables and fruit, flowers and meat. Also fresh is the fragrance of laundry dried in the wind, or newly cut hay. But the interactions between the sexes? The Ami is indeed naive to describe them this way. Anna imagines that, were she able to visit the caves in which people first dwelled, she would find scrawled drawings that have been omitted from museums and history books. There would be scenes of ritual aggression and submission, painted in blood, caked with dried seminal fluid. They are the very antithesis of fresh, the rites between men and women; age-old and rotten to the core.

49

THEY ARE WALKING, ANNA AND TRUDIE, ANNA WITH THE girl's hand clutched in her own. They walk through the streets of Weimar with the other townsfolk, all those who have not fled the city in a panic during the final deranged days before Null Hour. They walk as quickly as they can, which is to say not very quickly, since they are a malnourished, haggard lot, many of them with ill-fitting shoes or in stocking feet. But the Amis jogging among them with their guns drawn act as incentive, as do their stone-faced brothers on the truck that bounces over the street along-side. There has been an early morning roundup: cellars and attics searched; the Weimarians routed from their breakfast tables, beds, and bathrooms; dragged out by the hair or persuaded with blows from a rifle butt if they protest. And so they walk, Anna and Trudie amid the other women and children and old men who have not been killed or sent away.

It is a bigger group than Anna would have expected, num-bering in the hundreds. She recalls hearing that all citizens not working for the military have been evacuated to provinces far-ther south. Anna is not surprised that she was allowed to remain.

In servicing the *Obersturmführer,* has she not been fulfilling military duty? But she is not sure how the others have escaped the net. Perhaps the mighty machine of the Reich, grinding to a halt in its final days, had greater concerns than the tiny parts that splintered off, personified now in those who surround her.

They walk in obedient lines with their heads down. They pass once-grand houses and familiar storefronts decimated by shells. Though it is drizzling, and though the Amis have allowed the Germans to begin clearing the rubble, wisps of smoke still curl from piles of bricks and stone. A lady's hat lies among the ruins. A piano's backbone has been crushed by a fallen timber, its keys scattered on the pavement. Yet nobody dares gape at this grim scenery or elbow a neighbor to share a whispered comment on the destruction. Each stumbles along, eyes down, encapsulated in his own silence. The Americans might not be the SS, who would be using their rifles much more energetically by this time, but nor are they the friendly captors the Weimarians have come to know over the past two weeks. For no apparent reason, they have suddenly become hostile, and to fraternize might be to invite God-knows-what type of punishment.

Yet when Anna spies Frau Buchholtz trudging nearby with her brood, she angles through the ranks toward the woman.

What's happening? she murmurs to the butcher's widow from one side of her mouth. Where are they taking us, do you know? Why are they doing this?

Frau Buchholtz shoots Anna a narrow lateral glance, sucks her lips inward, and gives her head a tiny shake. Her eyes slide toward the soldiers in the truck, their weapons leveled at the Germans. Then, guiding her children, she drifts away from the reckless Anna.

I'm hungry, Mama, Trudie whispers. Is it much farther?

I don't know, little one, Anna says.

She stands on tiptoe to search for the Ami she knows best, Herr Lieutenant Jack Schlemmer. She finally spies him sitting amid the group on the truck. It was he who came to the bakery this morning, just as Anna was setting a bowl of farina in front of Trudie; Anna barely had time to register that he was wearing his helmet with its funny netting of mesh before the others came to take them away. Anna had thought that he was coming to reassure her following the previous day's attack. She had prepared a speech in English to thank him. Now she catches him staring at her, but when Anna meets his gaze, he severs contact by turning his head.

They reach the train station. Speculation ripples through the throng. Will they be loaded into the boxcars waiting on the tracks? But the Americans, shouting and waving their guns, indicate otherwise. Everyone turns left, onto a paved avenue that leads away from the city. Several streets spoke from this point, but Anna, with a little shock of fear, recognizes that the Americans are driving them up toward the forests of the Ettersberg. She is not alone in this realization. A moan rises from the crowd.

They're taking us into the woods, a woman wails, they're going to kill us all!

At this, there are screams and prayers. Some of the Germans break and run. They are swiftly caught and corralled back into place by the Americans.

They're going to shoot us, another treble voice insists, they're going to line us up and shoot us —

Shut up! somebody says. You're not making it any easier.

But they're going to —

Shut up!

One of the Americans on the truck stands and unslings his weapon. There are further screams at the staccato stutter of machine-gun fire, and some of the children begin to cry. But when it is realized that the bullets have been aimed at the low-hanging clouds rather than human targets, the multitude settles. Eventually all is quiet but for the shuffle of feet along the slippery pavement and the prehistoric moan of a tank in the distance. An elderly man near Anna recites the Lord's Prayer under his breath.

Trudie drags on Anna's arm. She is silently weeping, as is her new habit.

Mama, my feet hurt, she whispers.

The girl is far too heavy to be carried. Nevertheless, Anna takes Trudie on her hip. She will continue this way as long as she is able. It may not be that much farther now, depending on where the Americans are taking them. Anna has her suspicions. They are trudging up a steep incline, dark walls of pine looming on either side. A clammy fog warps the passage of sound; the grind of the truck's gears might be a meter or five meters away. It begins to rain. Anna registers her discomfort as if from a distance; she is thinking how strange it is to be traveling on this road rather than picking her way through the brambles alongside it, her usual path to the quarry. Surely this is where the Americans will take them if there is to be a mass execution. But when they pass the site of Mathilde's death and, a little beyond it, the dirt turnoff to the quarry, Anna feels nothing, no joy, no relief. She has the sensation of hovering outside herself, observing.

The command to halt comes so abruptly that, in obeying, people bump into one another. The man who has been praying prods Anna's foot with his crutch and apologizes. One of his legs is missing beneath the knee, his patched trousers pinned neatly over the stump. He is not as old as Anna first thought; he is probably in his thirties. The Weimarians mutter and jostle as the Americans herd them closer together. The soldiers leap from the truck, dark shapes coalescing in the gloom. Trudie shivers; it is cold here on the mountain. The girl's braids have come undone and strands of wet hair curve like commas on her cheeks.

It is raining harder now, with an accompanying wind. The fog has lifted enough to show Anna that they have reached the camp entrance. She pulls hastily away from the wall she has been leaning on. Inscribed on its stucco is the legend *RECHT ODER UNRECHT MEIN VATERLAND.* My Country, Right or Wrong. The archway over the iron gates bears a different, more ominous motto: *JEDEM DAS SEINE!* To Each His

Due! And what, Anna wonders, watching the Americans organize people into columns, is their due to be?

Two soldiers push the heavy gates open, then take up positions on either side. Another American, a barrel-shaped man with a checkerboard of bars pinned to his uniform, strides to the iron archway. Glaring at the fearful crowd, he makes a short speech. He gestures toward the crematorium, the chimney of which is just visible through the trees. Anna, trying to translate, has the feeling she has been here before. In a way, she has. She has often enough imagined the camp from the *Obersturmführer*'s descriptions, pictured him patrolling its streets with his adjutant and dogs, envisioned the prisoners sprinting toward the flaming forest. Snaking through the fog is a most familiar odor, sickeningly fatty: that of a smoking campfire on which bacon is being cooked.

The American officer concludes his announcement, his mouth wincing in a tic of disgust. For a moment, Anna expects him to spit. He does not. Instead, he makes a chopping motion with one hand, and the soldiers begin forcing the Weimarians toward the gates.

Although it is not clear whether the Americans' intent is to slaughter or incarcerate them, the Germans resist. Women balk, thrusting their children behind them; some try again to escape. The Americans are unimpressed, using their fists and rifle barrels to corral their captives. Anna, who is at the head of the crowd, struggles to maintain her balance. She shouts to Trudie to hold tight. The one-legged man is on the ground, reaching for the crutch kicked from beneath him. Somebody tramples on his hand and he shouts in pain.

A soldier drags the first woman toward the camp. She digs her heels into the mud; she clings to the bars of the gate, her head whipping from side to side. Then she spots Anna, who sees that it is Frau Hochmeier.

Wait, Frau Hochmeier screeches. She uses her free hand to claw at the soldier's arm. Wait, look. Her, over there, look.

The startled soldier glances at her. The people nearest the gate, sensing a possible diversion, quiet somewhat, and Frau Hochmeier uses the pause to her advantage.

Why imprison us? she yells. We've done nothing wrong. We just did as we were told, like good citizens. It's criminals like her you should lock up, that woman right there. She's an SS whore!

Frau Hochmeier points at Anna.

While the rest of us suffered and starved to feed our children, she was sleeping with an SS officer. I saw it, we all saw it!

That's true, that's right, Frau Buchholtz calls. I saw it with my own eyes. Put her and her kind in the camp and leave the rest of us alone.

There are shouts of Whore! Whore! The soldier looks bewildered. Frau Hochmeier places a finger on her upper lip to mimic the *Führer*'s mustache and marches in place; then she points again to Anna and pumps her hips back and forth.

That child she's holding, that's an SS bastard, she yells.

Somebody in the crowd whinnies hysterical laughter. A clod of mud hits Anna's arm. The crippled man, having regained his footing, quickly crutches himself away.

Anna stands pressing her daughter's face to her chest. She could attack Frau Hochmeier, defend herself by responding in kind. She too has only acted to protect her child. But she is paralyzed by the certainty that it will do no good to protest. She has simply awakened from one nightmare into another.

Two of the Americans shove through the mob to bracket Anna on either side. Initially, she thinks this is for her own protection. Then, to immense approval, they propel her with Trudie toward the gates. Frau Hochmeier draws back as Anna and Trudie are thrust past her; she cringes as if Anna were violent as well as morally bankrupt, as if Anna is going to hit her.

Anna doesn't look in her direction. Nor does she resist the hands that grip her. She concentrates on holding Trudie and keeping her balance. She wishes she had enough mastery of the soldiers' language to tell them that there is no need to force her.

She is light-footed and clearheaded; she could sing with relief. She has been praying, in some secret part of her, for this moment of expiation, this penance.

As she steps beneath the archway, somebody else shoulders through the crowd, the Ami who put a stop to the attack of the day before. His forehead is creased in furrows beneath his helmet.

Trust me, he says to Anna in his pulpy German. Then he lifts Trudie from Anna's arms.

The girl lets out a shrill scream and reaches for Anna. Anna lunges toward her daughter, but the soldiers restrain her. One of them shouts at Herr Lieutenant Schlemmer, who tightens his grip on the thrashing, shrieking child.

Hey, he says in his own language, *this is nothing for a kid to see.*

He turns toward Anna. You will not be hurt in there, he yells in German. But it is no place for your daughter. I will watch over her.

Despite his clumsy accent, Anna understands. She has a single second to convey her gratitude with her eyes. Then, as Trudie wails behind her, Anna is pushed along with Frau Hochmeier and all the others through the gates to *Konzentrationslager* Buchenwald.

50

LATE THAT NIGHT HERR LIEUTENANT SCHLEMMER BRINGS
Trudie back to the bakery, where Anna is sitting on a stool behind the display case, staring at nothing.

She's fine, the Ami says, urging the girl forward for Anna's
inspection. She's just fine—you see?

And indeed, though Trudie's braids are undone and her face
a streaky mess of what looks like dirt but is probably chocolate,
she seems to have forgotten the events of the morning. In fact,
she is more animated than she has been in months: she swings
the Lieutenant's hand in high arcs and hangs on it like a monkey,
babbling something about *tootsie pops.*

Anna's gaze wanders past her daughter to the window, the
walls. Her filthy hands lie limp in her lap.

The Ami watches her, blinking.

Where does Trudie sleep? he asks finally. I will put her to bed.

At this Anna stirs. She doesn't want him poking about upstairs, prying into their private quarters and seeing how she and
the girl have been living. Entering Mathilde's bedroom with its
stained and sagging bed.

Thank you, I will do it, she says.

But Trudie is already pulling her new friend from the storefront.

This way, she says; this way, in Tante's room, I'll show you.

Anna follows the pair to the base of the steps and stands there, arms crossed, slit-eyed and listening. She hears nothing more than the Ami's deep loud voice, mingling with the girl's soprano chatter. And after a while, quiet; then a clank and the squeak of water being pumped in the WC; then the Lieutenant humming to himself as he jogs down the stairs. Anna hastily returns to her stool.

The Ami comes into the storefront and stops when he sees her expression. He ducks his head, rubbing a wrist bone over his shoe-brush hair.

Are you *okay*? he asks.

Okay? What is this *okay*? Anna gives a curt nod, wanting nothing more than for him to be gone, to be rid of his earnest, well-meaning presence.

If you please, Fräulein, he says. Come upstairs. I've—

Whatever else he says is lost on Anna, who finds herself on her feet, hands clenched in fists. She is grateful, of course, for his taking care of the child, but this is going too far. So he too assumes she will express her appreciation in physical form, does he? He of all people, with his earnest, porridgy face, his sad bachelor's eyes, now shining at her with such hope and such pity!

How dare you, she says, her voice low and quivering.

The Ami flushes.

No, no, you misunderstand, he says. My fault. I put it badly. I don't— I don't have much experience with women. It's just that I have drawn you a bath. I thought you might like to wash, after...

He makes an awkward gesture in Anna's direction, encompassing her ruined dress, the clots of mud on her shoes and her earth-smudged face.

Please, he says. It will do you good.

Anna stays where she is, measuring him. He is by now so red that it appears as though he has suffered a burn, but everything in his posture signifies quiet insistence. If she spurns his offering, he may turn ugly, like the rest. If she complies, he may leave her in peace. She brushes past him and up the stairs.

The tub is full almost to the brim, steam curling from the undulating skin of the water. Anna slaps it with the side of a hand, sending a wave across the room. That he should assume such familiarity, such proprietorship, should interfere to such a degree! Yet he has her trapped up here, and there is nothing else to do. Anna removes her soiled clothes and climbs in, hissing in pain at the temperature. She immerses herself fully and surfaces. She sits dripping and staring at the wall. There is no need to bother with soap. She will never rid herself of the stench of corpses she has buried no matter how hard she scrubs. It is inside her. It will coat her nostrils and the back of her throat as long as she lives.

After some time there comes an uncertain knock.

Fräulein? Fräulein Anna?

The door opens a centimeter.

Is everything all right? I thought perhaps you...

Herr Lieutenant Schlemmer sidles sideways into the room, eyes conspicuously averted from Anna's nudity.

It's just that you've been in here so long and I didn't hear anything, he says. I was afraid you might have —

Anna turns on him, her face mottled and ferocious with shame.

Go away, she hisses. Go away and leave me alone.

The Ami ignores this. He steps around the puddles on the floor and comes to sit on the side of the tub, still looking anywhere but at her, heedless of the wet stain spreading on the seat of his Lieutenant's trousers. He reaches past Anna for the soap.

Please, he says again. Allow me.

Tentatively at first, then with more assurance, he lathers Anna's hair. He fetches the pitcher and rinses it once, twice. His touch is as gentle as a mother's. Anna submits, head bowed. Tears slip from beneath her smarting lids and into the cooling bathwater. She keeps her eyes closed the entire time.

THEY ARE MARRIED A MONTH LATER, IN AN OFFICE IN THE Rathaus, which the Amis are using for administrative purposes. The ornate furniture of the former government seat has long since been hauled away by desperate Weimarians and chopped up for kindling; it has been replaced by filing cabinets and folding tables and chairs. The rooms are full of men in olive drab, their footsteps echoing in the denuded halls.

Jack wears his uniform; Anna, the June bride, a clean workday dress; Trudie, who watches the proceedings with acute interest from a corner chair, swinging her heels, her least-mended dirndl. The thick sunlight of a summer afternoon slants through the dirty windows onto the couple, making them squint at the army chaplain as he performs the ceremony. He tugs at his earlobe throughout. The hasty mumbled rites are punctuated by the shouts of soldiers outside—*Hey, got a cigarette? Hey, Sarge, where do you want me to put this?*—and the grinding of truck gears in the square.

Within minutes they are husband and wife. After a quick glass of beer at the base, Anna will pack what belongings she and Trudie have and move into lodgings near Jack's barracks. He has already applied for discharge, he has told her; as a translator he is near the top of the list. They should have to wait no longer than four months, he promises Anna. Then they will board a ship for America.

51

AND WHAT DOES ANNA TAKE WITH HER FROM GERMANY?
Nothing.

Except:

A week before leaving Weimar for her new homeland, Anna surrenders the child to the care of a Red Cross nurse and returns to the bakery. It is a day in early September yet hot as summer: the air still, the sky white, the trees resigned and drooping. A sad afternoon, somehow; abashed, as if the weather is aware that it is acting improperly but lacks the conviction to change seasons.

The door to the storefront is unlocked. Anna opens it and steps inside. She has not been here since moving to her new husband's quarters three months ago. She walks through the rooms, rubbing her arms. It is cool inside these thick walls.

Crumbs, buttons, dust. Mouse droppings. Anna tries to feel something but cannot. In this place where she has spent the most important moments of her life! She lists each event under her breath as she revisits the site of its occurrence. *Here I gave birth to my daughter. Here she was baptized. Mathilde sat here, on the side of this tub.* Anna puts a hand on the porcelain. It is chilly; it gives nothing back. *Here, in this cellar, Mathilde hid them, people far more desperate than I. Are any of them still alive?* Anna looks at the abandoned pallet, the filthy sheets wrinkled as if somebody has just arisen from it, and marvels that she ever slept there. *Here I lay awake and thought of Max. At some point he must have walked over these floors, perhaps leaned against the display case. Sat at the worktable and had a cup of tea.*

Still she feels nothing.

Here I stood when he *first came for me. And here in Mathilde's bedroom the rocking chair where he deposited his tunic and trousers. Here the brushes with which he smoothed his dark hair, the mirror in which he smiled. Here the corner in which he made me stand, naked with my eyes closed while he walked toward me. His breath on my shoulderblades, stirring my hair. My back to him but still I knew he was grinning.*

Here this bed.

Why has she come back? What possible good can it do to try and remember, one last time, these things best forgotten? And if one must surrender the memory of the good along with the bad, well, perhaps this is not too high a price to pay. Better to remain so distant, a blessing to be so detached, as if all of this has happened to somebody else.

Anna gives the rocking chair a tentative push. It creaks wearily. The rush matting of its seat sags from years of carrying the baker's weight; its back is missing a slat. Anna stops the chair in its track and bends forward to look through the window at the view Mathilde might have contemplated in happier times. The road, the winding stone wall alongside it. The light is brownish and sad.

It is time to go. Anna turns to leave the room. As she does, she passes the bureau, where Mathilde's hapless Fritzi still smiles from amidst his shrine of dead flowers, now crumbled to dust. And next to it in a cracked china bowl in which Anna kept odds and ends, candle stubs and needles and earrings and some other jewelry the *Obersturmführer* brought her, is the small gold case with the swastika on its cover, containing the photograph snapped on her birthday. Anna takes this from the dish without thinking about it; it is as if her hand acts of its own accord. She slips it into the pocket of her skirt before she walks downstairs and away from the bakery for good, never suspecting that in the years to come her daughter will lift this sole relic of her mother's past from among layers of lacy undergarments in another bedroom across the ocean; that again and again she will stare at this portrait of what could be a family with longing and horror and a species of awe.

Trudy, April 1997

52

TRUDY IS HAPPY. SHE HAS NEVER BEEN THIS HAPPY. SHE IS not sure that, prior to this, she has even known what happiness is; she is awed by the force of it. It is like coming in from the cold, cheeks red and tingling and thighs blushing beneath one's clothes, and sitting down to a hot meal and suddenly discovering how ravenous one is, a hunger not recognized until this moment.

She is lying on one side in Rainer's bed, watching him as he stands by the window in his briefs and undershirt, a sleeveless cotton vest that Trudy's students would refer to as a wife-beater. Divested of its typical garments, Rainer's body in the astringent afternoon light looks old. True, the height of his frame does not belie the power within it, and he is bull-chested and covered all over with a smattering of grayish hair. But his flesh is powder-white and soft in places it wouldn't be on a younger man—for instance over his biceps, still apple-hard, it hangs slack and stretched from the muscle. Trudy doesn't care one bit. She is no spring chicken herself. And with Rainer, Trudy feels no shame; she is no longer plagued by images of blood, the smell of saliva paint-sharp on skin, the phantom gristle of pubic hair against bone—all things she has not realized have troubled her until now, in their absence.

Trudy stretches luxuriously and yawns, then says *Mmmm* to get Rainer's attention. It doesn't work; he doesn't turn from his pensive inspection of the yard. Unlike Trudy, Rainer is moody after lovemaking. Smoke curls against the windowpane. He is halfway through his second cigarette, a luxury he permits himself only postcoitus, tapping ashes into a small crystal bowl kept in a bedside table drawer specifically for this purpose, wiping it clean with a rag as soon as he is done.

When he lights a third Trudy sits up and reaches for the robe Rainer has bought her, a slippery silk garment of shocking and splashy pink Trudy would never have chosen for herself, so bright it verges on vulgar. Trudy loves it. She cinches the fringed sash around her waist and pads over to Rainer, the wooden floorboards cool against her feet. Standing behind him, she stretches on tiptoe to rest her lips very lightly on the back of his neck, where the silver hair is as short and prickly as that on a dog's muzzle.

Aren't you cold? she murmurs.

No. But you are. Your nose is like an icicle.

Trudy puts her arms around him.

Come back to bed, she says.

In a minute.

Rainer grinds out his cigarette and carries his makeshift ashtray from the room. Trudy hears the toilet flush down the hall and water running in the sink. When Rainer returns, he takes the cloth from the windowsill where he has left it and begins to polish the bowl dry. Trudy, observing this routine from the side of the bed, begins to laugh.

What is so funny? Rainer says, without looking up from his task.

You, says Trudy. You have to be the most German Jew in the entire world.

Rainer scowls. He drops the ashtray into its drawer and slams it shut.

And what, precisely, is that supposed to mean? he asks.

Oh, come on, Rainer. It doesn't mean anything. It's just that you're so obsessively neat. I've never met anyone as compulsive as I am before—aside from my mother, of course.

Rainer lifts his trousers from a chair, shakes them out, and steps into them, then turns to the closet for a shirt.

Hey, says Trudy. Aren't you coming back to bed?

No, says Rainer shortly. Get dressed.

But—

Rainer gives her a look over his bifocals. He points at Trudy's clothes, folded on the bureau. Then he leaves. Trudy sits bewildered in her robe, listening to him descend the steps. She takes a deep breath.

Okay, she says to the room, which is as large and square and neatly kept as its owner. Then she sheds the robe and pulls on her turtleneck and sweater and slacks and hastens down the stairs.

Rainer is in the kitchen, slapping sandwiches together, luncheon meat on brown bread. Trudy goes to the refrigerator and takes out the mayonnaise.

You forgot this, she says, setting it on the table.

A deliberate oversight. I do not want it.

But you like mayonnaise, Trudy says.

Don't hover.

Trudy retreats to the counter and leans against it, folding her arms.

Rainer, don't be angry, she says. What I said upstairs, I wasn't implying— I mean, I certainly didn't want to offend— Oh, hell.

Rainer cuts the sandwiches into triangles and puts them, tongues of bologna and lettuce protruding from their crusts, first into plastic bags and then a large brown paper one.

Get your coat, he says, adding napkins and a thermos.

Are we going on a picnic? Trudy asks. She ducks her head to glance through the window at the thermometer affixed to the garage. You must be joking. It's two degrees out there!

Get your coat, Rainer repeats. I will meet you in the car.

Bemused, Trudy complies. When she is all bundled up, she leaves the house through the back door and runs through the cold to where Rainer's white Buick is idling in the driveway, exhaust pluming from its muffler. It is a big low boat of a car with sharky tail fins, so absurdly long as to appear an optical illusion. The passenger's door cracks open at Trudy's approach and she gratefully throws herself inside.

This is crazy, she says, as Rainer reverses into the alley and accelerates out onto Fiftieth Street. Where are we going?

I want to show you something.

What?

In reply, Rainer reaches over and switches on the radio. He changes stations until he finds a Rachmaninoff prelude, then dials the volume up so that the swelling chords fill the car. Trudy sinks back in the prickly plush of the seat, watching Rainer from the corner of one eye. His profile is inscrutable, calm beneath the brim of his hat; he steers the big Buick with the twist of a finger, his hand relaxed on the wheel.

They drive through the quiet streets of Edina and the busier avenues of Uptown. Past Lake Calhoun, white and flat as a dinner plate — it being a weekday, there are no die-hard exercise fanatics on its paths, jogging in hamsterlike circuits or huffing along on skis. Onward over a bridge toward Lake of the Isles, where Rainer pulls right up to the shoreline and parks. He rummages in the backseat for the bag lunch and a tartan cloth, then gets out of the car and stands with the blanket folded over his arm.

Trudy looks at him and then through the windshield. Of all the lakes in Minneapolis, Lake of the Isles is her least favorite; its amoeba shape confuses her, turning her around on its walkways until she loses her sense of direction and can't tell whether the city is in front of her or to her back. There are no people here either, just a few ice-fishing shacks scattered about, smoke trailing thinly from their stovepipe chimneys.

This is silly, Rainer, Trudy says in her sternest tone. I'm not going out there.

Rainer shrugs, the wind whisking his streaming breath away into the air.

As you wish, he says.

He walks away from Trudy and out onto the ice, where he spreads the blanket and sits, fedora and overcoat and all, and opens the brown sack.

Trudy climbs from the car.

Get back here, you idiot, she yells. You'll catch your death of pneumonia!

Rainer appears not to hear her. He bites into a sandwich. He eats half of it with apparent relish, then sets it down and stands.

Come, he calls.

Trudy shakes her head, then slams the car door and picks her way over frozen mud and reeds to the ice. She puts a foot on it and hesitates. It appears solid, thick and rutted. And the temperature is certainly low enough that it should hold. And if people are still fishing...But there was a thaw a few days ago, and local newscasters have issued warnings to be extra cautious when venturing onto the ice, and Trudy has always thought that plunging through it would be a particularly terrible way to die. Flailing in frigid water, in the dark, bumping one's head against the hard ceiling, unable to breathe —

Come on! Rainer shouts, waving her forward.

Trudy takes another step. Then she runs out toward him, arms extended for balance, as pell-mell and clumsy as a child. Rainer catches her as she hurtles into him, so hard that they both stagger and nearly fall. But he rights himself in time and Trudy squeezes her eyes shut and pushes her face into the reassuring wool of his coat, which smells of the cedar closet in which he keeps it.

They stand for a minute like this, breathing hard.

Then Trudy hears Rainer say—or feels it, rather, his voice rumbling through the layers of cloth to her cheek: We have a problem.

What? What is it?

Rainer detaches her.

Turn around, he says.

Why?

Must you always be so argumentative?

Rainer grips Trudy by the shoulders and spins her so her back is braced against his chest. Then he takes his hands away. Trudy tucks her own into her armpits for warmth, even though they are gloved.

Look, Rainer says.

Trudy does. She sees nothing out of the ordinary: the gray-white lake, the overcast sky a darker gray above it, the dense black calligraphy of branches on the far shore. Behind them is a brilliant lemon-colored slash of light that somehow has the effect of making the afternoon seem even colder than it is. The wind rushes ceaselessly over the ice, teasing water from Trudy's eyes; her cheeks will be bright red when she and Rainer get back indoors. But this is also thrilling, like being, Trudy thinks, on the deck of a ship embarked on an Arctic expedition.

A brace of geese flies overhead, returning from some warmer clime, honking.

What is it I'm supposed to be looking at? Trudy asks.

Rainer chuckles and puts his arms around her from behind.

This is our problem, Dr. Swenson, he says into her hair. You think too much. Stop it. Don't think. Don't talk. Just look. Be.

53

THE FOLLOWING MONDAY TRUDY WALKS INTO HER SEMINAR TEN minutes late. The crosstown traffic from Rainer's has been horrendous: cars stalled in pools of standing water, the effect of intense April showers on highways whose drains are already flooded; tow trucks out in force, sending up wings of slush. Trudy, however, is whistling the Colonel Bogie March as she stamps her boots in the doorway. She has had it in her head for days, since to its tune Rainer is fond of singing in the shower, with bellowing enthusiasm and appalling pitch, this verse:

> *Hitler, he only had one ball*
> *Göring had two but very small*
> *Himmler had something similar*
> *And poor old Goebbels had no balls at all!*

Humming, Trudy crosses to the lectern and opens her briefcase.

Good morning, she says.

Some dispirited mumbles from the class. Trudy shakes the sleet from her hair.

What's wrong with you people? she asks. Granted, this is the sort of day the British would refer to as filthy, but it *is* technically spring, you know.

What*ever,* somebody says.

Trudy smiles and adjusts her scarf, a square of lime-green chiffon that she and Rainer bought over the weekend, Rainer insisting that Trudy make an effort to appear less funereal in public as well as behind closed doors. This caused a prolonged skirmish in the mall boutique, and Trudy smiles again at the thought of it: the saleslady at first flustered, and then, once the purchase had finally been rung at the register, assuming a conspiratorial tone and asking Trudy how long she and Rainer had been married.

Trudy walks to the board to write the topic du jour: Women in the *Schutzstaffeln*—Enforced Complicity or Lust for Power?

So, she says. Let's start with the female wardens in the camps. The lovely and heartless SS *Kapo* Mandel whom Fania Fenelon described in your assigned reading, for instance. What is Fenelon's assessment of Mandel's character?

She turns to her students. They stare vacantly at her or the floor, hollow-eyed from staying up all night. Their noses are rabbity and dripping from the eternal colds they swap back and forth. They are wearing baggy hooded sweatshirts and pajama bottoms with their big bulbous sneakers. They look completely uninterested in the topic at hand, and they are absolutely beautiful.

Trudy puts her chalk down and slaps the dust off her hands.

Oh, forget it, she says. Why don't you all go get some sleep? Or, God forbid, do something productive, like studying for your midterm.

Pens stop scribbling in margins. The students look at Trudy blankly or with dawning hope.

Go on, get out of here, Trudy tells them with a shooing motion. Enjoy your parole.

Hesitantly at first, as if this is a test they might fail by obeying, a few of them start stuffing their things into their knapsacks and struggling into their parkas. Then, before Trudy can change her mind, the rest leap up and funnel quickly from the room. Trudy watches benignly. The students are laughing and talking, animated, and this pleases her. This is the way they are supposed to be.

Now what's up with her? she hears Frick or Frack say to his counterpart.

Dunno. She looks—weird. Different. Like she's been getting laid or something.

Professor Death? You're on crack, man.

They shuffle out, grumbling.

When the door bangs shut behind them, Trudy repacks her materials and walks out too, without bothering to erase the board. But instead of heading toward the parking lot, she goes upstairs. She has something else to do before she leaves the university: she has had a wonderful idea. Singing under her breath—*Hitler, he only had one ball; Göring had two*—Trudy saunters through the History Department toward Ruth's office.

This, like Trudy's, is on the first floor, tucked away in a warren of rooms in the rear, and it is similar to hers in other ways as well: overheated, badly in need of a coat of fresh paint, smelling of coffee warmed overly long on a hot plate and dusty old books. But here the resemblance stops, for while Trudy's office is austere, Ruth is a collector of Holocaust memorabilia. A glass-fronted cabinet too big for the room displays her strange treasures: a swastika banner that once adorned the Reichstag; currency from the Warsaw ghetto; postcards sent from the camps, including Buchenwald, with their single lines of typed text—*We are being well treated, there is work here.* The walls are crowded with Nazi propaganda posters, the largest featuring a terrified Aryan woman who looks much like Anna being menaced by a grinning grizzled Jew. *Frauen und Mädchen,* its slogan reads, *die Juden Sind Ewer Ruine!* Women and Girls, the Jews Are

Your Ruin! Another, situated directly behind Ruth's head, shows a giant Hitler and Stalin shaking hands over a stream of tiny screaming Jews plummeting into a fiery abyss, startling Trudy every time she opens the door.

As Trudy has known she would be at this time of day, Ruth is at her desk, scowling at papers. She throws down her red pen at Trudy's knock.

Oh, thank God, Ruth says. You are my savior. These midterms are atrocious— Wait, don't you have a seminar now?

I do, says Trudy. I let my kids go.

You did what? That's unprecedented. Why?

Oh, I don't know, says Trudy. I guess I'm just in too sanguine a mood to talk about such depressing stuff today.

Ruth pulls her feet up on the edge of her chair, hugging her knees to her chest. She studies Trudy with her sharp little unblinking eyes.

All right, what's up.

Nothing, says Trudy.

Baloney, says Ruth. She squints at Trudy's tousled hair— which Trudy has left uncut so she will less resemble, as Rainer has commented, a tubercular young boy—and at the bright green scarf. You look— different somehow.

Trudy shrugs.

Don't be silly, she replies.

But she can feel herself grinning as she drops into the chair opposite Ruth's.

Listen, she says. That trip that you and Bob took to the Caribbean over Christmas. Do you still have the brochures?

Ruth leans back with a *squoink* of springs.

Why? she says. You're going?

Trudy nods. If the scheduling works out, she adds.

By yourself?

Well, says Trudy, actually no. There's a man...

Ruth pumps her fist in the air. I *knew* it! I knew that had to be it, with you grinning that way. It's about time! Who is he?

Trudy smiles down at her lap. Now that she is here, she can admit to herself that this is the reason she has come to see Ruth instead of calling a travel agent. Trudy wants to talk to Ruth about Rainer. She wants to talk to everybody about Rainer. She can barely go to the supermarket for toilet paper without announcing to the checkout clerk that Rainer uses the same brand. She can't pull her socks on in the morning without thinking that Rainer's are looking shabby, really; she should buy him some new ones. She has been bursting with the need to share all of this with somebody, to crow over her sudden good fortune. And she is certainly not about to tell Anna. But there is, thank heavens, Ruth.

Who is waiting for Trudy's answer, smiling in anticipation, so Trudy says, His name is Rainer. Rainer Goldmann. He's big and rude and preemptory and a former teacher and he must have been a terror in the classroom and I am completely smitten... What's wrong?

Nothing, says Ruth. She gives her head a little shake. The name sounds familiar to me, but I can't think why... Go on. Where did you meet him?

Trudy laughs. Through the Project, can you believe it? It was awful at the time. He'd read one of my flyers and he lured me to his house on the pretext of participating, but once we were on camera it turned out that he's really one of yours, a Jewish Holocaust survivor, and did he read me the riot act for even *attempting* to record the German side of the story. Which maybe wasn't unjustified, so I went back to his house that night with some latkes, and...

Trudy trails off, for Ruth is no longer looking at her. She has picked up her favorite toy, a Lego facsimile of Herr *Doktor* Mengele, and is bending his Lego legs to his waist, frowning at them. Trudy knows that Ruth has ordered Herr *Doktor* Mengele off the Internet, and that he has come complete with his own Lego operating theater, Lego assistants, and Lego victims, but these, unlike the Herr *Doktor* who customarily sits propped against a lamp, have been consigned to the supply closet. Trudy also knows that Ruth plays with Herr *Doktor* Mengele only when she is working through some thorny departmental problem or is otherwise upset. Trudy makes a face, perplexed.

What's the matter? she asks. I thought you'd be happy for me.

I am, says Ruth to the *Doktor,* bending him back and forth at the waist. Really, it's great that you're dating. But this guy, Trudy...I don't know. Because now I know where I've heard his name before: I called him myself, about participating in the Remembrance Project. And he seemed...

What?

A bit rough.

Rough?

Angry, says Ruth, setting the *Doktor* on the desk. He was really very rude, actually.

Trudy sits back.

Well, I already told you he's like that, she says. But that's just a front. He has some— some difficulty when he's confronted with talking about the past.

Ruth snorts.

No kidding, she says. Believe me, that came through loud and clear. Trudy, I hate to say this, but maybe you should rethink being involved with him. I'm not sure it's the wisest course of action.

Trudy bristles.

Oh, really? she asks. Why is that? Because I'm German and he's a Jew? You know how you're acting, Ruth? Like a Jewish mother, like any yenta who disowns her kids if they marry outside the religion and sits shivah if they do—

Ruth is tolerating this outburst with a patient, candid gaze, and Trudy stops, ashamed. She knows this is not the case at all. In fact, Ruth's husband Bob is only half-Jewish, and the couple has had to suffer the disdain of Ruth's family because of it. But why is Ruth treating her in this patronizing fashion, as if Trudy were a teenager dizzy with her first crush, as if she is incapable of seeing for herself that the boy who is taking her to the prom is really a juvenile delinquent?

I'm sorry, Trudy says. Please ignore everything I just said. But I don't understand why you're reacting this way.

I don't want to see you get hurt, says Ruth. That's all.

Ruth, that's not going to happen. Rainer's a good man. Really. He's the best person I've ever met.

Ruth reaches for her toy again.

I'm sure he is, she says. But you know, you've been out of the swing of things for so long that...I'm just a little concerned. Now listen. I really do think it's great that you're putting yourself out there again. So before you get too heavily involved with Mr. Goldmann, maybe you should consider dating somebody else too, for balance? As a matter of fact, there's a man I've been dying to introduce you to. A new colleague of Bob's at the firm, recently relocated here from St. Louis. Not divorced. A widower. Three children, but all grown, and he's really a wonderful...

Trudy watches Ruth throughout the rest of this sales pitch, smiling a bit acidly. She understands Ruth's objection now. For a long period after Trudy's divorce, the well-meaning Ruth, desperate to see Trudy remarried, introduced her to a parade of prospective candidates. And Trudy played along for a while, enduring countless dinner parties where she would be seated next to whatever available bachelor Ruth could provide—he could be pompous, balding, fat, flatulent, it didn't matter, as long as he was breathing and single. Trudy still remembers the scalding humiliation of Ruth's final attempt about seven years ago, which consisted of Trudy listening in horror while her date described, with huge enthusiasm, a recent singles' cruise where the introductory activity consisted of standing in the ship's pool passing a rubber ball from person to person using only one's chin. After this, Trudy gave up, telling Ruth that having a partner was perhaps simply not in her cards.

And Ruth must have been thinking of Trudy in this particular way ever since: the ungrateful recipient of social charity, the sad sole monkey on Noah's Ark. Of course she is disconcerted to see Trudy so suddenly changed. People hate it when others step out of their neatly labeled little boxes.

Ruth is looking at Trudy with bright expectation.

Well? she says. Sound good? I could set something up for next week.

Trudy smiles gently at her.

Thanks, she says. I'll keep it in mind. Maybe somewhere down the road...In the meantime, though, could I have those travel brochures?

54

ONCE THE PAMPHLETS RUTH HAS RELUCTANTLY GIVEN Trudy are safely tucked in her briefcase, Trudy drives back across the river to Rainer's house. She will now implement step two of her wonderful scheme: she will whisk Rainer off to lunch at Le P'tit, and there she will reveal the trip they will take together. The anticipation of Rainer's reaction—and of introducing her new lover to her ex-husband—is so delicious that Trudy starts to sing again, at the top of her lungs, smiling and waving at the other drivers who catch her belting like a Wagnerian soprano at stoplights.

But when she runs up his front steps and twists the key to his bell, Rainer doesn't come to answer it.

Trudy tries three more times. When Rainer still fails to appear, she walks slowly to his porch swing and sits, puzzled. Has Rainer mentioned some appointment this afternoon that Trudy has forgotten about? A routine checkup, a meeting with his accountant, the dentist? Trudy doesn't think so. Maybe he is running an errand. She sifts through the brochures while she waits. Palm trees, aquamarine waters, couples strolling hand in hand along sugar-sand beaches. Quite a contrast to what Trudy sees when she looks up, rain puddling on the sidewalks and street, ankle-deep over the ice. Canned game-show laughter and applause come from one of the neighboring houses: another retiree, perhaps, hard of hearing, the volume turned all the way up. Nobody else is home this time of day, except maybe an exhausted young mother or two stealing an hour's rest while her children nap. Everyone else is at work.

After forty-five minutes have passed, Trudy starts to grow concerned. Also cold. Unfolding herself stiffly from the swing— her limbs chilled, the seat of her coat damp—Trudy tramps through the remaining snow to the backyard. Rainer's car is not in the driveway where it usually is, and she feels a moment's relief. But when she checks the garage, peering through the dusty windows, the Buick is there among the cobwebs and garden tools: an improbably long white shape in the shadows, like a submarine.

Really worried now, Trudy rushes to the back door and pounds on it.

Rainer, she yells. It's me! Open up!

She backpedals to the middle of the lawn and squints up at the bedroom, cupping her hands around her mouth.

Rainer!

When there is still no response, Trudy retrieves from beneath an overturned flowerpot in the garden the spare key Rainer hides there. This is an effort, since the key has frozen into the ground. And it is an unnecessary one, for when Trudy uses it she locks the door instead of opening it; it has been unsecured all along. She hurries through the kitchen, the metallic taste of fear in her mouth. Has Rainer had a heart attack? A stroke? As he often jokes after an especially energetic session in bed, he is no longer a young man.

Rainer, Trudy yells. Can you answer me? Where are you?

She runs up the stairs and nearly collides with him halfway, as he is coming down.

Goodness, what a ruckus, he says.

Trudy grips the banister and lets out a shaky breath.

God, you scared me, she tells him. I thought something bad had happened to you.

Rainer smiles. Is it really so easy for you to give me up for dead, Dr. Swenson?

It's not funny, Trudy snaps. Why didn't you answer the door?

Rainer looks sheepish.

I wasn't expecting you until later, he says.

Didn't you hear me knocking? Ringing the bell?

I did indeed. I thought it was a particularly irritating salesman.

But Rainer looks away as he says this, and Trudy feels another frisson of unease. He is lying. Something is still wrong. She notices for the first time that he is holding an armful of sweaters.

What are you doing? she asks.

Packing.

Packing?

Trudy follows Rainer to his bedroom, which is in atypical chaos. On the bed is a garment bag, unzipped and bulging with trousers, and next to it is an open suitcase. For a bewildered second Trudy thinks Rainer has read her mind about the trip she has been planning, or even intended to suggest one himself. But the amount of clothes on the comforter soon puts paid to that idea. There are mounds of cardigans, pajamas, pairs of socks. Wherever he is going, he expects to be there for a long time.

What are you doing? Trudy asks again.

I should think it is fairly obvious.

But I don't understand. Is there some sort of emergency? Has something happened to your daughter?

Rainer wedges a packet of undershirts into the suitcase. He seems to be avoiding Trudy's eyes. Or is she imagining it?

I was going to leave you a note, he says.

A note?

A letter.

Trudy braces herself against the door. The rain has stopped, the droplets trickling down the windowpane casting sinuous shadows on the opposite wall, and the room is filled with watery gray light. She can hear the drip of melting icicles, the coo of a mourning dove in the gutter. The latter conjures images of green lawns, shadows at twilight, the clink of ice cubes in cocktail glasses. How can this be happening?

Where are you going? she asks.

Florida.

Florida?

Do please refrain from repeating everything I say, Rainer tells her, but without heat. He has yet to look at Trudy.

I'm sorry, she says. I'm just so...Why are you going to Florida?

To visit my daughter and granddaughter.

For— For how long?

Now Rainer does turn to face her.

Trudy, he says.

Trudy stares at him. The resignation in his eyes tells her everything she needs to know.

No, she cries.

Rainer shoves a pair of loafers into the suitcase.

It is for the best, he says.

How can you say that? That is the stupidest thing I've ever heard. How can you possibly think that's true?

Rainer stands with his hands in his pockets, studying the bed.

It *is* true, he says. And it is not the end of the world. In any case, I am not certain how long I will stay. I have deliberately left my return date open. Perhaps I will find I am not suited for a tropical climate after all.

His tone is sardonic, but Trudy sees the muscles working along his jaw. She crosses to him and tugs his sleeve.

Rainer, look at me. Please. Is it something I've done? Something I've said? That thing last week, about you being the most German Jew—

No, no, says Rainer. But he remains immobile, his forearm like a cord of wood beneath Trudy's hand.

Trudy takes a painful breath, tears building behind her eyes. Is it because of who I am? Because of *him*—my father?

Of course not. You must never think that, Trudy.

Then it has to be my Project. I'll give it up. Today. Right now. As of this moment I'll never do another interview—

Rainer sighs. Don't be preposterous. That is the last thing I want.

What *do* you want, then? Trudy says. Please, Rainer. Please don't go. Or take me with you—

Then she remembers her mother. What will happen to Anna if Trudy leaves? But Trudy is too frantic to care. She'll think of something.

Please, she says again. Don't do this. Why are you doing this?

Finally Rainer looks down at her and clasps Trudy's hands in his.

It has nothing to do with you, he says. You must believe that.

Trudy stares at their laced fingers and shakes her head. She feels nothing except the certainty that she is the butt of a cosmic joke. Has she really dared to think happiness is for her? She has been a fool. Somewhere the gods are slapping their giant robed knees and laughing.

Without you, she tells Rainer, I'll have nothing.

Ah, Trudy.

Rainer lets go of her hands to enfold her in his arms.

You will have plenty, he says, his voice a vibration on Trudy's cheek. You had a full life before we met, and you still do. Your classes, the students to whom you are so dedicated, your research, your project. You will be fine. Better than fine.

But Rainer—

As usual, I beg you not to argue. I must do this. You are only making it worse.

Trudy presses her face against the scratchy wool of his sweater and permits herself one last inhale of the cologne whose fragrance she has so rejoiced to find lingering on her own neck, in her hair; beneath this, Rainer's distinct scent, clean like wood chips, like cedar.

Then she pulls away from him.

You still haven't told me why, she says. You owe me that much, at least.

Rainer moves back to the bed. He selects a tie and holds it up, examining its subdued stripes as if he has never seen it before. Then he winds it into a roll and tucks it into the suitcase.

Why does any old man go to Florida? he asks, his voice not quite steady. A kinder climate. A perpetual summer. And in my case, the yearning to be with family. You forget I am older than you, Trudy. I do not know how many good years I have left, and I should like to spend some time with them.

All right, says Trudy. That sounds valid enough. But it's not the real reason. Is it.

Rainer gazes at his clothes, his fists clenched at his sides.

I do not deserve to have this, he says finally, very low. I am not meant to be this happy.

Trudy starts to protest this as well, but then she finds she can't. She suddenly feels very heavy. It is the weight of the inevitable. Who is Trudy to argue when she has felt the same conviction not a minute earlier? Part of her has known all along that this cannot last. The moment upon them now has been decided for them both long ago.

She releases a long trembling sigh and steps next to Rainer. She touches the pile of cardigans. She knows each and every one of them intimately. Something sharp catches in her throat, then swells until she can barely breathe.

Around it she asks, Why are you bringing all these sweaters?

Air-conditioning, Rainer replies. Everything down there is climate-controlled. My daughter's house is like a meat locker.

Ah, says Trudy.

She picks up the top cardigan and folds its arms behind its

back, then doubles it and sets it in the suitcase with the rest. Rainer fetches another suit from the closet and lays it in the garment bag. Trudy senses him standing close to her, so close she can feel the warmth radiating from his skin. He is breathing with effort in deliberately controlled measures, his breath coming short and hard through his nostrils, and Trudy knows he wants to touch her again. But he does not, and she helps him pack without saying another word. They orbit around each other in organized, well-choreographed rhythm, like husband and wife who have been sending each other off on trips for years.

55

WHEN TRUDY GETS HOME, SHE WALKS STRAIGHT PAST A startled Anna in the kitchen and down the hall to her study, where she slams the door. It occurs to her that Anna will find this behavior rude or even alarming. But Trudy doesn't spare it a second thought. She can apologize later. Or perhaps she won't. What does it matter now?

Without removing her coat, Trudy sinks into her desk chair and looks dully around the room. There are her texts and papers and books, the history periodicals to which she subscribes, her interview transcripts and *Lotte in Weimar* recording and CDs of German composers. The tapes of her subjects, alphabetized on a shelf in the television cabinet above the VCR. Headphones. Legal pads. Binders of class plans organized by year. Year upon year of them, in fact, stretching back through the decades. This, then, is the sum total of Trudy's existence. How has it come to be this way? This was not how it was supposed to be. Trudy tries to remember a time when she might have wanted something else and what that might have been, but she can't. And when Trudy attempts to picture simply going away, to Florida for instance, or one of the islands in those glossy pamphlets, what comes to mind is an image of herself on an old wooden ship, sailing and sailing until she reaches the end of the world and falls off.

You will be fine, Rainer has told her; your work, your students, your research, the full life you had before you met me.

Trudy leans forward and sweeps everything off her desk. She kicks her briefcase, which spills her lecture notes and the travel brochures onto the rug. Then she puts her head down on the blotter and covers it with her arms.

Some indeterminate time later there is a tentative tap on the door. Then it opens and Anna comes in. She switches on the floor lamp next to the sofa and Trudy looks up, blinking. She has not noticed how dark the room has become. It is already evening. And where is Rainer now? At the airport? On a plane?

Anna tucks the spatula she is holding into the pocket of her apron and extends her hands. Trudy stands, takes off her coat, passes it to Anna, and sits down again. Anna disappears with it, to hang it in the closet, Trudy presumes. She does not expect Anna to come back.

But Anna does. She stays in the doorway for a moment, assessing the mess on the floor. Then, with a small grunt of effort, she stoops and begins to tidy it up.

Leave it, Mama, says Trudy.

Anna blows at a long strand of white hair that has escaped her wreath of braids. Then she continues stacking the papers into orderly piles.

I said, leave it! Trudy says.

She puts her hands over her face.

Oh, God, she cries.

Anna straightens and walks to the side of the desk, setting a sheaf of transcripts on it.

So, she says. He is gone, then.

What? says Trudy.

Your man. The man with whom you have been keeping company.

Trudy lowers her hands and stares at her mother. Anna is looking down at her, neat and sturdy as always in a navy blue dress. There is a smudge of flour high on her cheekbone.

How did you know that?

Anna smiles.

Ach, Trudy, she says. Do you think I am a fool? Those times you did not come home for dinner. Those nights you did not come home at all. Where else would you be but with him?

Trudy nods and sighs.

He has gone away now, Anna repeats.

Yes.

For good?

I don't know, says Trudy.

She waits for Anna to offer some condolence, some platitude of reassurance or advice, but Anna says nothing more.

You know who it was, Mama? The man whose interview you watched. The night I came in here and you were viewing the tape.

Ah, says Anna. I suspected as much.

Did you?

Yes. It was written on your face the moment you saw him.

Trudy looks up at her.

So you know he was Jewish, she says.

Yes. I knew.

Doesn't that bother you, Mama? That I was involved with a Jew?

Anna continues to smile, a little sadly, Trudy thinks.

That is a silly question, Trudy, she says. Why should it? You are a grown woman. You may keep company with whomever you wish. It is no concern of mine.

Well, says Trudy. It's irrelevant now anyway. He's gone.

Then she covers her face again.

So, she hears Anna say. So.

She senses rather than feels Anna's fingers graze her hair, so light is the touch. It is more a fleeting rearrangement of the molecules in the air near Trudy's head, a momentary impression of movement, than anything. Yet it suddenly reminds Trudy of all the other occasions on which Anna has comforted her. *Nur eine Alptraum,* Anna would say, sitting on the side of Trudy's childhood bed when Trudy awoke yelling from nightmares she could never remember; *Ja so, es ist nur eine Alptraum.* Just a bad dream. A voice in the dark. A hand on Trudy's forehead. How Anna slapped Trudy and then held her on the morning of Trudy's first menstrual flow, when Trudy screamed and screamed and could not stop screaming at the discovery of the rusty stain on her drawers. *So. So. This is what it means to be a woman. Once a month you will pass blood. Like so,* nicht? The sight of Anna's rare smile, her fine strong white teeth, sun winking through clouds. And the tune Anna hummed, a favorite of Jack's to which Anna had not yet learned the words: *You are my sunshine, my only sunshine. You make me happy when skies are gray.*

But it is too late for such things now, or perhaps too much wariness has passed between the two women. For there is only the moth-light brush of Anna's fingertips and a trace of her lilac sachet, and when Trudy looks up she sees that Anna has already gone to the door.

I have made a cake, Anna tells her. A poppy-seed cake. Would you like some?

Before Trudy can refuse, she adds, I will put on a pot of your coffee to go with it.

Kaffee und Kuchen instead of *Komfort?* Trudy thinks. Well, why not? It is the best either of them can do.

Despite everything, Trudy's lips stitch in a rueful smile, and Anna looks pleased, and it is then that Trudy recalls the rest of the song: *The other night, dear, as I lay sleeping, I dreamed I held you in my arms. When I awoke, dear, I was mistaken, so I hung my head and cried.*

Thank you, Mama, she says softly. I would like that.

Anna and Jack,
New Heidelburg, 1945

56

HEIMAT. THE WORD MEANS *HOME* IN GERMAN, THE PLACE where one was born. But the term also conveys a subtler nuance, a certain tenderness. One's *Heimat* is not merely a matter of geography; it is where the heart lies. And Anna, lacking the vocabulary to explain this distinction to anyone in her new country, is no longer certain she has one.

For as alien as her own land has become to Anna, her husband's *Heimat* is more so. Everything about America is incomprehensible to her: the abundant food, the huge vehicles, the immensity of its flat horizons and the violence of its weather. Worse, despite the surface strangeness, an essential undercurrent remains the same. The people here regard Anna with suspicion, their hostility palpable beneath their polite smiles. Anna is dismayed to discover that she has carried Germany with her as surely as if she had imported the spores of its soil beneath her fingernails, as if the smell of its corpses still clung to her skin.

Christmas Eve, 1945, Anna's first experience of the holiday in her adopted homeland. She and Jack and Trudie will attend services at the New Heidelburg Lutheran Church. This is a good twelve kilometers—*miles,* Anna reminds herself—from the farmhouse. A long drive on a cold night. Anna would much prefer to stay home, putting the finishing touches on tomorrow's goose or tying ribbons on presents or simply sitting in the kitchen, toasting her feet by the range and awaiting Jack and Trudie's return. But over the past three months Anna has observed that it saddens Jack when she avoids going into town, though he never says it outright. And she has retained enough Old World schooling to know that a good wife should never disappoint her husband. So Anna bathes herself and the child, puts on her nicest dress and bravest face, and climbs into the truck.

This Lutheran church is a surprisingly plain affair: square and white and wood-shingled, only its steeple differentiating it from a dwelling. A far cry, thinks Anna, from her childhood house of worship, Weimar's massive stone cathedral with its soaring naves and disproportionately tiny red door meant to remind man of his relative insignificance. Yet Anna has never felt smaller than she does here, trying to evade the gawking of the curious by slipping into a rear pew. And tonight it is worse, since as a result of the farm truck balking in the subzero temperatures, she and Jack and Trudie are late. When they arrive minutes before the service is to begin, the church's modest interior is packed and riotous with New Heidelburgers and their overexcited children. But when Jack and his new little family appear, a hush falls over the crowd. Heads swivel in their direction. There is whispering. And aside from this and a baby's bleat, silence.

Jack stands surveying the room. He wears the stoic, friendly expression common among the people of this town, but in her side vision Anna sees his jaw tighten beneath his bumpy skin. And the reason is obvious: nobody is shifting aside to offer them a seat. Instead they stare, and nudge each other, and turn to stare again. Anna takes a firmer grip on Trudie's hand, hoping the girl will not notice her own trembling. She looks straight ahead at the altar, head high. It is like being in a dream, a bad dream, and

Anna has the odd sense that she has dreamed something very similar before.

Finally the minister's wife pops up from the front pew like the toy Jack has made for Trudie for Christmas, its name bemusing to Anna because it is the same as his: *jack-in-the-box*.

Here's some space for you folks, the woman calls, waving them over.

Anna and Jack and Trudie walk down the aisle past the rows of New Heidelburgers, Anna and Trudie a few steps before Jack as is proper, trailing a murmur in their wake.

Here you go, says the minister's wife when they reach her, moving her coat to make room on the varnished bench. She beams at Jack, her face round as a platter beneath shellacked poodle curls.

My, isn't it cold! she says, and turns to Trudie. But don't you worry, she adds to the child, it's not too cold for Santa to come. Not if you've been a good girl. Have you been good this year?

Trudie shrinks to hide herself behind Anna's coat. Anna doesn't blame her. The people here smile far too much to be trusted. But she whispers to the girl in German, Answer the nice lady.

Trudie peeks at the minister's wife and scowls.

Thank you, Adeline, Jack tells the woman, voice low. Merry Christmas.

Why, Merry Christmas to you too!

Then they face forward as the service begins. Anna comprehends little of it. The way the minister speaks bears scant resemblance to the language she learned in *Gymnasium;* these Minnesotans talk from the throat, with flat wide vowels. Anna makes a token effort to practice her English by translating, though she doesn't care much for the sermon on the glory of God and the miraculous birth of His son. But soon her mind returns, as always, to the bakery. The bakery with its worktable and rust-stained double sink. The bakery with mice scampering fruitlessly in the cupboards. The black rectangular mouth of the oven that assumed such horrible significance over the years as Anna shoveled loaves in and out. Mathilde's bedroom with its cracked gray ceiling and the *Obersturmführer*'s trousers slung over the baker's vacant chair.

The congregation stands to sing. If Anna doesn't completely understand the words, at least the music is familiar. Mindful of Jack watching her, she mouths the lyrics in English but rebelliously retains the German in her head: *Stille Nacht, heilige Nacht...* Then the service is over and the second part of this trial begins. Having been briefed by Jack beforehand, Anna knows what to expect, and she files with the rest of the town to the reception in the cellar. She looks around with curiosity, again startled by the humble appearance of the long room. When not being used for church functions, Jack has told her, it serves as a bingo parlor and cyclone shelter, whatever *bingo* and *cyclone* might be. In any case, it is tiled in faded linoleum and smells of old smoke, its only decorations lurid velvet paintings of Jesus and stags' heads, and the men and women immediately divide into separate groups at either end with tangible relief.

Anna gives Trudie over to Jack's care and approaches the folding table where the other wives have already set out their offerings. Such strange confections! A cake fashioned to look like a log, complete with a plastic sprig of holly; a gelatin mold with soft white sweets imprisoned in its wobbling confines. But for this too Anna is prepared, and she unwraps her *Stollen* and sets it among the other desserts as though it were no different from the rest. She regards her braided loaf of Christmas bread with pride. As Mathilde has taught her to do, she has folded dates and nuts into its dough, and before baking she brushed the top with egg white to make it shine.

As Anna steps back to further admire her handiwork, she notices the woman on her left inspecting it too. Mrs. Zimmerman, is that the woman's name? Whoever she is, she squints warily at the *Stollen* as if the candied fruit in its crust might explode in her face like shrapnel. Then she catches Anna watching her and smiles.

Looks tasty, she says, and scuttles off to where the other women are standing on the far side of the room in an exclusionary knot.

Tasty? Cheeks aflame, Anna wanders a few meters away and pretends to admire the Jesus portrait. The son of God is silhouetted against a yellow sunburst and wearing a bright blue robe; he clasps his hands in prayer, his eyes rolled up toward heaven to show the whites. Anna gazes at this without seeing it, counting the seconds under her breath: *elf ... vierzehn ... sieben und zwanzig ...* Once she has reached one hundred, she permits herself to look about for Jack. There he is, with the men, of course, discussing silage, drainage systems, crop prices and weather, a conversation as never-ending as the wind that scours this flat land. As is his wont, Jack is modestly listening rather than participating, but Anna notes the change in his stance: since importing and introducing his new family to the community, he stands at his full height rather than slumping in the way of a man accustomed to being invisible. Trudie is balanced on his shoulders, and Jack's hand is clamped to her rump to ensure she doesn't topple off. This mindfulness of the child, Anna has learned, is typical of Jack, as is his constant peripheral awareness of his wife. He now gives the room a quick scan as if to satisfy himself that Anna has not slipped away. She has grown used to this half-fearful reconnaissance, Jack's treating her as though she is a wild creature he has caught and must gentle into being unafraid.

She fields his glance and widens her eyes at him. Jack nods and Anna allows herself a sigh of relief. It is nearly over, this ordeal. After the obligatory good-byes, they can go home. She counts again to one hundred, then begins walking toward him.

As she does, one of the boys skating across the speckled floor in stocking feet nearly collides with her, swerving aside at the last moment. Anna forces a smile at him, assuming this is an accident. Why, she wonders, do the parents in this country not better discipline their children? She takes another step and it happens again with a second boy. And the next. And the next.

Heinie! Kraut! a little towheaded boy hisses, sliding close enough to tweak Anna's skirt and then veering away.

Did you see that? he shouts, darting back to the others. I touched her!

Timothy Wilson, you stop that, his mother calls.

The women break from their formation and descend upon their ill-behaved offspring, scolding the children as they haul them off by the arms. A few of them then crowd around Anna, standing much too close as they extend their apologies. In her discomfort they remind Anna of a pack of wild dogs; she thinks she even sees one woman sniffing her, then drawing back as if she has smelled something sour, boiled *Rotkraut* perhaps, on Anna's clothes and hair. But surely this is Anna's imagination, for she has used vanilla in her bathwater and after that, in antic-ipation of this occasion, an uncharacteristic spritz of *Pretty Lady* eau de cologne.

Sorry, the wives tell her, aren't they just awful, you know how kids can be, sorry, sorry—

Then Jack breaks through them, holding out Anna's coat.

Ready to go? he asks.

Anna nods, staring at the floor.

Where is Trudie? she whispers to the linoleum.

In the cloakroom, Jack replies. Putting on her boots.

Once he has helped Anna into her coat he guides her toward the door, lifting a hand in farewell. The crowds part for the pair, everyone smiling and nodding and wishing Anna a happy holi-day. Merry Christmas, they say, winking. Hope Santa's good to you this year! Merry Christmas.

But as the couple depart to collect the child, Anna looks back at the refreshment table. Among the empty trays and pans that contained the other wives' cakes and pies, Anna's *Stollen* sits untouched, its crust shining.

57

As if conspiring to foil Anna's escape from the church, in its lot the farm truck again refuses to start. Jack pumps the gas pedal and talks to the engine, which turns over sluggishly but dies time after time.

Come on, Jack mutters. Come on, that's it...Shitfire!

Anna huddles against Trudie, the two of them shaking helplessly. This is another thing Anna cannot get used to, this cold. She has given up trying to convert the temperature from Celsius to Fahrenheit, not because the mathematics are beyond her but because the results are surreal. Thirty below freezing, forty-five below—it is preposterous! Anna has heard that a dish of water, thrown skyward, will solidify before it hits the ground; that one's eyeballs, if left unprotected, will freeze. Prone as these Americans are to tall tales, Anna believes it. Such conditions are almost enough to make one nostalgic for the relatively tame trials of chilblains and aching joints, the damp Weimarian winters. Anna draws Trudie closer to her side.

Keep your scarf over your face, she reminds the girl.

Damn it, Jack says. Goddamnit—there we go! All right then.

He smiles sheepishly at Anna.

We'll just give her another minute or two to warm up, he says.

Anna nods, her teeth chattering.

Jack pushes his cap back on his head and ruffles the flattened hair there with a wrist, then cranes forward to examine the night sky through the windshield.

Least it's too cold to snow, he comments; that's one good thing.

Anna is too cold to answer. Instead, as they wait, she clears a small circle on her window with the side of her gloved fist. Jack has entreated her to wear mittens as Trudie does, explaining that they are more practical as the fingers are kept together for warmth, but here Anna has drawn the line. The bulky, childish things remind her of pot holders. She peers through the hole she has rubbed in the delicate fishbones of frost, watching the church. The reception is breaking up, the townsfolk coming through the door in twos and threes. Some of the women gather around the minister as he pauses on the step to secure the earflaps of his cap under his chin. Others inch toward their cars in pairs, arms slung around one another's waists, laughing at their halting progress over the ice in their spectator pumps.

Jack grunts. Be lucky they don't break their damn necks, he grumbles. Bet you're glad you wore your boots, huh, Annie?

Then he looks at Anna and his voice changes.

Oh, honey, he says. Oh, honey, don't. Don't cry.

Anna turns away.

I am not crying, she tells him. It is the cold. It is making my eyes to water.

It's *water,* not *to water,* just *water,* says Jack.

He blows out a breath and flexes his hands on the steering wheel.

You have to learn not to take it personally, he says. They don't mean to treat you wrong. It's just that— Well, the war being so recent and all. Give them some time to get used to you.

They'll come around if you make a little effort. They're basically good folks, you know.

Anna nods. There is some truth to what Jack says. They are not inherently bad, these New Heidelburgers. They are simply reacting to her own strangeness. The way her bones, even after months of beef and milk, are still too prominent in her face. The fact that her dresses don't hang right. The white spots and ridges in her nails, the pallor of her skin. Her clumsy English, uttered in an accent so thick that her tongue feels like a useless lump of meat in her mouth. Anna knows that despite the town's Teutonic name and the primarily German heritage of its citizens, they are Americans through and through, at least two generations removed from their original homeland. And thus Anna's mere existence in their midst must offend them by reminding them of what they have just lost. Almost every front window in New Heidelburg boasts a gold star or two, honoring the memory of beloved sons who have given their lives in service of their country, and from long experience Anna recognizes widow's black. No, she doesn't condemn these people for the way they treat her. If the situation were reversed, might she not do the same?

But Anna also knows that although the women may someday pretend acceptance, it is useless to *make a little effort,* for they will never truly *come around.* She has not told Jack what happened at the sole social function she attended, a few weeks after her arrival, a *bridge party* at the house of the banker's wife. Oh, the women were solicitous enough at first, insisting that Anna have the seat of honor on the *davenport* and making much of her pretty scarf, the elaborate coil of braids in which she wears her hair. Most of this took place in dumb show, naturally, although the women also brayed incomprehensibly in Anna's face — speaking loudly, as Jack initially did, as though Anna were not foreign but deaf. Yet Anna did understand some of what they said, thanks to Jack's insistence that only English be spoken at home, and indeed she comprehended perhaps more than they thought. For once their obligation to her was attended to, they withdrew to leave Anna on the *davenport* next to a plastic plant, a slice of *upside-down pineapple cake* in her lap for company, and as they chattered over their strange game of cards at tables of four, Anna heard the hostess utter the word *simple*. Glances in her direction. *Shhh! She'll hear you.* Then again, a statement this time, louder in agreement: *Well, sure she tricked him into marrying her, that poor simple man. Who else'd have him?*

Anna looks sideways at her husband. It is true that Jack is *simple* in that he requires only life's basic gifts to be content: a pretty wife, a lively child, healthy livestock and a well-run farm. But in the sense these women have meant it—befuddled, easily misled—Jack is not *simple*. He is shy, yet he is far from stupid. How much, Anna wonders, did he hear of Frau Hochmeier's denunciation at the Buchenwald gates? He keeps to himself, her husband, and this is one trait Anna understands and appreciates. Jack has never mentioned the scene, and Anna is certainly not about to ask him.

Whatever Jack suspects, however, there is one thing Anna is certain he does not: the other wives know about the *Obersturmführer*. Has Anna really been so foolish as to think she can escape him simply by crossing an ocean and half a continent? No. She knows what the women were sniffing for earlier. They may not have the specific facts at their disposal, but with the instincts peculiar to her gender, the wives can smell the *Obersturmführer* on Anna, even here.

Yet to cry further over this will be to risk the freezing eyeballs and upset Jack, so Anna summons a wan smile and picks up the thread of the conversation, winding it back to its source.

I will try better not to take it to heart, she assures him. Now can we speak of happier things? It is Christmas, after all.

Jack looks relieved, and Anna takes momentary advantage of his concern to slip into her own language, the ease of which is like a bath.

Did you see the jelly with the white things in it? she asks. Horrible! Like a science experiment.

Jack laughs.

Ambrosia, he says mysteriously.

He pats Anna's arm and shifts into gear, jolting the truck out of the lot.

Trudie, who has been dozing, stirs and nuzzles her head against Anna's coat.

What time is it, Mama? she asks. Is it Christmas yet? When is Saint Nikolaus coming?

Anna sits up straighter.

Saint Nikolaus doesn't come here, she says rapidly in German. In America we have Santa Claus, remember?

Yes, but I want Saint Nikolaus, Trudie says, and Anna's stomach goes cold.

Hush, Trudie, she says. Do not distract your father's driving. You will make us go into a ditch.

She waits fearfully for the child to say something else, but Trudie just shudders and yawns.

Somebody's ready for Santa, all right, says Jack.

On the county road the truck jounces over ruts of ice a half-meter deep. A *foot,* Anna reminds herself, her teeth clacking together; a *foot.* Already uneasy, she has to restrain herself from yelping when the truck fishtails on a curve; she tries to mimic Jack, whose expression remains unperturbed as he cranks the wheel in the direction of the spin. Anna bites the inside of her cheek and watches the headlights slice through the dark to reveal the icy road, the drifts and fencing on either side. She wonders, not for the first time, what on earth enticed people to carve out lives on this frozen plain. If she still believed in the religious teachings of her girlhood, Anna thinks, she would pray for two things: that they reach the farmhouse in one piece and that the child should hold her tongue until she can be put to sleep.

Devout or not, Anna is granted both wishes, and the truck is soon parked in the dooryard without mishap. Jack rouses Trudie and slings her over his shoulder like a sack of grain, jogging with her up the porch steps. Anna follows with her gloved fist to her mouth, feeling sick as the child shrieks with delight at this familiar game.

Can't I stay up just a little longer? Trudie begs. Please? Pleeeeeease —

Do you know what becomes of clever little girls who steal other people's names? asks the *Obersturmführer. They must go straight to bed.*

Trudie, behave, Anna calls. She knocks snow off her boots onto the plastic mat. Mind your father.

She holds her breath, but the only response is a drift of giggles from upstairs.

Frowning, Anna moves about the living room, picking up scarves and coats and hanging them in the closet. She wriggles her nyloned toes on the thick beige carpet and looks around at the Christmas tree with its gaudy bulbs, her own *davenport* with its new slipcover, the phonograph Jack brought home in September when soybean prices went *through the roof.* There is none of the shabby elegance of the *Elternhaus* in this room, nor the *gemütlich* trappings of the *Gasthof* in Berchtesgaden. And it is the furthest thing from the deprivation of the bakery. Life in this place is soft, made more so by wondrous amenities such as *deep-freeze units* and washing machines, *vacuum cleaners* and central heat. Anna wants for nothing. Nothing material, in any case.

In the kitchen, Anna sets out breakfast things on the Formica table: plates, mugs, sugar, jam. Returning to the front room, she stuffs Trudie's stocking with oranges and candy and clothes for her doll. She unplugs the lights of the Christmas tree so as not to start a fire. Then she switches off the floor lamp as well and stands in the dark, listening for noise from above.

But all is quiet. Anna taps her knuckles thoughtfully against her lips. What did the child really mean by her question? It is the first time Trudie has mentioned Saint Nikolaus since leaving Germany. How much does she remember? The numbing blow

Saint Nikolaus dealt her, the marching song he taught her, the tale they spun about the rabbits in the *Trog*? His clownish conducting of Brahms on the riverbank of the Ilm? The showering candlesticks and crashing china, the boot thudding on the wall near her head, Saint Nikolaus's stomach slick with her mother's blood? Playing in the kitchen, the cellar, the bakery dooryard, all the while listening to Anna's stifled cries.

Anna climbs the steps to the second story and pauses before Trudie's room. She taps on the door and pushes it open, shutting it quietly behind her. At first she thinks the girl is asleep, but then a sniffle comes from the huddled little ball on the bed, and then another, and when Anna sits on the edge of the mattress and feels for Trudie's face, her fingers come away wet.

So, says Anna. So. What is all this? Shhhhh. Hush now. You should be happy tonight of all nights. And you must go to sleep, for how will Santa ever come to bring your presents if you do not?

She strokes the girl's hair until Trudie stops crying and lies quietly, though her body still quivers beneath Anna's hand. Then there comes a sad mumble, muffled by the pillow.

What did you say, little rabbit? Anna asks, bending over her.

I don't want Santa, the child says. I want Saint Nikolaus.

Well, you cannot have him, Trudie. He will never come again. So you must not think of him any more.

But I want him, the girl wails. Where is he, Mama? Why isn't he here with us? I miss him—

Be quiet, Trudie! Do you want Jack to hear you? Now I will tell you something very important. You must never say such things in this house. You must never speak of that man at all. You must never even think of him. Never. Do you understand?

But I don't want Jack. I want *him*—

Anna grips Trudie's face on either side of the jaw.

I said you will not speak of him. He no longer exists. He belongs to the past, to that other place and time, and all of that is dead. Do you hear? The past is dead, and better it remain so.

Anna gives Trudie's chin a shake for emphasis, her fingers digging into the child's soft flesh. She despises herself for it— she would rather take a blade to her own face than hurt her daughter this way. But it must be done. The girl must be made to understand.

Never, Anna repeats. Do you hear?

Trudie tries to nod.

Yes, Mama.

That is my good girl.

Slowly, Anna relaxes her grasp. She touches the child's cheeks in the dark, then kisses her on the forehead.

Now we will not talk of it any more. You will sleep, and morning will be here before you know it, and then you may open your gifts. Won't that be nice?

Yes, Mama.

Well then.

Anna rises and makes her way to the door.

Sweet dreams, little rabbit, she says, as she closes it.

Then, legs weak, she wobbles the few steps to the window at the end of the hallway and stands clutching her elbows to stop their shaking. There is the dooryard. There is the truck, a dark shape against high snowbanks, its metallic womanly curves gleaming faintly in the light of pinprick stars. There are the pines standing guard along the drive, planted by Jack's grandfather shortly after the man emigrated to this country from a similar farm in Germany—from Rothenburg ob der Tauber, in fact. And beyond their silent boughs, there is only snow, stretching unbroken for kilometers in every direction. *Miles.*

Anna closes her eyes. She has done what she can for her daughter. She can only hope it is enough. And for the second time that night, Anna finds herself thinking that although she no longer places any faith in prayer, she will offer one up nonetheless: that the child be allowed to forget. Anna's first memory is of the radio on her mother's dresser speaking directly to her, admonishing her to eat her vegetables; she prays now that Trudie's recollections will assume the same jumbled, nonsensical quality of dream; that with time they will be expunged from that bright lively mind; that her daughter's childhood will consist solely of gamboling beneath this enormous American sky, on these flat broad planes as guileless as her adopted father's face.

A door opens down the hall.

Annie?

I am here, Anna whispers. I will be right in.

I wondered where you were. I thought maybe you'd fallen asleep downstairs.

Jack chuckles. What are you doing, anyway? he asks.

Nothing, says Anna. Telling Trudie good night.

Well, come to bed.

I will. In a moment.

Rubbing her arms, Anna takes a last look at the fields. Please, she thinks. Please, let her remember only what I have said. She stands a moment longer listening to the house settle around her, creaking in the wind. Then she turns from the window and walks to the master bedroom where her husband waits for her.

58

ANNA AND JACK ARE BOTH EARLY RISERS, JACK AS RE-quired by profession and Anna by dint of long habit from the bakery. But the next morning, Trudie is up and about before either of them. It is barely dawn when Anna wakes with a start to find the child staring down at her, a small ghostly figure in her long white nightgown and the room's slowly graying light.

Careful not to disturb Jack, Anna pushes herself up on one elbow, her vision half obscured by a curtain of hair.

What is it, Trudie? she asks. A nightmare?

Trudie shakes her head, her sleep-mussed braids unraveling.

Is it Christmas yet? she whispers.

Anna remembers what day it is and smiles.

So it is, she says. Merry Christmas, little one.

Did my presents come? Can I go open them?

May I, Anna corrects automatically. In a few minutes. When both your father and I will come too.

Jack stirs and grumbles something before burrowing deeper beneath the quilts, pulling the pillow over his head.

Merry Christmas, Dad, Trudie says, climbing onto the bed

between her parents. She plucks at Jack's undershirt. Merry Christmas Merry Christmas! Wake up wake up so I can open my presents, get up now, pleeeease—

Jack groans, rolling over.

Dad's sleepy, Strudel, he says.

Trudie pouts, pulling a wisp of hair on his chest.

Why are grown-ups always sleepy, she asks.

Because we're old, Jack tells her.

He taps his cheek with a finger. Trudie kisses the spot three times, then smacks the other side of his jaw, his chin, and his forehead.

Yuck, scratchy, she comments. Now will you get up? Please?

You go ahead, says Jack. We'll be down soon.

The girl catapults from the bed.

Only the gifts Santa has brought, Anna calls. Only those in your stocking, do you hear?

Yessssssss, Trudie shouts impatiently.

Anna sighs and grimaces at her husband as the child runs down the stairs.

You spoil her, she says.

I know, replies Jack without a hint of remorse.

He lifts the pillow and sweeps a palm beneath it. I like to spoil her mother too, he adds. Now where is that darned thing...? Oh.

He hands Anna a small velvet box.

Anna frowns. And what is this? she asks her husband.

A diamond? says the *Obersturmführer. Perfume, perhaps? A string of pearls for that lovely neck?*

You'll see, Jack says.

Anna turns the box over. On its underside is the imprint of the New Heidelburg jeweler, Ingebretsen's, scrolled in gold script.

You should not have done this, Jack, she scolds. It must be very expensive.

Would you just please open it?

Anna aims a mock scowl in her husband's direction. Jack smiles and lazily scratches his stomach. In the box, on cotton batting, is a silver locket.

This is very fine, Anna tells him. Such beautiful...

She fishes for the English word for *craftsmanship,* but when it doesn't surface, she repeats, It is very fine.

Look inside.

Anna does and again feels a nauseating *déjà vu.* The hinged oval reveals a photograph, inexpertly trimmed with nail scissors, of a family of three. It is not Anna and the child and the *Obersturmführer,* of course; in this locket she and Trudie are posed sitting with Jack at his HQ in Weimar, shortly before departing Germany. But the similarity is strong enough — down to Jack's dress uniform and ramrod posture — to cause cold sweat to form at Anna's temples and under her arms.

You don't like it, Jack says, crestfallen. I guess I should have gotten something else.

Anna daubs her forehead with the sleeve of her nightgown.

I love it, she says.

Really?

Anna hands the locket to him, gathering and lifting her hair.

Put it on me, please, she says.

After a few attempts, the fine chain catching on his callused fingers, Jack fastens the clasp. He kisses the nape of Anna's neck, and she shivers at the scrape of stubble on her skin.

How do I look? she asks, turning to face him.

Like a dream, says Jack.

Shyly, he touches her nearest breast through her nightdress, his signal. Anna is startled. He usually prefers such things to take place once a week, on Saturdays, only at night and always in the dark.

The child —, she protests.

Don't worry about her, Jack says. She's forgotten all about us.

She will love the bicycle, says Anna, stalling.

But Jack kisses her, his breath thick with sleep. He undoes the ribbon at the throat of the gown and draws the material aside to expose her breasts. As he buries his face between them, Anna stares over his cowlicked head at her curtains. They are not lace but dotted muslin; the walls have been papered, also at her request, with a pattern of violets. They are not dark wood or decaying plaster. There is nothing of Germany here. Except that, whenever Anna blinks, she sees the bakery. Blink: the cold ring of the overhead light in the storefront. Blink: the snow tracked in by the refugees melting in dirty puddles on the floor. Blink: the webbed cracks on the ceiling in Mathilde's bedroom, so similar to the tracery of veins in Anna's lids that they might have been tattooed there. The fleeting images are like cinders in the eyes, a constant irritant.

Anna screws them shut, but it is no use, it is in fact worse, for she then sees the *Obersturmführer*'s dilated pupils fixed on her. She feels his ersatz grin pressed to her throat, his mouth fastened and sucking on a particular spot between shoulder and neck. Her hips jackknife upward against her husband's and she cries out.

Jack rolls off her.

Annie? Did I hurt you? Look at you, you're shaking like a leaf. Are you cold?

The *Obersturmführer* drags his pistol down Anna's ribs. *Are you cold, Anna?* he asks. *You must not lie to me, I can tell you are.*

Is it— female trouble again? Jack asks. Let me take you to a doctor, Annie, please. We could go to Iowa City or Rochester. Nobody would have to know.

He reaches over to smooth Anna's damp hair. Anna ducks her head away.

I do not need a doctor, she assures him. I am fine.

In truth she is stiff with fright. This happens every time she and Jack perform the marital act, and Anna fears he suspects well enough what is wrong with her. There is no hiding anything physical from a man who works with animals, who guides lambs from the birth canal and calms skittish horses merely by grazing his weathered fingertips over their quivering hindquarters.

Anna searches for an excuse not already used.

I am just thinking of the child, she says. What if she should hear? And, Jack, in the daytime...?

But Jack is not listening. He is lying on his back, contemplating the ceiling. He runs a hand over his chin, skewing his jaw to one side. Then he sits up so he can see Anna's face.

I promised myself I wouldn't ask this, he says. I thought I didn't want to know. But it's been driving me crazy.

He looks down at Anna.

Anna, I'm only going to ask this once. That thing the woman said, the morning we brought you to the camp, the thing about the SS officer. Was it true?

Anna turns her head away, toward her curtains.

Yes, she whispers finally.

She feels Jack grow still beside her. She dares a glance at him. He has gone white; but for the rise and fall of his chest, he might be made of plaster. Then he turns his back on her.

Anna closes her eyes.

Jack, she says.

She hears him shove the quilts aside. She knows from the bed's sag that he is sitting on its edge, perhaps staring at nothing, perhaps talking silently to himself. Suddenly the mattress springs into place as he jumps up, and Anna is lying alone.

Please, Jack, she says.

She props herself on her elbows to watch him dress. He buttons his flannel shirt wrong so that one side hangs lower than the other. He thrusts his feet into his boots without lacing them.

Jack, please, she repeats. I had to. He —

Is he Trudie's father? She's a fucking Nazi's kid?

If you would let me explain —

Jack whirls on her.

Did you love him? he shouts.

Anna stares at her legs, fish-belly white and fully exposed now that Jack has flung away the covers.

Did you?

Anna compresses her mouth into a thin line and shakes her head. But her eyes brim with tears, and she knows her face is growing red.

I'm waiting, Anna. Answer me.

It was not as you think, Anna mumbles. It... You see... With him, I... We...

But she cannot choke out the rest of the sentence. Her throat feels as though it has been stuffed full of black bread. She looks miserably at Jack.

Goddamn you, he says, his voice shaking. Goddamn you to hell.

He slams out of the room with such force that the doorknob embeds itself in the wall. Anna sits listening to his heavy tread thudding down the stairs. The screen door to the porch bangs below.

Anna knows that he will be crossing to the barn, head low, breath steaming. She would like to put on her robe and go after him. She would at least like to open the window and call out. But she cannot, for she has seen his face, contorted by hate into that of a stranger. She should have known this would happen even with him; she should have known better than to tell him the truth. She can never tell him what she started to say: that we come to love those who save us. For although Anna does believe this is true, the word that stuck in her throat was not *save* but *shame*.

She reaches to pull down her nightgown, which is still rucked to her waist. Her fingertips brush the dark triangle of hair at her thighs and rest there. She has been unforgivably stupid. She has ruined everything. For how could she have hoped anybody would ever understand? How could her husband, this good and decent man, ever forgive the fact that during their conjoining it is always the *Obersturmführer* Anna feels, sees, smells; the *Obersturmführer*'s

sled-dog eyes glancing up at her face from where he kneels between her legs, dipping his head to lap delicately at her like a cat
and then using the pads of his thumbs so she can't tell which is
which; ceaselessly gauging her response; measuring, calculating,
why can't he leave her alone? but he ignores her *enough, please, it's
enough,* her gasping *stop stop stop*; he will not be satisfied until he
has felt her spasm twice, three times, five; until he has stolen her
reactions, taken her from herself, erased her; until she is as empty
as the kitchen cupboards below because all Weimar is starving,
everyone is starving to death; until she is burning and sore
around his fingers and pleads for him to be inside her, begs him
to mount her and be inside her in the real way because it is the
only way he is ever going to finish.

Anna snatches her hands from between her thighs and yanks
her nightgown down, weeping. She drives her fists into the mattress, pounding it over and over. She kicks it with all her strength,
her mouth working in a silent wail, the tears coming hot from
her eyes. But she cannot make a sound.

Of all the things the *Obersturmführer* has done to her, and
they have been many and terrible, this is the worst, the most unfair: he has blighted her ability to love. Everyone is born with it.
Anna knows that she herself has been. But because of the *Obersturmführer,* her heart is now only a sick and limping muscle, and
all she has left is her tie to the man, sometimes intense, sometimes not, but pulling at her always like an undertow. It is not fair
that he should have afflicted her thus, that thanks to the *Obersturmführer* Anna cannot truly love her good husband. It is not
fair that her dark heart should forever be yoked to such a man. It
is not fair and it is not forgivable, and Anna will never speak of
it again. To anyone. Ever.

After a time, when her tears subside, Anna gets up and
makes the bed. She pins her hair into a coil and dresses. She
ventures downstairs to find the living room a squirrel's nest of
shredded paper and discarded boxes. Trudie is shouting outside,
so instead of bothering to straighten this mess, Anna shuffles

through it to the closet and pulls on her coat. She steps onto the porch. The air sears her raw nostrils.

Jack is standing on the top riser, having finished attending to the livestock. He ignores Anna as she comes up beside him.

Lookin' good, Strudel, he calls. Not too fast now.

Trudie, her parka thrown carelessly over her nightgown, is pedaling her new bicycle in the circle Jack plows clear after every snowfall. The girl's face rosy with cold and excitement, the butter yellow of her disheveled hair, the blue of her coat—these are startling against the landscape, which looks as though it has been painted by an artist whose palette consists solely of whites. Oyster white, gray white, eggshell. The horizon is indiscernible, the sky shading into the ground. They will have more snow by midmorning. Such a place, this vast blank plain. But at the moment Anna doesn't mind it. It would be very difficult for anyone unfamiliar with these parts to find this farm. A former officer of the *Schutzstaffeln* bent on reuniting with his mistress, for instance.

Trudie races back and forth, skinny legs pumping.

Watch, Mama, she yells. Watch!

Anna draws her coat tighter at the neck, shivering.

Careful, she calls. There is ice beneath—

The girl pays her no mind, lifting her hands from the bicycle grips. Anna inhales sharply: one of Trudie's arms is extended in the Nazi salute. Then Anna blinks and sees only her daughter, showing off.

Anna turns to Jack, who is watching the child with his fists bunched in the pockets of his sheepskin coat.

Please, make her to stop, she says.

Jack doesn't look at Anna. All she can see of his face, his profile, is stony. He produces a match, ignites it with the flick of a thumbnail, and cups the flame to light his cigarette.

Please, Jack, tell her. It is dangerous. She could fall.

Jack chuffs smoke out through his nostrils. Then he calls, Not so fast, Strudel.

He slits his eyes at Anna.

Don't worry, he mutters. It's not *her* fault. I would never take anything out on *her*.

Jack, says Anna. Her voice falters. She clears her throat and tries again. Jack, I wish you would call her by her proper name. She is now American. We both are American. We have leaved Germany and everything in it far, far behind...Do you understand what I am saying?

Watch! Trudie screams.

Standing on the pedals, she topples into a drift, from which she emerges powdered head to foot with snow. She brushes herself off, laughing.

Anna touches Jack's sleeve.

Jack—?

Jack moves out of reach and drops his cigarette to the wooden floorboards. He grinds it out beneath the heel of his workboot. He bends to retrieve the stub and bounces it in his palm. Then he throws it into the bushes and goes inside.

Anna turns to follow.

Where are you going? Trudie demands of her mother, indignant.

To make breakfast, Anna tells her. You may stay out for a while. But not too long.

She finds Jack in the kitchen, head lowered, knocking his knuckles against the table. She catches his hand and raises it to her lips. She presses them to each callus on his palm. Then she leads him upstairs to the bedroom. He comes slowly but willingly enough.

Although the room is now full of light, Anna disrobes completely. She undresses Jack as well before guiding him to the bed. They are both quiet. There is nothing to say; there is so much to say that Anna will never say it. She will never tell him, although perhaps they both know, that as Anna presses against him, initiating the lovemaking that might bring them a child of their own, it is not her husband she thinks of.

Trudy, May 1997

59

MAY IN MINNEAPOLIS IS LILAC TIME. AS IF TO COMPENSATE for the punitive winter, the city explodes with flowers overnight—making it, if only for a week or two, one of the most beautiful places on earth. First there are sunny starbursts of forsythia; then the cherry and dogwood trees burst into life, showering petals everywhere, pink and cream, drifting thick as snow on the sidewalks. But it is the lilacs that truly herald the coming of spring: lavender and white and blue and sometimes a purple deep as grapes, they bloom in the alleys and over backyard fences and in graveyards. Beauty is everywhere, including the most unexpected places. There is no respite from it. And to Trudy, this abundance seems a personal insult, a trick of nature as cruelly calculated as certain forms of torture to inflict the maximum pain in the minimum time.

On this glorious Saturday morning, Trudy is in the passenger's seat of Thomas's van, en route to an interview in Minnetonka. She has asked him to drive, saying it is silly that they should take two cars to one destination—a point with which the ever-amenable Thomas instantly agreed. Of course, Thomas is agreeable by nature, but he is being so gracious that Trudy wonders if he suspects her real reason for wanting him to play chauffeur: without him, she might forsake the interview altogether. This is the first Trudy has conducted since Rainer's departure, and not only has she almost forgotten about it — having scheduled it a month in advance — she has lost her taste for the entire business. Despite Rainer's assertion to the contrary, Trudy can't help feeling that her Project must have played some part in his decision. She has done nothing to prepare for today's meeting other than making a halfhearted call to the subject, Mr. Pfeffer, to confirm the appointment; she has not done her research into his background nor come up with her usual list of questions, a breach of work ethic that would have been unthinkable in the days before Rainer left. She will have to wing it.

Thomas is driving past Lake of the Isles, the water throwing light into the cab of the van, and Trudy twists in her seat to watch it go by. Through the trees she sees families picnicking on the shoreline, lovers walking with their arms around each other's waists, the ubiquitous panting joggers. She cranes until it is out of sight, then faces forward again.

Are you okay? Thomas asks. Forgive me for saying so, but you look a little ragged.

Trudy is picturing Rainer standing by a man-made lake ringed with palms, its water like a bath; taking his daily constitutional along canals slithering with alligators. He would walk steadily through the simmering heat, his fedora replaced by a white straw Panama. Trudy roots through her briefcase for a Kleenex.

Allergies, she mumbles. Damned lilacs.

Thomas leans over, pops the glove compartment, and hands Trudy a somewhat elderly SuperAmerica napkin. She daubs the corners of her eyes.

Thanks, she says gruffly.

You're welcome.

Thomas turns onto Highway 7 and drives for a few minutes in silence. Then he says, I'm sorry to hear about Mr. Goldmann.

Trudy sits up straighter.

How on earth did you know about that?

Ruth told me.

Ruth! Trudy says, bridling. God in heaven, does everybody have to know everybody else's business around here? You'd think we were all in high school!

Sorry, Thomas repeats. I guess I shouldn't have brought it up. Clumsy of me. I apologize.

No, don't, it's fine, Trudy mutters.

She glares through the side window and applies the napkin again.

You know, says Thomas after a pause, I lost my wife two years ago. About this time of year. Car accident. I was driving.

Oh, says Trudy. Oh, Thomas, I didn't know. I'm so sorry.

Thomas cracks his joints on the steering wheel. It's all right. I mean, it's not, but of course you wouldn't know. It's not exactly something I advertise. And I only bring it up now to let you know I'm in your corner. Life is so often unfair and painful and love is hard to find and you have to take it whenever and wherever you can get it, no matter how brief it is or how it ends. So I understand. That's all.

Trudy looks at him. He is wearing black sunglasses that make it impossible for her to see his eyes, but his face seems serene enough. Yet Trudy feels bad, not only because of what he has told her but because she has never thought much about Thomas outside of the Project. He is just always there whenever she needs him, ready with his equipment and benign smile and words of encouragement. Trudy has a sudden flash, shocking but not unpleasant, of what Thomas would look like in the nude: a potbelly and slightly concave chest, either with scant hair around the nipples or completely smooth. She takes a small breath.

Thank you, Thomas.

You're welcome, Trudy.

They are in Minnetonka now, a privileged suburb of huge houses set far from the road on properties the size of golf courses. Old trees reach across the street to entangle in a canopy that allows only a few coins of sunlight to fall through. Thomas slows, canvassing the bronze nameplates and address plaques screwed into stone columns, and turns into the drive of 9311 Hawthorne Way.

Heavens, he says mildly of the house at the end.

Trudy silently concurs. Mr. Pfeffer's residence is more of a showcase than a house, a towering structure of glass and steel that seems to float on its vast green lawn, an architect's dream of contemporary angles. It is not the sort of place Trudy would choose to live in even if she could, in her wildest dreams, afford to: with those glass walls one would be as dreadfully exposed as in a dollhouse. Particularly at night. But Trudy has to grant that it is impressive, if only for the money it must have taken to construct.

And Thomas is apparently following a similar train of thought, for as they climb from the van he asks, What does this guy do?

I don't know, Trudy admits.

You don't? I thought that was one of the questions you always ask over the phone first.

Well, I do, says Trudy, but to tell you the truth, I don't remember.

She takes out her portfolio and flips it open. Of course, there is only Mr. Pfeffer's scrawled address, but the action prods her memory as to the long-ago contact conversation.

He was fairly evasive about his profession, now that I think of it, she tells Thomas. All he said was, *Oh, I do a bit of this and a bit of that; I'm a man of many interests, dear lady.*

Thomas gazes around as he and Trudy proceed up the flagstones of the front walk: at the manicured grass, the clever lack of any landscaping that would compete with the house, the wink of Lake Minnetonka behind it.

No wonder he was evasive, Thomas comments. He probably robbed a bank.

Probably, Trudy agrees, and then jumps, startled, for Mr. Pfeffer opens the door before she has pressed the bell.

Come in, come in, he says, ushering them into a foyer with the echoing dimensions of a cathedral. Welcome to my home! Is it not a lovely day?

He rubs his hands, then jumps aside to let Thomas pass with his cart. He is a small and dapper man, this Mr. Pfeffer, with the wiry build of a tennis player and a head as bald as a cue ball. His hair, when he had it, must have been black, for his eyebrows still are. They climb his tanned forehead in delight as he looks Trudy up and down.

But the morning is not half as lovely as you, dear lady, he adds. I suppose this is to your advantage as an interrogator, yes? I will be putty in your hands.

Trudy blinks and touches her hair, which now nearly reaches her shoulders. She has been too dispirited to have it cut. Surely Mr. Pfeffer is poking fun at her.

But he tilts his head and eyes Trudy with bright, robinlike appreciation. He is wearing a three-piece charcoal suit of fine Italian design, Trudy notices, and she is amused to see that the rose in his lapel is the exact shade of yellow as the silk handkerchief protruding from his breast pocket.

Tell me about yourself, Mr. Pfeffer says.

Well, as you know, I'm a professor of German Studies at the university, and I—

No, no. Please, something more interesting. Are you married?

No, says Trudy. I was once, but—

No? says Mr. Pfeffer. He makes a face of astonishment. But how surprising. How can it possibly be that such a charming lady as yourself is unattached?

Trudy tries to smile, but when her eyes fill she turns toward the glittering blue expanse beyond the clerestory windows.

Thomas, carrying a sound boom past them, says quickly, This is an incredible house, Mr. Pfeffer. What is it you do for a living?

Oh, a bit of this, a bit of that, Mr. Pfeffer replies, not looking away from Trudy. I'm a man of many interests, dear fellow...But how rude I am! I have not even offered you a refreshment. Please, this way.

Cupping Trudy's elbow, he escorts her into an enormous living room. Trudy gives Thomas a grateful glance as they pass. He reaches out to press her arm, then occupies himself with setting up screens near a white Steinway.

Mr. Pfeffer pats a leather couch.

Come, he says, sit here by me.

Trudy does. She is amazed to see, among the glinting chrome furniture, the sprigs of orchids in Meissen vases, a hotel tea cart at Mr. Pfeffer's elbow. It is stocked with a silver service and little crustless sandwiches and—can they be actual crumpets? They must be: a pyramid of small cakes, the hybrid of English muffin and scone.

Tea? Coffee? Crumpet? asks Mr. Pfeffer.

Just coffee, please, says Trudy.

She accepts a cup and smiles at him, more successfully this time.

Where in Germany were you born, Mr. Pfeffer?

Felix, dear lady, please. I come from the forests of Thuringia; I was born in a dank little hovel there, the seventh of eleven children, if you can believe that...The closest city was a small one, Weimar— but of course you would be familiar with it, given your field of study.

Trudy sets the coffee on her knee, feeling as though she has been doused in cold water. To hear the name of her own birthplace in the mouth of somebody who has actually been there produces not only a chill but the images so much a part of her that she is rarely conscious of their existence: more mood, almost, than memory. A muddy street running past a shabby storefront. The winding stone wall alongside. The field behind the bakery, gray and white with snow. The dark smudge of the Ettersberg woods at its edge. A bare lightbulb swinging. Melancholy. Fear. *Brötchen* under glass. And the officer, of course, standing in the doorway or upstairs in the bedroom. His light wolfish eyes.

Trudy manages a sip of coffee.

What a coincidence, she tells Mr. Pfeffer. I was born there as well. But closer to the center of the city.

Mr. Pfeffer rears back in delight.

Were you! But you are quite right: that is an extraordinary coincidence. However, I could have guessed you were a native German from your given name. Trudy is short for Gertrude, correct?

Yes, it is. I can't imagine what my mother was thinking.

Mr. Pfeffer laughs. It could have been worse. You could be a Helga, for instance... *Und sprechen Sie jetzt Deutsch?* Do you know what my name means in our original language?

Ja, natürlich. Auf Deutsch, Pfeffer ist Pepper.

Mr. Pfeffer claps. Ah, yes, your accent is Thuringian! But I was not referring to my surname. I meant my first: Felix.

That I don't know, says Trudy. Is there a direct translation?

No, says Mr. Pfeffer. But it means happy. Or, I should say, happy-go-lucky.

He wags a finger at Trudy.

My mother, Hannaliese Pfeffer, was a smart woman. She named me well. I have been lucky all my life.

In what way? Trudy asks.

In what way? Mr. Pfeffer repeats. His brows again rise, wrinkling skin the color and texture of caramel. Why, in almost every way. I am blessed with good health and an optimistic disposition. My business interests in this country have thrived, as you can see. And in Weimar, during the war, while so many of my compatriots were dying in such nasty ways in the Russian snow or the deserts of Africa, my business ventures exempted me and fed me and kept me warm. Until my unfortunate incarceration, that is. But I managed to survive, and here I am—whereas so many others of my generation are rotting in the ground...

Mr. Pfeffer pats Trudy's knee, his hand lingering perhaps a bit longer than it should.

And if that isn't lucky, dear lady, he says, his small brown eyes shining, what is?

60

THE GERMAN PROJECT
Interview 14

SUBJECT: Mr. Felix Pfeffer
DATE/LOCATION: May 10, 1997; Minnetonka, MN

Q: …You mentioned your business interests in Germany, Mr. Pfeffer. Can you tell me more about that?

A: With pleasure. To begin with, at fifteen I was an apprentice to an antiques wholesaler in Weimar—Fizel, his name was. I fibbed about my age in order to get the job, I must confess. But while my numerous siblings contented themselves with woodcutting and carpentry and other forms of manual labor, I somehow had been born with a taste for the finer things and a talent for persuasion, and within a few months I became Fizel's best salesman. When I had learned as much as I could from him, I advanced to working for a jeweler whose specialty was old stones in valuable settings. I traveled the Continent seeking such merchandise, and while doing so I met a great many influential people with an appetite for acquisition; in addition to gems, they wanted art, carpets, rare books. I soon discovered that I possessed, you should forgive my immodesty, an exceptional ability to procure for them whatever they asked for. By the time the war broke out, I had established quite a name for myself. I was only twenty-two then, but already on my way up. And as the Reich came to full power, other business opportunities presented themselves, of which I took quick advantage.

Q: What opportunities were those?

A: Well, I suppose you could say I became a broker [*subject laughs*]. Yes, a broker.

Q: A broker of…?

A: Why, people, my dear, of course. Jews escaping the oncoming juggernaut. It is true that many of them did not recognize the danger in time; they put their heads down and prayed it would pass. But there were plenty who were desperate to get out, and thanks to the numerous connections I had made, both among the wealthy and the, shall we say, less reputable element, I was able to help them. They were frantic to barter whatever they could to secure visas, new identification papers, passports. The supply soon overwhelmed the demand, I can tell you. I was swamped with furs, silver, paintings, heirloom jewelry, a grand piano or two. One family even convinced me to take [*laughs*] a canary in an antique cage. The bird naturally was worthless, but the cage was solid gold and I was able to find a home for it in short order.

Q: And what happened once you had accepted these payments?

A: I would put my Jewish clients in touch with the right people, and those people would get them out. Despite the Gestapo, there was a strong Resistance network in Germany, at least in the early days. As to what happened once I had turned my clients over to my contacts, that I do not know. I assume most of them got out.

Q: Did you ever feel guilty about making money this way?

A: No, dear, not at all. I did feel sorry for the Jews, but guilt? No.

Q: Then do you see yourself as a hero for helping Jews to escape?

A: [*laughs*] Oh my, no. Allow me to explain. In wartime there is always excellent business to be done, if one is only enterprising enough to spot the opportunities. As a historian you must know that certain men have always built fortunes from others' misfortune. If there must be wars — and given the nature of man, they are inevitable, sad but true — then why should one not profit from them if he is able? Business is business.

Q: How long did your business continue?

A: This particular sideline lasted until the, oh, I'd say, late thirties. Then the source dried up, as my Jewish clientele had already left the *Vaterland* with my aid or in less pleasant ways, at the behest of the Nazis. Yet I still had more business than I could handle, for the SS were by then entrenched at Buchenwald, that hellhole on the hill. Their demand for certain goods was more rapacious even than that of my former wealthy customers, and as my reputation had preceded me, I began to procure for them as well. Of course, the products were somewhat different.

Q: And they consisted of…?

A: Liquor, primarily. And drugs. Medicines, hashish, opium, cocaine. Also French cigarettes — the *Schutzstaffeln* had an unpatriotic preference for *Gauloises,* for whatever reason. At any rate, I knew everyone from Marrakech to Moscow, so whatever the SS requested, I could get.

Q: Who exactly asked you to get these things?

A: I had dealings with almost all the SS, but my main contact was *Kommandant* Koch, and he was my best client. You know, nowadays historians make a big hoo-ha about Göring having been an opium-addicted degenerate; I never had the dubious honor of making the man's acquaintance, so for all I know, they may be right. But from what I observed, he could not have held a candle to Koch. Now there was a fellow who enjoyed his pleasures. A sensualist. A hedonist. His position enabled him to do whatever he wanted, and believe me, he took full advantage.

Q: In what ways?

A: There were, for instance, the Comradeship Evenings, a little ritual Koch established during the early days of the camp. At least, that was what he called them. In reality, they were orgies. They occurred every Sunday, regular as clockwork, in the Bismarck Tower just outside the camp boundaries. There all of the officers would gather—their attendance being mandatory— to enjoy the company of prostitutes. Not the poor girls working in the Special Building, the Buchenwald brothel, but imports. And *Puppenjungen,* boys who were chosen from incoming transports specifically for this purpose. I supplied the champagne the officers drank and, when the evening's activities were concluded, in which they bathed. Also cigars, marijuana, the opium and cocaine I previously mentioned.

As you can imagine, this was a highly profitable venture, and it had the additional benefit of exempting me from service in the *Wehrmacht.* Nor was I the only one to reap the rewards of a contract with Koch, I can assure you. Some of Weimar's most respectable merchants did quite nicely for themselves. Herr Fischkettel, for one, a metalworks owner. Wohnmeyer, a purveyor of fine wursts and other meats. Frau Staudt, a local baker, made a tidy sum supplying bread for the officers, as well as the petit fours of which Koch was so fond.

Q: How long did your enterprise continue?

A: Oh dear, I was afraid we would come to this sooner or later...Well, I have told you I am a lucky man, but in 1940 my good fortune ran out for a while. Koch said that some of the cocaine I had provided was a bad grade—cut with sugar, he claimed, or some such nonsense. One of his deputies, an *Unterscharführer* Glick, had a somewhat nasty reaction to it: he died. I suspect overindulgence rather than any fault of the product, but one never knows. At any rate, the Gestapo caught and arrested me in late 1940, and I was taken to Buchenwald.

Q: What happened to you there?

A: It was a very nasty business all around. Firstly, I was classified as a Green Triangle, a *Berufsverbrechen,* which was the camp designation for professional criminal. Not a desirable occurrence, for the BVs were treated much more harshly than, say, the Jehovah's Witnesses or the Red Triangles, the politicals. And in some cases we were worse off even than the Jews, for often the Green Triangle guaranteed one time in the punishment block, being reeducated by the madman Sommer. Everyone called him the Hangman, for that was his preferred method of teaching: to string a man up by the wrists and let him dangle for days, from meat hooks or window bars. And that was his least creative method. A more inventive one was to force a garden hose down the throat of a hanging man and let the water run until his stomach burst.

I managed to avoid this initiation because of my connections within the camp. However, I was immediately assigned to the worst work detail, the stone quarry. I started making arrangements to be transferred to the laundry or the Gustloff armament works, where one would at least be inside, or to the kitchen, which of course was ideal because of the access to food. And that is where I did end up. Until liberation, in fact. But organizing the proper payments took some time, and meanwhile Koch was still irritated enough with me that I began my incarceration in the quarry. And that was a literal hell.

Q: What did quarry detail consist of?

A: We worked twelve hours a day, from six in the morning until six at night. We had the poorest rations, and we worked in all weathers, carrying enormous stones about. I never quite saw the point of it, but then I've never been one for manual labor. The exposure to the elements and the lack of food started to tear me down fairly quickly.

However, it was the guards who posed the greatest danger. They hated the monotony of overseeing the quarry; they called it

Shit Detail—you should forgive the vulgarity. They were very easily bored, as stupid men often are, and often hungover and most often drunk, and they had atrocious ways of combating their ennui. The favorite was to whisk the cap off the head of some unfortunate inmate and throw it across the sentry line. It was punishable by death to be without one's cap, and it was equally forbidden to cross the boundary. Yet the poor devil singled out would be commanded to retrieve his cap, and the instant he stepped over the line he would be shot. All of the guards found this endlessly entertaining. Gretel and Lard-Ass, as we called them, were two of the most willing participants. And *Wasserkopf*—water on the brain—a *Kapo* so nicknamed because of his abnormally large head and total idiocy. But the worst sadists, the originators of the game, were Hinkelmann and Blank, and more inhuman creatures I have never met to this day. As was the case with all the guards, they had been professional criminals before the war—real ones—and to keep them out of trouble, Koch posted them permanently in the quarry. I used to thank God I was adept at hiding behind the other prisoners, for evading the notice of Hinkelmann and Blank was one's only hope of surviving each day.

The sole benefit of quarry detail—and it kept some of the men alive long past the point at which they would have otherwise perished—was that bread was left for us just beyond the sentry line. It was sometimes possible, when the guards were involved in their sport, for one of us BVs to steal over and retrieve it and conceal it in our trousers. This duty often fell to me, since I was relatively small in stature and good at not calling attention to myself. Two women from Weimar, Aryan civilians, hid rolls for us in the hollow trunk of a large pine. They did this at great risk to themselves, of course, since *füttern den Feind*—feeding the enemy—was also punishable by death. We revered them; we called them *die Bäckerei Engel,* the Bakery Angels. Those who were religious prayed for them every night.

That was a miserable winter, but I managed to squeak by, and in the spring of 1941—

Q: Mr. Pfeffer, can we backtrack for a minute? Can you tell me more about the Bakery Angels?

A: Certainly. Let me see…Well, they made these Special Deliveries—as they were known—every Wednesday. And at the same time, they would collect messages we managed to smuggle out of the camp. We did so in a most unsavory way, I'm afraid; we wrote on tiny sheets of paper and hid them in prophylactics. I will leave it to you to imagine where the prophylactics were concealed. We were hoping to get word to the Outside about what was happening in the camp, so that it might be sent through the Resistance network to Israel or America. In the early days, before the SS put a stop to it, film was also left by the tree in this way. There was a photography department in the camp, and some of the more enterprising Red Triangles managed to use its equipment to take photographs for evidence. It was then up to the Angels to ensure that it got out.

I remember one poor fellow in particular who had been arrested for just this subversive activity: the Good *Doktor,* we called him, Herr *Doktor* Max Stern. I had known him before the camp as well, since he was the first link in the chain that enabled my Jewish clients to escape. He also once treated me for influenza. He was skinny even before the war, and after some time in the punishment block he was emaciated. They had beaten him to a jelly, too, of course. Yet he managed to last much longer than any of us thought he would, and I suspect this was a triumph of mind over matter. He'd had a love affair with one of *die Bäckerei Engel,* you see; she had hidden him until his arrest, and with her he had a child, a daughter he never saw, born Outside. I am convinced he lived for the messages about her. I remember well when she was born, November 1940, since I provided the cigars for the occasion. We smoked them in the barracks after lights out, though the Good *Doktor* was too weak to enjoy his by then—

My dear, are you all right?

Q: Yes. I'm sorry. Please go on. Who were the Bakery Angels? What were their names? Did you ever see them?

A: Of course. One was Frau Mathilde Staudt, whom I mentioned earlier as providing the pastries for the Comradeship Evenings. She was also in the Resistance, and I had helped her from time to time. Some of the men called her *die Dicke,* Fatty, and indeed she was quite plump. But I found this rather ungracious, considering what she was doing for us, and personally I have always preferred a woman to be buxom—

Q: The other one. The other Angel. What did she look like?

A: Her I did not know. She became Frau Staudt's apprentice during my unfortunate incarceration, and I had never had any prewar dealings with her, so I do not know her name. But I did glimpse her on occasion and once I saw her quite well, while Hinkelmann was squeezing the life out of some poor fellow by standing on his throat. She must have been so horrified by the sight that she had forgotten her caution, for she was standing too close to the quarry. I heard that later, after Frau Staudt was discovered and executed, the apprentice Angel managed to save herself and her daughter from the same fate by becoming the mistress of one of the camp's highest-ranking officers, one *Obersturmführer* Horst von Steuern, a colder-hearted murderer than even Hinkelmann or Blank. He was quite taken with her, I heard, and I can imagine why. She was very beautiful, small but generously curved, with light eyes and dark hair shot through with blond streaks—

Q: Stop the tape. Stop the tape. Stop the tape!

All right, Trudy, says Thomas, it's off, the camera's off. What is it? What's wrong?

Trudy shakes the contents of her purse onto Mr. Pfeffer's coffee table and seizes her wallet. Her hand is trembling so that she tears the photograph when she extracts it from its plastic sleeve. But it is still intact enough to show Anna at its center,

Anna in 1952 with Jack and Trudy on the farmhouse porch, on the Fourth of July.

Trudy thrusts the snapshot toward Mr. Pfeffer.

Is this the woman you saw? she demands. Is this the apprentice Angel?

Mr. Pfeffer holds the photograph at arm's length.

I cannot be sure, he admits. It was so many years ago... But there is a striking resemblance. I'm fairly certain this is her.

How certain?

Mr. Pfeffer purses his lips and lets out a *pssssh* of air.

Oh, I'd say, perhaps eighty percent?

He hands the photograph to Trudy, but she makes no move to take it. She stares at the rippling sun crescents on the wall over Mr. Pfeffer's shoulder.

My God, she says. My God.

Trudy, what is it? Thomas asks again.

After a minute Trudy shakes her head.

I'm not sure yet, she answers. But let's pack it up for now, okay?

To Mr. Pfeffer, who is observing her with keen interest, she adds, The woman in the photograph is my mother.

Mr. Pfeffer smiles.

Ah, yes, he says. I had surmised as much.

Would you mind terribly if we finished your interview another day? I'm feeling a bit overwhelmed...

Of course. I completely understand.

And if you have time, I'd so appreciate it if you'd come home with me —just for a little while —

You wish, naturally, to see whether I recognize your mother, says Mr. Pfeffer.

He produces a heavy gold pocketwatch and flicks back the cover.

I do have a dinner engagement, he says, but there is plenty of time. Until then, dear, I am all yours.

He stands, shakes out the creases in his trousers, and offers

an arm to Trudy. They adjourn to the front steps to wait while
Thomas disassembles his equipment. Mr. Pfeffer examines the
sky and removes his suitjacket, then blots his forehead with his
silk handkerchief. The sun is at its zenith, and the day has grown
hot.

Trudy gazes across the lawn and notices a border of lilacs at
the edge of the property, a hundred yards away. It is extraordinary, really: a solid wall of flowers over twenty feet high, all
shades of purple and white. She wanders a ways toward it, stopping in the center of the grass. There are little wooden doors set
at intervals in the hedge, presumably to allow one to walk inside
it. Trudy thinks of her *Trog,* of blinking up in wonder through
similar interlacing branches at the pale German sun. Her vision
blurs with tears.

There are paths in the hedgerow, calls Mr. Pfeffer. The
bushes are over a century old.

Trudy nods to show she has heard.

Their scent is powerfully nostalgic, is it not? It is the sole un-
tarnished memory I have of Germany. Weimar was lovely in lilac
time.

I know, Trudy thinks.

When she has collected herself, she returns to Mr. Pfeffer.

I have one last question for you, if you don't mind, she says.

Mr. Pfeffer inclines his head.

What happened to the Good *Doktor?*

Mr. Pfeffer turns and looks over at the drive, where Thomas
is loading the last of the tripods into the van.

Whom you suspect to be your father, says Mr. Pfeffer. If
your mother is indeed the apprentice Angel.

Yes. What became of him?

Mr. Pfeffer doesn't answer immediately. He tucks his hands
into the pockets of his trousers and bounces a few times on the
balls of his feet. In the distance there is a somnolent buzz, of a
mower perhaps, a gardener tending a lawn, or of an airplane, or
of bees.

Mr. Pfeffer?

Mr. Pfeffer clears his throat.

He was hanged, I'm afraid, he says finally. Poor fellow. Von Steuern himself kicked the chair away, then left the Good *Doktor* on the gallows for the crows to pick, as a lesson to us all.

61

Thomas lets Trudy and Mr. Pfeffer off at her house twenty minutes later, and Trudy again accepts Mr. Pfeffer's arm to guide her up her own front walk. She leans on him a little: her legs are shaking, her hamstrings weak. Inside, the living room, though in shade at this time of day, is as stuffy as if it were August, the furniture releasing the scent of wood in the sudden heat. There is also the smell of fresh-baked bread and some sort of boiled meat. Bratwurst, Trudy guesses. She leads Mr. Pfeffer to the kitchen, where Anna is sawing furiously away at a long loaf of dark pumpernickel, a wave of loose hair swinging in her face.

Mama, says Trudy. I've brought somebody to meet you.

She beckons Mr. Pfeffer from the doorway, where he is standing with his hands clasped behind his back like a maître d'.

Anna looks up. The sight of Trudy's urbane guest must startle her, for the serrated knife clatters to the floor.

Oh! she says. Her face, already pink from steam and exertion, flushes strawberry red. Forgive me, Trudy. I did not know you were having company. I will go upstairs—

Trudy bends to pick up the knife. She wipes it on her trousers and sets it on the breadboard.

No, please don't, Mama, she says. Mr. Pfeffer is here to see you. Mr. Pfeffer, this is Mrs. Anna Schlemmer, my mother. Mama, Mr. Felix Pfeffer.

She watches Mr. Pfeffer carefully for any sign of recognition, but Mr. Pfeffer merely smiles.

Enchanted, he says.

Anna, flustered, holds out a hand and then hastily retracts it and wipes it on her apron. When she extends it a second time, Mr. Pfeffer grasps it and bows low over it in the European fashion.

Will you join us for lunch, Mr. Pfeffer? asks Anna, once she has reclaimed her hand. We have more than enough. I will set another place at the table.

She turns to the cupboard, but Trudy takes her arm, staying her from the plates.

Leave it for now, Mama, she says. We'll eat later. In the meantime, could you come sit down for a minute? Mr. Pfeffer wants to talk to you.

Me? says Anna.

She pushes the damp tendrils from her forehead with a wrist, looking quizzically from Trudy to Mr. Pfeffer.

I cannot imagine—, she says.

But she obediently follows Trudy into the living room, Mr. Pfeffer courteously bringing up the rear.

No sooner have the three settled themselves, Mr. Pfeffer in the wing chair across from the two women on the couch, than Anna gets up again.

At least let me bring your guest some coffee, Trudy, she says. Or he would perhaps prefer something more refreshing, some iced tea—

Please, madam, says Mr. Pfeffer. I appreciate the offer. You are too kind. But please do sit. What I have to say won't take long.

Bewildered, Anna subsides onto the sofa, smoothing her apron over her knees.

Mr. Pfeffer studies her for a moment. Then he glances at Trudy and gives an infinitesimal nod. Trudy's breath catches in her throat.

Mama, she says. Mr. Pfeffer thinks—

But her voice breaks. Mr. Pfeffer waits politely for Trudy to continue; then, understanding, he splays his hands out before him, admiring the handsome signet ring on his little finger.

Your daughter tells me, he says, addressing it, that you lived in Weimar during the war?

Anna's face closes.

Yes, she says warily.

And that you worked in a bakery there?

Yes.

Mr. Pfeffer exhales on his ring.

I too am a native of Weimar, madam, he says, polishing the stone on his trousers. And before my incarceration in KZ Buchenwald, I came to know there a woman who owned a particular bakery, one Mathilde Staudt. A very brave woman, this Frau Staudt. She and her assistant risked their lives to leave bread for us, the prisoners, by the stone quarry in which we were forced to work. Furthermore, these two women couriered information back and forth from the camp to the Resistance. The film they smuggled out led to the Allied bombing of Buchenwald in August 1944. They saved many lives—including, obviously, mine.

Anna, who has been growing whiter by the second, flattens her palms on the couch cushions as if poised for flight.

Yes? she says. And?

Madam, says Mr. Pfeffer, one of those women was you.

A tiny muscle jumps at the corner of Anna's mouth, then is still.

I saw you, you see, Mr. Pfeffer adds. On several occasions, but the first time on the day *Unterscharführer* Hinkelmann mur-

dered an inmate in the quarry, an atrocity both you and I witnessed. I saw you standing by the tree in which you left the
bread. After all these years, that sight has never left me. It in-
spired in me the will to survive. It gave me hope.

Anna stares at him. She doesn't appear to be breathing. Only
her hands, rolling and unrolling the hem of her apron, betray her.

Finally Anna says, Obviously you have mistaken me for
somebody else.

Mr. Pfeffer smiles.

That is not the case, madam, I assure you. Yours is not a face
one forgets.

Forgive me, but you are wrong. I know nothing of this.

Don't you?

Anna gives a small shrug.

Hinkelmann, Blank, Staudt—these names mean nothing to
me. I did work in a bakery, yes. But there were several bakeries in
Weimar. I never did a thing out of the ordinary. I did only what I
could to feed myself and my daughter and keep us safe. Nothing
else. Nothing.

Mr. Pfeffer examines her closely.

Ah, he says after a few moments. I see.

In fact, I remember very little of what happened in those
days, Anna adds, getting to her feet. My memory is not what it
once was.

Mr. Pfeffer rises as well.

Some would call that a blessing, he says. I'm sorry to have
troubled you.

Anna bends to tuck the slipcover of the couch back into place.

It is no trouble, she says. I am sorry I am not the woman you
are seeking. Perhaps I can compensate for your disappointment
by giving you some lunch?

I would be delighted, Mrs. Schlemmer—if I may. We will
talk of happier things.

Very good, says Anna, and walks off toward the kitchen.

Mama, wait, Trudy calls.

She is crying. Not with the dignity of an adult, tears trickling down her face, but sobbing like a child, gasping and open-mouthed, hands helpless on her thighs.

Now, now, says Mr. Pfeffer. What is all this?

I'm sorry, Trudy says. I'll be all right in a minute—

A yellow silk handkerchief appears before her. Trudy gropes for it but doesn't use it. It seems a shame to spoil it by getting it wet. She twists it in her lap.

She is the woman you saw, she says to Mr. Pfeffer. The apprentice Angel.

Yes. I haven't the slightest doubt.

Trudy nods, head lowered. Tears spot the silk in her fist and the linen of her trousers. She is humiliated to be carrying on in such a way—in front of Mr. Pfeffer, no less. For what has she expected, really? That after all this time Anna would suddenly confess everything, simply because she is confronted by somebody who shared her experience, somebody who was there? Well, yes, apparently. Part of Trudy—the girl still carried within her, puzzled and stubbornly persistent—has been hoping exactly that.

But as Trudy sits trying to calm her breathing, she also remembers what Rainer has said: *Let the punishment fit the crime.* Anna has taken the burden of silence upon herself. It is her decision not to speak of the things she has done, valiant or otherwise. It is in fact her prerogative as a hero. And in another way, whether she is a hero or not is immaterial. Each person has this choice to make about how to live with the past, this dignity, this inviolable right.

Mr. Pfeffer puts a kindly hand on Trudy's shoulder. Trudy brings the handkerchief to her face. She wonders about him too, this man who gambled his life to help others. Perhaps his cavalier attitude about having done so is also not what it seems.

Better? Mr. Pfeffer asks.

Yes. Thank you.

Blow your nose, he commands.

Trudy laughs shakily and obeys.

There, Mr. Pfeffer says.

He stands and readjusts the cuffs of his trousers.

Now then, he says. Your mother has graciously extended an invitation to lunch, and I for one am going to accept. Won't you?

He strides with purpose toward the kitchen, where, from the sound of it, Anna is stacking a tray with plates.

After a time, Trudy gets up, walks quietly through the dining room past Anna and Mr. Pfeffer, and goes upstairs to the bathroom. She looks in the mirror over the basin and sees a stranger: eyes wide and astonished, tears clinging to the lashes. She washes her face and comes back down to join the other two, sitting and unfolding her napkin without saying a word. The afternoon sun falls in mild rectangles on the tablecloth. Mr. Pfeffer compliments the chef, who demurs and smiles, her cheeks again flushing bright pink. The three discuss Anna's views of what she hears on MPR, Trudy's summer classes, the weather's sudden change for the better. They eat the food that Anna has set before them: bratwurst and other sliced meats fanned on a platter, a sweet red cabbage salad, chilled cucumber soup. A dish of pickles. Bread.

62

AFTER LUNCH IS CLEARED FROM THE TABLE, ANNA SERVES iced coffee and tea and *Sachertorte,* over which she and Trudy and Mr. Pfeffer linger until well into the afternoon. By the time Mr. Pfeffer flips his watch open and exclaims at the hour, Anna is concealing yawns behind a napkin. She excuses herself to wash the dishes before retiring to her room for a rest, and at this announcement Mr. Pfeffer leaps up to help her pull back her chair. He thanks Anna profusely, again bowing low over her hand and then kissing it, and Trudy, watching, thinks that the rosiness of Anna's cheeks has to do with reasons other than drowsy post-prandial contentment and the warmth of the day.

Once this elaborate ritual of leave-taking has been concluded, Trudy drives Mr. Pfeffer to Minnetonka. In the car he seems happy to sit and watch the suburbs pass, attempting no small talk except, as they are setting out, to praise Anna's skills as a cook and to thank Trudy for her hospitality, comments that require no lengthy response. Trudy is grateful. She is tired now and empty, her face still tight from her earlier tears. She wants only to be alone and quiet, to sit and think and digest the events of the day.

So she says nothing until they reach Mr. Pfeffer's house, and then she says simply, Thank you, Felix.

Mr. Pfeffer smiles at his house, its glass walls and gravity-defying angles, with sleepy satisfaction.

It has been my pleasure, he says. I so enjoyed making your mother's acquaintance. Or, I should say, making it a second time.

Taking his suitjacket from the back of the seat, he drapes it over his arm and opens the door.

I'll be in touch about finishing your interview, Trudy tells him as he climbs from the car.

Hmmmm? says Mr. Pfeffer. Ah, yes. Please do.

He walks away a few steps, then suddenly turns on his heel and comes back.

With your permission, he says, ducking to look at Trudy through the window, I should like to visit your mother again.

Trudy nods.

I think she'd like that.

Do you? says Mr. Pfeffer. Good. That was the impression I received as well. I will call on her next week.

He winks at Trudy, the merest flicker of an eyelid. Then he pats the roof of the car in farewell and strides jauntily off across the lawn, whistling, his jacket slung over one shoulder.

Trudy watches him disappear into the house. Then, with a last wistful glance at the lilac border, she reverses into the lane and drives back the way she has come.

The winding tree-lined streets of Minnetonka give way to flat land and open sky once Trudy hits 394, and she cranks the window down to feel the breeze. It carries to her the smells of tar and cut grass, roses, cooking meat and charcoal from people's backyard barbecues. She can hear their lives, too, a mother calling, a dog barking, children shouting at play. A fragmented melody from a piano somewhere. The whistle of a train coming in from the prairie. The light is changing as the sun begins its descent, becoming sharp and pure, the shadows long and blue. All of this stirs in Trudy an exquisite melancholy that makes her throat ache. This evening, she thinks, she will go to her study and open the windows to the warm night, and then she may allow herself the luxury of calling Rainer. She wants to tell him all that has happened, that she better understands now how he must have felt when he first came to this country, stepping off the boat with land-shy legs and gazing about in fear and wonder, having left the freight of everything he thought he knew behind.

But not right away. Not yet. At the moment, Trudy wants to extend this odd feeling as long as possible. To prolong this sad and peaceful vacuum between one part of life ending and another coming to take its place.

So as the skyline appears before her, its simple building-block shapes refracting arrows of light into the car, Trudy passes the exit that would take her to her house. Then the next, which would bring her to Rainer's. Farther on, the turnoff that would lead her to Le P'tit, slumbering at this hour beneath its awnings while the waiters scramble to prepare dinner inside. Trudy turns onto the ring road and circles the city to the other side, emerging in the shade of the skyscrapers. The Mississippi flows beneath her to her left, its currents so slow and powerful that it doesn't appear to be moving at all. Across it is the university, its art gallery a blinding structure of crumpled tinfoil in the setting sun, the History Department behind it. At stoplights, Trudy inhales grease from fat fryers, exhaust, the heat rising from the sidewalks. People laughing, sitting at outdoor cafés with glasses of wine. Cars honking. The tinny *beat-beat-beat* of pop music from distant radios. All of this pushing, insistent life.

Finally, when the sun is touching the horizon, Trudy turns back toward the river, her mood dissipating. She drives onto the Nicollet Island Bridge with a mingled sense of regret and relief. She is halfway across it when she suddenly swerves to the side and parks. Something about the view has struck her as extraordinary. Something about the light. Trudy pops the hazards on and gets out, then walks to the railing to watch.

A front is moving in, towering cumulus whose tops glow cream and gold and pink. Its underside is dark blue, its edge as straight as if drawn by a ruler except for the curtain of rain that is slowly swallowing the skyline. From this vantage point, the city is all tension wires and smokestacks and turrets, girders and railyard warehouses and drab industrial buildings. It looks much, Trudy thinks, like German cities once did: Heidelburg, Dresden, Berlin. Weimar. Perhaps they still do. The sun makes one last valiant effort to shine through the mist, and for a few seconds everything steams, yellow and gray. Then the rain sweeps in and it is gone.

ACKNOWLEDGMENTS

ANY WRITER OF HISTORICAL FICTION OWES A GREAT DEBT
to the non-fiction masterworks of others. Though I consulted
dozens of invaluable sources while researching *Those Who Save
Us,* I was particularly reliant upon *The Buchenwald Report,* translated by David A. Hackett; *Frauen: German Women Recall the
Third Reich,* by Alison Owings; and that bible of World War II
material, William L. Shirer's *Rise and Fall of the Third Reich.*

I am also enormously indebted to the Steven Spielberg *Survivors of the Shoah* Visual History Foundation, for placing trust in
me as an interviewer and thus granting me access to Holocaust
survivors. And to the survivors themselves, who demonstrated
unparalleled courage and generosity in sharing their stories, I
cannot express adequate gratitude in words: Perhaps it will suf-
fice to say that you are living miracles and nothing you have said
will ever be forgotten.

On a personal front, there are a number of people who saved
me during the writing of this novel. For three years they endured
my ceaseless babbling about Nazis and understood when I didn't
pick up the phone. The prospect of honoring them was one of

my fondest fantasies; and I do so now, in roughly alphabetical order, with great joy. Thanks to: my family, Frances J. Blum, Lesley M. M. Blum, and Joseph R. Blum, for their lifelong belief and love; the B.U. CO 201 faculty for the cake and enthusiasm; Chris Castellani, master mentor; Jean and Adel Charbonneau for their innumerable readings and unflagging encouragement; Stephanie Ebbert Devlin, my goodiest editor, and her husband, Ted Devlin; Dan Ellingson, who always told me *I Think I Can;* Eric Grunwald for correcting my limping German and supplying the *Backe Backe Kuchen* rhyme; my Grub Street students, who taught me through allowing me to teach them; the Harcourt alchemists who have transformed this manuscript into a book; Phil Hey and Tricia Currans-Sheehan at the *Briar Cliff Review,* who gave the original story such a wonderful home; Julie Hirsch, my Puppet—she knows why; Ken Holmes; the Kenyon girls; Doug Loy for the inspiration; triumvirate of cheer Necee Regis, cool Ann Tracy, and Joanna Weiss; Sister Cecila; Dave Sandstedt for the sunflowers and champagne; Sarah Schweitzer, whose patient counsel helped me knock Trudy; Dr. Sherri Szeman, fellow laborer in the era of the Reich; and Steve Wilmsen, for listening and for taking me to Woodman's Clam Shack when I was blocked.

Special thanks to Stéphanie Abou, fierce and lovely superagent, and Ann Patty, incomparable *Über*-editor, for believing in this book.

It takes a village to raise a child, which is precisely what writing a novel is. If I have neglected to name anyone in this village, please know that it is not for lack of heartfelt appreciation: *Dankeschoen.*

Temple Israel
Minneapolis, Minnesota

IN HONOR OF THE BAR MITZVAH OF
STUART BAKER
FROM
DARCY & BOBBY SCHNITZER